NORTH TO CHEYENNE

The Long Road Home

Book 1
Home on the Range Series

NORTH TO CHEYENNE

The Long Road Home

Rosie Bosse

POST ROCK
PUBLISHING

North to Cheyenne
Copyright © 2020 by Rosie Bosse

ISBN: Soft Cover – 978-1-64318-049-6
ISBN: eBook – 978-1-64318-056-4

**POST ROCK
PUBLISHING**

Post Rock Publishing
17055 Day Rd.
Onaga, KS 66521

www.rosiebosse.com

PROLOGUE

As you read this novel, you will see that even though the story line is fictional, it is historically and geographically correct. Most of the characters are fictional. Other names are hidden in history. Perhaps their names will not be recognized, but maybe you will remember them after reading this book.

While Lance and Molly, the two main characters, are products of my imagination, I did choose names that were used in 1868. The name Lance is taken from the Germanic name *Lanzo*. The short form of this name began with the element *landa* which means land—quite fitting for a man who is passionate about land and cattle! The Rankin name was an established name in Georgia in the 1800's, and the Rankin House stands today as a landmark in the city of Columbus.

Both Lance and Molly grew up in Georgia although they didn't officially meet until they were aboard the *Frank Paragoud* or *Dandy Frank* as the riverboat was nicknamed. This was an actual riverboat that was on the Mississippi River in the summer of 1868. The riverboat scene was a fun one to create. Riverboats were often lawless in their early years, and the captain served as the final authority.

Each city traveled through was a functioning city or town. St. Louis, Kansas City and Manhattan were all vibrant and growing in the 1860's. As the characters moved through these cities, I tried to connect them with actual businesses that were established and flourishing during that time period.

Saint Louis, Missouri

The Barr Dry Goods Company was a large dry goods store open and operating in 1868. St. Louis was a gateway to the west, and many travelers passed through there. Of course, pioneers needed to prepare for their long trek west, and the Barr Dry Goods Company boasted to have everything one would need for that trip in a covered wagon. William H. Barr was a mover and a shaker in the young St. Louis. One could even say that the Barr Dry Goods Company was a precursor to Macy's but that is a story you will have to research for yourself. Sophie Barr is a fictional character, but I like to believe that is what Mr. Barr's wife would have been like.

The Southern Hotel was a lavish hotel in St. Louis for its time right down to heavy rugs. It was owned by Robert G. Campbell whom I incorporated into the story. I envisioned him as an astute businessman, and you will see him ensure that his hotel maintains its reputation for quality and service.

Kansas City, Missouri

Kansas City was originally known as 'City of Kansas' but as in many cases, the name was shortened, and the new town became known as Kansas City. The city developed first on the Missouri side of the river; growth on the Kansas side followed later. The Pacific House was considered one of the finest hotels there for many years. It was rebuilt after a terrible fire in 1867. In 1868, everything would have been lavish and new. I don't know if the rooms contained tubs, but I added them. After all, a bath in your own room in 1868 would have been a huge luxury.

Manhattan, Kansas

Manhattan was thirteen years old in 1868, and Kansas State University was already established there. Kansas State was the first land-grant institution created under the Morrill Act. It was established on Feb. 16, 1863 and was the first public institution of higher learning in Kansas. When it opened on September 2, 1863, it was only the second public institution for higher education in the United State to admit both women and men equally.

The Wolf House Boarding House was a two-story limestone house built by John Frank in 1868 as a boarding house and may still be toured today. While John Frank was a real person, his wife in this story, Nellie Frank, is fictional. Her gruff personality is fitting for a woman living on the edge of civilization with much manual labor to do each day, as well as a variety of characters to shelter each night.

I couldn't find the name of a saloon that was open in 1868, perhaps because it was such a new town or maybe because of the fires that burned through Manhattan in its early years. I chose to call the main saloon in my story *So Long Saloon*. That is actually one of our favorite eating places in Aggieville. The ornate wooden bar that runs the full length of the eating area is the original bar from an old saloon brought in from Kemmerer, Wyoming.

Fort Riley, Abilene, Salina, Ellsworth, Hays City and Monument Station, Kansas

The train route west in 1868 would have followed the described route. Indian uprisings were a problem, and the trains were often attacked. Wild Bill Hickok was known to have traveled this rail line. Who knows if he considered the train "his train" when he was alive and riding it—I like to think so since he did run for sheriff of Ellsworth County.

Perry Hodgden was one of Ellsworth's early residents and was a renowned business man. The Hodgden House which he built in 1873 still stands in Ellsworth today.

Monument Station was the end of the track in early June of 1868. Rail was laid by hand and seven to eight miles of track could be laid each day. As the rails inched westward, there was no organized travel in front of them. In June of 1868, one could take a stage from Monument Station to Denver, Colorado Territory. However, no stage or rails ran north. Monument Station was nicknamed Fort Pyramid by the soldiers because of the tall rocks around it. The Spencer and Fowler Boarding House was open and operating there in June of 1868. It served a large variety of meats, vegetables and other delicacies. This was nearly unheard of for such a new town and especially in such an isolated location. Monument Rocks National Natural Landmark is close Oakley, Kansas and is also known as the Chalk Pyramids. Monument Rocks are large chalk formations and reach a height of up to 70 feet. Monument Station was abandoned by the military in June of 1868. Nothing remains but scattered ruins of the small, one-company post. The unincorporated community of Monument, Kansas is about thirty-five miles northwest of the original Monument Station.

Arikaree Breaks

Arikaree Breaks was one of the most fascinating areas that I researched for this book. The trip north to Julesburg turned west around Arikaree Breaks. The breaks are a two-to-three-mile-wide stretch of badlands that run about thirty miles in length on the extreme northern edge of Cheyenne County in northwest Kansas. They reach north toward Nebraska and go west into eastern Colorado Territory. Much of Arikaree Breaks is on private land, but you can take a driving tour over some pretty rough roads if you want to see them closer. Horse Thief Cave was at one time a place where stolen horses were held. It can be seen from the road. Some of the material that I read talked about a spring and lush grass. Even though we didn't see any of that on our road trip, I added it to the story. Horse Thief Cave looks like it was dug out of a hill, but I glorified it here and made it an actual cave.

Rough Terrain and Lots of Rivers

In this book, I describe the terrain as well as some of the rivers that would have been crossed. My husband and I drove from Cheyenne down through Julesburg and then south, following the route that the characters in my book would have followed. It was an isolated and long drive even today. Many of the rivers we crossed were reported to have quicksand. A gentleman in Julesburg who was volunteering in the museum there stated that the sand on the river bottoms moves so maps across the rivers wouldn't have worked. However, I did find a map made by an army sergeant around the time of my story. He had drawn a route to follow to cross a river safely. It contributed a new twist of adventure and I added that to the story.

Julesburg, Colorado Territory

The South Platte River was the last river that had to be crossed by travelers from the south heading north to Julesburg. It looked benign when we crossed it but it was treacherous in its day. It too had lots of quick sand and sand bars that had to be navigated through or around.

The Indian outbreaks in Kansas in the spring of 1868 were light, although Indian hostility did pick up closer to Julesburg. Blue Feather and Broken Knife are fictional characters. The Arapahoe and the Cheyenne were the native tribes in the area covered by this story, and they were not always friendly.

I explain in this novel how the town of Julesburg moved three times. The citizens of Julesburg actually moved their town a fourth time in 1886 to connect with the new transcontinental railroad, and that is the location of the town today. The third location, as it was in this story, is where Julesburg earned the reputation of "the wickedest city in the West."

In the fall of 1867 when the first train arrived in Cheyenne from Julesburg, people were riding on top. It is hard to believe that in our day, but the top of the train was almost as full as the inside. Of course, that had to be added to the story as well!

Cheyenne, Wyoming

Cheyenne was first called *Crow Creek Crossing* because of its location. *Iron City* was also considered as a name, again because of its important railroad location between Omaha and California. The new city of Cheyenne went from being called *The City of Tents* to *Magic City of the Plains* in just a few months because of how rapidly it grew. Cheyenne wasn't even a year old in June of 1868.

The Rollins House was one of Cheyenne's first hotels and was owned by John Quincy Adams Rollins. It stood across the street from the Ford and Durkee Hotel owned in part by ex-slave, Barney Lancelot Ford. Mr. Ford is sometimes called a "fast food pioneer." He arrived in Cheyenne in 1867, shortly after the town was formed. The earliest known ad for his restaurant, the Ford House, was published on October 10, 1867. By January of 1868, he was offering fresh oysters daily to his customers. In his 1870 ads, he offered free carriage rides from the train station to his eating house about a block away.

I was absolutely amazed by Barney Ford's story. He was born on farm in Virginia, the illegitimate son of a white plantation owner and a slave. He grew up as a slave on a South Carolina plantation, and escaped when the riverboat he was working on docked on the "free" Illinois side of the river. He made his way to Chicago where he learned to read and write.

His wife, whom he met in Chicago, helped him choose his middle and last name. They were taken from a steam locomotive called the *Lancelot Ford.* The Fords chose to travel by ship to the gold fields in California but stopped in Central America. Together they opened and lost their first hotel in Nicaragua.

Throughout his life, Mr. Ford was a civic leader who fought for black suffrage and education. He also worked closely with the Underground Railroad. He eventually became one of the wealthiest men in the west.

I did take liberty with Mr. Ford's personality as I read about his accomplishments. The manner in which he handled the many difficulties he encountered said much about his tenacity and resilience. I made his restaurant a main eating place for the Rocking R cowboys although the Ford House was known as one of the best eating establishments in Cheyenne during the short time it was there. You will see more of Barney Ford in novels two and three.

I truly hope that you will enjoy reading this novel as much as I enjoyed writing it. Here's to reading, writing and following your dreams.

Rosie Bosse

CHAPTER 1

HEADED HOME

L ANCE STROLLED ACROSS THE TOP DECK OF THE *DANDY FRANK* and stared down into the murky water of the Mississippi. He liked it up here, away from the noise and commotion below. He ran his finger around the inside collar of his shirt and scowled.

"There are just too darn many people on this boat," Lance muttered. "All these people and this heavy air make it hard for a man to breathe."

He paused and then growled, "But at least it's quieter up here."

Although the day had been fairly warm, as evening came on, Lance could feel the chill coming off the water through his long-sleeved shirt and vest. The two low-hung guns looked as natural on him as the neckerchief that he used to wipe his face. When he turned his head, the lights from the pilot house shined for just a moment on his face. It was a strong face, tan and smooth-shaven. As the light glinted across his eyes, laugh lines showed the humor that lurked just below the surface.

The *Frank Paragoud* or the *Dandy Frank* as she was called was moored for the night because the captain was a careful man. The boat needed to move faster than the water to navigate safely; otherwise, the treacherous water would control its course. The Mississippi was a dangerous river to navigate at any time, and the captain refused to travel after sunset.

It was 8:00 p.m. now and quiet. Supper was served on the boiler deck at 7:00 p.m., and by 8:00 p.m., most of the passengers had retired to their cabins. Lance was hungry, but he wasn't in a hurry to eat. The food was bland, and the coffee was weak. He had never cared if a meal was fancy as long as he didn't leave the table hungry, but this food left a lot to be desired. He scowled as he thought about the salty stew he'd had for dinner.

"I think that cook spilled the salt when he was cooking," Lance muttered.

Lane's eyes glinted as he thought of his own cooking.

"I can make some pretty mean biscuits, but a man gets tired of biscuits and beans every day." Then he laughed out loud. "Of course, I could get hitched!"

He had known quite a few women over the years who would have been glad to oblige, but Lance took marriage seriously.

"I think I will stick to my own biscuits," he laughed to himself.

It was May of 1868, and Lance Rankin was headed back home to Cheyenne, Wyoming. He hadn't ridden a riverboat before, and it had sounded like a grand adventure. However, now he was wishing he had taken the train because it would have been faster. Lance had been gone eight long months and he was anxious to get home. The trip upriver from New Orleans to St. Louis was supposed to take six days with good weather, but it could take seven days if they ran into fog. It was only day five, and Lance felt like a caged animal.

His six-foot plus frame was lean and solid with muscle. He flexed his shoulders. Lance was used to working with his hands and was most comfortable on the back of a horse. He frowned at the stiffness in his arms.

"I need to get back to work," he muttered.

There was a slight breeze on the deck, and it stirred the dark hair curling slightly from under the brim of his hat. As he stared up at the stars, Lance considered all that had taken place this last year.

It's been a heck of a ride, he thought as he pushed back his hat and scratched his head. He took a small packet from his pocket. It contained a single gold band that had belonged to his mother and a pocket watch engraved 'J.R.' that had been his father's. Not many things had survived the fire when the warring armies from the North and the South had burned the old family home to the ground.

Just about a year ago, his ranch boss, Old Man McNary, had taken a bullet from some cattle rustlers. He was a tough old codger and after Lance and the other ranch hands removed the bullet, they had captured and hung the rustlers with the Old Man leading the way. This time though, at seventy-five years old, Old Man McNary just didn't bounce back like he had in the past. The Rocking R ranch hands with Lance as foreman kept working without a hitch, but Lance was worried about the Old Man.

Lance had been at the Rocking R for four years and foremen for three of them. He loved the isolated ranch south and west of Cheyenne even if the winters were rough. If a man knew how to prepare and had enough feed, winter was doable.

Then came the letter from his aunt in Georgia; Lance's father had died, and Lance was needed at home to settle the estate.

Most of Lance's childhood memories were good ones. As a youngster, Lance had been outside any time he could, hunting in the forests, and racing their long-legged thoroughbreds down the worn roads. Lots of cuts, scrapes and bruises had been incurred. There was even a broken collar bone when he convinced his little brother to try to ride his horse standing up. Paul fell off but wanted to do it again as soon as the sling came off his arm.

As Lance grew older though, he became more restless. His father could never understand but Lance felt like he was choking. The constant flow of people and the heavy, damp air weighed him down.

Abigail Rankin, Lance's mother, had died when Lance was three years old. He didn't remember much about his mother other than she was always smiling, and she kissed him a lot. Sometimes, he almost remembered her smell. He could vaguely see long black hair, coiled around her head and green eyes. "Eyes the color of grass in the springtime." That was what his father always told her. They were eyes that often flashed bright with laughter and rarely showed anger. Lance's mouth turned up briefly. *Father was always able to make her smile*, he remembered. Lance tried hard to remember her face. As he stared at the ring, he realized that he didn't even have a picture of his mother.

"I wonder if my memories are just childhood wistfulness," he muttered softly as he wrapped the ring back up and placed the package in his pocket.

Jonathon Rankin, Lance's father, had inherited the plantation in northern Georgia from his father, Thomas Rankin. Thomas had died in a buggy accident just a month before Jonathon's wedding, but in his will, Thomas gave the plantation to his only son as a wedding gift.

The first thing Jonathon did was free all the slaves. He offered the freed men their jobs back at the going wages. Most of the neighbors thought he was crazy, but Jonathon didn't care. He didn't hold with keeping people against their will. He often told Lance, "Slavery is an evil practice. God created all of us and color isn't important."

Most of the freed men and women stayed on at the plantation as both Jonathon and his new bride were fair employers and good to their workers. Every harvest, Jonathon took part of the profit and bought back family members of those in his employ. These new members were promptly given their freedom as well. The farm hands as well as those employed in the gardens and house became very loyal to Jonathon and

Abigail. They also adored the two boys who were born from that union, first Lance and then three years later, Paul.

Their mother had died giving birth to Paul. Lance was too small to know what happened, and their father never discussed their mother with either of the boys. Lance just knew that one day she was there and the next day, she was gone. Lance stopped asking questions about his mother because it always made his father sad.

As he looked down into the dark waters of the Mississippi, Lance frowned and shook his head.

"I didn't really ever know either of my parents," he muttered. "Mother died too early, and I was mad at Father for letting her die." He frowned again. "Kids can be pretty unreasonable."

Lance looked up at the sky. Dark clouds were sliding over the moon, and only a few stars twinkled in the night. *That was a hard time*, he thought.

"I'm sorry, Colonel," Lance whispered. "I was an unreasonable kid who didn't understand death or grieving. I sure wish I could have known you as a man."

Paul had been so full of life. Lance smiled as he thought about his brother. He laughed as he remembered shaking the small tree that Paul had climbed until Paul fell out. Paul had cut his head on a rock as he hit the ground, and he bled so much that Lance thought he was going to die. Granny Mac, their nanny, had stitched it shut and Paul didn't cry. Paul never told anyone that it was Lance's fault. "I fell out of a tree," was all he ever said. Lance's smile became a little sad as he thought of Paul. They had always been close as brothers. As they grew older, most people thought that they were twins. When at sixteen, Lance decided to leave the plantation and head west, Paul wanted to go with him. Lance wouldn't let him.

"You're too young," Lance argued. "Besides, the Colonel will need someone to help run things here."

Paul had stayed. Horses were his passion and he enjoyed working beside his father. Then the Civil War broke out in 1861 and Paul enlisted as a Confederate soldier.

The Colonel was angry. "You are fighting for slavery!" his father accused Paul as tears filled his eyes.

Paul shook his head, "I am fighting for the South," he replied quietly as he left.

Mail was slow and Lance didn't receive the letter that Paul sent saying he had enlisted until nearly a year later. He wrote Paul a long letter. He missed his brother and he wanted him to stay safe.

Lance hadn't written to his father since he had come to the Rocking R, but Paul must have given the Colonel his address as Lance received several letters from his father. In the last letter, the Colonel told his oldest son that Paul had been killed in the Battle of Columbus. The bitterness that their father felt came through in his words.

"Your brother was killed fighting for a flawed cause. He died in a battle that should have never been fought as Lee had already surrendered days before."

Lance read the letter and sadness seeped through him. All of the anger and resentment he had for his father came to a head. He tucked the letter under his mattress and that night, he showed it to his best friend, Slim. After Slim read the letter, he looked hard at Lance. "Write yore Pa, Lance. Stop carryin' this around. It wasn't his fault that your Ma died any more than it was yore fault that Paul died. Forgive 'im an' be glad ya have a Pa."

Lance did write a letter to his father. He thanked him for all he had done to raise Lance, teaching him to be an honest man and a gentleman. He talked about their mother and how sad he was when she died. He shared stories about Paul. It was a long letter when he finished, and Lance felt the weight roll off his shoulders as the words poured out of him.

His father never read that letter though as he died before it arrived. Lance hadn't cried since his mother died, and he didn't cry when he received his aunt's letter telling of his father's death.

"His heart just quit," she wrote.

Lance just wished that he had been able to know his father as an adult. He was quite sure they would have had a lot to talk about.

CHAPTER 2

OLD MAN MCNARY

OLD MAN MCNARY BLESSED THE DAY LANCE RODE IN, TRAIL WEARY AND HUNGRY. Lance had been working on ranches from South Dakota to Montana for nearly eight years by the time he arrived at the Rocking R. He was considered a top hand on every ranch he worked. However, he never found one to call home. He looked around as he rode into the headquarters of the Rocking R. He had been pointed there by another rider, and he liked what he saw. Lance was tired of moving from spread to spread, and was ready to put down some roots.

The sixteen plus cowboys on the Rocking R made sure the new rider could prove his salt before they accepted him as one of their own. Within the first four months, Lance had fought and whipped almost every one of them at one time or another. Sometimes the riders fought for the joy of fighting and other times, it was to work out a slight or a problem.

Tiny was the only one who hadn't challenged Lance. Tiny was huge. He stood well over six foot and pushed nearly three hundred pounds. Tiny didn't challenge anyone. He just grinned and said, "If I fight you,

you might mess up my purty face!" Tiny wasn't much to look at but all the hands loved him like a brother.

Most of the cowboys had been there several years before Lance signed on. Now four years later, they accepted him as foreman. For his part, Lance never asked them to do anything he wouldn't help with or do himself. He was also willing to listen to suggestions from the men, something not all foremen were willing to do. The cowboys of the Rocking R were tough, work-hardened and mostly young. Although they broke into groups in the bunkhouse, when it came to the workings of the ranch, they rode for the brand. Like most ranches, the Rocking R had an "all for one; one for all" attitude, and they never walked away from a fight.

When Lance received his aunt's letter, Old Man McNary told Lance to go home and to take his time getting things settled. Although he had never told Lance, the Old Man loved Lance like the son he had never had. It bothered him that Lance and "the Colonel" as Lance called his father had never reconciled. Of course, travel was slow and Georgia was over two months of travel time east of Cheyenne, Wyoming. They decided that Lance would leave in mid-October.

As he sat in his office the morning before Lance left, Old Man McNary thought about how Lance had improved the daily workings of the ranch. He knew the Rocking R benefitted from Lance's knowledge and cow savvy. Even more than that, he appreciated how Lance ran the operations of the ranch as if it was his own.

Old Man McNary looked around the office he had spent so many hours in.

"I should have had a son," he told himself. "I dumped all my energy into this place and forgot that someday I would get old. Well, I'm old and I have the opportunity to turn this place over to a man who will love it as much as I do. I just hope that he takes the time to have a family."

He grunted a little as he shifted in his chair, and his knees cracked as he stretched out his legs. Old Man McNary was a tall man and had only begun to stoop in the last year. The evening before Lance left, the Old Man asked him to come up to the ranch house.

"I want to talk to you about some business before you take off. You may be gone for a year, and there are some things we need to work out before you go."

Most of their discussions about ranch work took place with Old Man McNary sitting at his beat-up wooden desk. Lance would lean against the wall in the small room, and they would talk for just a few minutes.

Old Man McNary would turn sideways in his chair, stretch out his long legs with the tall, scuffed boots and say, "Here's what I think we need to get done this week," whether it was moving cows, cutting off tall grass, or riding range. Then he would wait for Lance's suggestion to put that job into action.

Lance was constantly thinking of what could be done to make the ranch more efficient and profitable. When it came to the daily workings of the operation, Lance wanted everything planned and thought through.

Old man McNary looked up as Lance walked in. His fierce eyes softened as he studied this man he had come to love as a son. He didn't like to waste words and as Lance sat down, he began, "Lance, I can't run this place like I used to. I never married because I was married to my cows, so I don't have anyone to take it over. I would like to you run it—Heck, I want you to have it! I know that you are too proud to have it give to you, so I want you to buy it."

Lance was stunned. This was not a conversation that he ever saw coming. He had come to love the old man, but he never expected this.

Old Man McNary continued, "I will make you a fair deal if you are interested."

Lance couldn't believe it—it was a dream of his to run his own ranch. He had been saving back, but $40 a month didn't allow for much to be saved. *This is going to be a long haul*, he would think to himself each month as he added $15 more to his ranch fund.

Then, just like that, he was offered a 5,000-acre ranch with prime water and winter grazing.

Lance stared at his boss and Old Man McNary laughed.

"I know that I'm no good at showing my feelings, but you have become like a son to me. I want you to stay here and run this place, and I want you to have a family. Don't do like me and get so busy with making a living that you forget to live."

As Old Man McNary waited for his answer, Lance looked down and then cleared his throat to keep the emotion out of his voice.

"I would be proud to buy the Rocking R, if I could figure out how to pay for it." He looked directly at Old Man McNary and his voice cracked as he added, "I've ridden for a lot of brands, but coming here was the first time that I ever felt like I had come home."

He put out his hand to shake Old Man McNary's hand, and the old man pulled him into a bear hug.

"Now let's see if we can figure out a way for you to buy this spread!"

Old Man McNary showed Lance some numbers of what plantations in the south were bringing after the war. Lance was surprised. Surely, land couldn't be worth $50 to $75 per acre. After all, the buildings were mostly destroyed, and the fences would have to be replaced.

"With good fences and buildings, some places are bringing over $100 per acre."

Lance was amazed and he agreed to take the necessary time to prepare the plantation for sale, even if it meant being gone longer than he had anticipated. He was sure the place was in massive disrepair. The work hands were run off when the two armies fought each other back and forth across the fields. The Union soldiers couldn't believe that free men wanted to stay, and the Confederates didn't believe the work hands were free.

When Lance and The Old Man finished going over the numbers, Lance was almost giddy.

"Why I can sell the plantation and buy you out!" he exclaimed.

Old Man McNary smiled.

"Shore can! Now let's finalize some details here so we can get you headed east."

Now, at 28 years old, Lance was headed back to Cheyenne to take over a ranch he was once foreman of.

"Shoot," he pondered out loud, "*Most* fellas have to marry the boss's daughter to get a ranch and as crotchety as Old Man McNary can be, I'm kind of glad he didn't have a daughter!"

That thought brought him back to the money belt around his waist and once again, he wished he was back in Wyoming. *Soon*, he thought.

"The *Dandy Frank* will drop me at St. Louis. From there, I'll ride the cars to Kansas City. Then, I'll pick up my horses and head northwest. There won't be many roads to follow on that route, but I'm not concerned about roads. I will push west across Kansas and then cut north through the Colorado Territory.

"I will have to go a little east to skirt the mountains in the Colorado Territory, but I should still be able to make forty-plus miles per day." He could almost smell the fresh air blowing across the prairie.

CHAPTER 3

RESCUE ON THE MISSISSIPPI

A YOUNG WOMAN CROSSED THE DECK TO STAND BY THE RAILING. Her small frame was topped with a pretty face, once tanned and flushed but now pale from being inside for so long. A wealth of red-gold hair wound around her head. Her dark blue eyes reflected the storm of emotions coursing through her. She sucked back a sob and squared her shoulders.

"You are on your own, Molly Brewster, and you had better get used to it," she lectured herself quietly.

The dank water lapped the sides of the boat, and she turned up her nose at the smell of rotting vegetation.

"Oh, how I mess the rolling pastures and green hills of Georgia!" she whispered as she leaned over the railing.

Still, Molly was glad to be out of her cabin. For four days she had fought morning sickness, and the swinging movement of the riverboat hadn't helped. What she wanted was someplace quiet where she could breathe some fresh air and not be bothered. The captain had told her that the top deck, or hurricane deck as he called it, would be the emptiest. Finally, she could see the stars.

Unconsciously, she touched her round belly and the baby growing inside of her moved.

The slight movement by the railing broke Lance's contemplation, and he realized that he was not alone on the deck. He could see the small figure of a woman standing alone against the rails just a few feet away. Lance narrowed his eyes and looked harder.

"Why that is the same little gal that rode the cars all by herself from Atlanta to New Orleans!" He knew because he recognized her red-gold hair and trim shoulders.

All through that trip, he had made sure that no men had set down next to her. She seemed to want to keep to herself. He had positioned himself about four rows back, and made it clear she was to be given some space. No one was too eager to question the tall young man with tied down guns and icy blue eyes.

A grandmotherly woman had set down next to her and they visited awhile. Lance moved up few seats and listened in on their conversation. After all, she was quite a looker and it never hurt for a fellow to know as many details as possible. It was when she stood up at one of the stops that he realized there was something more to the bulge in her skirt. That little gal was in a motherly way and he didn't see a wedding band.

He heard her say, "I am a widow," as she talked to the older woman, but she fidgeted when she gave her name. Now Lance didn't know much about women, but he did recognize a lie when it was told and he scowled.

Then he shrugged his shoulders. Regardless of what was going on, she should not be traveling by herself. *Since we are traveling the same way, a least to St. Louis, there is no reason I can't keep an eye on her* Lance thought. After all, no young woman should be traveling alone, let alone one who was pregnant.

Loud voices broke the silence of the night. Two drunken men stumbled out onto the top deck for a smoke, and it didn't take them long to notice the young woman at the railing.

"Hey, Girlie," the first one slurred, "how about keepin' us company?"

"Joe," the second man hissed, "let's don't bother her. Folks don't like havin' their women trifled with."

"Shoot, Hank," leered Joe, waving off his friend and coming closer to the girl, "this little gal's already been trifled with! Look at 'er belly and no ring or man in sight. Come on, Sweetheart—how's about a hug for ol' Joe?"

As the drunken man reached for her arm, Lance stepped out of the shadows. "Back off, Friend," Lance growled, "The lady doesn't want your company."

"Lady!" Joe shouted, "She ain't no lady!"

A rock-hard fist connected solidly with Joe's chin, and he dropped to the floor. Lance stepped toward Hank, his blue eyes flashing.

"I want nothin' to do with you!" Hank exclaimed, "I warned 'im." He pushed at Joe with his foot. "Is he daid?"

Lance's voice was angry as he answered, "No, but he'll think his jaw is broken when he wakes up. Now get. If I see either of you bother this lady again, I will break you in half and dump you in the river."

Joe grabbed Hank under his arms and hauled him toward the stairway. Hank was a big man, and Joe was grunting as he drug the limp body. Finally, Hank was close enough to the edge of the stairs and Joe pulled him head first. Banging could be heard as Hank was drug down the stairs. His boots hit each stair as he slammed down to the decks below.

Lance turned toward the young woman. Her deep blue eyes were so large that they nearly consumed her pretty face. She was standing with her back to the rail, trembling hard enough that he was afraid she would fall overboard.

"Here now," Lance spoke softly as he stretched out a hand in an offer to steady her.

"They were just drunk. Chances are, Joe will be apologizing in the morning. Regardless, they won't be bothering you again."

He pointed at himself, "I'm Lance Rankin, and you are?"

The young lady paused just a bit before she answered.

"My name is Molly, Molly Gallagher." As she offered Lance her small hand, she added, "I mean *Mrs.* Molly Gallagher."

Those eyes! Why a man could lose himself in those eyes, Lance thought. He doffed his hat and grinned at her, showing her a head of wavy, dark hair.

"Would you be willing to dine with me tonight, Mrs. Molly Gallagher?"

Molly paused for a moment. Her hands were still trembling, and she gripped them together to make them stop. She almost refused but as she studied Lance's face, she relaxed.

"Yes, I would, just this once." She took his arm and smiled up at him. "Thank you, Mr. Rankin. Thank you for rescuing me. I thought for a moment I was going to have to take a swim."

Lance laughed and drawled, "Well, I am sure glad you didn't. It was a whole lot easier to just punch that fellow than to jump in the water after you! Call me Lance, Mrs. Gallagher. And you are very welcome."

His blue eyes twinkled as he added, "I'm always perfectly happy to help a lady in distress, and if she is as pretty as you, why that is certainly a bonus!"

Molly looked startled and then as she saw he was teasing, her face slowly turned pink and she laughed along with him.

Lance pulled out Molly's chair for her and held it until she sat down. As he moved to the other side of the table, he pointed out different parts of the dining area and told her what was on each deck of the boat.

She looked at him in surprise. "It sounds like you have been all over this steamboat!"

Lance laughed. "Well, we have been on it for five days and there are only so many men to punch," he drawled with a wink and a crooked grin.

Molly was easy to talk to, but Lance had never been a man who just chattered pointlessly. He looked seriously at Molly.

"Mrs. Gallagher, women especially young women, don't travel so far unescorted. Are you running from somebody or to somebody?"

Molly froze. She looked down at the plate for a moment and then looked up at Lance with wide eyes. "The men in the south are rarely this brazen." Her voice was tight, and her breath caught as she spoke.

Humor flickered through Lance's eyes, but he nodded soberly. "In the west, we don't have time for games. I guess that can make us seem abrupt at times."

With a waver in her voice, she asked, "Do you want the whole story?"

"Kit and caboodle," Lance responded with a grin.

Molly placed her small hands on the table and clenched them together. She took a deep breath and look up into Lance's face.

"Have you ever heard of Whispering Pines Ranch?" Molly asked.

Lance nodded. "If I remember right, it is in southeast Georgia."

Molly nodded as she continued, "That was my home. My mother died when I was fourteen. She was always sickly, and the summers were hard on her. I played outside a lot. I loved horses. My father let me ride my pony all over. By the time I was eight, I could saddle him by myself."

Molly smiled and looked directly at Lance. "We went everywhere. I didn't have any brothers or sisters, so my pony was my friend. I rode where I wanted and spent as much time as possible on horseback. I played in the creek, made mud pies in the soft dirt, and created forts from hay. My childhood was really quite idyllic."

"No brothers to bother you or knock you out of trees. Sounds like a pretty good life!" Lance replied with a smile on his face.

"Mother always worried about me, but Father believed I was safe. We had quite a few ranch hands, and they kept an eye out for me as well. Mother wanted me to stay in the house and learn to be a lady."

Molly wrinkled her pert nose and Lance laughed.

Molly couldn't help but smile back as she continued, "Finally, she and Father compromised. I would learn those things but only if I spent half of my day outside." Molly paused and a cloud passed over her face.

"After Mother died, Father was heartbroken. He stayed more in the house and didn't ride as much as he had before."

Molly was twisting her hands tighter now. Lance quietly reached over and placed his big hand over hers.

"It's tough to lose your mother," he agreed quietly. "Tough for you and your father."

Molly nodded. She took a deep breath and continued, "Then the war started, and Father didn't want me to ride all over like I had. I missed it terribly. After the South surrendered, I thought the war was truly over. I didn't realize that things were even more dangerous than before."

Molly hesitated and there was a catch in her voice. "I think my Father understood the dangers, but he didn't know how to talk "*woman things*" with me. Our ranch hands were rough, but they were all kind and gentle to me. I didn't know that all men weren't that way…" Molly's voice trailed off a little as she looked across the ship towards the darkness outside.

Lance was silent. He could feel the irritation for her father rising in him, but he pushed it down and just listened.

CHAPTER 4

"SPAWN OF THE DEVIL"

"I HAD A BEAUTIFUL BAY HORSE NAMED BABE, and I took her out one day in early November. It was warm and sunny—just a perfect day for a ride." Molly smiled softly to herself. "The air was crisp, and I just wanted to feel the wind in my hair and the sun on my face. It was like I had been tied down forever. I left my father a note—I didn't ask him if I could go riding because I knew he would say no, but I did tell him where I was going. Babe and I took off. She loved to run, and I loved to ride, and oh did we run that day. We raced over the hill towards the creek on my father's property. I didn't see the men camped there until we were in the middle of their camp." Molly stopped and quietly sobbed.

Lance cursed silently as he took both of her hands. "You don't have to tell me any more, Molly," he stated softly. Fury raged through his body and he fought to keep the anger from showing on his face.

"But I need to tell someone," she sobbed. "There were eight of them. They cornered Babe and pulled me off her back." Molly paused and a slow tear slid down her cheek.

"They did me wrong. I fought to get away, but I couldn't. They all had their way with me. After what seemed like forever, I heard horses and guns. Father and the ranch hands found me. They shot six of them. Four were killed right away and the fifth one died before they could hang him. They hung the sixth one. Gus, our cook, took me back to the house so I didn't see all of that."

Molly began to cry, soundless shuddering sobs.

Lance was quiet. He didn't know what to do as he squeezed her hands tighter. He looked down as fury seared through him. Molly twisted her hands and Lance realized that he was gripping them.

As Lance relaxed his hold, her voice calmed and she continued, "We didn't have any women in the house, so Gus went to town and found the woman who ran the saloon. She came out and talked to me. I think I cried forever."

Molly looked up at Lance with such raw hurt in her eyes that Lance could feel his own heart break for her.

"My father couldn't talk to me. I think he felt responsible—responsible for teaching me to ride, for teaching me to roam, for teaching me to play by myself, for encouraging me to be fearless, for allowing me to be too much of a tomboy." She paused.

"It wasn't his fault, of course, but he still felt responsible for not keeping his little girl safe. And then, I found out that I was with child. Father lost it. He was furious. I knew he wasn't actually angry with me, but it came across that way. He wanted nothing to do with 'that spawn of the devil.' I didn't see it that way. I was terrified of being pregnant but when I felt this baby growing inside me, I fell in love with it." Tears leaked out of Molly's eyes and dripped down her cheeks.

"Father told me that I needed to give it away. My aunt in New Orleans had a friend who dearly wanted a baby. She and her husband couldn't have children, and it looked like the perfect situation for everyone. Well, for everyone except my unborn baby and me." Molly pulled her hands back from Lance and clasped them tightly together.

"I took the train to New Orleans to meet my aunt and her friend. When we arrived at the station, I took my bags and started up the walk. I saw my aunt and a very severe looking couple with her. I don't know if they were the future parents or not, but I panicked. I was terrified at the idea of anyone so joyless raising my child. I bought a ticket on the nearest boat I could find and here I am."

She looked up directly at Lance.

Her voice quavered, "Now I have hardly any money, a baby on the way and no way to make a living to support a wee one."

Molly tried to square her shoulders, but the tears came anyway. At first, her teardrops were large and slow. Then, steams of tears ran down her face as she cried quietly.

Lance handed her his neckerchief. He was raging inside. *How could her father send her off by herself on such a long and dangerous trip? Truly, the man was either uncaring or unaware of how lucky his daughter had been to make it this far safely.*

Finally, he asked, "Did they catch the other two men?"

Molly's face went white. "No, they disappeared. I wouldn't know them if I saw them, so I wasn't much help in the search. I would recognize their voices though."

Lance sat quietly. *Men like that always come back,* he thought. He hoped the west was big enough for her to never meet them again.

For the second time that day, Lance missed his mother. She would have known what to do. He felt so inadequate. He cursed silently again. *I was raised with no mother and no sisters--I have no idea what to say or what I can do to help this woman.* As he twisted in his chair, his arm bumped the package in his pocket.

Suddenly, an idea came to him. "Miss Gallagher—" Lance began.

"Brewster," Molly interrupted with a small smile. "My name is Molly Brewster. Father told me to go by Molly Gallagher so no one would know who or where I was. Gallagher was my mother's name."

"Miss Brewster, that has a nice sound to it." Lance continued with a smile. He took the small gold band from his pocket.

"This belonged to my mother. It is the only thing I have of hers." Lance paused as he looked at the small ring.

"My brother Paul died in the war and had no wife or girl, so how about you become my widowed sister-in-law? Folks will question you less if you are a widow wearing a ring. Paul wouldn't mind and my mother, bless her soul, would be glad to help—I can see her smiling now!"

Shock and surprise passed over Molly's face as she stared at Lance.

"I've just met you! I can't take your mother's ring," Molly protested. She started to hand the ring back, but Lance pushed her hand down.

He asked seriously, "What am I going to do with it?" He slipped the ring over the tip of his smallest finger. "I don't wear rings and there is no Mrs. Rankin—nor will there be any time soon," he told her with a wry smile.

Molly studied the gold band. It was engraved with, "Abigail, my love." Molly slipped the simple band onto her finger and smiled up at Lance as a single tear slid down her face.

Lance reached over to wipe it with his thumb.

"My mother died when I was three and my father died a year ago. Paul was my only brother. Take it, Molly. Better that you wear it than for it to get bent and dusty in the bottom of a cowboy's warbag. "

Molly turned her hand and the light from the riverboat shined on the ring. It sparkled on her finger, and she looked up at Lance with a soft smile. "Thank you, Lance. I can't think of a more wonderful gift."

"Well, it does come with a few strings attached," Lance drawled as he smiled at her.

Molly stilled and her face paled.

Lance quickly added, "Maybe you will have breakfast with me in the morning, so I don't have to chew on tough eggs and hard biscuits by myself?"

"Perhaps," Molly smiled at him as she stood up. Lance rose when she did and she looked back once as she started for her room. Lance tipped his hat and gave her a crooked smile.

As she hurried to her cabin, Molly scolded herself, *"Molly Brewster, don't you be taken in by a good-looking cowboy just because he was nice!"* Then she thought of his ornery smile, and she smiled in spite of herself.

CHAPTER (5)

A Friend to Talk to

THE NEXT MORNING, LANCE WAS UP EARLY AND WAITING FOR MOLLY by the door into the dining room. As she came down the hall from her room, he tipped his hat and drawled, "Good morning, Mrs. Rankin. You look as pretty as a new born calf on a spring morning."

Molly was startled and then she laughed. The smile stayed on her face and Lance saw dimples that he hadn't seen the day before. She replied, "Thank you, Mr. Rankin. I see you have been practicing your charm." Lance grinned at her as he offered her his arm.

"Why Mrs. Rankin, I am just plumb full of charm."

Molly laughed out loud and the two of them entered the dining hall, catching the eyes of the other diners.

When they were done eating, Lance gave Molly a small derringer.

"It only has two shots," he told her. Molly studied the gun. It was small and could be hidden easily.

Lance showed her how to load it and asked her if she had ever fired a gun.

"I am actually an excellent shot," Molly replied with a shy smile.

Lance looked at her thoughtfully. *She certainly holds it like she's familiar with guns,* he thought. He hoped she wouldn't have to use it. *If she does, I hope she won't hesitate.*

As Molly slipped the small gun into her pocket, Lance added, "It is only accurate up to about four feet. Keep it with you. It won't do you any good if you need it and it is in your cabin."

The Captain announced that they would be arriving in St. Louis the next evening. That meant tonight there would be a celebration. The gala was known as the Captain's Ball and all on board were invited.

"Well, Mrs. Rankin, how would you feel about a little dancing tonight?" Lance asked as they finished breakfast.

"Lance, are you inviting me to go dancing with you? What would your brother think?" Molly asked as her eyes sparkled.

Lance laughed, "Why I believe that Paul would be tickled. He was never one to be morose or sad," Lance answered with a twinkle in his eye. A brief cloud passed over his face, and Molly stood to take his arm.

"Please tell me about Paul," she asked softly. "I would like to know more about your brother."

Lance looked down at her intently and then led her to the ship's railing where they could look over the side.

"Paul looked a lot like me, but he was three years younger. He was always a little more serious. He loved horses. In fact, he was the best horseman I ever met although Slim, one of our riders, would be a pretty close match. He ran the plantation at home until the war broke out."

Lance paused and then added softly. "I wish he had lived. He would have loved the west."

Molly looked up Lance's profile. "He sounds like he was a wonderful brother," she whispered softly.

Lance looked down at her and smiled. "He was. Thank you for that, Molly."

40

They visited most of the morning and then Molly left to do her laundry. She had very few clothes that fit although she didn't tell Lance that. She worked right through dinner and then napped for a bit in the afternoon. She was almost ready to go down for supper when she heard a knock on her door.

Lance was standing at her door with a smile on his face. "I thought I might escort my pretty sister-in-law to supper tonight, and then maybe she would dance a few steps with me," he drawled as he smiled down at her.

Molly laughed as she took his arm. *It is nice to have a friend to talk to*, she thought. *It has been so long since I was able to laugh with someone.*

MAN OVERBOARD!

AFTER THE EVENING MEAL, THE TABLES IN THE LARGE DINING ROOM WERE PUSHED TO THE SIDE to make room for dancing. Soon, the room was full of people. Lance was visiting with some men on the side of the room while Molly was about six tables behind him.

A bold man swaggered into the ballroom. His voice had a nasally twang and he talked loudly. Molly froze and went completely white. His voice pierced her memory and her eyes were terrified. The hair came up on the back of her neck as she whispered, "He is one of them!"

The man glanced toward Lance and then his eyes settled on Molly. With a leer on his face, he angled across the room towards her.

Some instinct made Lance turn, and he saw a burly, unkempt man advancing deliberately towards Molly. As she stared at the man, the color drained from her face, and she clutched at her chest with one hand. Lance began to push through the crowd, knocking tables out of the way as he forced his way back to her.

Before Lance could reach her, he heard the pop of a small gun. The leering man was less than four feet from Molly when he fell. The crowded room erupted into chaos as people stopped to stare, and then pushed each other as they fled towards the doors and stairways. The boat lurched and people slammed into each other.

Molly fell and Lance saw the derringer drop from her hand. It slid across the floor, stopping next to his foot. He quickly put his boot over it and then squatted on the floor beside Molly.

She looked up at Lance with terror in her eyes and whispered, "He was one of them. I recognized his voice."

Lance removed his hat, placed it over the gun and in a swift motion, slid the gun under Molly's body. Her face was completely white, and she was gasping as if she couldn't breathe. People were talking excitedly and soon, some of the men began to point in their direction. No one knew where the shot had come from but since the man and Lance seemed to be heading toward each other, many assumed it was Lance.

One man reached out his hand. "Let me see your guns, son. I want to see if they have been fired."

Lance looked up coldly at the man. His eyes were as hard as glass.

"No one takes my guns," he grated. "I will be glad to show them to the captain, one at a time. And if you knew your guns, you would know that hole was made by a shot from a derringer, not from a 45. Perhaps you would like to check all of the men—and women—present here to see who is carrying such a gun."

People began to mill around and mutter uncomfortably at the mention of the small gun.

The shot man's coat was open, and items were spilling from the pockets.

"That's my bracelet!" a woman exclaimed as she pointed to a small bangle beside the fallen man.

A rough-looking fellow knelt beside the dead man. "Why this is Rib Slater! He rode with Quantrill's Raiders some time back. I thought he'd been hanged back in Georgia last year for hurtin' some gurl. Guess he finally got his just due!"

The room went silent, and then angry voices took over. The man was stripped of his gun, his pockets searched, and his body promptly heaved overboard.

Just then, the captain arrived.

He asked, "What is the problem here?" Most of those present had just walked away, leaving the captain standing next to Lance. The Captain was confused.

"I thought there was a shooting."

"There was," Lance informed him. "One of Quantrill's raiders was shot just a few feet from Mrs. Rankin. Some of the men heaved his body overboard."

The captain looked at Lance and then at Molly. She was trying to sit up but was still shaking.

"Are you all right, Ma'am? I can have one of the cabin crewmen carry you to your room if you like."

Lance answered quietly but firmly, "Thank you, sir, but I will carry my sister-in-law to her room. This was all very upsetting to her."

The captain nodded. "As you wish."

He turned as he walked away and looked back at the two of them. Shaking his head and still a little puzzled, he headed back to the bridge.

Lance was already picking up Molly, keeping the small gun in his hand and hidden beneath her skirts.

As he carried her to her room, he scolded her.

"Molly, what were you thinking? You could have hit the wrong person or you could have been killed yourself!"

Molly looked up at him. Her voice shook but she answered quietly, "I told you I could shoot what I was aimed at. Now there is only one left."

Lance stared down at her and started to answer. Then, he just hugged her tighter to him and was silent. *This young lady is proving to have more guts and nerve than is even healthy.* Ruefully, he shook his head. He stood her up at the door of her cabin and handed her the derringer.

"Reload this right away before you hide it again." He started to walk away but paused a few feet down the hall and turned to face her again.

"Good shooting, Molly," he added quietly.

Molly smiled shakily and closed her door.

CHAPTER 7

An Honorable Man

MOLLY WAS QUIET ON THE LAST DAY and Lance was as well. They were standing side-by-side on the hurricane deck, leaning on the railing as they watched the water rush by. Both were thinking of what was to come. Finally, Lance stood upright and turned toward the small woman beside him.

"You know, Molly, you could come west with me. I'm sure we could find you a job in Cheyenne. Women are in real short supply in Wyoming, and just about any store would give you a job."

He added with a grin, "Just for the business you would bring in!"

Molly's blue eyes sparked and then widened,

"You are serious!" she exclaimed. "Oh, Lance, do you think so? I would be able to make a living for myself and my baby?"

"I sure do."

With devils dancing in his eyes he gave her a lop-sided smile and added, "Or you could just become Mrs. Lance Rankin and then you wouldn't have to tell any stories at all. I think I like that idea better anyway. I am going to have an awful lot of competition for your time once you get to Cheyenne."

Molly elbowed him and they both laughed.

The pier in St. Louis was packed with people as they moved down the gangplank from the *Dandy Frank*. Lance was edgy in the crowded city and wanted to get out of town as quickly as possible. However, the train to Kansas City didn't leave until the next day at 9:00 a.m..

Molly seemed to be in awe. She tried to look in all directions at once; she had never seen so many people nor such a large town.

"I think we need to get you some riding clothes if you are going with me," Lance stated as they maneuvered through the crowded streets of St. Louis.

Molly was quiet.

Lance looked at her and then down at her stomach.

He frowned and asked, "Are you sure you will be able to ride a horse all the way to Wyoming? No roads go all the way through."

Molly answered earnestly, "Lance, I'm as anxious to get up on a horse as you are. I know that I may have to relearn my balance, but I want to do this."

Lance studied her face. Molly's eyes were sparkling with excitement and her cheeks were glowing. He wasn't sure how this was all going to work but Molly was excited; and she certainly knew more about babies, and all that went along with them than he did. Lance smiled and pulled her arm closer to his side.

"Well then, Mrs. Rankin, let's get you some riding clothes!"

The William Barr Dry Goods Co. seemed to have everything. Lance didn't need much as most of his gear was stored in Kansas City. Still, he had never seen such a well-stocked store. The Barr's prided themselves on having everything one would need for a trip west in a covered wagon, and Lance was pretty sure that claim was correct. Dried food and goods, gear, fabric and every kind of cooking utensil were all under one roof.

Molly only had one dress that fit her and nothing to ride a horse in. They were hoping that they could find something here that would work for both riding a horse and riding the train.

The store keeper's wife, Mrs. Barr, was a seamstress and soon Molly and she were chatting it up like the best of friends. Mrs. Barr was a kindly woman, and she loved to help young mothers. She quickly began to measure Molly, talking the entire time.

"So, where are you and your husband headed, Mrs. Rankin?" Mrs. Barr asked.

Molly only hesitated a moment before answering, "To Cheyenne, Wyoming. We are riding the cars to Kansas City and traveling by horseback the rest of the way."

Mrs. Barr stopped pinning. "Well, I hope you have a place in mind where you are planning to stop and have this baby. You look like you are just a month or so away to me."

Lance overheard their conversation as he wandered between the stocked shelves, waiting on Molly. His hands, twirling a rope, went completely still.

A month! "I thought that we would have plenty of time to get back to the ranch before the baby came," he muttered. He frowned as panic began to rise. *What if it's early? What if there are problems? I can't deliver a baby! Why, just the ride to Wyoming alone will be over a month!*

Lance began to fidget, mashing his hat brim as he turned it in his hands.

Mrs. Barr continued to measure, pin and tuck Molly's new dress. Neither seemed to realize the stress their conversation was causing Lance.

"Now you come back in the morning, Molly, and I will have this waiting for you at 8:00."

Molly was chattering away as they left the dry goods store. She was clearly excited about their venture, but Lance was more concerned now than before.

Besides, he didn't like lying of any kind and it looked like they were going to have to continue to lie to make this all work.

"What is it, Lance?"

"Well, other than the fact that you passed us off as husband and wife, it seems that you are calving earlier than I had planned. I know how to calve a cow, but I don't know how to calve a lady!"

Molly stopped and looked up at him with sparks flying from her eyes.

"First of all, women don't have calves, so I am *not* calving. And second of all, I *know* when I became pregnant so unless this baby comes early, we have two months."

With a stomp of her foot, she began marching down the street. However, her steps became slower and slower until finally, she turned around.

"I guess I don't know where we are staying," she admitted.

"Come on," Lance laughed as he took her arm. "We will do it up right tonight since we'll be sleeping on the ground for the next two months. Of course, if we are going to pose as man and wife, I will only get us one room," he drawled as he winked at her.

"Mr. Rankin, how dare you! I most certainly will not share a room with you!" Molly emphatically stated as her eyes flashed a deep blue. She pulled her arm away and once again, the stomping resumed.

Lance caught up with her and pointed at a sign across the street from them that read, The Southern Hotel.

"How would that one be?" he asked.

Molly stopped and stared in amazement. She had never seen anything so elegant. Then her eyes quickly became worried. "I can't. I only have a little money left and I'm sure I can't afford that…" Her voice trailed off as she looked up at Lance.

Lance laughed. "Well, only the best for my favorite sister-in-law!"

As they walked into the lobby of the Southern Hotel, Molly looked around and gasped. The vaulted ceiling loomed high above the lobby, and a huge, curved staircase led to the upper floors. The floor was marble and vast pillars supported the massive structure.

Lance wasn't comfortable with all the gilded walls and sparkling chandeliers, but Molly seemed to be eating it up. Even so, she was still very concerned about the cost.

"Perhaps we should go somewhere less expensive," she whispered. "I don't want you to pay for my room, and I'm sure that I can't afford this."

Lance pushed her forward. He gave the clerk his most charming smile.

"I would like two rooms, one for my sister-in-law and one for myself."

"Names, please?" she asked.

"Mrs. Paul Rankin and Lance Rankin," Lance answered.

"And would you like those to be adjoining rooms, Mr. Rankin?" she asked with a smirk.

Lance's eyes became an icy blue.

"And for what purpose would we need adjoining rooms?" he asked dangerously soft.

Startled, the clerk looked up, suddenly aware that she was on very thin ice with a man who looked exceptionally dangerous at the moment.

"Uh, oh, I meant nothing, sir," she stammered.

Lance leaned in until his face was next to hers, boring into her with his furious eyes. "My sister-n-law will receive nothing but respect from you and if that is too difficult, we can go someplace else," Lance grated.

Mr. Campbell, the hotel owner, suddenly appeared, quick to identify a bad situation.

"Is there a problem, sir?' he asked.

Lance returned to an upright position.

"No," he answered as his blue eyes glinted with anger. "There seemed to be a misunderstanding, but I believe we are perfectly clear now."

Mr. Campbell whispered something to the clerk, and she took two keys from a special rack beneath the counter.

"Mr. Rankin, Mrs. Rankin—your rooms are to the left. There will be no charge for your stay—welcome to the Southern."

Lance thanked her, his voice still steely.

Molly took his arm and they started up the stairs. She could feel the tension and white fury seething through him.

She patted his arm and whispered, "Relax, Lance. It is okay."

He stopped mid-stride and stared at her.

"It is *not* okay! I will not have people smirking or tainting your reputation in any way," Lance spat angrily. "She had no cause to talk like that, and I won't tolerate that kind of rude and disrespectful behavior."

As they continued upstairs, Molly thought about the things that Lance had done to protect her reputation. She whispered a prayer of thanksgiving to God for sending such an honorable man to be her friend and protector.

When Molly opened the door to her room, she gasped, "My own tub!"

The windows looked out over the city. A chandelier hung from the ceiling and the room was done in rich, red brocade. The floor was covered with a large rug.

"Oh, Lance, this rug looks so soft that I just want to take off my shoes and dig my toes into it!"

Molly bounced on the side of the bed. She ran her hands over the velvet cover.

"This bed is huge compared to the one I had in Georgia and amazingly soft," Molly murmured as she touched the cover again.

Lance growled something about food, but Molly wanted a bath.

"Oh, please, may I take a bath first" asked Molly as she eyed the tub.

Lance growled again about food and turned to leave.

As he strode out of her room, he hollered over his shoulder, "Knock when you are ready."

He went to his room, lay down, and was instantly asleep.

When Lance awakened, it was dark outside. His pocket watch showed 8:00 p.m.. He jumped out of bed, ran his fingers through his hair, and slapped his hat on as he rushed down the hall.

"I hope Molly didn't go to eat by herself," he muttered as he beat on Molly's door, hollering for her.

"Molly! Are you in there?"

A sleepy Molly answered the door. "Not so loud, Lance." she whispered. "Yes, I am here. You were sleeping so hard you didn't answer the door earlier so I took a nap myself. Give me five minutes and I'll be ready." She smiled again as she shut the door.

As Lance lounged outside her door, he took in the foot traffic in the hall.

Once again, he muttered under his breath, "I sure will be glad to be back on a horse!" He pulled off his kerchief and went to work buffing his boots. Then he knocked the dust off his hat, slapping it against his leg as he waited for Molly.

When the door finally opened, Lance could only stare at Molly. Her red hair was drawn up on her head with a long curl running down one side of her neck. The midnight blue hair ribbon made her eyes look as dark as the Wyoming sky at night. Lance stared as he offered her his arm.

"Molly, you are prettier than a fresh-born foal taking its first steps," he drawled as he smiled.

Molly looked up at Lance and her blue eyes sparkled. She primly took his arm.

"Thank you for escorting me to supper."

Molly turned lots of heads in the restaurant as she entered. Men bowed to her and she curtseyed daintily.

Lance tried not to snort. He had been raised to be a country gentleman. While he always practiced chivalry and manners around the ladies, some of that other business was just overkill. He was not going to kiss a woman's hand—although he might punch a guy for trying to kiss Molly's.

There were three restaurants in the hotel and all of them were still serving. Lance ordered a steak--rare, cob corn and pie. Molly chose fried chicken.

"I can't remember the last time I ate chicken that I didn't pluck myself," Molly stated as she stared at the menu.

Both were quiet during the meal. Lance was already planning ahead. He would need a horse for Molly and a second pack horse for her things. That was going to delay getting out of Kansas City.

Just as their food arrived, they heard a voice shout Lance's name from the back of the room.

"Lance! Lance Rankin!" Lance turned to see a friend from Georgia.

For just a moment, Lance panicked. The man calling him was Jack Sneld, and as Paul's best friend, Jack would know that Paul was not married. They would have to pretend that Molly was Lance's wife.

Lance hissed, "Molly, that man is a friend of Paul's and he will know that Paul wasn't married."

Molly looked startled but she was perfectly composed when Jack Sneld appeared at their table.

Lance stood and put out his hand with a smile. The man took in Molly appraisingly while he grasped Lance's hand.

"Well, Lance, it looks like you have been busy. Who, pray tell, is this beautiful young woman—other than your wife, I mean?"

Molly smiled back at the man as she put out her small hand. "Molly Brewster, well Molly Rankin, I mean. And you are?"

"Jack Sneld, and the pleasure is all mine. Paul and I were best friends and were together at Columbus." A shadow passed briefly over Jack's face.

He shook Lance's hand vigorously. "What are you doing on the Mississippi? I never figured to see you this side of Denver!" Jack exclaimed.

Lance laughed. "I've been back home. The Colonel died and I sold the plantation. Our business is completed, and we are headed back to Wyoming."

Jack looked surprised. He glanced at Molly's rounded stomach.

"Not by horseback, I hope?"

Molly spoke up with glowing eyes, "Oh, yes indeed! I grew up riding horses and I am as excited as Lance to be on a horse again."

Jack looked at Molly admiringly and shook his head.

"I don't know where you found her, Lance, but I am betting they don't make many more."

Lance agreed and the men shook hands again. Jack headed back to his table and Lance sat down.

CHAPTER (8)

THE PROPOSAL

LANCE'S BROW WAS FURROWED AS HE STUDIED THE **TABLECLOTH**. He finally looked up. "Molly, I'm afraid we are not going to be able to continue this charade. That man is a cattle buyer, and I guarantee you he will show up in Cheyenne just to see if you made it all the way."

Molly laughed but Lance shook his head.

"No, I'm serious. He thinks we're married, and he will expect us to be married when he arrives. He usually comes by the ranch in late August or early September to look over the calf crop, and that is just a little over three months away. Then there is the prospect of taking you across the plains for two months unchaperoned. I don't want to be the one to destroy your reputation before you even arrive in Cheyenne."

Molly became very quiet. "Lance, are you saying that you don't want me to come with you? If so, I will understand. I know that I am a lot of baggage that you didn't plan on." Her heart felt tight, but she tried to stay calm as panic rose inside of her.

Lance looked shocked and then a little embarrassed. "No, that is not what I am saying. I think that we should, um, well maybe—I think we should just get married in Kansas City before we leave." He hesitated as he looked at her and then added, "Then we won't have to lie anymore."

Lance was fidgeting in his chair and turning his hat around as he crushed the brim. When he looked up, Molly could see that his face was tense.

Molly was stunned. She stared at Lance for a moment and then a pink flush rose over her cheeks.

Her voice was brittle and her face tight when she responded, "Lance Rankin, I will not marry you out of your pity for me. I will go on to Kansas City with you since we have the tickets. From there, you may leave for Cheyenne on your own, and I will find work in Kansas City."

Molly's face was tight as she stood up and ran from the restaurant. With tears streaming, she let herself into her room and slammed the door. As she leaned her back against the cool wood, she buried her face in her hands and sobbed.

After a moment, she turned her tear-stained face up and asked, "Why, God, did you have to send someone so wonderfully kind that he would change his life for me?" As she listened to her own prayer, Molly was ashamed of herself. *Look what God did for me! How ungrateful He must think I am! Lance has been nothing but kind and caring, and I have been ungrateful and selfish.*

Taking a deep breath, Molly opened her door. Lance was just returning from the dining room. His face was tight and he barely looked at her.

Stepping out into the hallway, Molly touched his arm, "Lance, I'm sorry. I was very rude and you have been nothing but kind. I have thought it over, and I accept your proposal." Then before he could see her cry again, she stepped back into her room and closed the door.

"Oh, I so wanted to marry for love!" she whispered. "Instead, I am tying a good man to a marriage that he doesn't want because he is too much of a gentleman to walk away!" Molly cried quietly as she climbed into bed.

Lance had been embarrassed when Molly turned him down. Still, his proposal hadn't been all out of pity. *Part of it was based on selfishness,* he thought— *I don't want to share Molly with other men.* Lance paused as he studied on that.

It was true. He liked Molly and the idea of her spending time with another man bothered him. "I'm jealous!" he muttered as he turned red. "I have never been jealous of a woman in my life".

Lance shook his head. "I'm pleased as punch that she said yes, but I feel bad that she thinks she has to marry me, that I'm her only option."

Life is surely getting more complicated and all over a little bit of a thing with midnight blue eyes!

This time, Lance was the one who took a soaking bath, and then he fell asleep in the tub. When he awoke, the water was cold, and he was shivering. He toweled off quickly and jumped into bed.

Why this might be my last bath as a single man. Funny, Lance thought. *I am not even afraid.* As he pondered on that, Lance was surprised. Marriage had always made him uneasy. He liked women but Molly was the first one he hadn't shied away from when marriage was discussed.

CHAPTER 9

LUMPY SMITH

JACK SNELD WAS NOT THE ONLY PERSON WHO NOTICED MOLLY. Another man sitting in a dark corner saw her and recognized her as a girl he had known briefly.

So, the little gal got married, huh? Wonder if she told 'er young husband that a bunch of us took 'er fer a roll in the hay 'fore she snagged 'im? He smirked at the thought. *Not likely,* he thought, *or he sure wouldn't 'a married 'er.* "She prob'bly tricked him into thinkin' that kid is his," he sneered under his breath as he stared at Molly.

Lumpy Smith was a short man with dark, snaky eyes. His lack of hygiene made it difficult to tell if his skin was dark or just dirty. Greasy hair hung down in ragged strings from under the beat-up cowboy hat on his balding head, and a heavy paunch hung over his belt. He stretched out his short legs and leaned back in his chair. He had fled Georgia that fall day on a stolen horse and hadn't slowed down until he reached New Orleans. He had ridden the cars to St. Louis, and he intended to go on west where there weren't so many people who might recognize him. He managed okay just picking pockets but Lumpy was always looking for that next big deal.

"What I need is a new gang," he muttered to himself. It never occurred to Lumpy that he wasn't smart enough to lead a gang of men, but then his opinion of himself had always been overblown.

Say, that young cowboy looks like he might be wearin' a money belt. I might have to foller along behind those two an' introduce myself, smirked Lumpy.

Lumpy saw Molly run out of the dining room and Lance follow slowly.

"Ain't no such thing as love," Lumpy laughed to himself as he left the hotel to sleep in the livery barn. He planned to be up early to see where the two of them went next. *Any couple stayin' in as swanky of a hotel as the Southern has to be packin' some cash.*

Lance was up early. He tapped lightly on Molly's door but there was no sound from inside. He slid a note under her door saying that he had gone for breakfast. First though, he decided to stretch his legs a bit. The livery barn was just down a block or two. He thought he might stop in and see what a barn in a big city offered that the small liveries didn't.

As he stepped inside and looked around, he thought to himself, *not a thing.* Then he saw the blood bay horse in the first stall. She was a beauty. The bridle hanging on a hook by the door was engraved "Babe".

Lance's heart stopped. *Could this be Molly's horse* he wondered? He reached over to pet her, and Babe stretched out her soft nose to nibble his arm. *Probably not the same horse*, he thought. *I mean, what are the chances? She would be the perfect horse for Molly though. She could be a wedding present*, he thought excitedly.

Lance checked the horse over. She appeared to be sound. She was a little thin but overall, Babe was in good condition.

The hostler appeared as Lance was checking the horse's teeth.

"Some feller come in a couple of days ago. He paid for two days and then come in last night. Decided he wanted to sell her. He didn't have a bill of sale so I only gave him $50. If you want her, you can have her for $75 but you won't have a bill of sale neither."

The man scratched his bristly chin. "Funny thing. His rig almost looked like it was set up for a woman. He had the stirrups extended as far as they would go but it is kind of a girly saddle and blanket."

The hostler added, "The horse is real tame. I would say whoever owned her before treated her well, and I am guessing it was a woman." He looked slyly at Lance.

"You buyin' her for a lady friend?"

Lance only grunted. "Do you know where the horse came from?"

The stock tender shrugged his shoulders. "Don't know. I ain't seen that feller around here till the last few days so I'm guessin' that he come in on the cars. From the east, prob'ly. That ain't no western horse."

Lance rubbed his chin. "Since you don't have a bill of sale, I'll give you $60. We have a ways to go and there is always the possibility that someone will step up and claim her as stolen."

The hostler studied Lance. *That for sure is a possibility*, he thought. *I'd be better off to unload her fast and make $10 than lose my original $50 if the sheriff shows up.*

He nodded slowly, "Deal but I want 'er gone first thing. An' you take all that rig as well. When that horse leaves here, she warn't never here."

Lance grinned to himself and paid the hostler. He saddled Babe and laughed as he led her down the street to the stage station.

"Never know what a seed can do once it's planted," he told the horse. "You probably were stolen but I doubt anyone is looking for you. Still, I like to dicker and you saved me $15."

He chuckled again as he picked up the pace. He was committed now so he certainly hoped there was room in the livestock cars. Lance was excited to get Babe but since he didn't want Molly to see her until after they arrived in Kansas City, he needed to arrange for her loading as quickly as possible.

The station agent grumbled a little, but he was more cooperative when Lance flipped him a $1 gold coin on top of the fare. Then he promised to see to the loading himself.

"In fact, I'll make sure she is the only horse in her car," the agent promised.

Lumpy Smith saw Lance take the horse to the train station for shipping and he cursed his luck. *Who woulda' thought her man might actually find that horse let alone buy it? Well, it don't look like he showed it to her. More'n likely, her man's got no idea that it used to belong to his purty little wife.*

He tried to con the station agent into telling him where the horse was headed. "So where's the young feller takin' that there horse? Headed west, is he? She sure is a purty little thing. Bet he bought 'er fer his gurl."

The station agent stared at Lumpy and then turned his back to work. He saw nothing in Lumpy Smith that he liked, and he could close his mouth when he was paid well. When Lumpy continued to hang around his ticket box, the station agent looked hard at him. "I suggest you find someplace else to hang around. If I see you here again today, I am going to tell the sheriff to check the bill of sale on that fancy horse you just sold."

Lumpy cursed again and turned up the street. He settled down in front of a saloon. The train would be in soon and he would see which one they boarded. *I cin foller 'em all the way to Californy' if I have to. In fact*, he thought with a sneer, *the farther from people and settlements that they git, the easier it'll be for me to pick 'im off. Then, I'll take that little wildcat fer my own.*

Molly had bitten him when he raped her and the teeth marks still showed on his face when it was clean. Lumpy rubbed his cheek.

"I'll get even with that little hellcat," he muttered. Lance's tied down guns bothered him for a bit and then he shrugged it off. Being the braggart that he was, Lumpy assumed that any man who didn't brag was a coward.

Lance made it back into the hotel just as Molly was coming down the stairs.

Molly was surprised. "I thought you would be eating already—or are you done?"

Lance shook his head. "I went for a walk. I wanted to wait and eat with my new girl," he drawled and then he grinned.

Molly blushed and looked down. Lance was feeling pretty chipper this morning as he pulled her chair out for her. Then he thought again about the horse. *I really do hope it is Molly's Babe, but then that means that the last man could be around here.*

Another thought pushed its way into Lance's mind. *Why would a fellow sell a horse all of a sudden? Maybe to ride the cars? What if Molly's abuser was on the same train as them? Neither of them knew what he looked like. How was he going to protect her?* With a frown on his face, Lance sat down.

Molly noticed Lance's quick change in mood, but she decided to stay quiet. When Lance was feeling ornery, he always embarrassed her, and she didn't want to blush again.

CHAPTER (10)

A New Dress and a New Friend

MRS. BARR HAD PROMISED TO HAVE THE DRESS DONE BY 8:00 IN THE MORNING, and true to her word, the traveling dress was ready. She invited Molly to come back to her sewing area to try it on. When Molly came out, she had on her riding boots and a long skirt with an overlay. The skirt beneath was split for riding. The overlay could be buttoned on to make it look like an actual skirt or taken off for riding. Mrs. Barr had made the skirt waist band adjustable to ride above Molly's stomach so there was room for more growth. The fitted jacket had long sleeves. Both the skirt and jacket were in a dark blue and the blouse was light blue. The neckline and hem of the jacket were trimmed with small beads.

Molly fingered the trim, and then she turned around. She had unpinned her hair, and it was hanging in a long braid down her back. Her hat was in her valise and with that, she would be ready to go.

"Isn't it beautiful?" Molly exclaimed. "Mrs. Barr, you must have worked on this all night!"

Lance looked at her admiringly. *She sure is a pretty little thing. And look at that hair*, he thought to himself. Then he turned his head. He hoped that neither of the women had seen him staring. *I'm acting like a school boy*, Lance thought disgustedly. He snorted and shook his head.

Molly glared at him and it was Lance's turn to blush.

She must think I am making fun of her dress, Lance thought. *I just can't win*. He thrust some money into Molly's hands and headed outside to wait.

Molly gave Mrs. Barr a hug and thanked her. "Oh, Mrs. Barr, thank you so much," murmured Molly with tears in her eyes.

Mrs. Barr squeezed her arms and whispered, "My name is Sophie and it was my pleasure. Now you take care of that baby and that good man you have. Maybe I will see you again someday."

This time, Molly hugged her hard.

As Molly came out of Barr's Dry Goods, Lance wasn't sure what to say so he stayed quiet and waited for Molly to talk.

Molly was excited about her dress. "Mrs. Barr added some baby garments as well as some cloths to use as diapers once the baby is born at no charge," Molly told Lance as she lifted some of them out of the bag. "She even threw in this travel bag for my extra things. Mrs. Barr insisted that I take it. She said it was just gathering dust because as she stated, 'I sure never get out of here to go anywhere.' She must have stayed up all night to finish this."

Lance was caught off guard. "I guess I didn't think about how long things like that take to make," he admitted with genuine surprise in his eyes.

Molly looked at him for a moment and then laughed. "No, I don't suppose you would know that," she agreed as she smiled up at him.

Then she frowned. "And just what didn't you like about my dress? I heard you snort in there like an old bull."

As she glared up at him, Lance thought about how to answer.

68

His blue eyes began to twinkle and he drawled, "Well if I snorted like an old bull, then you shouldn't have to ask yourself why!" A devilish smiled flickered across his face and Molly eyes opened wide as she turned red.

"Lance Rankin!" she sputtered, as she faced forward and Lance laughed.

This little gal is sure fun to tease, he thought to himself.

Molly didn't stay quiet for long. There were so many things to see in St. Louis that she just had to talk.

"Oh, Lance. Wouldn't it be wonderful if we could come back someday and introduce the Barr's to our little one?"

Lance patted her hand as he tucked it under his arm and gave it a squeeze. "That would be fine, Molly—that would sure be fine." he replied with a smile.

Sophie Barr watched them go with tears in her eyes. Only Mr. Barr knew that she had lost four little ones long before they were ready to be born and a fifth had died during birth. Sophie knew she would never have any babies of her own, but that just gave her more time to help young mothers when she could.

"I hope that young girl makes it to Wyoming safely. Such a long ride and such harsh conditions." She sighed as she began to ready the store. It was going to be a long day with no sleep, but it would be worth it.

Mr. Barr looked up as Sophie walked around the counter to organize the goods and ready the store for the day. He took one look at her face and put his arms around this woman who had been his wife for thirty-five years.

Yes, he thought as he kissed the top of her head, *my wife is a fine woman*.

Sophie looked up at him and smiled as she brushed the tears away. She put out the open sign and greeted the young family coming through the doors.

"How about some hard candy for your youngsters?" Sophie asked as she held out the candy jar with a smile on her face.

CHAPTER 11

NEXT STOP, KANSAS CITY

THE TRAIN WAS RIGHT ON TIME. Once Lance had Molly settled, he returned to the platform for his war bag and Molly's bags. He deposited those by Molly and then hurried to check on Babe. He called to her over his shoulder, "I'll be right back. Enjoy that real seat, Molly. You get to ride the cars in style to Kansas City. No benches on this train!"

Even though he knew the train wouldn't leave until all the passengers were on board, Lance hurried back to the livestock cars. He wanted to make sure Babe was loaded as he had instructed.

Babe had her own car, just as he was promised, and she nickered to him as he climbed up on the side of the car. He gave her a couple of carrots he had snatched out of the kitchen as they left. The cute little waitress had offered him a whole plate with a smile, but three were all he needed—just one for him and two for Molly's horse.

"Ready to go to Wyoming, Babe?" he asked. "It's going to be a new life for all of us!"

Molly scowled as she waited. She really had wanted a carrot too, but she didn't think it would look very lady-like to munch on a long carrot.

"Oh, to have the freedom of a man," she muttered irritably as she watched Lance lope down the steps of the train station. He had a look of pure enjoyment on his face as he munched his carrot. Instantly, she was ashamed of herself. *Why,* she wondered, *am I always looking for things to complain about?* As she thought more about it, Molly began to giggle.

The waitress who had given Lance the carrots had looked at him with pie eyes and he didn't even notice. He was totally into the carrot. Ducking her head so people wouldn't see her grin, Molly tried to keep from laughing out loud. *Soon,* she thought, *I really will be Mrs. Rankin but this time it will be Mrs. Lance Rankin.* That name had a fine sound. Molly pinched herself to make sure it was not a dream and she smiled contentedly.

The baby kicked Molly hard as if to remind her that she hadn't been very attentive lately. She rubbed her stomach and talked softly to him.

"Be patient, sweetheart. We don't want you to come too early. In fact, if you can hold off until we get home to Cheyenne that would be best."

Molly smiled as she felt the baby move. Her skirt showed the jumps and rolls as the baby catapulted inside of her stomach.

"A little life inside of me," she murmured in amazement as the baby kicked her hand. *It could be a girl,* she thought, but somehow referring to her baby as "he" seemed more appropriate.

A dark man in dirty clothes climbed the steps. He leered at Molly and she felt a deep shiver run through her as her neck hair rose of its own accord. She could almost feel the menace in the man. He sat down in a seat catty-cornered from hers and continued to stare at her. Molly looked around for Lance, but he was outside visiting with one of the train attendants. The dirty man smirked at her, and she turned her head away from him.

"What's the matter, Missy? Don't ya like 'ol Lumpy?" he asked.

Molly froze. Pure terror welled up inside of her. *I know that voice!*

Molly's breathing was ragged and her face lost its color. As she clutched her hands together, her right hand bumped the derringer in her dress pocket.

The fear flowed out of her and a cold calmness settled over her. Molly forced herself to breathe deeply, to slow down her breathing. When she turned her head to face him, she was cold and collected. She was afraid but she knew this evil man would never hurt her again. Her derringer was pointed at him through her skirt pocket. One tiny squeeze of the trigger—then Lance was beside her and she turned away.

Lumpy was confused. He knew the girl was scared, real scared of him at first. *But just now,* he thought, *when she turned to look at me, I saw no fear, jist a coldness like I ain't never felt in a woman. Why she almost gave me the willies.*

Lance bounded up the steps and sat down by Molly. He took in everyone in the car and catalogued in his mind where every passenger was seated. His cold blue eyes rested on the greasy man, and the man faced forward. Lance's eyes narrowed as he studied the man's back.

"He's a no-good fellow if I ever saw one," Lance muttered.

He turned to say something to Molly but she was looking out the window. Lance touched her arm and when she turned to look at him, he noticed that her face was pale.

Lance studied her face and Molly smiled.

"I'm glad you're back," she whispered as her eyes flitted to the man's back before they returned to Lance.

Lance scowled as his eyes drilled into the man's back again. Then he took Molly's arm and looped it through his. He smiled at her as he patted her arm, and he could feel her relax.

Lumpy could still feel those piercing eyes cutting into his back, and he didn't like it one bit. He slid down farther in his seat. *No way does her man know who I am. Heck, she doesn't even know,* thought Lumpy.

A cold shadow passed over him. *Some folks say it feels that way when someone steps on your grave*, Lumpy thought. He shrugged it off. *I won't make my move here anyways. I'll wait 'til they's a lot farther from people.* Lumpy was a bushwhacker from way back, and he had no problem with shooting people in the back.

Suddenly, the loading area was filled with noise and scuffling. A mother and ten unruly children were getting ready to board. She had them lined up and was talking to each one, eye-to-eye, *probably telling them the kind of behavior she expects*, Lance thought, chuckling. Once she released them, they all made a mad charge for the steps and exploded through the door pushing and arguing.

Lance grinned. *Looking at their behavior so far, maybe her expectations weren't as high as I originally thought.*

One sat down beside the greasy man and began to talk to him. Three more were in the seat in front of him. When two more sat down behind him and began to kick his seat, it was too much. The greasy man moved to another car and Lance almost laughed.

As soon as the train started, Lance pulled his hat over his eyes and went to sleep.

Molly glanced over at Lance, irritated at his ability to sleep anytime and anywhere. Her eyes widened as she recognized his hatted figure as the cowboy who had set behind her on the first leg of her journey west.

"Lance!" she whispered loudly as she elbowed him.

Lance grunted.

"Were you on the train from Atlanta to New Orleans with me?"

Another grunt came from under Lance's hat.

"You were that cowboy about four rows back who slept the entire trip!" she exclaimed. "The one who moved up closer so he could hear my conversation with the older lady."

Lance pushed his hat up and looked at her with one eye as he grinned. "Could have been but there were several cowboys riding those cars."

"Yes," she agreed," but not one of them tried to sit any closer than four rows away."

"Well," he drawled, "They *might* have but they were discouraged from doing so."

Molly was silent.

Lance pushed his hat up on his head and this time, his voice was serious.

"You looked like you needed a little peace, and each time a man came close to your seat, you froze all up. I figured you deserved a comfortable ride. Then, when you stood and I saw that you were going to have a little one, I figured you needed your rest more than ever."

He winked at her as he drawled, "Of course, that didn't stop me from getting a little closer so I could hear your conversation."

He grinned at Molly, pulled his hat back over his face, slid down in the seat and promptly went back to sleep.

Molly was perplexed.

So Lance was watching out for me the entire trip. Molly whispered a little prayer of thanksgiving. Even when she had been alone and afraid, Lance had been there to make sure she was safe.

She thought again about the greasy man. She was almost relieved to know that he was on the train. Now she knew what he looked like and she knew he would be in Kansas City.

Molly put her hand in her pocket and touched the derringer that Lance had given her. This time she had a gun and she had Lance. *That man will never hurt me again*, she promised herself. Molly relaxed and as she fell asleep, her head tipped to rest on Lance's shoulder.

The train ride to Kansas City was six hours and even the rowdy kids drifted off to sleep. As the train stopped and the doors began to open, there was a commotion in one of the front cars.

A man was shouting, "I've been robbed!"

Lance looked up from under the brim of his hat as the greasy man who had been seated in their car plunged through the door and down the aisle. The man's eyes were on the open door and he looked furtively behind him as he tried to rush by Lance. Lance's boot came from nowhere and tripped him.

The man went down on his face, and a wallet flew from his coat. By the time he opened his eyes, Lance was standing over him, his face steely cold. Lance picked up the wallet and handed it to the passenger who was rushing into their car.

Then, without a word, he grabbed the man by his greasy coat collar, hauled him to the gangplank and kicked him down the depot steps. The passengers began to clap and Lance looked startled.

Once again, Molly thought, *Lance acts and reacts not because he should, but because that is who he is.*

CHAPTER 12

A Wedding Gift for Molly

THE TRAIN PLATFORM IN KANSAS CITY WAS CROWDED with people of every nationality. Languages of all kinds could be heard. Rough-dressed people with hard work written all over them brushed shoulders with the elite who seemed afraid to touch those around them. Everyone had a story, including the young pregnant woman with the protective cowboy by her side. Molly's bright eyes and friendly smile reciprocated smiles from many of those she met as they exited the train.

Lance was watchful as they stepped off the platform. Still he could hardly wait to show Molly her horse, and he was almost bubbling with excitement as he took her hand.

"I have something to show you," he told her, anticipation sparkling in his eyes.

As he led her back toward the cattle cars, a horse whinnied.

Molly stopped and grabbed his sleeve.

"Lance, I just heard Babe whinny! I would know her neigh anywhere—I raised her from a colt!"

Lance patted her hand and smiled down at her.

"I have a wedding present for you."

Lance unlatched the door to the cattle car that held Babe.

It was hard to tell who was more excited, Babe or Molly. Babe's head was over the side and Lance was afraid she would try to push the door down as he opened it. Molly rushed into the car and cradled Babe's big head. Babe nuzzled her shoulder, nickering softly and pushing her head into Molly's chest.

Molly turned a tear-stained face to Lance. "Where in the world did you find her? I thought she was gone forever."

Lance smiled. "Remember that morning in St. Louis when I took a walk before breakfast? I wandered down to the livery stable and there she was, in the first stall. The stock tender told me that he had just purchased her from a man with no sale bill."

A scowl formed on Lance's face. "There is a good possibility that the man who took her from you is the one who sold her, and that means the last man was in St. Louis."

Molly's face went white.

"No, he is here. He's the man you threw off the train."

Shock drained the color from Lance's face. His fingers dug into Molly's shoulders as he jerked her towards him.

"And you didn't tell me? Molly, he could be after you! How can I protect you when you don't tell me these things?"

Molly looked up at Lance quietly. Even though her face was white, she was calm.

"Because you already have. I had my Derringer pointed at him when you boarded the train in St. Louis. You came between his chest and my gun barrel or he might already be dead," she stated quietly with steel in her eyes.

Lance searched Molly's face with his eyes and then folded her in his arms.

"Molly girl," he uttered hoarsely, "I'm here. Let me be in charge of the outlaws. You just take care of that little one growing inside you."

Molly had never felt safer in her life than she did at that moment.

Lance released her from the hug, but he kept his hands on her shoulders.

Laugh lines began to show on his face. "Now let's go get hitched so I only have to pay for one room tonight."

As fire started to grow in Molly's eyes, he laughed and picked up her saddle.

"How about we saddle Babe right here and you can ride her to the livery? The little gal I'm traveling with has me hauling so much stuff that there is no way I can carry a saddle too."

Molly busied herself bridling Babe although the thought of sharing a room with Lance made her fidget and blush uncomfortably.

Once Babe was saddled and Molly mounted, Lance kept one hand on Babe's reins so they didn't get separated in the crowd. He stopped at the platform to get his war bag and Molly's bags. The war bag he tied behind Molly's saddle. Then, he handed her the valise and the bag Mrs. Barr had given her to hold in front of her. He wanted to keep one hand free.

Lance scanned the crowd for the man he had thrown off the train. He viewed everyone in the crowd as a potential danger, and once again was anxious to head out.

CHAPTER (13)

SKULLDUGGERY IN KANSAS CITY

L UMPY HAD LOST MOLLY. He cursed as he looked around the packed station with people going all directions.

The logical thing to do would be to go to the livery and wait for them to get horses, but Lumpy was thirsty. Besides, he had to steal some money or steal a horse, and it was easier to pick someone's pocket.

He bumped into a well-dressed man and almost knocked him down. As the gentleman staggered, Lumpy offered his hand and apologized. "So sorry, Mister. I shore didn't mean to bump ya like that."

The gentleman nodded and dusted himself off. He didn't realize that his wallet was missing until he arrived at his hotel ten minutes later; of course, nothing could be done.

Lumpy turned the opposite direction and found a saloon close to the train station. He ordered a bottle and stood at the bar listening to the talk. A man could learn a lot just listening. There was talk of gold, land, timber, Indian uprisings and travel routes to just about anywhere you could think of. The railroad was moving west and taking people with it.

The bar was packed with people, most of them hard-working people with hope for a better future on their faces. Those who were immigrants had already made the long trek from Staten Island where they were processed as they arrived in America. However, there were also many people from the east moving west. Kansas City was a vibrant patchwork of humanity in 1868.

There were also the thieves and no-accounts like Lumpy. They seemed to be able to pick their kind out of a crowd as well, and it wasn't long before Lumpy had picked out two possible cohorts to join him in his plan to rob Lance and steal Molly.

Bede Benson was a squat, swarthy man. His short neck grew out of thick shoulders and supported a heavy head with cruel eyes. Bede had killed his share of people and had no problem with killing a woman. No one knew what Bede stood for and no one ever asked.

The second man told everyone that he was Bede's partner. He was a slow young man known as Slick. Slick Jackson's real name was Roosevelt Jackson, but he earned the name Slick because he liked to wear his greasy hair combed back over his head. Slick did anything and everything that Bede told him to do. He was convinced that Bede was the smartest man around.

If he was ever asked about Slick, Bede snorted, "Slick is as dumb as a door, and as loyal as a cur dog."

Lumpy first saw the two men standing at the bar. He sidled up to them and began to visit. The one called Bede stared at Lumpy and then turned away; Slick, the younger one, was willing to talk.

"So are you boys lookin' for a little side work?" Lumpy asked as he pushed his bottle their way.

Slick grabbed the bottle and eagerly poured himself a drink. Bede reached for the bottle and took a long pull. He slapped the bottle down on the counter and wiped his lips on his shirt sleeve. He grinned at Lumpy, and Lumpy looked away as the irritation rose in him.

Bede laughed and then sneered at Lumpy. "So what job ya have in mind? Mebbie we's interested an' mebbie we ain't."

Lumpy's plan was simple. "I'm after a feller carryin' a money belt. He's travelin' with a little tramp. I want his money an' I want that gurl."

Bede studied Lumpy. He didn't know this man, but they were short on cash and stealing was his game. He had no problem with killing a man, but a feller had to be careful when it came to women.

Bede asked carefully, "So what ya gonna do with the gurl? Western folks is touchy 'bout ya triflin' with their women."

Lumpy's small eyes glinted. "Ain't nobody carin' about this gurl. She's just a travelin' with this feller. "

He pulled himself up taller as he bragged, "I already done had 'er onct back in Georgia anyhow."

Bede's eyes narrowed down. *There's somethin' here he ain't tellin,'* Bede thought as he sorted through what Lumpy had just said.

"I'm a guessin' that little ol' gurl wasn't willin'," smirked Bede, "or ya wouldn't be so all fired up ta get 'er again." He gave a nasty laugh as he added, "An' I bet it's got somethin' ta do with that there scar on yore face."

Lumpy's face turned red and his small eyes stared hard at Bede. Then they crumpled under Bede's gaze and slid away.

Bede laughed again and smirked again at Lumpy. "Shore. Tell us yur plan. We ain't busy at the time an' we could use a little cash."

Lumpy explained excitedly, "We'll foller 'em outa Kansas City. Once they's out there west a ways, we'll circle around 'em, wait at the next water hole, kill the feller an' take the gurl. The money we'll split two ways—half fer me since it's my deal an' you fellers can split the other half."

Bede listened and then snorted. "Why foller a man all the way west when ya cin roll 'im in a back alley right here in Kansas City?"

Lumpy leaned forward as he answered, "'Cause there'll be less folks around."

Bede stared at Lumpy closely. "What 'bout Indians? I hear they's up in arms 'bout the railroad crossin' their lands."

Lumpy waved his arms in dismissal. "We'll be in an' out so fast that the Injuns won't even know we was there."

Bede stared at Lumpy. *How this man managed ta live as long as he did is a pure miracle,* Bede thought. *I ain't gon' nowhere with him an' he sure ain't goin' ta plan no job I'm part of.* Bede hooded his eyes and pretended once again to listen.

Lumpy continued, "The gurl 'ill go ta me first an' when I'm done with 'er, you boys can do whatever ya want with 'er. The most important part o'' this here deal is that little wildcat disappears an' never comes back."

Slick was a little uneasy about that. He didn't believe in hurting women.

Then he relaxed. *I'm sure Bede would never hurt a woman neither* he told himself.

Although Bede wasn't impressed with Lumpy's plan, he pretended to agree. He lowered his heavy head and bared his teeth in a cruel grin. *Lumpy don't know it but his life's 'bout ta take a hard left turn* thought Bede.

CHAPTER 14

No More Lies

LANCE WANTED TO TAKE MOLLY STRAIGHT TO THE HOTEL SO SHE COULD REST, but she insisted that she see Babe stabled herself.

"Please, Lance. Let me make sure that Babe is taken care of. Didn't you say we will be here overnight? That means that we have a little time."

Lance growled an answer as he headed toward the livery.

Molly looked at him and laughed. "Lance, anytime you are crowded by too many buildings or too many people, you just get cantankerous!"

Lance looked back at her in surprise and then gave a little laugh. He nodded in agreement.

"Yep, you have me all figured out. I'm not a fan of crowds or cities," and he growled again as he picked up the pace.

There were horses and rigs of all kinds on the streets. Men and women headed west with hope in their eyes while discouraged families and broken-down men headed back east. The dreams they had followed had proven to be too difficult. Horses were a needed commodity but were in plentiful supply.

"So how are you on horse trading, Molly?" Lance asked.

Molly was startled but her eyes sparkled with excitement. "I love to dicker on horses! I used to help my father and I always looked forward to the day when I could do a deal on my own."

Lance laughed at that. "Well, polish up your skills because we will be working with one of the best around. Badger McCune was one of the first people to buy land here and is a good friend of Old Man McNary's. The Old Man told me that Badger purchased every acre around this city that he could acquire. Now he is reselling those plots and making a fortune."

The first time that Lance met Badger was on his trip to Georgia when he dropped off his horses. The two men had agreed on a price for Badger to board Lance's horses and the old man was quite the haggler.

Lance knew that Badger was a long-time resident of the small but growing town named City of Kansas although most folks shortened it to Kansas City. Old Man McNary even hinted that Badger was a wealthy man, but you sure didn't see that wealth if he was. He lived simply with one weakness—he loved top hats.

Lance hadn't intended to buy any horses here, but now he needed another pack animal for Molly's things. Besides, Badger had some fine mules that he was pretty proud of. Lance was hoping to trade his pack horse for a couple of mules, and he knew it was going to cost him. No one bested Badger on a horse trade, but just maybe Lance could soften him up with a top hat.

Of course, Lance had no idea that he already had the best deal-maker available in the small person of Molly. Badger was a gruff old codger who had never married, but he was a sucker for a little gal with a big smile. If she could carry on a conversation with him, why she could talk him out of just about anything he had!

Lance decided to send Old Man McNary a telegram to let him know that he had made it to Kansas City. He told him that his trip home would take a little longer, but he didn't say why.

It was now May 25 and Lance had wanted to be home by late June. Anything later than July 15 and they could hit some bad weather, not to mention Indians. Alone he could make thirty to forty miles per day depending on the roughness of the route, but he didn't know if Molly could do a forty-mile day. Sometimes she rubbed her back when she didn't think he was looking so he was pretty sure that sleeping on the ground all the way there as he had planned wasn't going to work either.

The most important thing now is to have her at the ranch before the baby comes, he thought. Lance shook his head. *If the baby comes early or we run into trouble, this trip could prove to be pretty hard on both of them.*

CHAPTER 15

ONE ROOM, PLEASE

THE PACIFIC HOUSE HOTEL WAS CONSIDERED ONE OF THE FINEST HOTELS IN KANSAS CITY. After the 1867 fire, it had been rebuilt. The rooms were clean and comfortable, even considered elegant for the time. Lance had ridden by it on his way back east, and thought it would be a nice place to spend their first night as newlyweds.

He dropped their bags in front of the counter. "One room, please."

Molly blushed and looked down.

When the clerk asked for their names, he answered, "Mr. and Mrs. Lance Rankin, Cheyenne, Wyoming."

The clerk looked up and then down at Molly's stomach. "I have a very nice room on the first floor," she stated with a smile. "It is on the corner so has a little more privacy and no stairs."

Molly blushed again and replied, "Thank you."

"When is your little one planning to arrive?" the clerk asked with a smile.

Molly smiled back. "In about two months."

The clerk then smiled at Lance. "I am sure you are very proud and excited, aren't you?" she asked.

Lance grinned at her. "We both are."

Then he asked, "Say, can you tell me where to find a sky pilot in this town?"

When the clerk looked startled, Molly interjected sweetly, "We want to talk to a preacher about our baby and baptism."

"Oh," the clerk responded with a big smile, "there is one right down the street. His name is Pastor Jenkins and you will find him tending his garden if he is not in his office."

As they walked out of the hotel, Lance looked down at Molly.

"Baptism?" he asked.

"Well," answered Molly. "I just didn't want the conversation to go the direction it did in St. Louis. Besides, I am actually looking forward to being a real Mrs. Rankin." She paused and then added with a giggle, "Although, I do feel badly about ditching your brother so quickly."

Lance looked startled. Then threw back his head and laughed.

"If you had known Paul, you would know how delighted he would have been to help. But you are right; he would never have let you live down dumping him for me."

Taking her arm, they started down the street toward the pastor's house.

Suddenly, Lance slowed down and stopped. Turning to look seriously at Molly, he asked, "Do you want to change clothes or freshen up? Some women make a big deal out of marrying, and you are only going to do it once."

Molly looked up at Lance. She thought he was the best looking man she had ever seen and she really didn't care about what she was wearing. A white wedding dress was not in her future. However, this man was and that was what counted. She smiled up at him.

"Let's do it now. What I wear doesn't matter as much as who stands beside me."

Lance's heart turned over. He knew he cared for Molly but was this love? He had never been in love so he had no idea. Whatever it was, he liked it. He gave her a little hug and they walked arm in arm down the street to Pastor Jenkins's house.

As they knocked on the door, Lance looked at Molly. "No more stories. We are going to tell him the truth." Molly breathed a sigh of relief. Living a lie was hard, and she was glad it would soon be over.

A woman opened the door when Lance knocked.

"Is this the home of Pastor Jenkins?" he asked.

"Yes, and the pastor is in," she replied with a smile. She led them through the house to the pastor's small office in the back, but she never asked them their names.

Pastor Jenkins was a tall man with a kind face. He stood as his wife lightly knocked on his door. She presented the couple to him and then quietly shut the door.

Pastor Jenkins invited them to sit.

Molly did but Lance continued to stand, turning his hat in his hand.

"Pastor, I am Lance Rankin, and this is Molly Rankin, I mean Molly Brewster. We have come to be married."

The pastor studied the tall young man before him and the small woman sitting in the chair. He cleared his throat.

"Perhaps you can tell me a little more about your situation first. Are both of you willing participants in this marriage? After all, pregnancy is a difficult way to start a relationship."

Lance began to turn red and Molly spoke up quickly.

"Pastor Jenkins, about seven months ago I was raped by a group of men whom I encountered on our property. I became pregnant as a result of that rape. My father sent me to New Orleans to give the baby away. He didn't want me or the baby around."

Pastor Jenkins cleared his throat and nodded for Molly to continue.

"I met Lance on that long trip, and he has been my friend and protector. We pretended that I was his deceased brother's wife as it made traveling easier for me if I was a widow. Now, we are going on to Cheyenne, Wyoming and we would like to be married before we make that long trip across country by ourselves." Molly's hands trembled as she spoke but she held her head high.

Pastor Jenkins could see that Molly was a young woman of rare beauty and strength. As he looked towards Lance, he almost smiled. Lance's teeth were clenched, and he was crushing the brim of his hat as he held it in his hands. *Yes, this man is very protective. I believe these two young people may very well be in love and are not even aware of it,* he thought. Pastor Jenkins studied both of them again and then he smiled tenderly at Molly.

"Young lady, what you have done has taken considerable strength and fortitude. And you, Lance, I can see that you are protective of this young woman. I believe God chose you specifically for this special job. To be husband to a woman who was abused but with so much love to give, and father to a child who isn't yours but whom you are willing to raise as such. It is my pleasure to marry the two of you. Please come this way."

Lance quietly let out a huge breath of relief and his stiff figure relaxed. He looked over at Molly and she smiled at him. He didn't know if all women were beautiful when they were pregnant, but Molly certainly was. Lance smiled at his bride as he offered her his arm.

CHAPTER 16

A Big Step

PASTOR JENKINS LED MOLLY AND LANCE OUT THE BACK DOOR of the house and into the quiet little church next door. As they went inside, Lance noticed the name on the sign in front, 'St. Paul's Church.' He smiled ruefully.

Well, brother, I guess you did us one more good turn by helping us to find the right pastor. I just wish you could be here with me today. You would love Molly. Mother and Father would as well.

Moisture collected in the corner of one eye, and Lance wiped at it in surprise. It had been a long time since he had teared up over anything.

Then he frowned and growled to himself, "She is making me soft!" The frown was followed by a grin. Somehow, Lance didn't care.

I'm getting married! The Rocking R hands will sure be surprised when they see what I'm bringing home, he thought as he laughed silently.

Molly's face was pale and her chest was tight. She clutched her hands together as panic overtook her. *What am I doing here? I am marrying for convenience and not for love."* Her eyes began to fill with tears, and she stole a glance sideways at Lance just in time to see him wipe his eye. He growled something that she didn't hear but then he smiled. Molly was trembling and Lance felt her arm shake.

He smiled down at her and pulled her closer to him.

Molly felt a sense of peace. *It is going to be alright. I am marrying a good man who cares about me.* As she thought about her father, Molly almost cried again.

She whispered, "Oh, Father, I wish you were here."

Mrs. Jenkins saw her husband lead the young couple into the church, and she hurried to follow. This was another wedding where she would be the witness, the organist and the musician. She quickly gathered the needed papers along with her music, and hurried to join her husband in the church.

She squeezed Molly's hand and handed her a small bouquet of daisies from their garden. "For you, Sweetheart. A woman should always have a few flowers on her special day," she whispered. Then, she fixed three daisies in Molly's hair and hugged the surprised young woman.

The tears that were in Molly's eyes began to leak out and Molly hugged her back.

Lance was startled but he smiled when he saw how happy that little gesture made Molly. *My Molly likes flowers*, he thought to himself. *I need to remember that.*

The service was short and to the point. Pastor Jenkins talked about love and honor. When he mentioned submissiveness, Lance glanced uneasily at Molly from the side of his eye. She never moved but he still questioned if she agreed to that part. He liked what the pastor said about love and protection. It was Molly's vulnerability that had drawn him in but he hadn't known early on just how strong she really was.

Pastor Jenkins asked Lance if he had a ring and they both looked at Molly's hand. Molly slipped Lance's mother's ring off of her finger and placed it in Lance's hand. As he slid it back on her small hand, he could feel his mother smiling.

Suddenly, it was over, and Mrs. Jenkins was playing *Amazing Grace*. Both Molly and Lance liked to sing although neither of them had ever heard the other sing before. Molly didn't think she had ever heard a song sound prettier than they all sounded that day.

As the last note ended, Pastor Jenkins looked at the young couple in front of him. "I now pronounce you husband and wife. You may kiss the bride!"

Lance stared at the pastor for a moment. He had never been to a wedding before but he sure didn't think you did things like kiss in church.

Molly turned a little pale and dropped her head.

Lance looked at Pastor Jenkins, "Well, if a kiss is part of this deal, then let's make it a good one!" He turned to Molly, scooped her up, and kissed her soundly.

When he finally put her down, Molly was unsteady, and Lance was laughing.

The pastor smiled and Mrs. Jenkins started playing *Bringing in the Sheaves*.

Lance shook the pastor's hand. "Thank you for fitting us in today. And you too, Mrs. Jenkins, for the flowers." Molly smiled and nodded in agreement.

"How much do we owe you?" Lance asked.

Pastor Jenkins replied, "You don't owe me a thing for doing the Lord's work. However, the church is going to need a new roof so a donation for that would be wonderful if you can afford it."

Molly took the few dollars that she had left and gave them to Pastor Jenkins.

As they walked out, Lance whispered, "You didn't have to do that, Molly. You should have kept your last few dollars and let me take care of the payment."

Molly smiled. "I know but I felt like I needed to. Besides, now you can tell all your friends how you were drug to the altar and your new bride even paid to make it happen!"

When she laughed up at him, Lance almost scooped her up a second time. His gaze lingered on her face, and it was so intense that Molly began to blush.

Then his eyes began to twinkle and he drawled, "Molly girl, you are so pretty that you put the sunset to shame."

As Molly smiled up at him, her blue eyes seemed to swallow him up.

Lance coughed to cover his emotion. He took her hand and they started to walk back to the hotel. The young couple was quiet; they had just taken a big step together and were wondering what was to come.

Both were hungry so they stopped at the first place they found, "Grandma Nell's Steak and Pie House." Molly was learning that two of Lance's favorite foods were steak and pie. This time Molly tried the meat loaf. Lance ate all of his and then cleaned up what she couldn't eat. Grandma Nell's portions were huge; even a slice of pie was one fourth of a pie.

As they left, Lance pointed down the street. "Now you have to help me buy a top hat."

Molly stopped and looked up at him in surprise. "A top hat? You would wear a top hat?"

Lance looked startled. "Not for me—for Badger McCune. I want to use the top hat to soften him up."

Molly smiled sweetly at him.

Lance looked at her suspiciously. Whenever she gave him one of those sweet smiles, he knew he was in for trouble. *Now what*, he wondered?

Molly giggled, "Maybe you should let me soften him up."

Lance snorted. "You probably could do it because you know how to get what you want, but do you know anything about mules?"

"No, but I know horses *and* I know how to work a deal," Molly answered. "You point out the mules you want, and then let me take it from there. If I fail, you can bail me out."

Lance was about to disagree but as he thought about it, he agreed.

"This could just be a lot of fun! Now come on. Let's go find that top hat!" Laughing together, they walked down the street.

Lumpy stepped out of a saloon as they went by. He pointed at them and elbowed Bede.

"They's the couple I was tellin' ya 'bout. Why don't ya have yore partner keep an eye on 'em but don't let 'em see 'im."

Bede nudged Slick who was sleeping with his head back and his mouth open.

"Slick! Wake up! Foller that couple there an' see what they're doin'. Find where they is stayin' and then come back. *Don't let 'em see ya.*" Slick nodded and glided out the door. As slow as he was to understand, he was hard to lose when on a trail. He had grown up in the woods and was most at home there. He sauntered down the street, keeping Lance and Molly in view. When they stopped at Wilson's Haberdashery and Millinery, Slick crossed to the other side of the street and picked up a stick. He sat down and began to whittle. He could see the door easily from where he sat on the boardwalk, and it was comfortable there in the sun.

Lance was beginning to regret bringing Molly with him to find a top hat. She made him try on *every single one*. The clerk helped for a time and then became busy with other customers.

"Maybe that clerk just figures that Molly is in charge, and I will buy whatever she tells me to buy," fumed Lance under his breath. Then he had to grin because he knew that was exactly how this would work.

"They all look ridiculous." Lance complained. "And why do you need to see them from the back each time?"

He is actually pretty cute when he is irritated and confused, Molly giggled to herself. However, as Lance's scowl became larger, she decided that the games were over.

Molly pointed at a silk hat with beaver skin around the band and a large red feather.

Lance's eyebrows shot up. "*That* one? Why it is the gaudiest, ugliest one here!"

"Trust me. If Mr. McCune has a collection, he will love something totally over the top," Molly smiled. "It will stand out and be different from everyone else. And, from what you have told me about him, he doesn't care what people think. He lives his life totally as he pleases."

Lance had to agree with her but still, at two bits, that hat was going to cost him half as much as their room.

"Good thing I'm only paying for one room tonight," Lance muttered.

At the thought of the single room, Molly's smile faded just a bit. She bit her lip. *I hope he will be understanding,* she thought. Looking at Lance's face from the side, she could see the smile lines around his eyes and lips. *Still,* she thought, *I have seen his face as hard as stone and his eyes glittering like chipped glass.*

Lance suggested that Molly pick a Stetson for herself as well.

She shook her head. "Thank you, but I already have a hat in my valise."

As they walked out of the store, Lance noticed a young man sleeping across the street. He was leaned up against a support pole. His whittling knife hung loosely in his hand, and the stick he had been working on lay on the boardwalk.

Lance studied his face. He didn't recognize the man and it didn't look like he would be moving anytime soon. The warm sunshine had wooed him to sleep.

Lance took Molly's arm and they strolled toward the hotel.

Molly was quiet as they walked the short distance to the Southern Hotel.

Lance was doing some thinking too. After what Molly had been through, he wasn't sure how she would feel about sleeping with a man in her bed.

I will sleep on the floor, he thought. *I'm used to it, and she could probably use the extra room to get comfortable.*

Of course, he hadn't shared his plan with Molly, and she had chewed on her bottom lip until she had almost drawn blood.

Lance opened the door and lit the lamp. Then he stepped back out to let Molly walk in first. This room was newer and quieter than their rooms in St. Louis had been. Lance knew that the hotel had burned, and only reopened this year.

They sure burn down a lot of hotels around here, he thought. *Best not tell Molly. She will have just one more thing to worry about.*

"I will sleep on the floor if you don't mind letting me have one of those blankets," Lance told her. "Do you want me to see if they will bring you some water for a bath?

"I would dearly love a bath," Molly answered. Then she looked away as she blushed, "but there is literally no privacy in this room."

Lance grinned at her. "I will put my blanket over here and turn my back. You can have all the privacy you want. Just know that I am taking a bath in the morning and I don't care about privacy at all." he added. There was a devilish twinkle in his eye. When Molly blushed a deep red, Lance laughed again—he had accomplished what he wanted.

Lance headed down to the front desk to arrange for their baths. When he came back into the room, Molly had taken her hair down and was brushing it. It reminded Lance of his mother and how she used to brush her hair at night. He had always loved his mother's hair.

Lance picked up a lock of Molly's hair and slid it through his fingers. Even though his hands were rough, he could still feel the silky softness. "Your hair is softer than the silky mane of a well-groomed horse, Molly."

His compliment startled Molly and then she smiled. Lance's compliments often compared her to something he admired, and she smiled at him again.

Lance made a bed in the corner, removed his shirt and began to undo his britches. Molly quickly turned her back, and Lance dropped onto the blanket. He was quietly snoring in no time and by the time the water arrived, Lance was breathing deeply, sound asleep.

Molly enjoyed her bath. She discovered that she could look over the city when the curtains were open or have the room completely dark when they were closed. She looked over to where Lance was asleep on the floor.

"Thank you for not asking me to share a bed with you tonight, Lance," she whispered softly.

When she finally climbed into bed, she fell immediately asleep too.

CHAPTER 17

BADGER McCUNE

BY THE TIME MOLLY AWAKENED, LANCE HAD THE HORSES SADDLED and tied to the hitching rack in front of the hotel. When he walked in, she was just sitting up in bed.

Lance grinned at her. "Good morning, Mrs. Rankin. Are you ready for some breakfast? This will be the last meal you don't have to cook for me in some time," he teased. "How about I meet you downstairs in say, ten minutes?"

Molly nodded. "I won't be long," As he closed the door, Molly rushed to get ready. She almost worked up a sweat just fastening her dress.

Soon I am going to have to ask Lance to help me, she thought as she blushed a deep red.

"We are going to ride out to Badger's this morning, so I hope you are ready to do your horse trading," Lance told her as they found a table "Badger lives about five miles out, and has eyes like a hawk. He will have us spotted, analyzed and a stamp on us long before we get to his place."

Lance ordered beef, eggs, bacon and scrambled eggs. "Whatever you don't want, I will clean up," he told Molly as she stared at him in surprise. Lance couldn't remember the last time he had eaten eggs twice in one week and it had been almost a year since he'd had any bacon.

"We might have to get a few pigs," he commented as he chewed contentedly. "I sure do like my pork!"

"And chickens?" asked Molly hopefully.

Lance nodded as he ate. Then he paused and added, "But no milk cow!"

Molly was wearing her new riding outfit. It fit nicely over her growing belly. She looked up and saw Lance's eyes on her.

"You are prettier than a painted pony, Molly," he commented softly as he studied her.

Molly blushed and then smiled happily. "Thank you, Mr. Rankin," she answered primly. "You are looking quite handsome yourself."

Lance looked surprised and then reached across the table to squeeze her hand. When she looked up again, the lights were sparking in his ornery eyes and he winked at her.

"I think I am going to enjoy this marrying business."

Then his face became more serious.

"Molly, this ride today will be a test run to see how you do on a horse. I am thinking we need to change up our plans. I just don't think you can handle pushing so hard by day and sleeping on the ground."

"Oh Lance," Molly pleaded, "Please just let me try at least one week. I am so ready to ride again. I am tired of being locked up in trains and boats and hotel rooms. I want to feel the fresh air and see the world between Babe's ears!"

Lance slowly nodded but he was already studying the route in his head. The problem was, there were few options and none of them were easy. His brow furrowed and he was quiet through the rest of their meal.

As they walked down the steps of the hotel, Molly handed the box that held Badger's top hat to Lance to tie to her saddle.

"Unless you want to wear it!" she giggled as she to keep a straight face.

The look that Lance gave her broke her composure and she folded over laughing. "You did look quite dashing."

Lance glared at her and her eyes crinkled with humor.

"I like this hat just fine," he growled as he jammed his Stetson down on his head.

Lance gave Molly a leg up into her saddle, mounted his horse and they headed out of town.

He noticed the young man with slicked-back hair come from behind and ride past them. Lance recognized him as the man sleeping across the street when they had come out of the top hat store. As he dug back through his mind, Lance couldn't find a memory of such a man anywhere. *Still*, he thought, *I'd better keep an eye out for him.* "Twice might be an accident but three times would not be, even in a town the size of Kansas City," he muttered under his breath.

Now that Lance knew the last of Molly's attackers was in Kansas City, he was even more vigilant. Molly looked over at him as he muttered under his breath. He glanced up and laughed apologetically.

"I guess I am too used to riding alone. I talk to my horse and myself a lot." He added more seriously, "I will be glad to get back home. I'm suspicious of everyone here because I don't know anyone. Back home, I know when a stranger comes around. Here, everyone is a stranger."

Molly was quiet. She had always tried to be strong, but it was nice to have someone watching out for her. She smiled at him.

"Thank you, Lance. I feel safe when you're around."

Lance reached over to squeeze her shoulder and they urged their horses to a cantor.

It was a beautiful morning for a ride. The air was still cool, and everything was green.

Lance looked over at Molly and she smiled at him again. Her eyes were shining and her long braid hung down her back. Babe had a smooth stride, and Molly was enjoying her ride. Slowly, Lance's concerns were disappearing; Molly looked completely at home on her horse.

Lance pulled on the reins. "Let's slow down. I don't want Badger to shoot at us with that big buffalo gun he carries around."

Molly looked at him in surprise, but they slowed their horses to a trot as they moved closer to Badger's Lane.

Badger spotted them when they were almost a mile away. He also saw the rider hiding back in the brush about three hundred yards to the right of his gate.

"A feller who cain't use the gate is shore up to no good," growled Badger as he aimed toward the horse.

His shot was right over the horse's neck, just low enough to graze the mane. The horse exploded in the air, dumping its rider on the ground before it raced away, reins trailing.

Badger grinned and spat out some tobacco juice. "That thar horse won't even slow down 'til it gits ta the livery an' mebbie, not even then."

His second shot was close to where the unseated rider crouched, and the man dropped flat on his face.

Badger shouted, "My next shot'll cut ya in two, stranger. Now come on outa there with yur rifle an' point it ta the sky!"

The rider whined, "My rifle is on my horse."

"Then hold up yur six shooter an' git on down here," ordered Badger.

Lance reined his horse in as he heard the shots. He recognized Badger's buffalo gun and waited for return fire. When he heard nothing else, he led Molly on down the road, listening for anything out of the ordinary as they rode.

The man's hands were high in the air and he walked toward Badger as he whined, "My name is Slick Jackson. What are ya shootin' at me for? I ain't done nothin' to you."

Badger kept his cold blue eyes on Slick. "Ya was a sneakin' 'round on my place. Any feller what don't use the gate is a gonna git shot at. Now take off yer boots."

Slick started to protest so Badger pointed his gun at him and cocked it.

"I could drop ya where ya stand an' not a person 'round would miss ya or never find ya if they did. Now I suggest ya stay on my good side, an' do as I say."

Slick pulled off his boots and stood up in his dirty socks. "You'ins socks too," ordered Badger, "an' whilst you'ins is at it, git rid o' the gun belt an' those 'spenders."

"I won't be able to hold my pants up!" cried Slick. Badger gave him a wolfish grin. "Well as long as ya have one hand busy holdin' up yur pants, that is one less hand ta git in trouble. Now git!"

Slick's eyes opened wide. "You 'spect me to walk all the way back to town?" he gasped.

Badger pushed the gun a little closer to Slims' chest. "I don't rightly care how ya git ta town, whether ya walk or if'n I haul ya in the back of that there wagon. Ya come out here lookin' fer trouble an' ya found it. Now *Git!*"

Lance's eyes narrowed as a meek version of the young man with the slicked-back hair hobbled by, carefully picking his way over the rocks. One hand was holding up his pants. His feet were already bruised, and he had nearly four miles to go to get back to town.

Lance turned in the saddle to watch him, but the man didn't look around. Once again, Lance turned the man's face over in his mind but found no memory of him.

Lance frowned. *Everyone is a stranger to me here*, he thought. *Where does that man fit in, and what was he doing with no boots on?*

Badger turned his eyes back to the riders coming down his road. He could tell one was a woman by the way she sat her horse and he recognized the second as Lance Rankin, the fellow who had left his horses for Badger to board while he went east.

That there kid is a horseman, Badger thought as he watched the easy way that Lance rode. Then Badger's sharp eyes returned to the woman. "By George," he chuckled to himself. "That little gal is gonna drop a wee one real soon. This here is goin' ta be an entertainin' day!"

"Howdy there, Kid. 'Bout time ya picked up yur horses," Badger greeted them. "I thought mebbie I would git to keep 'em an' make a few bucks." Badger let fly with a trail of tobacco juice. "Thought mebbie you went an' got yoreself shot up or dead or somethin'."

Lance grinned at him. "Not this trip, Badger! Lance looked back over his shoulder where the walking man could be seen picking his way carefully over the rocks. "Any trouble this morning?" he asked casually.

Badger grinned. "Naa. No trouble 'tall. Jist a feller who come a walkin' out here this mornin' with no shoes an' no gun. Guess his hoss got away from 'im."

Lance looked down at the boots, socks, and gun lying on the ground. Badger gave an evil chuckle, and his bright blue eyes glistened.

"Feller should be careful where 'e falls off'n his hoss!" Molly had been watching Badger as he talked and she was smiling. He looked fierce but she wasn't buying it. She had him pegged as a softie from the get-go. Molly had grown up around gruff men with soft hearts, and this one wasn't going to fool her. She laughed out loud and Badger gave her an ornery grin.

Before Badger could say anything more, Lance nodded toward Molly. "And as far as me taking longer, let me introduce you to my wife, Molly Rankin. Molly, Badger McCune."

Badger swallowed so fast that he choked and swallowed some of the tobacco juice. As he tried not to cough, he moved toward Molly. He was grinning and his blue eyes were full of orneriness.

106

"Well, ain't you a purty little thing. How 'bout you dump that there slow cowboy an' marry ol' Badger? You won't have ta work near's hard. Just rub my feet at night an' scrub my back!"

Lance looked completely irritated but Molly laughed.

"No thank you, Mr. Badger. I think I will keep the man I have. However, I do have a gift for you!"

Molly handed Badger the box that held the top hat.

Badger's eyes opened wide as he tried to appear nonchalant. When he opened the box and saw the top hat, Badger couldn't contain himself.

"WhooWee! Ain't that a purty one!" He put the hat on his head and began to dance fast jig, totally delighted.

Lance rolled his eyes and refused to look at Molly. He knew the look on her face would be a sugary sweet, "I told you so!"

Badger went to the horse tank to admire his reflection in the water. As he turned around, his ornery blue eyes were twinkling.

"So, Mrs. Rankin, I know ya didn't ride out here just ta' give me a hat. What is it that you'll be a wantin' from Badger?"

Molly's eyes were shining as she slipped off of her horse.

"Mules, but not just any mules. I want two of your best for packing my things across the prairie to Cheyenne." She paused and gave him a sweet smile as she added, "I hear that you are known for your mules, and that you are particular about who you sell them to. That is why I wanted to talk to you myself."

Molly gave him another big smile as she waited for his answer.

Badger looked down at Molly and grinned.

Lance was incredulous. He had never seen Badger so cooperative. Molly was going to get her mules and he hadn't even told her which ones he wanted.

Badger looked over at Lance who just folded his hands across the saddle horn and shrugged his shoulders. He was trying to be nonchalant, and then Badger winked at him. Lance ducked his head to hide the grin.

That ornery old cuss, Lance thought as he chuckled to himself. *Badger is going to make her work for those mules and they are already hers!*

"So which mules do ya think ya want, Missy? They's all fer sale 'cept that mean-lookin' feller over thar. His name's Mule an' he's mine."

He walked by the big mule, talking to him as he passed. "Now, Mule, these here folks is friends. Ya jist be on good behavior today. Ya ain't gonna chaw on no one jist yet."

Molly stared at Badger and then at Mule. The mule yawned and wobbled his lips at her, but Molly didn't touch him. Somehow, she knew that Badger was telling the truth about that mule.

Molly looked back at Lance and then at Badger.

She whispered, "Mr. Badger, I have a confession. I don't know a thing about mules, but I told Lance I was an excellent horse trader so he would let me do the negotiating."

As Molly smiled up at Badger, his old heart just went squishy.

He took her arm. "I tell ya what, Little Missy. I'll show ya the mules an' then we'll dicker. Let's jist see if we cain't make yur feller proud!"

Lance watched as Badger showed Molly the mules. Badger had her feel their backs and look at their feet. They looked inside the mules' mouths to check their teeth for age.

"It's the length o' their teeth, Missy. Ya don't want a mule that's long in the tooth 'cause he'd be an old feller."

Badger already knew the age of each, but he wanted Molly to see for herself. Each of his mules had its own personality and all were exceptionally tame.

Lance grinned as he watched them. Molly was totally enthralled with the process, and Badger was having fun explaining all the attributes of a good mule to her.

When the deal was done, Molly had three mules with pack saddles and bridles, five days food supplies, a new blanket for Babe, a bed roll, and a blanket for the new baby. Badger took the pack horse that Lance had left and $50 cash.

Lance was stunned. He hadn't uttered a word the entire time. Molly did know her horse flesh, and now she knew a little about mules as well.

Molly's face was flushed, and she was laughing as Badger and she shook hands.

Badger winked at Molly. "Now, little missy, ya come back here an' see me any time ya want. An' if'n that there cowboy don't treat ya right, you'ins jist let Badger know."

Badger reached up to shake Lance's hand. "You'ins got yerself a prize filly there, son. Treat 'er right now. Give 'er a little rein an' let 'er know she's special ta ya," Badger said softly.

Lance looked at Molly and then back at Badger.

"I will do that and know that you can always come to Cheyenne if things get too crowded here."

Badger grinned. "Why ya never know when I might jist show up. 'Nother year or two an' I'll be able ta ride the cars all the way ta Californy! I jist might stop in. 'Sides, it's good fer youngins ta have a grandpappy!" he declared with a wink as another stream of tobacco juice shot out of his mouth.

Molly laughed and Lance shook his head.

As they rode away, Lance pondered, "I don't know what kind of grandpa Badger would be. Somehow, I just can't see that."

Molly smiled as she looked back to wave at Badger. "I think Badger would be a wonderful grandfather, and I do hope that he comes to Cheyenne to visit!"

Badger watched the Rankins ride off and his wise old eyes narrowed.

"I think it's time I took a trip ta town. That kid I sent packin' warn't smart 'nough ta plan anythin' on his own. I think I'll find out who he's a runnin' with an' what they's up to."

He rolled up the boots, suspenders and gun belt in a blanket. "I b'lieve I'll jist return these ta that there feller," he cackled with a wolfish grin.

Badger adjusted his top hat, whistled for his favorite mule and headed for the barn. When he was almost to the barn, he stopped.

"Now wouldn't those two kids be plumb surprised if'n I showed up in Cheyenne. I think I'll plan me a little trip. Me an' ol' McNary ain't had a good argument in years! 'Sides, that little ol' baby needs more than one grandpappy, 'specially if the other's ta be Old Man McNary!" By the time he arrived in town, Badger's trip to Cheyenne was completely planned. He would leave next week on the stage.

CHAPTER 18

MULE INTRODUCES HIMSELF

L ANCE LED THE WAY BACK TO TOWN but he didn't take the pack mules in. Instead, he hid them outside town in a thick grove of trees. The Rankins rode into town by a different route than they had taken when they left, coming to the livery on the back side. They quickly slipped in a side door. Lance switched his gear to his mustang. He grabbed their bags that he had stashed in the barn early that morning and tied them onto his horse. He bought several bags of oats which he tied to Molly's horse. In just a few minutes, they were headed back out of town. It was barely 10:00 a.m. and Lance wanted to put as much distance as possible between them and anyone who might be following.

By the time Slick made it to town, his feet were raw and bleeding; Bede showed no sympathy.

"Well, where are they headed an' when are they headin' out?"

"I don't know 'cause that crazy old man shot at me. He just cut lose for no reason!" Slick was sitting on the ground, trying to pull some stickers out of his bloody feet.

Lumpy's eyes narrowed and Bede kicked Slick as he cursed.

"Stick them in that horse tank over there, and next time, don't get caught," he growled.

As Slick hobbled toward the tank, a small man on a large mule rode up. He threw a bundle at Slick's feet. "Lose somethin'?" he asked casually.

When the bundle fell open, Bede saw Slick's gun belt, dirty socks, and boots. Slowly he looked up at the little old man to see a large buffalo gun trained on his stomach.

"I been a doin' some thinkin'," stated the old man, "an' I'm a tryin' to figger why this here kid would be a hidin' in the brush out ta my place."

As he talked, the old man moved the gun from Bede to Lumpy. Bede didn't know Badger McCune and neither did Lumpy. However, Slick had experienced the old man's shooting skill first hand, and he hit the ground, crawling towards the horse tank as fast as he could crawl.

Bede's face twisted into a snarl as he jumped to the side and went for his gun. Badger shifted the barrel of the buffalo gun and shot Bede in the brisket. The man was thrown backwards five feet. Bede tried to stand but was only able to sit up. He stared down at the large hole in his stomach and then looked up in surprise. His lips moved but the words couldn't be heard.

Lumpy threw down his gun and cried, "I ain't holdin' a gun!" as Badger moved Ol' Betsy to cover him.

Badger stared at Lumpy. His finger flicked back and forth over the trigger of the gun as he asked, "What's yer in'erst in those two kids?"

Lumpy's mind worked hard to come up with a believable story. He didn't think of Molly's man as a kid, but he guessed someone as old as this old coot might. He looked over at Bede.

He's dyin' anyways, Lumpy thought. "Bede here thought they had money. He wanted to rob 'em. I tried ta talk 'im out of it but he sent Slick there out to keep an eye on 'em. I got nothin' to do with this."

Bede stared up at Lumpy. His last thoughts were, *the little coward. That's how he lived this long. He's a lyin', lowdown coward.*

Badger kept his big gun trained on Lumpy. He knew Lumpy was part of it, but as with any lie, there was just a touch of the truth to Lumpy's story.

Badger kneed Mule closer to Lumpy. "I jist want ya ta know," he threatened with a deadly look on his face, "that I takin' a likin' ta that little gurl. I'm a gonna be 'round an' ya won't see me. But if I ever see you'ins even *look* at that little gurl, I'm agonna turn Mule loost on ya. An' ya ain't never been stomped till ya been stomped by a mule!"

Just like that, Mule reached out his head, laid back his ears and proceeded to take a bite out of Lumpy's arm.

Lumpy screamed and fell back.

Had Badger not stopped him, Mule would have followed Lumpy to finish the job.

Badger spoke softly, "Not yet, Mule. Mebbie someday." As he turned and rode away, Badger looked back one more time. "Someday."

Lumpy felt a chill of fear sweep over him, but he sneered at Badger's departing back.

"That crazy ol' man. Com'on, Slick," Lumpy demanded as he held his bleeding arm. "Let's go get a drink an' get me bandaged up."

Slick looked down at Bede and shook his head.

"Not me. I'm done with that old man. No sir. There's a little spread out south o' town that's a lookin' to hire someone ta swamp out their barn. I'm a gonna go get me a job that ain't so hard on a body!"

Lumpy looked at Slick in disgust. "You'll never be nothing!" he snarled at Slick.

He tripped over Bede as he tried to reach for Slick. He kicked the dead man. "You ain't nothin' neither but Lumpy is still alive!"

As Lumpy disappeared between the buildings, Slick crawled into the horse tank and carefully positioned his sore feet on the side. He could hear someone hollering for the sheriff.

"Bede's dead," he muttered as he slid around on the bottom of the tank, "an' that coulda' been me. I'm a reformed man."

Slick sank down into the water and let the coolness soothe his feet.

CHAPTER (19)

WHERE NO ROADS GO

LANCE WASTED NO TIME TYING THE MULES TOGETHER. He attached the traveling bags and checked the bindings before he led west at a fast trot. As they came out of the trees, he put his horse into a slow lope hoping to make the pace easier for Molly. He turned in his saddle to look at her and she was smiling. Babe was loping easily and Molly was completely enjoying herself.

Lance smiled. *This just might be a fun ride. Easy-riding horses, a girl to talk to and my wife at that!*

Although there had been few Indian uprisings that spring, Lance kept a sharp eye out. They had a long way to go, and he didn't want to be caught off-guard.

They made camp that evening near a trickling spring, and Lance made a quick meal of biscuits and beans. Water was plentiful in eastern Kansas but the further west they rode, the more scattered the creeks would be.

Molly rested her hand on her stomach. The little one didn't seem to mind her riding a horse but after being calm all day, he was bouncing inside of her tonight. Still, it was a wonderful day and she gave Lance her bright smile.

"We made about twenty-five miles today—not too bad for such a late start," Lance commented as he handed her a plate. "Babe seems to be keeping up the pace well. How are you doing?"

"It was a wonderful day, Lance. The weather was beautiful and the baby traveled well. I think he likes to ride."

"Well, he better," Lance laughed. "We have a ways to go."

The nearby spring could be heard and the sound of the water was tempting.

"You might want to take advantage of the waterhole, Molly. We won't have this fresh of water at every stop." Lance suggested.

Molly studied his face. Her first inclination was to decline, but then she nodded, "A bath would feel good after that ride. I would love to wash off some of this trail dust."

Lance turned his back and Molly quickly stripped down to just her knickers and her blouse. She didn't really want to get them wet, but she had to get out once she was in, and she certainly didn't want to rely on that ornery man for her clothes. She hurried down the bank and into the cool water.

The water felt wonderful, and Molly swam across the pool. Suddenly, she heard a large splash. Lance had jumped in too but just for Molly, he kept on his union suit.

As he shook the water out of his hair, he grinned at her.

"Now you didn't think I was going to pass up a dip in this water, and with the prettiest girl around, did you?"

Every time Lance started to swim toward her, Molly would squeal and back away. Finally, he settled on splashing her a couple of times and then swam downstream a ways. Lance relied on his mustang and the mules to alert him to danger. As long as they grazed, he wasn't worried.

A branch snapped in the trees and Lance's mustang snorted. Lance quickly climbed up the bank and grabbed his guns. He tossed their clothes into a thicket and signaled to Molly to be as quiet as possible.

Silently, he disappeared into the brush. Molly slid toward the other side of the bank and slipped into some tree roots where she was barely visible. The horse's ears stayed pricked for several minutes; then the mustang nonchalantly went back to eating. Molly's heart was pounding as she waited, but soon Lance appeared and grabbed their clothes.

"Must have been a cat. The horses didn't like it but they are okay now."

Molly quickly swam to the bank where Lance was standing. Her heart was beating hard as Lance put out a hand to help her out of the water. Molly slipped as she stepped onto the bank and fell against Lance. He caught her and for a moment he stared. Then he shifted his eyes and his neck slowly turned red. Molly's wet clothes were stuck to her body and Lance had a view of every curve. She turned a bright red, and Lance handed her a blanket without speaking. He walked away as she wrapped it around herself.

As Molly came up to the small fire, he looked up at her and grinned.

"Maybe next time," Lance drawled, "we should just strip down to our skivvies. Then we wouldn't have to deal with wet underclothes."

Molly blushed a deep red again and was silent. Lance chuckled and then set about fixing her bed.

As she dozed off, Molly heard him talking to the horses and the mules as he picketed them on new grass.

Morning came early, and Molly awakened to the sound of birds chirping and bacon snapping. Her undergarments had nearly dried during the night and she quickly dressed.

Lance didn't look up until she walked up to the fire, fully dressed.

Her stomach was rumbling and her hair was down, flowing around her shoulders.

He stared at her for a moment. "Good Morning, Beautiful!" Lance greeted her as she sat down. "You know, I could get used to looking at you in the morning," he added with a lopsided grin.

Molly could feel her face heating up, but she looked him in the eyes and sassily responded, "Well, since we are married, I guess you will see a lot of me in the mornings!"

Lance's smile became bigger and he started laughing. "Well, I think I would enjoy that too," he insinuated.

Molly's blue eyes went wide as she realized how he had interpreted her response and then they flashed sparks at him.

"You are an incorrigible man!" she sputtered.

Lance laughed and he nodded. "That is probably true but you sure are fun to tease. Life on the ranch is going to be different with you around, and I think I am going to like it."

The food smelled good and when Molly took the plate Lance handed her, she noticed that the horses were packed except for her bed and the cooking utensils. Yesterday's stubble was gone from Lance's face, and he had already eaten.

Molly was surprised. "What time is it? You look like you have been up for several hours!" she exclaimed.

Lance chuckled. "Well, I sure have been up awhile. Eat up. We're burnin' daylight!"

Molly quickly ate while Lance put out the fire, rinsed the frying pan and refilled the canteens. She had slept well but she was stiff this morning.

She hurried to take Babe's reins and Lance gave her a leg up onto her horse. He stood smiling up at her with his hand on her leg.

"I'm glad you came along, Molly," Lance stated softly. He squeezed her leg and smiled again before he mounted his mustang.

As they rode, Lance told her about the plants, grasses and trees they passed along the way. He talked about trail drives and cattle. "You will like our ranch, Molly. We have five thousand acres of deeded grass with water and protection for winter graze." His blue eyes were shining.

As Molly listened to her husband talk, it was clear to her that Lance was passionate about cattle and land.

CHAPTER (20)

MANHATTAN, KANSAS

THEIR FIRST FIVE DAYS ON THE TRAIL WERE RELAXED
and to Molly, they were wonderful days—like a ride and a picnic
every day.

Then, about ten miles east of Manhattan, the rains came. They
were both drenched within minutes, and the horses plodded down the
sodden trail into the rain.

Lance helped Molly into her slicker and then wrapped a blanket
around her. She was still shivering, and Lance could hear her teeth
chattering.

"Manhattan is just a few miles away, Molly. Wrap your blanket tight
around you and hold it. Let Babe follow me. She is not going to wander
off the road in this storm."

Molly nodded as she pulled the blanket closer and looped the reins
over the saddle horn.

Their voices could barely be heard over the rain, and neither of them
talked as they ducked their heads.

Finally, they could see the lights of the new town of Manhattan,
Kansas, one of the last more-populated settlements on their route west.

"We made it, Molly. Manhattan is just ahead. Soon, you will be dry and in a warm bed."

Molly's teeth were chattering too hard to answer but she tried to smile at Lance.

He patted her shoulder and urged the horses on.

Lance presented a soggy and exhausted Molly at the door of the Wolf House Boarding House around 8:00 p.m.. Molly's face was pale, and her teeth were chattering loudly.

"Do you have a room available for the night?" Lance asked. "My wife is pregnant and really cold."

Mr. Frank, the proprietor, took one look at Molly and hurried to find his wife.

Mrs. Frank helped Molly to a clean room, found her some warm, dry clothes and put her to bed. As she clucked at her, Mrs. Frank scolded, "Shame on your husband for bringing you out in weather like this!"

Molly looked up at Mrs. Frank and smiled as she answered softly, "Isn't he wonderful? I don't know what I'd do without Lance."

Mrs. Frank's mouth fell open. "Well—" she started to respond but Molly was asleep.

Lance took the horses and mules to the livery. He was dead on his feet and was not prepared for the wrath of Mrs. Frank when he arrived back at the boarding house. As she started to raise her voice and shake her finger at him, Lance turned his back and walked down the hall to Molly's room.

Mrs. Frank was not used to being ignored and she shouted after him. "I want to have a conversation with you! Shame on you for bringing that poor girl out on a night like this. No good husband would consider such a thing."

Lance stopped and almost turned around. His shoulder's bunched and he was ready to release some wrath of his own, but he stopped himself. "Calm down and walk away. The old bat is probably a very nice woman and is just concerned about Molly," Lance told himself as he let out his breath and walked away.

After checking on his wife, Lance stripped down, rolled up in a blanket and went to sleep. Neither of them woke up until late morning the following day. Lance shaved, dressed and checked on Molly again. Her face was pale, and he knew she needed more rest.

Lance was anxious to check his livestock, and he hurried to the livery. Molly's Babe looked tired, but his mustang and the mules were ready to go. Lance shook his head. *I am sure gaining a new respect for mules*, Lance thought to himself.

Both horses and one mule had loose shoes. The smithy couldn't get to them until that afternoon.

"I'll check all of their feet. They look like they have come a ways," he offered.

Lance agreed, "Give them all extra rations. They have put in some hard miles."

He wandered down to the train station. The tracks had reached past Hays just days before and all of Manhattan was excited. The word was that they were laying between seven and eight miles of rail per day. Even Lance felt a surge of excitement. Twelve to thirteen hours on the train would put him a whole lot closer to home. He made an immediate decision that they would go as far west as they could by rail.

The next train was in two days and was filling fast. Lance bought tickets for Molly and himself. He also arranged for two livestock cars for their horses and mules.

There was talk of Indian trouble so the engineer asked that every party have at least one person who could shoot. The tracks would end at Monument, Kansas on the western side of the state.

The ticketing agent gave Lance a map and he was studying it when the engineer passed by.

"Headed home, young man?" the friendly engineer asked.

Lance nodded as he looked up.

"My wife and I are. She is nearly eight months along, and we are trying to get home before the baby comes."

The engineer let out a low whistle. "You are in a tough spot, son. Normally, I would tell you to go north by rail from here in Manhattan up to Lincoln, Nebraska, and then catch the train west. This past week though, there has been a lot of flooding, and the tracks are under water for part of the route. Your only option is to go west."

Lance studied the west routes and found that he could arrange a stage for Molly from Monument Station in Kansas to Denver, in the Colorado Territory.

The engineer looked over his shoulder as he scratched his chin, "The stage does run from Monument Station to Denver, and then another one runs on into Cheyenne. Just remember, the stage will be crowded, hot and dirty not to mention rough. Those roads aren't the best." He paused and then studied Lance's face. "Will she know anybody on the stage? That line handles some pretty rough characters. Lots of folks headed to the gold fields or towards Denver to work on the rails," he warned.

The engineer tapped the map. "If you could get from Monument Station to Julesburg in the northeastern part of the Colorado Territory, then you could take a train right on into Cheyenne. That first stretch is one hundred fifty or two hundred miles though so I would try to get a few more folks to go with you, was it me."

Lance put out his hand. "Lance Rankin is my name and I sure do thank you, Mister. None of those options are ideal but at least I can explain the benefits of each to my wife."

The engineer smiled and took Lance's hand. "John Oakley is the name and good luck to you, Mr. Rankin."

As the engineer walked away, Lance shook his head and muttered, "I am going to have to run these options by Molly and none of them look very good."

Then he smiled ruefully. "I for sure didn't know on my way east that I would be bringing a pregnant wife home!"

CHAPTER 21

OUT OF OPTIONS

MRS. FRANK MET LANCE AT THE DOOR OF THE BOARDING HOUSE WITH WRATH IN HER EYES.

"What were you thinking when you drug that poor girl across the prairie in that storm last night?"

Lance stood and looked at her for a full minute. He was tired, hungry, and stressed. He certainly had no reason to explain anything to this woman. On the other hand, she was just concerned about Molly, so he held himself still to calm down.

Mrs. Frank pulled back. She could feel herself shrinking under his hard gaze.

"If you'll excuse me, ma'am, I need to check on my wife," Lance grated out and walked away.

Mrs. Frank stared after him. "What a terrible man," she spat out.

Mr. Frank just smiled at her. "Now, Nellie, not all folks think like you. That man seems to genuinely care for his wife. Maybe she was in agreement about this trip." He patted her arm and kissed the top of her head. "Be nice!" he whispered as he winked at her.

Nellie Frank glared up at her husband and then slowly smiled. "Well, she does think that that man is wonderful. I suppose that I should try to be nicer." She snorted and began to wash dirty bedding.

Molly was up and dressed when Lance entered the room, and she gave him a quick smile.

"I can be ready to go any time," she said as she smiled brightly.

Lance took Molly by the shoulders and looked hard into her eyes. Then he gave her a quick hug.

"You are quite a woman, Molly Rankin," he murmured into her hair. As Molly smiled up at him, Lance could feel his heart thud in his chest.

He released her and held out his arm with a grin.

"We have time today—let's go see what this new town is like."

Molly was excited. "Let's look at *everything*! Oh, I hope Manhattan will be around for a while. So many of these little towns pop up and then are gone as the people move on with the railroad." She smiled up at Lance again as she took his arm.

Mrs. Frank was quiet as they walked by, arm in arm. Molly had a sparkle in her eyes and was laughing as she looked up at Lance.

"Why she is perfectly happy with that man!" Mrs. Frank muttered to herself. "For the life of me, I will never understand what young women look for in a man. Beyond being handsome, that man has just no redeeming qualities."

With a shake of her head, she went off to clean the rooms used last night to ready them for the next round of travelers.

Lance pointed to a large building across town. "Look, Molly—there is a college in this town. I hear they even allow women to attend!"

Molly's eyes were shining. "Oh Lance! Maybe we will have a little girl someday and she will attend here." Molly was trying to take everything in and was unaware of what she had suggested.

Lance caught it though and gave her hand a squeeze.

"Well, Manhattan is thirteen years old and growing every year. It just might still be around then."

Molly's stomach growled loudly, and Lance asked with a laugh, "Hungry, Molly?"

"Starving!" she exclaimed as he guided her into the next eating house they came to.

Their eating house was next to the stage station, and people were gathering as the stage was to be arriving shortly.

As they sat down, Lance looked closely at Molly's stomach. Her bump looked bigger and he could even see movement inside her skirt.

"Molly, what is going on inside your stomach?" Lance asked as he stared.

Molly laughed. "That is our baby doing his morning exercises. I think he lies on his back and tries to see how hard he can kick me."

Lance looked surprised. "They kick in there? I thought they just laid there until they were ready to come out!" Once again, Lance was reminded of how little he knew about babies.

The route map was in his shirt pocket and Lance ran the travel options by Molly.

She was all for the train ride to Monument, but if Lance was going from there by horseback to Julesburg, she wanted to go along.

"Lance, I don't want to travel by stage." Molly's breath was catching as she tried not to cry. "It won't be any easier than by horseback and I won't know anyone."

A sob slipped out as she whispered, "What if something would happen to you? I would be waiting and have no idea where you were!"

Lance squeezed her hand as he tried to smile. "Molly, please don't be afraid. I will figure something out," he promised. He smiled at her and was once again lost in her blue eyes.

Still holding her hand, Lance turned his head to look out the window. He didn't want Molly to see the worry in his eyes.

Lance was at a loss as to what to do, and he was out of options.

CHAPTER 22

WHOA THERE, MULE

THERE WAS A HOLLER FROM DOWN THE STREET, AND THE STAGE RACED INTO TOWN. The driver hauled on the lines to bring the team to a stop in front of the stage station. A spry old man with a large buffalo gun jumped down from where he was riding shotgun. Following behind the stage, a mule came running into town, stirrups flapping.

Badger McCune stepped out in front of the mule and hollered, "Whoa there, Mule. We'll jist stop here fer the night."

Lance leaned forward in his chair and stood up, still looking out the window. He pointed out the window with a grin.

"Molly, look who just came in on the stage!"

Molly turned to look out the window. Her fears were forgotten as she recognized the old man.

"Badger!" she squealed in excitement as she jumped from her chair and ran outside.

Badger turned around as he heard Molly squeal, and he held out his arms to the young woman who was running to meet him.

"Hello there, little missy!" he beamed as he hugged her tight. He looked over her head at Lance who was following her.

"I see ya kept that cowboy ya done runned off with!"

Lance stepped forward with a laugh and he shook Badger's hand.

"Good to see you, Badger," he smiled as Badger released Molly.

Molly asked breathlessly, "What are you doing here, Badger? Will you be going through Wyoming? Surely you will stop in to visit us!"

Badger kept one arm around Molly as he answered, "Oh, I'm jist a headed out ta see Old Man McNary. I brung a jug an' we'uns is a goin' ta have us some arguments over corn whiskey!"

He stepped back to look at Molly and his ornery face broke into an even bigger grin.

"Say, little missy. I see you'ins ain't dropped that little one yet. By George, I'm in time ta see a baby birthed!"

Molly looked stunned and Badger laughed. He gave her a peck on the cheek.

"Well, I figgered since I was agoin' ta be a grandpappy that I had better git out here. That kid's agoin' ta need a grandpappy more cheerful than Old Man McNary an' that's a fact!"

Molly laughed and hugged Badger again. "I am so glad you came," she whispered softly as she smiled.

Lance grinned at Badger and drawled, "That smile jist kind a melts a feller, don't it?"

Badger grinned again and Molly's dimples became bigger.

The wheels were turning in Lance's head. "So, you are going on into Cheyenne? What would you think about riding the cars with us? We can put Mule in one of our livestock cars."

Badger rubbed his bristly chin and looked closely at Lance. He could see from the intent way that Lance was waiting for his answer that something was going on.

"Say, that would be jist fine. I do like ta ride the cars. I'll jist go on down an' git me a ticket. You kids order me a steak. Tell 'em ta cook it on one side till it stops bellerin'. Then flip it over an' cook it till it quits a movin'." With that, Badger headed down the street.

Badger wasn't gone long. "Say, it's a good thing I got me that ticket now," Badger commented as he dug into his steak. "The feller behind me bought the last one. That train is gonna be plumb full."

"I am so excited you will be traveling with us, Badger!" Molly exclaimed. She was beaming with delight. "Even the mules will be excited to see each other."

The food was good and the coffee was hot. Badger was careful not to share any information about Bede, Stumpy or Slick. He would talk to Lance later but for now, he just wanted to enjoy his food and their company.

Lance quizzed him about Mule.

"Why is Mule following the stage? That's a long day, even for a mule."

"Well, the ol' sidewinder follered me outa town. I tried ta tie him ta the back o' the stagecoach but he pulled back so hard that the driver allowed that I couldn't bring 'im. Once I untied 'im, he follered along like a baby. I stop ever' day or two when it looks like he's a gittin' tard. Purty hard to wear down a mule though," Badger stated with a grin.

Although he had never before complimented a mule, Lance agreed.

After they ate, Molly and Lance walked with Badger down to the livery. Badger didn't lead Mule. He just told him what they were doing and Mule seemed to understand as he followed along at his own pace.

At the livery, Badger gave the hostler strict instructions. "Don't try to pet 'im an' keep away from his hind legs. That mule cin take a door down an' done already tried ta eat a feller jist a few days ago."

The hostler stared at Badger a moment and then looked at the big mule. The mule yawned wide and flapped its lips at the man. The hostler felt his neck hairs stand up.

"You lead your own durn mule to that back stall, an' don't worry—I ain't a goin' in there," the hostler stated as he watched the two of them walk away. The mule turned to look back and it almost seemed to laugh.

Molly decided that a nap sounded good, so the men walked her back to the boarding house and then sat down in the shade behind the building.

Lance told Badger what he was considering. "I have been thinking that we could maybe ride the cars to end of the tracks at Monument Station, and then go by horseback northwest to Julesburg. From Julesburg, we could ride the cars right into Cheyenne."

He paused and looked intently at Badger. "Any chance you would ride with us?" Lance asked cautiously. "We could sure use an extra gun."

"Say, that would be jist fine. I would be plumb tickled ta ride with ya kids," declared Badger.

The men visited some more and soon Badger told Lance about Bede as well as how Mule took a bite out of Lumpy.

Lance frowned. "Where did the kid that was walking fit in? I have never seen him before."

"That kid were jist a taggin' along with that Bede feller. The kid's out of it."

Badger added cautiously, "Those boys was a gonna foller ya out here, an' I think it were more than that money belt youin's a wearin'. I b'lieve it has somethin' ta do with our gurl."

Badger's sharp eyes studied Lance. As Lance looked up, Badger knew Lance wasn't telling him everything.

"That Lumpy feller were a hurtin' when I left Kansas City, an' the kid that ya seen walkin' back ta town were plumb again' goin' with 'im anywhere. 'Course, ya know, he could pick up some more fellers an' foller ya out here. In fact, I think he will." Badger paused and looked hard at Lance before he continued, "Don't ya worry though. Mule is a hankerin' ta chaw on 'im some more, an' if'n I see that feller anywhere close ta our gurl, I'm a gonna turn 'im lose."

Lance's face hardened as he scowled.

"This Lumpy fellow you're talking about—is he a short, greasy-looking fellow with stringy hair and little pig eyes? Paunchy and walks off the sides of his boots?"

Badger nodded.

Lance cursed under his breath. "He was on the train with us from St. Louis to Kansas City, but I haven't seen him here in Manhattan. I didn't know if he was after Molly, or the money belt, or if he was just traveling the same way," Lance growled as he scowled again. "I can tell you that I want to hurt him bad but that is all I am going to say."

Badger nodded as he listened to Lance talk. Then he slapped him on the back.

"Come on, Kid. Let's go get us a beer an' ol' Badger'll even pay," and the two men headed to the main street to find a saloon and a cold beer.

They were quite the pair. Lance was a tall young man who moved easily down the street. His blue eyes were piercing and drilled into everyone he met. Badger was a short little bandy-legged man. He almost bounced as he walked, and his bright eyes moved constantly as he studied his surroundings.

Between the two men, not a detail was missed on the streets of Manhattan.

The Lucky Lady Saloon was busy at 2:00 in the afternoon as Manhattan was a hopping little town. They drank their beer quickly and left. Neither of them liked elbow to elbow people nor loud crowds, and the Lucky Lady was full of both.

Lance and Badger ambled over to the smithy to see how the shoeing was going. Lance's horse had a cracked shoe, so it was a good thing the smithy had checked it. His horse would have been lame in no time, and in fact the mud probably kept that from happening on the last day.

While they were there, they had ten offers to buy their mules and their horses. Horseflesh of any kind was scarce in Manhattan. Lance was amazed at not only the money offered but the variety of people who wanted to buy. From city slickers to range riders, Manhattan was full to the brim.

From there, they moved on to the bath house. Each paid for a bath and took a good soak in the tub. Baths were ten cents and Lance thought it was money well-spent.

The next stop was the dry goods store for a new pair of britches and shaving soap. As he was waiting on the clerk, Lance wandered over to where all of the fabric was stacked up in piles. He was amazed at all the color choices. Lance approached a woman who was folding britches and stacking them on a shelf.

"Do you have dresses for women that are—." He paused and blushed.

The woman turned to him and smiled.

She finished his sentence, "for women who are expecting?" she asked gently.

Lance laughed as he nodded.

"How far along is your wife?" the woman asked.

Lance held his hands in front of his stomach. "About this far," he answered seriously.

Mrs. Good of *"Everything Good"* could barely keep from laughing at Lance's description. Her eyes twinkled as she answered, "If you can bring your wife in this afternoon, I would be glad to measure her and see what we can do."

Lance agreed and showed Mrs. Good the britches that he needed. As he started to leave the store, he paused again by the fabric.

"Can you set back this cloth?" he asked as he held up some blue fabric with yellow daisies. "I think my Molly would like this color of a dress."

Mrs. Good smiled, "I would be happy to, Mr.?"

"Rankin," Lance answered. "Lance Rankin and my wife's name is Molly. I will bring her by this afternoon, and thank you."

Badger grinned at Lance as they left the store. "Yer Molly is a fine little woman—mebbie more than a slow cowboy like you'ins cin handle," he commented as he winked at Lance.

Lance stared at the little man for a moment and then laughed.

"She might be at that," he admitted as they headed for the boarding house.

CHAPTER 23

My Wife Makes Pies!

AS LANCE AND BADGER WALKED INTO THE WOLF **HOUSE,** they could hear Molly laughing. She was in the kitchen helping Mrs. Frank prepare supper.

Mrs. Frank fixed one meal per day, and she had a reputation of putting out quite a spread.

Molly was up to her elbows in flour—making pies.

Lance's mouth began to water. *My wife makes pies! This marriage business just keeps getting better*, he thought.

Mrs. Frank was no longer grouchy, and Lance didn't glare at her any more either. Of course, Molly had no idea of their exchange, or at least that was what Lance thought.

Once the pies were in the oven, Lance asked Molly to go with him to the dry goods store.

"The woman there said she might be able to make you a dress and she has lots of cloth." He grinned at her and added, "Maybe you will even like the same cloth I liked."

Lance held out his arm and Molly linked hers through his as she smiled up at him.

The *Everything Good Dry Goods Store* was just a few blocks away from the Wolf Boarding House, and the Rankins arrived quickly.

The clerk hurried over to greet them.

She put out her hand, "You must be Molly. Your husband was in here earlier and said he would be bringing you by. My name is Mrs. Good, Mrs. Harriet Good."

Mrs. Good had placed the blue fabric with the daisies next to bolts of pinks, lavenders and greens.

Molly's eyes went immediately to the blue fabric.

"Oh, I so love daisies!" Molly murmured as she fingered the soft cotton fabric.

Lance was pleased with himself as he sauntered out the door.

Mrs. Good was a genius with her needle and thread. She showed Molly a stylish dress that would be comfortable to ride the rail cars in. She also suggested that Molly let her make a bonnet to wear with it.

"It will help keep your hair clean and out of your face in the wind."

Molly nodded. "A bonnet would be nice to have on the train," she replied. Molly loved her Stetson, but it wasn't something typically worn by women when traveling by train.

Lance was happily smiling as he came back into Mrs. Good's store. *Maybe I am getting to know this little gal after all*, he thought. Lance paid Mrs. Good and they agreed that Molly would pick up the completed dress around 4:00 the next afternoon.

As Mrs. Good marked the time and date down, she remarked, "Why that is June 2. We are having church service here tomorrow morning if you would both like to come. We have a new church," she stated proudly.

"It was just completed. Our first service in the church will be tomorrow and will be followed by a box dinner. All of the proceeds are going toward the purchase of the church bell." Mrs. Good smiled at them again. "I do hope you will be able to attend. We have a wonderful pastor who just gives the best sermons!" she gushed.

When Lance didn't say anything, Molly thanked her again. "That sounds wonderful. We haven't been to a service since we were married. Yes, we will plan to be there."

Lance was grinning as they left the store, and Molly eyed him suspiciously. When he grinned with devils in his eyes, she knew that she was probably going to blush.

"And just what is so funny, Mr. Rankin?" Molly asked with just a glint of fire in her eye.

Lance's grin became bigger. "Well, I was in there earlier today and picked the very same cloth. Guess we're getting to know each other a little," Lance replied happily, quite delighted with himself.

Molly studied Lance's face.

His eyes were twinkling, and he was almost strutting; he was quite proud of himself.

She laughed up at him and took his arm. "Yes, we are," she replied softly as she gave his arm a squeeze.

As they walked, Molly glanced up at Lance and her eyes were sparkling. "I'm going to put a meal together for the box social Mrs. Good was talking about. So, Lance, if you want some of my delicious pie, you have to figure out tomorrow which box is mine."

Lance stopped and stared at her, "But how will I know? Back home, we know everybody and people talk. Here, I won't know anyone. How am I going to figure it out?"

Molly smiled up at him and batted her big eyes. "Don't worry—you'll know."

Lance almost frowned but he just couldn't be grumpy when she looked at him like that. He pulled her arm closer to his, and they headed back to the Wolf House.

Supper at the boarding house was delicious. Lance tried three different kinds of pie. He didn't know that Molly had made all of them;

he thought just the cherry was hers. All three were delicious and he was eying a forth piece when Mrs. Frank glared at him.

I have to admit it, Lance thought to himself. *That woman is just a little scary.*

Molly offered to help with cleanup, but Mrs. Frank declined.

"You have had a long day, Molly. You get off of your feet and get some rest tonight," she ordered.

The boarding house was quiet by 8:00 p.m., and that was fine with Molly. She had given up her nap to help make pies and her bed looked inviting.

Lance began to roll out his bed on the floor.

Molly watched him a moment and then hesitantly offered. "Lance, if you want, you can have the bed tonight."

Lance looked at her and grinned.

"Sure, I'll take it as long as you are in it too."

Molly blushed and stuttered, "Well, okay but you have to stay on your side."

Lance's eyes twinkled as he drawled, "Why, shore, I can do that—at least until you fall asleep."

Molly stared at him for a moment and then she looked away, "You really are a cheeky man, Lance Rankin. You turn everything I say around just to embarrass me."

When Molly looked back at Lance, he was laughing. "Molly girl, you are a lot of fun to tease."

Mrs. Frank had drawn a bath for Molly that morning so both of them were clean and refreshed. Nellie Frank prided herself on a clean boarding house and was happy to accommodate travelers when it came to bathing. Her mantra was "Dirty bodies make dirty beds."

Lance pulled off his shirt and britches. He had cut off his long john because they were too hot, and his legs below the cut line were a sharp contrast in color from the dark brown of his face and arms.

Molly started giggling and Lance jumped into bed.

"Now, Mrs. Rankin, it is your turn to change clothes…and just maybe this time I won't turn my head," he chuckled with a devilish grin.

Molly's eyes became quiet and when she looked down, Lance relented and rolled over so his back was to her.

"Just know, Mrs. Rankin that I am going to peek someday."

Molly undressed quickly. With the curtains pulled, the room was quite dark. As she started to slide into bed, Molly realized that Lance had rolled over and was watching her. She quickly pulled the covers up to her chin.

He continued to study her face. "You are a rare beauty, Molly Rankin," Lance commented softly.

A slow blush began to slowly climb up Molly's face.

Lance watched her a moment longer and then he rolled over. He was almost asleep when he heard Molly whispering.

Molly couldn't sort out all her feelings and she was so confused. She wanted Lance to hold her, and yet she was terrified to have him touch her beyond a quick hug.

Tears leaked from the corners of her eyes.

"Why did those men have to hurt me? Will I ever be able to let go of that terrible time? I hope that someday I will be completely comfortable around Lance," she whispered softly.

A quiet sob slid out of her chest as Molly rolled over to face her side of the bed.

Lance heard her whisper and almost turned over to hold her. He forced himself to lay still as his heart broke for his wife. *Molly girl, I will help you heal*, he promised her silently.

"I so hope that we have some women neighbors on the ranch," Molly whispered to the quiet room. "Never in my life have I had another woman to talk to. That would be so nice."

Finally, she fell asleep. She didn't even notice during the night that Lance rolled over and gathered her to himself. Briefly he held Molly, breathing in the smell of her. Then quietly, he rolled over and went back to sleep.

CHAPTER 24

A KILLER MULE

ONCE AGAIN, WHEN MOLLY AWAKENED, LANCE WAS GONE. She could see that he had shaved, and she could smell the scent of his shaving soap.

Molly smiled. "I like to wake up to that smell in the morning."

She dressed quickly and went in search of Lance.

The local men were all around the church setting up makeshift benches from boards and barrels in preparation for the box supper.

Neither Lance nor Badger was anywhere to be seen. Molly assumed that Lance was checking the livestock. She had no idea where Badger was. Sometimes, he just disappeared. He had taken Mrs. Frank's last small room so she knew he had stayed at the boarding house.

Molly didn't know that both Badger and Lance were looking for Lumpy. They had each risen that morning with the same goal and were in the process of searching the liveries and the bars for the outlaw. Although neither had seen him, both were convinced he was around.

Lumpy was around. He had found a drunk who slept in the livery stable in Kansas City where Lance had kept his horses and offered him a drink. The man was happy to share all he knew about the couple who had slipped in the back door and back out so quickly. He had staggered outside to watch them because he had never seen a pregnant woman ride astride before.

The drunk pointed to the west, "They went thata way. Didn't have no pack animals but the man bought some oats so they was plannin' ta travel."

Lumpy handed the man the nearly-empty bottle and hurried to the train station. He cursed when he found that the train was full for that day.

"You'll have to be here early to get on," the ticket agent told him. "We fill up fast."

"Now I'll have ta roll a drunk or pick a pocket fer money," Lumpy growled to himself. It never occurred to him that he could save the money he had for one more day.

Lumpy missed the train the second day too because he awoke too late. On the third day, he slept close to the station.

He had just enough money to buy a ticket to Manhattan. As he studied the stops in between, Lumpy decided that was where he would go.

Lumpy wandered around Manhattan for a day and didn't find them. Then, on his second day in Manhattan, he saw their mules in one of the liveries.

When he saw Molly walking toward the church, he couldn't believe how big her stomach was. He started to follow her but something warned him to look around. Coming up the street carrying that big buffalo gun was that crazy old man who had sicced his mule on him! Lumpy ducked back inside the nearest saloon and ordered a whisky.

Badger paused in the doorway of the So Long Saloon and slowly scanned the room. It was early for a bar crowd, and not many of the tables were full. Only a few people were at the bar, and Badger saw the back-shooter he was looking for.

He moved down the bar to stand close to Lumpy, and purposely bumped him.

Lumpy was irritated but moved down a little without acknowledging Badger.

Badger ordered his whisky, held up the glass and toasted loudly, "How about a drink to all the back-shootin', thieven', no 'count fellers in this here town!" he hollered as he looked directly at Lumpy.

Lumpy's face turned dark. *I'd like ta grab my gun but I'd never git it out as close as that old coot is standin' ta me.* No way was he going to respond to that crazy old man. He cursed under his breath and moved a little farther down the bar.

The conversation in the room paused. Those present knew something was going on, and they waited in silence to see what happened next.

Badger repeated his invitation but this time he hit Lumpy's drink with his own, spilling some of it on the counter. "Well, drink up there, ya sidewinder, an' then ya cin tell me jus why you'ins in this here town."

Badger turned around to the room and announced, "This feller were travelin' with a couple o' men who intended ta do harm ta some friends o' mine. Now this feller says he warn't involved but I'm a thinkin' he were. One o' those friends is a little gal 'bout ready ta have a baby. Now if'n I find that this here feller is lookin' to hurt her in any way, why I'm a gonna turn my mule loost. When ya see that mule a ruunin' down the street, get out a the way, boys. He likes ta stomp an' chaw on folks that's no good. I guess he knows that if'n I don't like somebody, they must be purty bad."

Then he turned again and looked hard at Lumpy.

"An' you, I don't like a'tall."

With that, he drained his drink and slammed the glass down on the bar. He tossed some money towards the bartender, then turned and bumped into Lumpy again as he stomped out of the saloon.

Lumpy was seething. He stepped away from the bar and grabbed for his gun. Before he could aim it at Badger's back, every gun in the room was lined up on him.

The bartender cocked his double-barreled shotgun and Lumpy froze.

"Get out of here and don't ever come back," the bartender ordered quietly.

Then the bartender addressed the room full of customers. "Take a good look at him, boys. If anyone gets shot in the back while he is in town, let's have us a little necktie party—right under that beam." The bartender pointed at a high beam that ran the length of the room.

Lumpy shoved his gun back into his holster and stumbled toward the swinging doors. He was raging but he knew better than to face a stacked deck. He was going to kill that old man.

"I'll wait for him early in the mornin'. He'll go down an' check that mule. It cain't get out a that heavy pen an' I'm a gonna cut 'im down."

Still seething from the humiliation, Lumpy pushed through the swinging doors of the saloon. He almost fell onto the wooden boardwalk that ran along the street. Still muttering to himself, he ran right into Lance.

Lance didn't pause. He let go with a right hook and laid Lumpy out on the street.

He was breathing hard and his face was white. He knew that if he unclenched his fists that he would either kill the man with his fists or with his gun.

Badger glanced back. He was almost to the livery and kept walking. Suddenly, a mule came racing up the street, teeth bared and neck stretched out.

Lance jumped out of the way and the mule charged Lumpy.

Lumpy was trying to stand. He screamed and attempted to run. The mule grabbed him with his teeth and tossed him up in the air. As he came down, the mule landed on Lumpy with both front feet. Lumpy was dead but the mule continued to stomp and kick him until Badger arrived and called him off.

The mule calmly walked over to Badger.

As he snapped the halter rope onto Mule, Badger addressed the crowd. "This here mule has no tolerance fer folks with bad behavior." Then he turned and calmly led the mule back toward the livery.

The bystanders were shocked. They looked at what was left of Lumpy on the ground, and then turned to stare after Badger. Soon the crowd was murmuring amongst themselves.

The bartender from the So Long Saloon stepped outside with his shotgun in his hand.

"We all saw the dead man try to shoot the fellow with the mule in the back as he left this bar. I say the mule took care of a problem for all of us." He scanned the crowd, looking for anyone to oppose what he'd said. "Now someone go get the undertaker." He glared at the crowd one more time. "And tell him to bring a shovel," the bartender growled over his shoulder as he went back into his bar.

Lance let out his breath. His face was still white. Slowly, he unclenched his fists and turned down the street towards the livery.

Badger was leaving the barn. He started back up the street. He had his top hat on and was whistling a jig. As he met Lance, he slapped the younger man on the back.

"C'mon, son. Let's have a drink. We cin drink ta safer streets!" He guided Lance into a bar and ordered whisky for both of them. Lance rarely drank whisky, but he had three shots in fast succession. His entire body was as tight as a steel cord and his face was still pale. As he finished the third one, he turned to Badger. "Thank you for turning your mule loose. I was going to kill him."

Badger studied Lance with his wise old eyes and answered, "I saw that. I figger you cain't arrest a mule an' old Mule was hankerin' ta help." He continued to watch his friend and waited for Lance to say more.

Lance signaled for another whisky and downed that one. As he set the glass down, he turned again to face Badger.

"He did Molly wrong. There were eight of them, and he was the last one." Lance's hand clenched the shot glass tightly.

"I was going to kill him today but Mule got to him first."

Badger pulled himself up straight and threw some coins on the bar. He pulled Lance away from the bar. Badger's face was drawn into hard lines and neither man spoke as they left the saloon.

CHAPTER (25)

CHURCH SERVICE AND A BOX SUPPER

MOLLY WAS WAITING FOR LANCE IN FRONT OF THE CHURCH. The service was going to start in just a few minutes. As she turned and smiled, Lance picked her up and squeezed her so hard that she could hardly breathe. The baby inside of her kicked him soundly and he relaxed his hold.

He gently put her down and kissed her forehead. Molly was startled and as she looked up at Lance, he breathed, "Lumpy's dead."

Molly's eyes opened wide. "Oh, Lance," she whispered as she took his arm. "Did you—?"

Lance shook his head. "Mule got him first."

Molly's heart was beating fast and she could feel the tension in Lance. She looked up at Lance and big tears formed in her eyes. As Lance pulled her close, Molly's body shook with silent sobs and she buried her face in his chest.

Finally, the shuddering stopped, and Molly pulled back. As she looked up again at Lance, he promised softly, "It's over, Molly. It's all over." He wiped off her tears with his thumbs.

Lance put his arm around his wife and pulled her close as they walked into the little church.

Molly leaned against this man who had done so much for her. She turned her tear-stained face upwards and Lance kissed her gently.

As some of the older women began to wag their tongues, Lance looked around.

"What? Can't a man kiss his wife in church? The last time I was in a church, the pastor told me to."

The little church was full, and Lance guided Molly to an open seat just as the pastor began the service. He felt someone bump him and as he looked around, Badger pushed his way into the seat next to Lance.

Badger stood Ol' Betsy up between his knees and grinned at the older woman he had stepped on and over. He leaned over and whispered loudly to her, "If'n you'ins a good cooker, tell me what box is you'ins an' I'll run 'er up."

Then he winked broadly at the startled woman and faced forward. People behind were craning their necks to see what was going on. The woman turned beet red and snickers came from the seat behind.

The little church was packed, and the pastor gave the best sermon of his life. He was excited to have such a willing congregation.

Lance thought the sky pilot banged on the pulpit a mite too much, but no one seemed concerned. Molly certainly enjoyed it.

Badger was a model participant for the rest of the service; he was totally immersed. His "Amens!" were among the loudest in the congregation. And each time he hollered one, he banged Ol' Betsy on the floor, narrowly missing the toes of the woman next to him.

When the service was over, the woman whom Badger had embarrassed leaned over to him and whispered, "The one with the big blue bow!" Then she primly marched out of church and left Badger sitting with his mouth gaping open.

Badger began to laugh and he thumped his thigh.

"When was the last time a woman 'vited Badger ta buy her box supper?" he wondered out loud. He grabbed Ol' Betsy and hurried out of church.

Everyone moved from the church to where the tables were lined up. They were covered with boxes of all shapes and colors. Lance was worried about finding Molly's box. Then he spied one wrapped up in blue fabric with little yellow daisies and he grinned.

"This is turning out to be just a fine day," he commented to the startled woman beside him. He grinned at her again as he walked toward the benches.

Lance spied Badger in front of another table and moved over to join him. Badger seemed to be studying the boxes intently.

Badger moved boxes around. Then he stepped back to study them.

Lance watched Badger for a moment and then moved up beside him. "What are you looking for, Badger?" Lance asked with a smile showing in his eyes but trying to look serious.

"Well, I be lookin' fer one with a big blue bow but they be five of 'em here with blue bows," Badger answered.

Lance was beginning to grin. He hadn't seen Badger work so hard at anything. Lance pointed at the one on the end that had a *huge* blue bow on it.

"Well, that one has the biggest bow," Lance suggested helpfully.

Badger picked up the box and smelled it. A look of pure joy came over his face. "Fried chicken with taters an' gravy, apple pie, corn an'—" He sniffed it one more time. "Raisin cookies!" He put the box down and happily walked off. He stopped abruptly and slapped his leg. "I fergot my top hat!"

He rushed back to the boarding house and returned in a few minutes with his hat in place. Badger caught the attention of the woman whose box he intended to buy and gave her another wink. Again, she turned a proper red.

The bidding started and the boxes were going for $1.50 all the way up to $5.00.

When Molly's came up, Lance started the bidding at $10. He grinned at Molly who smiled prettily at him. The auctioneer closed the bidding and Lance had his box.

"It was worth it. I bought the prettiest box, and now I can eat with the prettiest girl!" he drawled as he took Molly's arm. Molly rewarded him with a show of her dimples.

Badger wasn't about to be outdone. When the auctioneer held up the box with the big blue bow, Badger stood up, waved his hat, and hollered, "$20!" The people present let out a single gasp in union—except for the older woman to whom it belonged. She beamed at Badger.

No one bid Badger any higher. He crossed the church yard to the woman, doffed his top hat, bowed and introduced himself.

"Badger McCune at you'ins service, Ma'am. If'n that there food tastes as good as she smells, it be worth ever' cent."

He placed his top hat back on his head, took her arm and guided her over to sit with Molly and Lance.

"Molly, this is the best fried chicken I have ever eaten!" Lance exclaimed with a pleased grin as he wiped off his chin.

"Potatoes and gravy, cob corn and four pieces of pie of four different kinds. I'm in heaven," he murmured as he ate with half-closed eyes. Large pieces of peach, cherry, apple and rhubarb were tucked down inside the box. Lance offered to share the pie with Molly but she was full. She giggled as he felt compelled to eat all four pieces.

"And Mrs. Frank isn't here to stop me!" he crowed in a loud whisper as he winked at Molly.

The woman's name whose box Badger had bought was Martha. She had never seen such a small man each such a large quantity nor enjoy it so much. Her box had everything in it that Badger had smelled *plus* a bag of donuts or bear sign as they were often called. Badger was ecstatic. He ate and smacked his lips, rubbed his stomach, and ate some more.

Martha had been a widow for nearly five years and she loved to cook. She had a nice little house in town and invited Badger for supper the next evening. Unfortunately for Martha, Badger was leaving in the morning. It was with great regret that he turned down her invitation for supper and for the rest of the day, Badger talked about nothing but Martha's food.

CHAPTER (26)

NELLIE FRANK'S APOLOGY

LANCE WANTED TO FINALIZE PREPARATIONS FOR TRANSPORTING THE HORSES AND MULES, so Molly asked Mrs. Frank to go with her to pick up her new dress. Mrs. Frank was glad for a break, especially since Molly was helping with supper again.

When Mrs. Good showed Molly the new dress, Molly gasped with delight. The bodice was fitted, and the skirt flared out to fit over her stomach. The sleeves were three-quarter length. The yellow bonnet coordinated with the daisies in her dress perfectly. Mrs. Good had also altered some knickers and a petticoat. The fabric was lightweight and even with the undergarments, it was cool and easy to move in.

Mrs. Good asked, "Would you like to try it on, Molly? I would like to make sure that I gave you plenty of room for your stomach as it grows." Molly looked down at her stomach as she nodded. It was already quite large. She wondered just how much bigger it was going to grow.

As soon as Molly stepped into the dress, she knew she was going to love it. The fabric was so soft and draped nicely over her rounded stomach. She looked at Mrs. Good with glowing eyes, "Oh, thank you! I love it!" Molly exclaimed.

Mrs. Frank was clucking like a mother hen and beaming at Molly. "You just look lovely, dear. Let's hurry back so you can bathe before we start supper. You will probably want to wear your new dress tonight."

Molly agreed and again thanked Mrs. Good who smiled. "I had lots of help." Three young women were peeking out from the living quarters and smiling shyly.

"These are my daughters, Constance, Meredith and Rosanna. If they hadn't helped, I could never have finished it in such a short time. Now you run along and enjoy your dress."

As Molly and Mrs. Frank hurried from the store, Molly turned around to wave. "I so appreciate how hard you worked," she called. "Thank you again for my beautiful dress!" She couldn't wait to see what Lance thought.

Molly's bath was quick as it was past time to finish supper. Mrs. Frank had prepared much of it earlier, but they needed to bake bread and Molly wanted to make more pies.

As they baked, Mrs. Frank and Molly visited. Molly could tell that Mrs. Frank was preoccupied.

Finally the gruff woman stopped working and placed her hands on her hips as she faced Molly.

"Molly, I need to apologize to you. I have been rude to your husband. I was horrified the first night that you arrived so cold and wet. I thought he was a terrible man and I proceeded to tell him so."

Molly was startled as she looked up and then she giggled, "And he didn't stick his face in front of yours? Well, that is a surprise!"

She put her arm around the older woman. "Mrs. Frank—"

Mrs. Frank interrupted her, "Call me Nellie, please. I want to be Nellie to you."

Molly smiled and hugged her.

"Nellie, Lance is a wonderful man but he grew up in an all-male household. He can be pretty abrupt, and he is clueless about women. In fact, I don't think he understands me at all," Molly giggled.

Then tears filled Molly's eyes as she whispered, "I'm not sure where I would be if he hadn't come into my life. Lance met me after I was raped and he has been wonderful."

Nellie Frank hugged Molly tightly as the young woman sobbed.

"There, there," Nellie whispered huskily as she sniffed loudly herself. She used her apron to wipe Molly's tears and held her face between her hands.

"Molly, I am so glad your husband brought you to my boarding house. Why, I have only known you for a few days, and you already feel like a daughter to me."

Nellie's eyes were red and her big face was soft as she wrapped Molly up in her arms.

When Mrs. Frank released Molly, she cleared her throat. Her voice was rough with emotion as she turned Molly back around to her pies.

"We had better get busy—we have a lot of men to feed tonight, including that man of yours."

Supper was served at 7:30 and the tables filled quickly. Mrs. Frank was known to "set a good table" and her clientele was mostly male. Molly had an apron on over her new dress and was hurrying back and forth as she carried large plates of food to each table.

Lance stepped through the door. He looked tired and dusty but when he saw Molly in her new dress, his eyes lit up. Lance worked his way between the tables and put his arm around her.

"Say, Little Lady, you are just about the prettiest thing I ever did see. How about you run away with me and we'll get married?"

Molly giggled and blushed. She responded, "Thank you, kind sir, but I am a totally committed married woman."

Lance grinned and kissed her.

Of course Molly turned red and everyone around them started to laugh and harangue them. Lance just grinned bigger and went to look for an open spot.

Badger was scanning the room to find Lance, so Lance waved. Badger pushed through the crowded tables to join him. By 7:35, there was not an open chair in the room, with another group waiting outside to see if there was food enough left to feed a few more.

Mrs. Frank always fixed extra so she had Molly fill some plates and take them outside for those who could not get in. When Molly came back in and started to pick up more plates, Nellie shooed her away.

"Go squeeze into a spot beside your husband, Molly. You have been on your feet long enough and I can take it from here." She paused and then smiled as Molly began to take off her apron.

"You know, Molly, I have always worked alone, but after having you here, helping me for two days, I think I might hire some help. I believe I will stop at Goods tomorrow and talk to Harriet about hiring one of her girls. I just didn't realize how much difference one more person could make. Those girls are friendly young women, and they just might enjoy helping out."

Molly smiled in agreement and hurried to find Lance.

As Nellie Frank watched Molly and Lance, she was ashamed of how she had treated him that first night. It was obvious that he adored Molly, and she could tell that Molly loved him.

"My goodness," mused Mrs. Frank to herself as she rubbed her eyes, "I am certainly going to miss Molly."

CHAPTER 27

RIDE THE NEW RAILS WEST

TRAIN TIME WAS 7:00 A.M. Lance had confirmed all of the arrangements for the animals the day before, but he was still up early to see that they were loaded. He hurried back to the boarding house to collect Molly. She had her bags ready and waiting by the door.

Mrs. Frank walked with them to the train station. She handed Molly a package.

"I packed a few sandwiches and such. It is just left over roast beef from last night but it might taste good on the train."

She looked hard at Lance and added gruffly, "There is some pie in there, maybe even more than one piece."

Lance shifted his feet and thanked her. *I still think she's scary*, he thought to himself.

Badger rushed up carrying a box and looking extremely pleased with himself.

Lance looked curiously at the box.

"Is that food, Badger? What did you do—ask for your breakfast to be put in a box?"

"Nope," Badger replied. "I et breakfast with Martha this mornin' an' she packed it fer me. Laudy, cin that there woman cook." With his box carefully tucked under one arm and Ol' Betsy on the other, Badger hopped onto the train.

Molly tearfully hugged Mrs. Frank and promised to let her know when the baby came.

"Thank you, Nellie. I will always treasure my days here," she whispered as she smiled through her tears.

Lance put out his hand to shake Mrs. Frank's but she pushed it aside and gave him a bear hug.

"Now you take good care of that little gal," she ordered with a fierce look on her face.

Lance promised and quickly took Molly's arm to help her up the steps.

Mrs. Frank grinned at his back. She knew she scared him—and him being such a tough man and all. She waved until the train was almost out of sight and then wiped the tears out of her eyes as she hurried to talk to Harriet Good about hiring one of her girls.

The passengers on the train were talking about the possibility of Indian raids. Many were new to the west, and there was much confusion over the conflict between the Indians and those invading their lands.

Badger summed up the conflict in just a few words.

"The Cheyenne an' Sioux is up in arms. They's ready ta defend they's home. See, too many folks is shootin' their buffalo an' invadin' their lands. The Injuns use ever' bit o' the buffalo while, the white folks, they jist takes the hide, mebbie the tongue, an' leaves the rest ta rot. Why sometimes, they's miles a dead buffalo just a layin'out there with all that meat goin' ta waste. Them hides is worth money an' some a them fellers cin kill a hundred buffalo in an hour or two."

A gentleman from the East pressed, "But we have treaties. Don't the Indians abide by the treaties they make?"

Lance interjected, "Treaties are made and broken by both sides. The young warriors want to fight while many of the older leaders understand that they can't kill all of the 'white eyes.' More just keep coming. Now with the advance of the railroad, the movement of people west just keeps getting heavier."

Molly was quiet. She was new to the west but it sounded pretty unfair. She frowned and shook her head.

Badger saw her face. "Now don't ya go a feelin' sorry fer those red devils. They's the finest group a fightin' men you'ins 'ill ever meet up with. That's what progress does. Helps one group a folks an' hurts 'nother. They's a fightin' fer their way a life, but too many a us is a movin' in an' they cain't kill us all."

The conversation moved on to other things and Molly asked Lance, "Do you think we will be attacked on this trip?"

Lance looked at her and then shrugged. "The railroad boys say there's a good chance. We need to be ready."

Lance had brought his rifle and had plenty of extra rounds of ammunition. He hoped that he didn't need it, but from all the talk, he was pretty sure there would be some fighting along the way. He had studied the route and was trying to figure where the Indians would be most likely to attack.

As the train left Manhattan, it headed west past Fort Riley and Abilene towards Salina. From there, it angled south towards Ellsworth before it went back north toward Hays City.

A loud murmur moved through their car as a tall man with long blond hair and two low slung guns appeared. His eyes were bright and careful, studying each person.

He paused in front of Badger and put out his hand. With a huge grin on his face, he pumped Badger's hand.

"I heard you were on this train, Badger!"

As Badger grinned up at him, the man added, "I couldn't believe you would actually leave Kansas City."

"Billy Boy!" Badger exclaimed as his bright blue eyes twinkled. He jumped up and pointed toward Lance and Molly. "Shore now, I'm a goin' ta resettle in Wyomin'," Badger told him. "I sold my little spread by Kansas City, an' I'm a gonna start over with these here kids."

Lance was stunned. He had no idea that Badger was planning to *move* to Wyoming. Then he thought of Badger's top hats and laughed. *Cheyenne needs a few more colorful characters*, he thought to himself.

Molly beamed. She knew that first day that Badger was a softie under all that bluster, and she loved him to pieces.

Badger turned to Lance and Molly. "This here is Bill Hickok." Then, turning to Hickok, he pointed at Molly and Lance, "These here kids is Molly an' Lance Rankin. I'm a travelin' with 'em ta their spread south an' west o' Cheyenne. Old Man McNary's a friend o' mine an' I ain't seen 'im in a while."

"Did you bring Mule?" Hickok asked. "That is one animal I just don't want to cross."

Badger winked at Lance. "Why now ya know ol' Badger don't go nowhere without Mule an' Ol' Betsy," he answered as he patted his buffalo gun.

Hickok and Badger visited a while longer, and then Wild Bill continued on through the cars. It was his custom to know who all was on "his" train.

The murmur started again as Hickok walked on.

Lance looked at Badger and laughed as he shook his head. "Badger, for a man who claims to not get around much, you sure know interesting people."

Badger gave Lance his evil laugh. "It ain't where ya go, Lance—it's who ya know." he declared as he winked at Molly.

Molly leaned over to Badger with a surprised look on her face. "Badger, it was so exciting to meet Wild Bill Hickok but I am even more excited that you are going to be moving to Cheyenne! Do you want to live on the ranch with us? I am sure we could make arrangements," as she looked questioningly at Lance.

Badger's eyes twinkled. "Nope," he answered. "Martha's a goin' ta be movin' out ta Cheyenne, an' we's a gonna get hitched."

Both Molly and Lance stared at Badger and then Lance threw back his head and laughed. He thumped Badger on the back and pumped his hand.

"You old devil! Well, I sure hope we get invited to the wedding."

Badger grinned. "Oh you'd a better be there. I'm a gonna' need a bestest man."

Slowly, the talk died down and everyone tried to get some sleep. It was a long trip, and who knew if it would be a quiet one the entire way.

Lance leaned back in his seat. *Badger is getting married and moving to Cheyenne.* He laughed again and shook his head.

Molly was almost asleep but opened her eyes when Lance laughed. "I was just thinking about Badger," he explained. "That old rascal. I wonder if Martha knows what she is in for. I sure hope his place is close enough that we see a little of him."

Molly smiled contentedly and went to sleep. She snuggled closer to Lance in her sleep and he gently kissed her forehead. It seemed to Lance that every day, she healed a little more.

CHAPTER (28)

INDIAN ATTACK!

THE TRAIN STEAMED STEADILY PAST FORT RILEY AS MOLLY SLEPT. When she awakened, the train was just outside of Salina.

Lance smiled at her as she raised her head.

"We will have two stops to restock water and wood. The first will be Ellsworth and then Hays City. I think Ellsworth will be the best place to get off and we should reach there in a few more hours. Hays City is pretty rough from what I hear. We'll be on here about twelve hours, thirteen if we have any problems." He grinned down at her. "Now might be a good time to catch up on some more sleep."

Molly stood up in her seat to stretch and an arrow came crashing through the train window.

Lance jerked her to the floor, and there was a mad rush inside the cars as the men took position.

Wild Bill was running through the cars yelling at everyone to keep an eye on the couplers between the cars. "Those redskins may have figured out how to unhitch the cars! Watch those couplers!"

The Indians were racing their horses beside the train. They had picked a slight grade to attack so that the train had to slow. If they were able to get into the locomotive or kill the fireman, the train would be immobilized.

The cow catcher on the front of the train could sweep a person or livestock off of the track; however, it could also be used to try to shoot into the locomotive if anyone was able to jump on it.

Wild Bill rushed back to the front of the train to protect the engineer.

He hollered at Lance and Badger as he went through their car, "I need someone to watch the fireman and to make sure he isn't shot."

Lance gave Molly one of his pistols and some ammo. "Use the gun, Molly. We need everyone who can shoot. Stay low and don't get too close to the window!"

Lance and Badger ran for the front of the train. As they opened the door to the next car, a large Indian jumped onto the gangway. Lance shot him and he toppled to the ground. They continued through the cars until they were right behind the tender that held the fuel.

Lance opened the door to see the fireman in a hand-to-hand battle with a brave while another was on top of the train. Badger let go with his buffalo gun, and the brave on top of the train was blown backwards onto the ground below.

Lance jumped into the tender car and used his Bowie knife to dispatch the Indian. He crouched down inside the car as the fireman went back to work, giving the train more fuel to pick up speed.

Badger had climbed on top of the train and was shooting down at the Indians trying to climb up the sides of the train.

Gunfire could be heard everywhere. As quickly as they had appeared, the Indians dropped back. Gradually, the firing in the cars died off and people began to take account of family and friends.

Five Indian ponies were running with no riders. One man inside the second car was dead with an arrow through the chest. The fireman had a bad cut on his arm which was making his job difficult. Lance had just stood up to help him when he heard a single shot from one of the back cars.

He jumped out of the tender car and raced back, pushing through the crowded cars as he ran.

An Indian was hanging halfway in the window, dead from a bullet through forehead. Lance's gun was in Molly's hand and her eyes were large as she stared at the dead brave.

Lance grabbed Molly. Her hair was pulled down where the brave had grabbed it to pull her out of the car. She was shaking but unharmed. Lance lifted the Indian's body up and pushed him out of the window. He turned to Molly and gently held her by her shoulders.

"Are you okay?" Lance asked as he studied her face.

Molly only nodded. She was pale and her hands were trembling. Lance hugged her tight before he released her.

"I need to help to keep the fuel in the train. Can you handle being here alone?" Molly nodded again. Lance helped her to her seat and kissed her cheek. He dropped down in front of her, took her face in his hands and kissed her gently. His eyes were dark and showed the flood of emotions that he felt.

"I will be back as soon as I can."

Lance quickly moved through the train and jumped back into the tender car with the firemen. The man was pale and bleeding. He told Lance how much fuel to feed the engine. Then he shakily climbed out and crawled into the locomotive to get help.

After Lance had been feeding the fuel for about forty minutes, another man crawled out to spell him, and Lance was glad for the break.

He climbed out of the tender car and headed back to sit down by Molly. Her face was still pale, and she was twisting her hands together. She looked at Lance. He was covered with soot and dirt from the smoke and wood. He didn't want to get Molly dirty, but he opened his arms and she collapsed against him, crying softly.

"I thought he was going to pull me out of the train and I shot him."

Lance released her and then looked to make sure she had no cuts.

Badger tossed Lance a blanket, and Lance wrapped it around Molly before he pulled her close again. He patted her back.

"Molly girl, you are one heck of a woman," he whispered to her. "You are headed into a rough land, but it is a good land, filled with mostly good people. Bad folks are everywhere, but that Indian was just doing what you or I would do. He was defending his home against invaders. The difference between the Indians and the whites is that the Indians understand that. They have always been warriors. They fought with each other for generations, and now they are fighting with us. We "white eyes" have lives that are a little softer. We haven't had to fight every day just to survive, so it is harder for us when we do. I don't think that either the settlers or the Indians are right or wrong. We just happen to be on one side and they are on the other."

He spoke quietly, "And if you hadn't killed him, you would be dead now."

Molly nodded slowly as she laid her head back down on his shoulder.

"I know it feels like this is different than the situation with the fellas that hurt you," Lance consoled her softly, his voice soothing. "They had already shown you their evil, and you wanted to make sure they didn't hurt you again. That is okay, but it doesn't change the fact that he would still have killed you."

He set her upright again and kissed the tear trails on her face. "I'm glad you came west with me, Molly," Lance whispered. "I may not always be right beside you, but you will always be here." Lance pointed at his heart.

Molly smiled at him as she wrapped her arms around him. "I'm glad you rescued me, Lance. And I'm glad I'm in your heart. I like it there." She snuggled against Lance, and he wrapped his arms around her tightly.

Wild Bill came through the cars and announced that they would be refueling in Ellsworth.

"We will be there a little longer than normal to check the train over. You have forty-five minutes to stretch your legs," Hickok drawled."

He looked at Lance and laughed. "You might want to use that time to take a bath." Lance wiped his hands on his britches as he agreed.

"Just be back on time or plan to live in Ellsworth!" Hickok suggested with a wink.

CHAPTER 29

A Bath and some New Britches

WHEN THE TRAIN PULLED INTO ELLSWORTH, LANCE STOOD. "Molly, I am going to take a bath. I need some britches and a shirt. Do you want to get them or would you like Badger to pick them up?"

Molly felt a lot better. She smiled at him. "I will pick them up. It might feel good to stretch my legs."

The people of Ellsworth gathered around the passengers as they stepped off the train. Lance and the other volunteer headed down the street to find some place to take a bath.

Molly squared her shoulders and set out to find a place to buy Lance's clothes.

A sign to her right read Hodgden's Dry Goods, and she hurried through the door. Molly quickly realized that she had no idea what size of britches Lance wore. She turned around and rushed back outside. Further down the street, she could see a sign with an arrow that read: Bath 15 ¢.

Now she would have to find Lance, and she knew he would embarrass her. As she hurried toward the back, she saw a tall man in cut-off long johns just beginning to strip.

"Wait!" she cried, "I need to know what size of britches you wear!" Lance started laughing. He took her hands and put them on the sides of his hips. "That big," he showed her and the devils danced in his eyes. As Molly jumped back, he held his money belt out to her laughing even harder. Molly grabbed the money belt and fled, her face a deep red.

She tucked the money belt into her bag and tried to compose herself. "That man," she sputtered. "I think he lives to embarrass me."

Once again, she returned to Hodgden's Dry Goods. As she walked in, she prayed that a woman would be helping. No such luck. The gentleman behind the counter asked if he could help her.

"I would like to purchase a pair of men's britches and a shirt," Molly stated. The clerk looked at her stomach and arched an eyebrow. "Do you know what size you need?"

Molly blushed deeply. "This big," she whispered, holding her hands as they had fit on Lance's hips.

The clerk tried not to laugh, but his eyes gave him away.

"I am sorry, Ma'am, but could you hold your hands up here so I can get a better idea of size?"

Molly was so mortified as he held britches up, one after another to match them to her outstretched hands. Finally, he found a pair that fit Molly's hand measurements. She picked a red shirt that looked like it should fit, speaking no more than she had to. She paid the man and almost ran out of the store.

Now if I can only find Badger, she thought to herself. *I am not going back down there.*

She heard Badger calling her name before she saw him. He was walking up the street toward her with a grin on his face.

When he was a little closer, he hollered, "Molly, Lance wants ta know where'd ya leave his durn pants when he tooked em off?"

People walking down the street turned to stare at her.

Molly's face turned crimson, and she handed the clothes to Badger without speaking. Mortified, she turned and ran toward the train. She could hear Badger laughing behind her.

"Oh," fumed Molly. "Men are all alike!" She stopped at the horse tank to wash her hands. Taking a hankie out of her bag, she wetted it and wiped her face. She scrubbed at her dress where the soot from Lance's clothing showed and then dabbed the cloth on her neck. As the coolness spread through her, Molly sighed. It felt so good to rinse off the grime.

"I hope I will be able to take a bath when we reach Monument," she murmured as she scrubbed her hands a second time. Then, she straightened her shoulders, repinned her hair, and marched onto the train.

When Lance slid into the seat next to her, she was calmly eating a sandwich.

He grinned at her but the sandwich smelled so good that he ate one instead of bothering her.

She turned to him sweetly. "Your britches look very nice. You know, I told the clerk that I needed some this big," she drawled as she stretched her hands far apart.

Lance choked on his sandwich and they both started laughing. Lance looked at her again and shook his head.

"Molly girl, you are truly a special gift."

His eyes changed as he remembered what else was packed for their lunch.

"Say," he exclaimed, "where is that pie?"

Molly pulled out not one piece of pie but four. Lance's mouth began to water. He offered Molly a piece and she chose the apple. He took the peach and was eating it with such total enjoyment that Molly rolled her eyes.

"I can't believe how much you like pie, Lance."

Mmmmm—" His eyes were closed. "Just promise me that you will continue to make pies when we get home."

Molly smiled. "I promise," and she kissed his cheek.

Lance's eyes flew open, and the pie was forgotten for a moment as Lance wrapped his arms around his wife and kissed her soundly.

The passengers were beginning to board the train and Molly pulled away. Her face was flushed and her breathing was uneven. "You shouldn't do that here, Lance. I almost feel faint," she whispered breathlessly.

Lance's eyes were a dark blue and they penetrated her with their intensity. Then he smiled his ornery smile, "Home is looking better all the time."

CHAPTER (30)

FORT PYRAMID

HAYS CITY WAS THE NEXT STOP. Badger stood up to look out the window. "Yessir, this is one humdinger of a town. Why they must be over one hundred bus'nesses in this here town. The saloons sell beer an' whiskey whilst the liquor houses sell whiskey an' beer! Jist looky there at all those tents. Those is the bus'nesses. This here town is so new that there ain't hardly no wood buildin's."

Molly agreed that it looked like a wild and wooly place. The land around Ellsworth had been green and the grass was long but at Hays City, it was much shorter. She was glad that Lance had taken his bath in Ellsworth.

I don't think I would want to roam around those tents at night, she thought with a shiver.

Refueling in Hays City was going to be much shorter, so most passengers stayed on the train or searched for someplace close to relieve themselves. In less than fifteen minutes, the whistle blew and the train was on the move again.

The train was due to arrive at Monument Station about 8:00 that evening. It had been nearly a thirteen-hour trip, and Molly was ready

177

for a bed. She hoped this town wasn't as rough as Hay's City looked, but she wasn't sure as she listened to the conversations on the train. Monument Station or "Fort Pyramid" as it was nicknamed because of the tall rocks surrounding it, was being abandoned. Soon there would be no military presence at all.

"Why is the army abandoning this post?" Molly questioned Lance.

He shrugged. "Who knows? Probably because the town packed up and moved with the railroad. End-of-rail cities move with the track as it's laid down. Or maybe the army just doesn't need a fort in this location anymore."

Lance pointed to the west where the rail was just starting.

"See it just inching across the prairie toward Denver? The mountains between Denver and Cheyenne are going to be tough to build over; that stretch of rail will be some of the last to be built."

Molly was a little uneasy. Still, she was excited as this was the last leg of their rail trip across Kansas.

As the train pulled into Monument, troops could be seen moving around. There was an urgent energy in the air.

One of the passengers seated next to Lance was from Monument. He pointed out the window at all the activity.

"The army is abandonin' this post in the mornin'. By noon tomorry', there won't be a soldier anywhere 'round. Word is, some of the officers' wives are goin' up to Fort Sedgewick." He shook his head. "They'll have to go by ambulance as there ain't no roads or coaches that go that way. Those army gals have to be almost as tough as their men," he noted with admiration.

The scene from the train was ordered chaos. It almost looked like a beehive as men rushed around. The entire post had to be dismantled. Supplies and gear of all kinds had to be packed and loaded for transport.

Lance listened intently and then spoke excitedly to Molly, "If the ambulance is taking the wives to Fort Sedgewick, they will pass right through Julesburg! Maybe we can tag along with them. That would be a much safer way to travel. If they are abandoning this post, they may allow another woman to travel along, especially since we can provide extra protection."

His eyes shifted to Badger. "Will you be in charge of getting Molly off the train? I want to talk to the officer in charge as we don't have much time."

From the train window, they could see a big sign advertising the Spencer & Fowler Dining Hall. Lance pointed toward it.

"I will meet you at that dining hall as soon as I can. Once I make our travel arrangements, I will try to find us a place to stay."

Molly was delighted. Lance hadn't mentioned the stage since Badger had joined them and this sounded like a great solution. She was so tired though that she just wanted to go to sleep. *I hope I have a bed but if I don't, I am pretty sure I can sleep anywhere I can sit.*

As soon as the doors opened, Lance leaped down and hurried to find the camp commander while Badger gathered their bags and helped Molly off the train.

Molly offered to help carry their things, but Badger winked at her as he stepped out lightly and she had to hurry to keep up with the spry old man.

He hauled their traveling bags right into the Dining Hall and deposited them on a table.

"Shouldn't we leave them outside or at least by the door, Badger? The Dining Hall may be crowded," Molly questioned nervously.

"They's too many folks up ta no good in this here town," Badger argued, giving a stubborn shake of his head.

CHAPTER (31)

LITTLE JOHNNY LEWIS

CAPTAIN JOHN LEWIS WAS THE CAMP COMMANDER. He looked up as Lance was presented. When he saw a civilian, he scowled but signaled for him to come in.

Lance stepped forward.

"Thank you for seeing me, sir. I am Lance Rankin. I understand that you are abandoning this fort, and that you have a group of soldiers headed to Fort Sedgewick. I believe you will pass through Julesburg?"

The Captain nodded, waiting for Lance to make his request.

"My wife and I are traveling to Cheyenne. I was hoping we could join your party. We plan to catch the train at Julesburg."

The captain leaned back in his chair and studied Lance. "I assume that you can shoot but are you willing to fight? " he asked.

Lance replied quickly, "Both my wife and I are excellent shots, and yes, we have no problem with helping to protect the party. Badger McCune is traveling with us as well, and he is deadly with his buffalo gun."

Captain Lewis dropped his chair back down on the floor and leaned forward with a surprised look on his face. "Badger! Does he still have that crazy mule?"

Lance was a little surprised that the captain seemed to know Badger.

"Badger just seems to know people from Kansas to Colorado Territory, " Lance answered with a laugh. He added, "He does still have Mule, and Mule made the trip as well."

Captain Lewis placed his hands on his desk. "Well, I'll be. I grew up just outside of Kansas City, and I used to help him some on his little ranch. Mule was a pet when Badger handled him, but no one else ever tried to touch him."

He stood and walked around his desk.

"You are welcome to join the Fort Sedgewick party. I'm glad to have two more men who can shoot."

Captain Lewis frowned as he added, "The main body of soldiers is going on west with the rail crew to guard the workers as they lay rail. They are to set up a temporary outpost at Downers Station." He shook his head. "I am spread too thin."

He turned to face Lance again. "Be ready to leave at 0700 tomorrow. It is nearly two hundred miles to Julesburg and some of it will be pretty rough. Are you familiar with the route?"

Lance shook his head, "No, I'm not. I have been to Julesburg but not this far south."

"Several of the soldiers are familiar with the route. Sergeant O'Malley will be in command." He reached to shake Lance's hand.

"Welcome to Fort Pyramid, Mr. Rankin. I'm headed over to the Dining Hall. Would you care to join me? Or perhaps I should ask if I may I join you? I would enjoy seeing Badger while he's here."

As the two men walked toward the Dining Hall, Captain Lewis asked if Lance had made sleeping arrangements. Lance shook head.

"Not yet. I wanted to talk to you first."

"Your wife is welcome to stay with my wife and me. My quarters aren't large but they will be better than any accommodations available yet tonight." He paused and added, "Badger and you can stay in the barracks. It is against regulation but, nothing is working according to regulation tonight,"

Lance was relieved. "Thank you, Captain Lewis. Now let's see if we can find Badger."

Captain Lewis laughed. "If he is wearing one of his top hats, he should be easy to find!"

Both men were still laughing as they walked into the Dining Hall.

The first thing they heard was, "Lance! Over here!" Standing on the table, waving his top hat was Badger.

"Badger, that is terribly inappropriate," Molly giggled. Still, she just couldn't help but enjoy his pure zest for life.

When Badger saw Captain Lewis walking behind Lance, he leaned forward and squinted like he couldn't see. He didn't fool any of them because they knew how sharp his eyes were.

"Well, little Johnny Lewis! Look at you, all growed up! Did ya ever marry up with that little gal ya pined over all the time or did ya leave her cryin' for someone else?"

Captain John Lewis reached up to shake Badger's hand. "Hello, Badger. It is certainly good to see you. I hear you brought Mule with you. Will you be visiting Cheyenne long?"

Badger shook Captain Lewis's hand and then hopped off the table. "Visit? I'm a gonna move there!"

When Captain Lewis looked surprised, Molly spoke up. "Badger is getting married."

Captain Lewis looked stunned. "Badger? Married? I would never—" He paused and shook his head, completely surprised as he continued to stare at Badger.

"She's a good cook," Lance explained with a grin.

Everyone began laughing and then Lance introduced Molly.

Captain Lewis was quite the gentleman and other than his wife and a few of her friends, he hadn't seen many ladies in Monument.

Lance thought for a moment the captain was going to kiss Molly's hand, and he almost laughed at his own irritation.

The men claimed a space on the bench quickly as food lines were forming. The Spencer & Fowler Dining Hall was full.

The meal was excellent. Vegetables, meats of all kinds and other delicacies were spread out on a huge table. People helped themselves. It would have been an amazing spread anywhere but for an end-of-rail town, it was incredible.

When the meal was over, Badger headed to the barracks, and Lance walked with Molly to Captain Lewis's house.

Mary Lewis was delighted to have a lady guest. She invited Molly in and offered to arrange for a bath. They left Captain Lewis and Lance standing by the door.

"I am sure your wife will want to ride in the army ambulance with the other women," Captain Lewis stated, looking at Lance.

Lance grinned ruefully. "Let's don't assume that. Molly loves to ride and I am guessing she will be on her horse and ready to go, at least for a few days, anyway." Captain Lewis cocked an eyebrow but didn't reply.

CHAPTER (32)

NORTH TO JULESBURG

LANCE AND BADGER WERE UP BEFORE REVEILLE. As the bugle echoed through the lively town, Molly hurried to get ready. The music was haunting and beautiful.

Molly's men had the horses and mules ready to go. Lance had been able to buy some supplies from the local sutler. The prices were high not only because of the cost of shipping, but because the sutler knew what he could charge for his products on this small outpost. The man didn't appreciate being awakened before 6:00 in the morning either so that might have added to the cost. Two mules were loaded with food and supplies. The third mule was loaded with their traveling bags and all of the items that Molly had collected on the way.

Lance tied the mules to the back of the loaded wagons and stepped back to survey the little group.

He shook his head. *I sure never dreamed I would be packing all of this back to Cheyenne,* Lance thought with a wry grin. *I left the ranch with one saddle horse and a pack horse. Now I'm returning with two horses, four mules, a pregnant wife and an ornery old man.* Lance laughed. *Life is good,* he thought.

Molly was standing by Babe, and was searching the sea of activity for Lance.

She looked so beautiful that Lance's breath almost caught in his chest. Her long red gold braid hung down her back beneath her Stetson. In the sun, it glinted with highlights of gold. She had the stampede string on her hat pulled up under her chin and had removed the outer apron skirt from her riding outfit. Somehow she had been able to clean her clothes, and she was sparkling with excitement.

Molly's eyes found Lance in the chaos, and she gave him her glorious smile as she led Babe toward him.

Lance's heart jolted in his chest. He pulled Molly close to his side and whispered down to her, "You make my heart tingle, Molly."

Molly smiled up at him and Lance lost himself again in her blue eyes. He would have kissed her but the sergeant was yelling at the men to mount. Lance quickly gave Molly a leg up and mounted his mustang.

The rough soldiers were on best behavior, although some of them were rather uncomfortable around the women. Even Badger seemed to behave himself, at least so far.

At promptly 0700, Sergeant O'Malley gave the signal and the small unit moved out. There were six mounted soldiers, plus three more driving two light wagons and the army ambulance. In addition to Molly, three women were making the trip. They were Mary Lewis, Kate O'Malley the sergeant's mother, and his eighteen-year-old sister, Marion. Marion was a sassy young lady with hair more red than Molly's and a sprinkle of freckles across her turned up nose. Her eyes sparkled all the time, and she thoroughly enjoyed the attention that she received from the young soldiers. She especially liked to tease the shy ones. Her brother had his hands full trying to keep her in line along with the young men whom she kept stirred up.

The sergeant along with several of the older soldiers had been over the route many times. Indian activity had been low so far this year but

Sergeant O'Malley was not a trusting man. Besides, even if the Indians weren't a problem, there were renegades. Outlaws had always been plentiful but after the war, even more were moving west. Besides, the sergeant knew he had some pretty desirable cargo. A caravan with loaded wagons, women and mules could make them a target.

Everyone was armed. Even the women were asked to carry a gun of some kind. In addition to his pistols, Lance had a rifle in his saddle boot and he had purchased one for Molly at the sutlers that morning. Molly immediately checked to confirm it was loaded and thrust it into the boot on her saddle. He handed her some extra ammunition. Some she placed in her pockets and the rest went into her saddle bags. Lance watched the comfortable way that Molly handled the long gun. *My Molly is a rare girl*, he thought to himself.

The army used mules to pull their wagons, and the soldiers led off at a brisk trot. They hoped to make twenty miles per day, although there would be days it could be much less, depending on the terrain. The 200 mile journey from Monument, Kansas to Julesburg in the northeast corner of Colorado Territory should take ten to twelve days.

Lance and Molly rode at the front of the caravan with Sergeant O'Malley while Badger followed the wagons with the other five soldiers.

Lance's three pack mules kept up with the wagons easily. Their packs could be removed, and they could be used to pull a wagon if needed. Both of the wagons were lightweight. However, each was loaded. One held the personal items that belonged to the women, and the other held supplies for the trip as well as some items that Captain Lewis wanted to transport to Fort Sedgwick. Four mules pulled each wagon and two pulled the ambulance.

The ambulance was lighter than the wagons and not as rough. The women could ride wherever they chose. However, the ambulance was more comfortable. Of course for Marion, comfort was not her only concern.

"Are you expecting lots of hard pulling, Captain?" Lance had asked as he studied the teams before they departed. Typically, two mules would have been sufficient to pull each wagon.

"I don't want those mules too fatigued by the end of the trip. You are going to need power all the way through and if a few more mules make that possible, then I want that extra insurance," Captain Lewis had responded.

Captain Lewis was not a man who left anything to chance. He had chosen Sergeant O'Malley to lead the little caravan because the sergeant was one of his best men. In addition, the sergeant was familiar with the route, and had been over it multiple times.

The first day was fairly easy but hot. The prairie was rolling and there was hardly a tree to be seen. Water was the main concern as even streams had to be crossed carefully with wagons. Two water barrels were attached, one to each side of both of the wagons, and were to be filled every day if possible.

"Most of these rivers will only flow for just a bit after the rains," Sergeant O'Malley explained. "The sand is more of a concern than the water, although the streams can flood too if the rains come too fast."

One of the mules pulling the ambulance didn't want to cross but followed when another wagon went first.

The route chosen went due north of Monument, and they traveled about twenty-five miles on their first day before camping by a small creek. May rains had filled some small waterholes although not enough to make the rivers they needed to cross too difficult. Tents were set up and the women prepared an evening meal. Molly was able to bring three pies and even though Lance hated to share, they were enjoyed by all.

"We will cross the Saline River tomorrow. It's a dark, briny river. There are salt springs under it that feed into the river and taint it with salt. It won't be deep but we'll have to be careful because the base will be a bed of mud and sand," the sergeant explained at supper that evening.

Lance made up a bed for Molly and then checked the picket pins on all of the animals before calling it a night. His horse was a mustang and like a watch dog, it would alert him if it smelled something out of the ordinary. The horses and mules had been watered and now were eating contentedly.

Sergeant O'Malley asked, "Any of you ladies want to rinse off? The water we see tomorrow may not be as clean as this stream is."

The women were eager to clean up although Molly was a little nervous with the men so close.

The sergeant assured her that they would have complete privacy. "Besides, my own mother and sister will be with you."

Molly grabbed a blanket and headed for the water with the rest of the women. Their chatter and laughing could be easily heard but not understood. The sergeant made sure that the men, especially the young ones were busy.

Soon the women's voices could be heard coming back up from the creek. Molly's hair was wet but all of her clothes were dry. Lance grinned at her. Molly knew what he was thinking so of course she blushed. Lance laughed and stood up.

"That water looks mighty inviting. I think I will take a dip before I turn in too."

He grabbed the blanket that Molly had used and headed for the creek. He placed his guns within each reach but out of the water. The money belt was rolled up in his clothes and stuffed under a rock. Several of the soldiers joined him in the water. Unlike the women, they listened more than they talked. All of the men were a little edgy and that was not a good sign.

Lance washed out his shirt. He would have liked to wash his britches, but he didn't bring the second pair down with him. *Those ladies wouldn't appreciate my cut-off long johns*, he thought with a laugh. Most of the soldiers were already bedded down when Lance climbed back up the hill to their camp. Captain Lewis had sent a tent for the women to sleep in plus another for the men, but Lance preferred to sleep outside. He could hear the women talking softly as he went to sleep.

Yes, he thought, *it is going to be different having a woman around, but I am starting to get used to it.*

CHAPTER (33)

JUST ONE SHOT

THE MORNING WAS COOL WITH JUST A LITTLE DEW ON THE GROUND. Sergeant O'Malley had asked for no bugles on the trip. He hadn't asked for the group to be quiet. He just didn't want any unnecessary noise. The men were all talking about the possibility of fresh meat.

"I was thinking of taking a shot at a deer today if I see one. Do you have any problem with a gunshot?" Lance asked Sergeant O'Malley.

The sergeant thought for a moment and finally, he nodded in agreement. "I would like to keep things quiet, but we could use some fresh meat. One shot," he added as he grinned at Lance.

Molly was ready to do a little exploring, and was delighted when Lance asked her if she wanted to join him.

The wagons were quickly repacked, and once again, the group was on the trail by 0700. Sergeant O'Malley announced, "I would like to leave an hour earlier tomorrow. We can stop mid-afternoon and maybe save the livestock a little. This heat is going to get worse."

They reached the north fork of the Saline River within an hour. The north and south forks of the Saline were fairly close together; however, they would only have to cross the north one.

Molly stared at the water. It was a brown color and the mules snorted as they smelled it. Molly could smell the salty water and she turned up her nose as well.

"Everything is so vast—so open," Molly commented as she looked around. She could see no trees in front of them. She felt small in such a big country.

Sergeant O'Malley led off followed by Lance and Molly. Lance had his lariat ready in case someone or something needed help. The mules snorted at the brackish water but were sure-footed and had no trouble. Two of the soldiers were riding young horses and their horses didn't want to go into the water. Badger popped one with his rope and it sprang into the water, hitting the second horse. The second horse almost went down, and the young private was ready to jump when it regained its footing. Both animals buck-jumped through the water. Lance watched them carefully. *I will be ready for them on the next crossing,* he thought.

Once everyone was on the bank and headed north, Lance and Molly turned off to hunt. Sergeant O'Malley sent Private Most with them as he was familiar with the country.

"One shot," Sergeant O'Malley repeated," and stay alert."

"Where did you grow up, Private?" Molly asked.

"Billy," he answered with a shy smile. "My name is Billy. I was born in Julesburg. It was just a trading post then and my Pa traded with everyone."

"I'm sure you met lots of exciting people!" Molly exclaimed. "Did your mother enjoy it there? I've heard some of the posts could be quite isolated."

Billy nodded. "It was isolated. I didn't mind it, but Ma was really lonesome. Sometimes we didn't see anyone but trappers for days. One day, Ma got sick and then she died. Pa loved it there but he was sad after Ma died. He said that the frontier was hard on women, and he blamed himself for her death." Billy paused as he looked across the prairie.

"When I turned eighteen, I joined the army and Pa sold out of everything. He told me he wished he'd a left when Ma was alive." Billy's smile was a little sad as he looked at Molly.

"Pa said he was going to take his stake and start a dry goods store in Denver. That was two years ago. I ain't heard from him in over a year but in that letter, he told me that he'd bought him a little store there like he planned. When I get out of the Army, I want to go to Denver and see if I can find 'im.'"

"Oh, that means that all three of us lost our mothers when we were young. So hard," Molly whispered with tears in her eyes. "Yes, I think you should go to Denver and look your father up. He probably has a big store by now, and could use some help." Molly assured him with a smile.

Billy smiled back at her. "You're a nice lady, Miss Molly."

Lance listened to their exchange quietly. *Everyone has their own set of heartaches,* he thought.

Molly started to point at a flower when Lance reined his horse in. He held up his hand and pointed downhill as an antelope tentatively walked out of the brush below.

"We are pretty far away. I'm not sure I can take it with one shot," he whispered.

Before either Billy or Molly could respond, a shot sounded, and the antelope dropped. The three slipped quickly from their horses and pulled them into some brush by the side of the trail.

Voices carried to them from below. "Nice shot, Sam! 'Bout time you shot somethin' we cin eat 'stead of settlers. Now throw that buck over yore saddle an' git back to camp. That little ol' gurl cin gut this thing an' work some fer 'er keep."

A garble of sound followed and then a man's voice added, "Well, she better git it done fast 'cause we're pullin' out in the mornin' an' she ain't comin' with us."

Soon two men in buckskin rode into view. One was carrying a buffalo gun, similar to Badger's. The other had a rifle and six gun. The first man grabbed the antelope and swung it over the saddle in front of the second man, and they rode out of the clearing.

Lance let out his breath.

Molly's hands were sweating and she felt faint. She gasped, "We are going to follow them, aren't we? They have a girl prisoner!"

CHAPTER (34)

LET THE COYOTES
HAVE THE COYOTES

LANCE REACHED OVER AND TOUCHED MOLLY'S HANDS. "We'll find her, Molly," he promised, "but I don't want you along. It's too dangerous."

His eyes moved to Private Most. "Billy, you ride back with Molly to the wagons. Get Badger. I'm going to start following them, and Badger can track me. And if he can't see tracks, that mule of his will smell them."

For once, Molly didn't argue. The two walked their horses slowly at first. When they were a distance out, both spurred them and took off.

Lance was worried as he watched Molly ride out of sight. He hoped that O'Malley would find a protected spot and hole up—someplace that could be defended. Molly was right though. They did need to find the girl, and it needed to be soon.

He mounted his horse and slowly eased down the hill. The mustang's ears were pricked, and it picked its steps carefully as it went down and over the rocks. The two men were out of sight but Lance still took his time. He really didn't want to come up on them until Badger was there to back him up. Before long, he was in a dry creek bed surrounded by scrub trees and bushes.

Lance could hear voices coming from ahead. He stepped down from his horse, removed his spurs and hooked them on the saddle horn. He ground-tied his horse and squatted down to wait for Badger. The sound of the men's voices carried back to him, but he couldn't hear what they were saying. He was just starting to get antsy when his horse pricked its ears, and looked back down the trail. Lance grabbed his horse's nose to stop the whinny just as Badger and Billy came into view, walking their animals carefully. As they stepped down, Billy tied his horse to a tree while Badger dripped Mule's reins.

Lance looked at Badger and in a quiet whisper asked "I'm not sure how many there are. Any ideas?"

Badger grinned with a wicked look in his eyes. "I say we send Mule in an' foller behind. He cin be tame as a baby an' then turn on 'em when I give 'im the signal. We cin foller along. His walkin' an' snufflin' will help cover the sound of us boys sneakin' up on 'em."

Lance grinned and nodded.

"I sure am glad you are on our side, Badger—and Mule too."

Badger took Mule's face in his hands and talked to him. Then he pointed down the trail and waved his arms. Mule started towards the outlaw's camp. He walked, then stopped. He smelled the ground and snorted. Then he walked farther, brushing the trees as he went by. The three men followed silently behind, staying in the cover of the small trees.

The camp ahead of them became quiet. "Who's out there?" a voice asked loudly.

Mule continued to walk with his head down, smelling the trail.

A man stepped out in front of Mule and Mule stopped with his ears pricked forward.

"Hey boys, it's just a mule. Looks like somebody lost their ride."

Another voice growled, "Mebbie but it also means they's somebody out here 'sides us."

Two more men came into view. One reached out and grabbed Mule's bridle. Mule meekly followed the man.

Lance and Billy looked at Badger who gave them both a wicked grin. Badger nodded his head towards their fire.

"Let's move a little closer an' spread out ifn' we cin. An' don't shoot my mule!" he hissed as they faded into the brush.

Three hard-looking men were standing around Mule. A fourth man was sitting down back from the fire. A young girl of eighteen or so was butchering the antelope. She handled the knife skillfully when they weren't looking, but made her motions look awkward when the men were watching.

The girl glanced up from her work and looked right into Lance's eyes. The knife paused in motion and Lance put his fingers to his lips. He signaled to go into the brush if she could. She looked back toward the men who were still standing around the mule, discussing where it came from. The fourth man finally stood up and started to walk towards them. Just as he turned his back, the girl darted into the brush.

Badger whistled and Mule exploded. He reared up on his hind legs, pawing the air and knocked both men in front of him to the ground. He whirled around and kicked the third one so hard that the man few backwards twenty paces. The fourth man was staring in horror when Mule laid back his ears and charged him. The man screamed and tried to run. Mule grabbed him with his teeth and tossed him in the air. As he hit the ground, Mule once again reared up on his back legs.

Badger whistled again and Mule stopped. He dropped his feet to the ground and stood calmly as Badger climbed out of the brush. The man on the ground was still screaming and Billy's eyes were so big they looked like holes in his head. The girl was peering out of the brush. Her face was white but she was silent as she stared.

Badger stalked toward the man lying on the ground.

"Now we'uns have some questions fer ya, an' ya better answer 'em right or I'm a gunna turn my mule loost on ya agin!"

The man was holding his arm and blood was seeping through his fingers. His wrist was dangling at an odd angle. As Badger reached to pull him up, one leg started to give out. The man cringed and started to moan but clamped his mouth shut as Badger glared at him.

Lance walked over to the other men. The two who had caught the full force of Mule's front feet were dead. The man who was kicked had hit a tree or a rock and his neck was broken. The girl had come back into the clearing. She was shivering and Billy gave her his jacket.

Badger snarled, "He's all you'ins," and shoved the outlaw toward Lance.

"Who are you and why do you have this girl?" Lance asked coldly.

The outlaw was silent and Badger led Mule closer.

The man's eyes bulged out. "No!" he screamed. "Don't let him bring that devil any closer to me!"

"Then answer!" Lance snapped.

"I am Hughie Uting and these are my partners. We was just campin' here when this girl wandered in, lost or somethin' and we offered to help her."

Lance's eyes narrowed into a hard glare. He turned to the girl.

Her face was pale with fright. She sobbed as she cried out, "He's lying! They attacked our cabin and killed my parents. I hid my baby brother under some potatoes and then I hid. They found me and brought me here. That was last night. I don't know if my little brother is still alive or not but they certainly had no intentions of helping me!" Her hands were trembling so hard that the skinning knife that she held was shaking.

Hughie smirked. "I never done nothin' to ya that ya didn't want."

The girl raised her knife and ran toward Hugie screaming.

Lance grabbed her and took the knife from her hand. As he held her, she began to cry.

He looked around at Badger and Billy.

"I've heard enough."

Badger was silent and Billy's hands were clenched at his sides.

Hughie's eyes opened wide. "You can't hang me!" he screamed. "That ain't fair! I get a trial!" Hughie lunged for Billy's gun.

Billy shoved the outlaw and Badger turned Mule loose. This time Badger didn't stop his big jack mule.

The clearing was quiet. Billy's face was pale as he stared at the dead men.

"Are we going to bury them?"

Badger spat. "Let 'em lay. "Let the coyotes have the coyotes."

Lance turned to ask the girl about her brother. She didn't look much more than sixteen. Her face and arms were bruised, and her fingernails were broken. Lance had noticed the scratches on several of the men's faces. He scowled as he shook his head.

Billy had his arm around the young girl. He had turned her around as Mule was killing Hughie, and now she was crying softly.

Lance recognized that cry and cursed under his breath. *Well, she can talk to Molly. Molly will know what to say*, he thought.

"What is your name?" Lance asked gently.

The girl stared at Lance. "My name is Emma Mosier and my little brother's name is Sammy." Tears began to run down her face. "He's afraid of the dark," she sobbed.

Lance cursed under his breath and Billy talked softly to Emma. He walked her to the horse Badger had saddled for her and helped her up.

They left the outlaws where they lay and gathered up what food supplies were available. The men mounted and leading the extra horses, they all quietly left the clearing.

The only talking on the trip back to the wagons was done by Lance. He turned to look back at Emma.

"We will look for your brother tomorrow if you think you can tell us how to get there. Otherwise, Badger will backtrack your trail." Lance turned back around in the saddle, and they rode on in silence.

CHAPTER (35)

LETTING GO

MOLLY WAS WATCHING FOR THE MEN. Her stomach turned into knots as they rode up, and she saw the young girl's face. Lance caught her eye and for a moment, Molly was paralyzed. The terrible memories she had tried to put away came rushing up, and she felt sick. Then she squared her shoulders and walked up to the young girl.

"I am guessing you would like to clean up. Would you like to go down to the creek with me?" Molly asked with a quiet smile. Molly noticed that she was wearing Billy's coat.

Marion wanted to help. "I have a dress she can borrow if she needs something clean." As Molly nodded, Marion ran to fetch some clothes, and Private Most helped the young girl down.

"Mrs. Rankin, this is Emma."

Molly smiled at Emma again and then at Billy. "Thank you, Billy." Molly touched his shoulder. "You are a kind man."

Molly grabbed two of her blankets and took Emma's hand.

Emma followed Molly to the creek. She was shaking, and Molly put her arms around her.

"Oh, Emma. I am so sorry," Molly whispered through her tears. She hugged the girl, and Emma began to cry. Her crying was almost silent but it shook her body with great shudders. Molly held her until the shudders subsided.

"How about we clean you up? I will help you wash."

As she helped Emma to take off her outer clothes, Marion ran down the hill, out of breath. "Here are some clothes. Mother said to keep them; they are getting too tight for me. She sent some soap, a hair brush and some new undergarments as well."

Emma didn't look up, but Molly smiled with gratitude. "Thank you, Marion, and please thank your mother for us."

Marion stood unsure of what to do, and Molly signaled for her to go. As she walked up the hill, Marion glanced back. Molly had dropped her own dress on the ground but had left her undergarments on. Then she helped Emma with her clothes. They were filthy and torn. Molly removed all of Emma's clothes. She set Private Most's coat aside and then tossed the rest of Emma's clothes over toward the bushes.

I will ask Lance to burn those in the morning.

Molly took Emma's hand and together, they stepped into the water. The water had pooled under a tree and even through it was moving slowly, it was still a little warm from the sun. The pool was deep enough that it came up to Emma's shoulders. Molly helped Emma wash her hair. Emma began to cry again but this time out loud.

"They did me wrong, Molly!" she cried. "It was horrible. I will never be able to love a man. They have ruined me," she sobbed.

Molly turned her around to look in her eyes. "Yes, they did you wrong and there is nothing any of us can do about that, but you are not ruined. You cry and let this go. Don't hold it in."

Emma sobbed, "Men are just terrible. I will never be able to look at a man again without remembering this."

Molly turned Emma back around and began to brush her hair.

"You will never forget it, that is true; but it doesn't need to define you. Most men are good and decent. Look how Billy gave you his coat. Billy is a kind man. I believe that all of the men who are with us would do anything they could to help you; they just don't know how."

Emma confided, "I was going to kill the last one, you know. The tall man with the hard eyes stopped me. He shouldn't have—I wanted to do it."

Molly paused in her brushing. "That was Lance. He is my husband."

She turned Emma around again and smiled at her. "He didn't want you to have to live with that memory if he could help it. Lance knows what you are going through. He met me after I was raped."

Emma's eyes became large. "You were? And now you are married? Does he hold it against you that he was not your first?"

Molly shook her head and answered softly, "But he is my first. He is the first man I have truly loved. Rape has nothing to do with love, and I love Lance deeply."

Emma was quiet. She had scrubbed her skin so hard that is was raw in places.

As she began to shiver, Molly took her hand. "Let's get you dried off."

The two women stepped out of the water and Molly wrapped Emma in the blanket.

Molly and Emma walked up the hill and into the campsite. Emma was pale and quiet. She had put Private Most's coat back on but was still shivering.

Lance took one of his blankets and wrapped it around her.

Molly looked at the quiet group and gave them all a smile.

"Let me introduce you to the newest member of our party. This is Emma—why, Emma, I completely forgot to ask you your last name."

"Mosier," Emma replied quietly. "Emma Mosier." A look of panic washed over her face.

"My little brother!" she gasped. "He is at our house alone!"

Badger spoke up. "I tracked ya back ta the west, but I didn't foller far. Do ya know how far ya come?"

Emma shook her head. "I don't know how far. I don't even know where I am," she answered with her eyes full of tears.

Badger looked at Sergeant O'Malley. "I'm a guessin' that they come a ways. They woulda wanted ta put some distance behind 'em. Mebbie we should wait 'til first light."

"I want to come with you," pleaded Emma. "I want to make sure that my parents are buried, and I know where I hid my little brother. Oh, he is probably so afraid," she sobbed.

The men shifted their feet uncomfortably and Sergeant O'Malley nodded. "Wait till morning." He patted Emma's shoulder awkwardly and sat down.

Mrs. O'Malley had supper ready and conversation eventually picked up throughout the meal. Slowly laughing and joking picked up around the fire.

Lance moved up to sit by Molly. She was very quiet but gave him a smile. He put his arm around her and kissed the top of her head. *Gosh, how I love this woman*, he thought. Molly snuggled up next to him and soaked up his warmth.

The men had put up the tents and fixed a bed for Emma. They didn't have an extra cot but Marion gave Emma hers. The O'Malley's and Mary Lewis surrounded Emma and took her back to their tent.

"Someone had better clean up that mess or there won't be any breakfast!" Mrs. O'Malley hollered as she dropped the tent flap.

The men looked surprised and Lance started to laugh.

"Don't look at my wife. I'm taking her for a walk. You boys are on your own." He pulled Molly to her feet and led her out of camp.

Molly pulled back, "I should probably stay. The men might—"

Lance cut her off. He grabbed her and hugged her tightly. Then with a big smile he drawled, "Those men are just fine. If they don't know how to wash dishes, they can learn tonight. Now I, on the other hand, have not had my wife alone for nearly two days."

He scooped her up as he had done on their wedding day and kissed her. This time, there was no one watching, and Molly certainly didn't tell him to put her down. Finally Lance released her, and they sat down on the ground.

He looked seriously at Molly. "Are you okay? I know this was hard on you today as well."

Molly smiled although her face paled just a little. "I'm fine. It did bring back some terrible memories and I almost threw up. However, it was good for me to talk to her. Some of the things that I told her, I needed to hear myself." Molly paused and looked intently at Lance.

"What happened to the men? Did you hang them?"

Lance shook his head. "No, we took all four of them without firing a shot."

At the question on Molly's face, Lance responded quietly, "Badger turned Mule loose."

Molly was quiet. Lance had warned her not to get close to the big jack but he certainly didn't look like a killer.

Mule always acts like he wants me to pet him, she thought, a little puzzled.

When Molly and Lance returned to camp, the site was clean as a whistle with the wood laid out for breakfast. Some of the men were in the creek and others were lounging around the fire.

The sergeant told Lance, "We need to be out of here by 0600 tomorrow. We only made ten miles today."

Lance agreed. "Can you let the women know, Molly?" he asked.

Molly nodded her head. She smiled goodnight to all of those present and went back toward where the women's tent was staked. The murmur of voices from the tent picked up just a little as she went in and soon some soft laughter could be heard.

"Thank Heaven's we had women with us," Sergeant O'Malley muttered.

Lance was thinking the same thing.

Lance sat down with the sergeant, "Emma is insisting that she go with us in the morning. Are you okay with that?"

Sergeant O'Malley slowly nodded. "The girl can go if she wants. Let's let her decide. If she goes, I will send Private Most. She seems to be comfortable with him. Do you think you will need an extra horse? How old is this boy?"

"I'm not sure but I would say pretty small. He can ride double with his sister, but I'll take one of my mules in case she has anything she wants to bring back."

Lance grinned at the sergeant and drawled, "I don't think you brought enough wagons although we seem to be gaining horses."

The sergeant laughed and then his face drew into serious lines.

"I'm a little concerned though. We didn't make it as far today as I would have liked. I called for an early stop when we found a place with water and good natural defense. We are now behind and I can't afford to waste any more time."

Sergeant O'Malley frowned and then looked hard at Lance. "I hate to split the party but we need to keep going if you fellas think you can handle it."

Lance nodded. "I'd like to take Badger since he is the best tracker," and O'Malley agreed.

Badger stood up. "Good. We'uns leave first light," and tromped off to find a place to put his bed.

Lance walked back to the women's tent. "Emma?" he softly called.

The flap came open a bit and five women's faces appeared. Lance almost laughed.

Women seem to like to travel in packs.

"We are leaving at first light, Emma. You will need to be ready if you want to go with us."

"Oh, yes! I will be ready!" Emma exclaimed.

Lance could see the question in Molly's eyes and he shook his head slightly. Molly could stay with the wagons. He didn't want to put her in any more danger than necessary.

CHAPTER (36)

RESCUE OF SAMMY

THE SUN WAS JUST COMING UP AS BADGER LED THE WAY OUT OF CAMP. He was followed by Emma while Private Most and Lance brought up the rear. Badger set a fairly fast pace until he came to where he had stopped tracking. Still, he could see the trail through the grass as the outlaws had made no effort to cover their tracks. They had obviously not been concerned about pursuit. The tracks had been leading from the west but now they turned north.

The sun had been up for five hours when Emma exclaimed, "I know where I am!" She spurred her horse and raced ahead at a dead run.

Badger shouted, "Now don't race off like that, Missy—" but Emma didn't slow down.

"Durn fool gurl," growled Badger. "She don't know but what there could be more trouble."

The men urged their horses to a lope as they kept Emma in sight. All three had their guns out and ready as they followed Emma towards the farmstead. They saw her pull up in front of a small house and jump down. She ran into the house calling. When they arrived, she was running out of the house, terrified.

"Sammy isn't answering!" she cried.

Private Most spoke softly. "Calm down, Emma. Where did you hide him?"

"I put him in the potato barrel, but he's gone!" she cried with a sob. Private Most patted her hand. "Well, he probably had to go to the bathroom. Let's look around outside but try to be calm. If he is afraid, he may be hiding from everyone."

Badger waved his arms as he directed the search. "I'll take that there tree grove, an' Lance, you'ins check that there creek back o' the house. Missy, looky all over in that big barn, even up in the loft there, an' Billy, ya check that there little buildin' an' the house again. That thar little feller is jist a hidin' 'cause he's scaint."

Private Most turned toward the small shed and Emma ran for the barn.

Emma called frantically, "Sammy! Sammy, where are you?"

A sob sounded in the back of the shed as Billy entered and blond, tousled hair could just barely be seen sticking up from between two saddles.

Billy stepped out of the shed and whistled sharply; then he ran to the barn and called softly, "Emma!"

As she rushed towards him, Private Most pointed, "He's in the shed."

Emma ran for the shed as the other two men came back into the yard. Sammy was crouched down in a corner. He had piled saddles and tack round him until only his head was visible. His eyes were big, and his face was stained and dirty from tears. When he saw his sister, he stood up and reached out his arms.

"Sissy!" Sammy cried as his big sister wrapped her arms around him. Sammy's eyes were a bright blue but were red from crying. "I didn't know where you were," cried Sammy as the tears welled up in his eyes again.

"Now, Sammy, I told you that I would be back for you." Emma whispered softly as she hugged his little shaking body to hers. The tears ran down both of their cheeks.

Private Most had brought an extra blanket and he wrapped it around both Sammy and Emma.

Lance studied the little boy. He didn't know how to judge age in children, but the boy was small. He had just spent nearly a day and a half hiding, with his parents' dead bodies lying in the yard.

"I like old Mule better all the time," Lance growled out loud.

Lance asked, "Private Most, why don't the three of you water the horses?" Lance didn't want Sammy or Emma to look at their parents' bodies, riddled with bullets.

CHAPTER 37

A Good Day to Meet the Maker

BADGER HAD ALREADY STARTED TO DIG TWO HOLES under a big tree about one hundred yards from the house. The dirt was softer there, and the big branches hung low enough to offer shade if anyone ever wanted to plant flowers.

Lance pulled a couple of boards off the shed. He made two crosses to mark their graves.

Once the bodies of their parents were wrapped, Lance called the children over.

He asked gently, "Do you want to see their faces before we bury them?"

Emma nodded but Sammy wouldn't look.

Emma kissed each of them. "Momma, Papa—we will miss you," she whispered as tears ran down her cheeks.

Lance and Badger lowered the bodies into the graves, and Samuel and Josephine Mosier lay in their final resting place under the big tree that they loved so much.

Private Most spoke a few words and read a passage out of the little Bible he kept in his saddle bag.

Lance thought that it was a fine farewell. The birds were singing in the trees and several hawks glided overhead. "It's a good day to meet the Maker," Lance murmured softly as he touched Emma's shoulder.

"Emma, would you like to get anything from the house before we leave?"

Emma nodded as she walked toward the house. She was back quickly with two small packs, one for Sammy and one for herself.

Billy muttered softly, "Not much to show for sixteen years of life." He kept quiet but he wondered what they were going to do.

The only animals that hadn't been killed or stolen were a milk cow and a pig. Lance looked at the milk cow with distaste. They surely didn't have time to drag a stubborn cow along, and he was not going to milk her. The pig on the other hand made his mouth water—he could almost taste the side pork.

"Do you have any neighbors, Emma?" Lance asked.

She nodded. "The O'Toole's live about three miles north."

Lance put Emma on one of the extra horses and Sammy rode behind her. He hooked a rope onto the cow and with the pig running behind them, the unlikely troupe headed north.

Well, at least we are headed in somewhat the right direction, Lance thought.

The O'Toole's hadn't been aware of any problems, and were surprised to see the Mosier children.

Lance explained what had happened.

Mrs. O'Toole covered her mouth and then hurried to comfort the children.

"You poor children," clucked the kind Mrs. O'Toole, 'You will stay with us, of course."

Emma didn't want to stay. She liked the O'Toole's but there was nothing for her here.

Lance could see that Emma was hesitant. "You do as you wish, Emma, but you are both welcome to come on up to Wyoming with us. You can stay with Molly and me for a year or so, and then we can help you get established in Cheyenne if that is what you choose to do."

Emma looked at Sammy. "Sammy, do you want to stay here or go to Wyoming?"

Sammy's blue eyes lit up. "Go to Wyomin' an' be a cowboy!" he shouted as he drummed his heels on the horse's side. Lance tried not to grin.

"If you don't mind, Mr. Rankin, I would really like to come with you," Emma requested shyly. "I like Molly a lot."

Emma smiled at the. O'Tooles. "Mrs. O'Toole, we really appreciate your offer but I think we will go on to Wyoming. I don't want to farm, and Sammy wants to be a cowboy. Thank you though, and thank you for being such good neighbors and friends to all of us."

Mrs. O'Toole was shocked. "Why, Emma, you can't be traipsing across country with three men!"

Emma looked confused and then she realized what Mrs. O'Toole thought. "Oh, we are not alone. Lance's wife and three other women are traveling to Julesburg with some soldiers. Private Most is part of that unit." As she named them, Emma pointed at each of the men.

Badger hadn't spoken but when Mrs. O'Toole looked in question at him, he winked at her. She turned a dark red and glared.

Lance shook his head and Private Most was oblivious.

"Did your folks buy their ground, Emma, or were they homesteading?" Lance asked as he studied the O'Tooles' small homestead.

"They were homesteading and Papa had just filed on it."

"Mr. O'Toole, you might want to check into how their land is filed. I doubt that Emma will be back." Lance commented as he looked at Emma.

Emma shook her head and Mr. O'Toole looked surprised.

Lance wrote up a quit claim and showed it to Emma.

"This deeds the land over to the O'Tooles, Emma, but only sign this if you are sure you don't want to return."

Emma quickly signed the paper and handed it to Mr. O'Toole.

"I have nothing to give you for it," he faltered, embarrassment showing in his voice and on his face.

Emma replied, "If you would plant some flowers on my parents' graves and carve their names into the markers, that would be enough. You were always good neighbors and I know that Momma and Papa would want you to have it."

Mr. O'Toole shook her hand and with tears in his eyes, smiled at Sammy. "Son, if you ever decide to come back, that land will be yours." Sammy just stared at him with big eyes but didn't respond.

Lance then asked Mrs. O'Toole, "Would you like the cow and the pig? We can't really take them with us." Mrs. O'Toole was delighted to take them. She hadn't had a milk cow in some time. The O'Tooles' had no cash money but Mrs. O'Toole sent them away with a cured ham and some bacon.

Lance had tied the Mosiers' small packs to the mule. He added the ham and the bacon. As they rode away, he turned around and looked longingly at the pig and then laughed softly.

As Badger looked over at him, Lance grinned.

"I was just thinking of the scene we would make if we had tried to get that pig onto the train to Cheyenne. My wife would be blushing!"

Badger's sharp eyes twinkled as he nodded, and then he led the way northeast.

CHAPTER (38)

QUICKSAND!

BADGER LEAD THE WAY NORTHEAST. He knew that Sergeant O'Malley was going to start angling west before long but either way, they should cross his trail. They had left at daybreak and the sun was hot now.

"Sammy, you need to hang on. You almost fell off again!" Emma scolded as the little boy dozed behind her saddle.

"But Sissy, my belly hurts. I'm hungry, don't ya know?"

Badger reached over and lifted Sammy off to sit in front of him. He pulled a biscuit out of his saddle bag for the little boy, and Sammy sagged back against Badger as he chewed. Soon, he was asleep, with the crumbs of the biscuit trailing down his chin.

Lance looked at Sammy and his face colored.

"Shoot. That little feller hasn't eaten in a day and a half and I didn't even think about it. We had better take a break."

Badger nodded and pointed at the bacon. "Durn shame ya didn't bring a skillet too so's we'uns could have some of that thar bacon." He grinned at Lance and added, "Shore now, ya jist need ta think ahead more an' do more figgerin'."

Lance laughed ruefully and the two men began to look for a suitable area to rest.

They had followed the tracks that morning for five hours. The sun was high in the sky, and everyone was hungry.

Private Most had filled the canteens when he watered the horses and it was a good thing. The river beds were there, but they were dry.

"Folks been talkin' 'bout what a dry spring it's been. This here country needs a good drink in the spring or it jist burns up." Badger added quietly, "Tough place to start a farm."

Private Most dropped back to ride by Emma. "What kind of a job would you like to get, Emma? I hear that Cheyenne is growing fast so you might have lots of opportunities to learn a trade there."

Emma perked up as she answered, "I always wanted to be a teacher. I love children. Papa taught me to read but we could never afford any books. If I could teach children and read more than the same book over and over, that would be wonderful!"

Her eyes sparkled as she talked and Private Most thought she was just about the prettiest girl he had ever seen.

"I like to read too," he responded softly. "My favorite book right now is by Charles Dickens, 'Our Mutual Friend.'"

Private Most pulled it out of his saddle bag. "You can read it if you want," he offered shyly. He blushed as he added, "Or we could read it together."

Emma held the book in her hands. "It is a beautiful book, Private Most."

Private Most answered, "Billy. Please call me Billy."

Emma smiled. "Thank you, Billy. Maybe I will read some by myself and then we can read together later."

Billy smiled at her and Emma remembered what Molly had told her. "Billy is a kind man." *Molly was right. Billy is a kind man.*

As they rode on in silence, both were smiling.

Lance rested the little group for about twenty minutes. They chewed on hardtack and jerky, then were quickly back on their horses. This time, Lance put Sammy in front of him and they moved out at a fast trot.

As they topped a rise, Lance's mustang perked up its ears. They slowed up and then stopped their horses. They could hear a man talking, but only snatches of the conversation could be understood.

"Grab…Pull….Can't…Sinking."

Badger rode ahead to check while the rest of the group followed slowly. Pretty soon, he waved them in.

A man was in the water struggling with a horse. He couldn't get close enough to the back end of the horse to wrap the rope around its rump. The horse was in quicksand and the more it struggled, the deeper it sunk. The man's wife was on the bank trying to hold a second horse that had the rope attached to the saddle horn. He looked up as Lance's party appeared.

"I'm too heavy," he blurted out. "My weight will push it down even farther and I have to get that rope behind it."

Emma spoke up quickly. "I can do it."

Lance started to protest but before he could open his mouth, she was sliding over the head of the horse with the rope in her teeth. She pulled up his tail, slid the rope under it and shimmied backwards pulling the rope as she went. She dropped the loop under its neck and was back on dry ground in no time. Emma had done it so fast that the men were standing open-mouthed.

She looked around at them. "Well, let's pull!"

Lance moved the rope from the saddle horse to his mule and the mule leaned forward. The horse's back was coming up but it wasn't moving its front feet. Lance clucked at the mule and it heaved again. This time the horse pulled out one foot and threw it forward. Lance moved the mule to the opposite side to change the angle of the pull and the mule heaved again. The horse pulled out the second leg and the mule almost threw the horse up on the bank. The horse was trembling as it stood there but it didn't appear to have any broken bones.

The man had fallen down on the bank. He stood up, wiped his hands on his pants and put out his hand to Lance.

"You sure did come along at the right time."

He pointed at the creek. "I have the route marked to cross this river to avoid where the quicksand usually collects, but the horse spooked when a bird flew up. I think it was a crane. Whatever it was, it was big, and its wing slapped Old Jessie on the side of her head. She reared up and almost dumped me. When she came down, she was in quicksand and we were in trouble." The man paused, "I don't have any cash money to pay you but we could sure give you a meal."

His wife spoke up. "Dinner is ready. I came out to see where he was and found this mess. We are so thankful you stopped to help."

Lance looked at his group. They were all tired and hungry. He wanted to keep moving but he relented, and they all followed the couple to their house over the little rise.

As they walked toward the house, the man introduced himself. "My name is John Sable and this is my wife, Mary Sue. We sure do appreciate you folks stopping to help." Mary Sue smiled in agreement.

The smell of food greeted them as they entered the Sables' home. Lance's mouth started to water. And what was that other smell….did he smell *pie*?

Mrs. Sable saw Lance perk up as he walked in the door and she laughed.

"I see you smell the apricot pie. I just picked them this morning so you will get to try our first harvest of the season." She beamed at Lance. Mrs. Sable loved to make pies but her husband wasn't much on sweets. He ate them to make her happy, but was delighted to share.

The meal was delicious and Mrs. Sable invited them to spend the night.

Lance shook his head.

"Thank you, Mary Sue, but we really need to get on down the trail. We need to meet up with the rest of our group by tonight."

Badger stepped forward. He squeezed Lance's shoulder as he suggested, "I shore think a little nap would be good fer those young'ins. Mebbie we could bed 'im down for a bit."

Lance looked at the tired children and slowly nodded his head. Mrs. Sable took Sammy and Emma into the bedroom. She studied the tear-stained little face with the big eyes and just gave Sammy a hug. He hugged her back and rewarded her with a smile that melted her heart. Mrs. Sable gave Sammy a bath and put one of her husband's night shirts on him so she could wash his clothes.

"You climb in there by your sister, Sammy, and I will tuck you in."

Emma was already asleep, and Sammy cuddled up next to his sister. He threw one arm over her back and with a deep sigh was asleep.

"Oh, how I wish we could have children," she whispered as he lay sleeping.

Mrs. Sable quietly shut the door and went into the kitchen to clean up.

Lance was talking to her husband, and he told them how Sammy and Emma had come to be with them.

Mrs. Sable nearly cried. Neither she nor her husband could understand the cruelty of some people. Lance did leave out a few details, like how Mule had killed all four of the outlaws. He never told them that Emma was raped either but they both understood.

At 3:30, Lance asked Mrs. Sable to wake up the children. He was anxious to connect with the wagons.

"There's a good bivouac area about five hours due north," Mr. Sable explained as he drew a map on the ground for them. "If they find the camping place, and I am guessing they know where it is, you should catch up with them by tonight."

Mrs. Sable helped Sammy dress.

Sammy told her, "I don't have a Mommy or a Papa anymore."

It broke Mrs. Sable's heart. She so wanted to tell him that she would be his mommy.

Instead, she hugged him again and replied, "No, but you have a wonderful sister who loves you very much."

Sammy giggled. "I know she does. Sometimes she slips me hard candy when Momma isn't looking,"

Mrs. Sable squeezed him before she put him down and her eyes filled with tears as she watched Sammy run outside to his sister.

Lance's eyes lit up when Mrs. Sable handed him an entire apricot pie. It was wrapped in paper.

"That is not going to travel well," Mrs. Sable stated as she gave Lance a big smile. "In fact, you might want to eat part of it right away so it doesn't all get mashed."

Lance grinned and thanked her as the little group mounted up.

CHAPTER 39

A Grandpappy for Sammy

WHEN SAMMY FOUND OUT HE COULD RIDE WITH WHOMEVER HE WANTED, he decided to ride with Badger on Mule; and he was full of questions.

"Badger, do you have any kids?"

Badger's bright eyes sparkled, "Nope but I do have lots a' mules!"

Sammy hesitated. "Are they like yur kids?"

"Wal now, they shore is. I help birth'em, I raise 'em an' I train 'em, I love 'em. Shore nuf, they's like kids!"

"What's this mule's name?"

"This here mule is my fav'rite. His name's Mule an' he's been with me nigh on fifteen years. 'Course a mule cin live 'til they's nigh on forty years, so he has lots o' good years left in 'im."

Sammy thought a little bit. "Forty is really old. Are you forty yet, Badger?"

Badger cleared his throat to keep from laughing. "Wal, let's see. I done had my fortieth birthday sometime back so I must be most fifty."

"FIFTY years old! Why you's old enough to be my grandpappy!"

Sammy twisted in the saddle to look up at Badger. "I ain't got no grandpappy. Would you like to be my grandpappy?"

Badger laughed as he hugged the little boy closer. "Why I shore 'nuf would like to be yur grandpappy! So what's a grandpappy do?"

Sammy thought a little bit. "I reckon he would take his grandkids fishin'. Do you like to fish, Badger?"

"Why I shore 'nuf do! I like hard candy too. Do ya think a grandpappy would keep hard candy 'round?"

Sammy's blue eyes were shining. "I bet they do keep candy. And maybe some cookies?"

Badger scratched his head. "I don't know how ta make cookies but I could mebbbie marry me up ta a gal what makes good cookies. How does that sound?"

Sammy's face lit up, "Say, I would like that just fine! Do you think she would be my grandmammy?"

Badger grinned into the back of Sammy's head. "I reckon she would but you'ins have ter ask her yerself. We'll be a pickin' 'er up in Julesberg so ya cin ask 'er then."

Then Sammy teared up, "But I don't have a momma anymore. Or a papa. Those bad men hurt them and now they're gone."

Badger didn't know what to say so he was quiet for a bit. "Wal, ya know, lots a folks don't have mommas. Molly don't, Lance don't, Billy don't, an' I don't. But I think they's plenty of mommas on this here trip. Maybe ya could jist borry one for the trip!"

Sammy liked that idea. "I guess I'll have ta think on that. I might want more than one!"

Badger shifted Sammy in the saddle. "Wall, I think that'd be jist fine. A feller cain't have too many friends so I reckon he cain't have to many mommas neither."

Sammy was getting tired again, and he leaned back against Badger.

Lance rode up beside Badger and laughed. "Did you just acquire a grandson, Badger?"

Badger gave Lance his ornery grin but the sparkly blue eyes looked a little watery.

"I shore did an' a finer grandson I jist couldn't find. This here kid's a special boy."

"Sammy is a lucky boy," Lance replied softly as they rode on toward the camping area.

Badger found the area Mr. Sable had directed them to around 8:30 p.m. Sergeant O'Malley had found it as well, and camp was set up.

Lance almost fell off his horse, he was so tired.

Mrs. O'Malley and Mary Lewis met them and took the children as they were lifted off of their mounts. They led them to the women's tent and the beds that were prepared. Neither Emma nor Sammy was awake enough to eat and they were quickly bedded down.

Sergeant O'Malley barked for some soldiers to take care of the livestock, and all three men just wrapped up in blankets and went to sleep by the fire.

Molly was cleaning dishes in the creek when they rode up and Lance was asleep before she even made it up to the camp. She looked down at him tenderly and thanked God for such a wonderful man. Leaning down, she kissed his cheek. He smiled in his sleep but never moved.

The little convoy had covered twenty-eight miles, their best day yet; Molly knew that Lance's party had covered a lot more miles than the wagons.

CHAPTER 40

Travel by Night

JUNE 8 WAS GOING TO BE A HOT DAY. Molly joined Sergeant O'Malley as he stared ahead at the faint trail leading north. The land was almost flat and where it did rise, the hills were so low they were almost unnoticeable.

"The land looks flat here, but we are climbing," the sergeant stated. "You will see it in the way the mules pull today. I'm pleased that Captain Lewis sent two extra mules for each wagon. It shorted him on his end, but it is sure going to help us out."

So far, the riverbeds had mostly been dry and those that weren't had been easy to cross. Still, flat riverbeds always made Molly leery.

"So where does the water go if it comes really fast? These riverbeds look really flat."

"I'm sure they can have some pretty nasty flash floods out here," the sergeant agreed. "I guess it just depends where the rains are." Then he added, "I don't think we need to worry about that as much as we do a lack of water for the next day or so. The spring rains were light and early. With all these dry river beds, we need to pack all the water we can for the next few days."

The sergeant walked away, barking orders to his men. "Make sure all those water barrels are full. Today will be a dry day. Ladies, make sure your canteens are full."

Molly watched the sergeant and smiled.

As Lance handed her Babe's reins, she commented,

"The men like Sergeant O'Malley. He puts them first and makes sure the animals are cared for."

Lance nodded as he watched the camp come alive and prepare for another day.

"O'Malley knows this area well and wants to take as few chances as possible. He's a western man, and he knows how fast problems can arise."

Lance pointed at a group of young soldiers. Marion was in the middle of them, and she was flirting outrageously.

"There's the sergeant's biggest problem," he chuckled.

"And Marion, you leave my soldiers alone!" Sergeant O'Malley snorted in frustration to his sister.

"Why she has those boys so addlepated that they can't even think at all," he fumed to himself. "Women."

Molly was giggling as the sergeant stomped away.

One of the young soldiers that Marion tried to toy with was Private Smith. Marion was very interested in Private Smith but he was not yet under her spell. Of course, that just made her all the more determined. She tried everything to get his attention.

Private Smith was very polite and he always answered the questions she asked him. Then he would quietly excuse himself and go check on the animals, or do anything else that needed done. Private John Smith had grown up with sisters, and he knew all about the games girls played.

As he watched Marion flirt with the other soldiers, Private Smith scowled.

"Women just mess with your mind and cost you money," he muttered as he walked out to check the picket lines.

Molly covered her mouth and laughed out loud as she watched Private Smith's reaction.

Lance was grinning widely as he helped her up on her horse.

"And while you are laughing, look at Badger."

Sammy was following Badger like a little shadow, talking constantly. Badger's ornery eyes were twinkling as he answered the boy.

Molly laughed softly as she watched them and then looked down at Lance with an "I told you so" look on her face.

"Didn't I tell you Badger would be a great grandfather? He has even stopped chewing tobacco."

Lance had to agree as he mounted up.

O'Malley had his little caravan on the road by 0500, and the sun was hot three hours later. No shade could be seen for miles.

By noon, the sun was an orange globe in the sky, and the winds had picked up. Not that they didn't have wind every day, but this wind was terrible. O'Malley finally called a halt.

"Line up those wagons for a windbreak and unhitch the mules," the sergeant barked.

The horses and mules stood with their backs to the wind, and the people crowded beside the wagons to seek protection.

Even though the ambulance was partly covered, the gales of wind furiously blew anything it could pick up, and the wind stung their faces with dirt, sand, small rocks and even pieces of dried grass. Even a few sticks hit them.

Lance picked a stick up. It looked like it had broken off of a small tree.

"I wonder how far this blew?" he wondered out loud as there were no trees to be seen in any direction.

A few of the women stayed inside the ambulance but Molly thought it was worse in there than on the ground beside Lance. He protected her as much as possible.

"Pour a little water over your bandana and tie it around your mount's nose. Get something over your face as well," the sergeant ordered, "and under no conditions are those water barrels to be opened until this wind goes down."

The wind continued to blow until evening when it finally relented. As the members of the small caravan picked themselves up and shook out their clothes, they could see dirt and sand piled everywhere. The mules had fared better than the horses but all of the animals were thirsty.

"Wipe those animals' noses and faces off. Then give each two gallons of water," O'Malley barked.

One barrel was immediately drained along with part of the second. Oats were then given to the livestock. The people sipped some water and then wiped their faces, eyes and noses using as little water as possible.

"There will be no cooking tonight so chew on your hardtack and jerky," O'Malley grunted at the bedraggled party.

Finally, Sergeant O'Malley hollered, "Hitch up. We're moving out!"

The women stared at him incredulously.

Even Mary Lewis asked quietly, "Sergeant, do you really think that is a good idea?"

"We have a full moon tonight, Ma'am," O'Malley informed her with a grim look on his face even as it turned a little redder than usual. "This is no place to deal with another day like today. We need to go as far as we can while it is cooler and then take any cover we can find."

There was a little grumbling but everyone understood that the sergeant was correct.

Private Smith offered Marion the second bandana that he always carried. Then he patted her shoulder and walked away. She was so miserable that she forgot to flirt.

The mules seemed to be glad to be leaving the dirty piece of ground. The wind had completely buried the sparse grass in places.

O'Malley used his compass and then set his route looking at the stars. He estimated that they had only made about eight miles. He cursed silently and led out.

The mules pulled through the night. They could see shelter nowhere. Finally, O'Malley stopped beside a large buffalo wallow and had the mules unhitched. They arranged the wagons the same as the night before. This time though, the people were able to lie down on the soft dirt in the bottom of the wallow. Again, each animal was watered but they were only given one gallon of water. Now the third barrel of water was only half full.

"Wipe off your canteens before you fill them and be careful not to spill any water," O'Malley told the group.

Once the canteens were filled, only the fourth barrel had water. While it was full, it was not enough for two more days of this hot weather.

Again, the animals were given oats and everyone bedded down for the night.

O'Malley knew the situation was grim.

Lance pulled Molly close and tried to shield her from the wind. He handed her his canteen.

"Drink some of my water, Molly. You need more water than me."

Her lips were cracked. Her face was red and wind-burned. "I don't think I have ever been so miserable," she whispered to Lance.

He put some water on his handkerchief, and wiped her face off. Then he wrapped her in a blanket and they both went to sleep.

The wind came up with the sun and blew again the next day. Everyone was miserable and hungry. Tempers were beginning to fray and the buffalo wallow was crowded.

O'Malley ordered people to relieve themselves in twos and to stay close to the hollow.

"Stick together. It will be easy to lose your direction and wander off."

Molly had never endured such a miserable day in her life. There was nothing to do but wait and everyone was antsy. Finally, evening came and the winds subsided a little. The sergeant ordered each of the mules' and horses' noses to be wetted and each received a gallon of water.

The wagons were hitched and the hungry, bedraggled party moved out.

"We covered fifteen to twenty miles last night," O'Malley informed the group. "We need to pull farther than that tonight and if we can, we won't have to spend another night out in this wind."

Again, the sky was clear and the moon was bright.

"And we can thank the Good Lord that we have a clear night and a bright moon. This trail would be hard to find if it was a black night," O'Malley added grimly.

Around midnight, one of the mules pricked up its ears, and soon all of the animals were pulling to the left.

Lance's mustang was jerking his head and trying to run; he gave the animal its head but kept it at a gallop. Badger fell in beside him. As they dropped off a small rise, they saw a small pool of water. Some dirt had sifted in but it was protected on all sides by rocks.

The wagons were slower to arrive and O'Malley told his little party, "Fill your canteens and then we'll water the animals."

The water was brackish and warm but it was wet. One by one the horses and mules were watered. They didn't get as much as they wanted but they all had some. Then, O'Malley had them rehitched, and they moved out.

The mules pulled well into the night but now they were showing fatigue.

Lance could tell that O'Malley had a location in mind. He was pushing the animals and angling slightly toward the west. Around 0300, he saw some bluffs ahead.

"Look, Molly—we are headed toward those bluffs. The sergeant must be planning to camp in there somewhere."

Molly looked up and stared dully ahead.

"Are they close? They look like they are just a few miles away."

Lance shook his head, "No, they are closer to five miles but we will have protection tonight." He patted her arm.

"Not too much farther, Molly. Give Babe her head and all you have to do is slow her down."

O'Malley rode along the exhausted column.

"We are stopping there," as he pointed toward the bluffs.

"Keep pushing those mules. There's a spring-fed creek ahead. The mules will smell it soon so give them their heads. Just use your brakes because it will become much rougher the closer we get."

One of the older soldiers stood up in his stirrups.

"Arikaree Breaks! Sarge is takin' us to the canyons. We will be campin' in Horse Thief Cave tonight, boys!" he exclaimed. Then he let out a whoop and waved his hat in the air.

CHAPTER (41)

ARIKAREE BREAKS

SLOWLY THE LITTLE PARTY STARTED TO PERK UP. Once the mules smelled water, it was hard to hold them back. The ground was now rougher and some of the women chose to ride instead of being slammed around in the ambulance. With the outlaws' horses, they now had twelve horses in addition to fourteen mules.

Lance's mouth twisted with humor. *Most drives lose livestock but we just keep gaining.*

As he laughed out loud, Molly looked over at him. He just grinned at her.

Molly studied Lance's profile. He was dirty and dusty, but he didn't look as bedraggled as the rest of them did. His lean, hard body seemed to be in tune with nature, and he just adapted. Molly smiled in spite of her cracked lips and then focused on helping her horse to navigate the rocks.

The mules had pulled thirty-five miles that night with little water and still looked better than the army horses or Babe. Lance's mustang was tired, but he seemed to be as tough as the mules.

Finally, they arrived at Arikaree Breaks.

O'Malley began barking orders.

"Privates Smith and Most, unhitch those teams and start watering those animals. Limit them and bring them back down every two hours. The rest of you soldiers, get those tents up and get a fire started."

He paused as he studied the women.

"Ladies, there is a pool up-stream from where the horses are being watered if you would like to clean up. My men will be busy packing and setting up camp for a while."

The creek was spring-fed and the water was deliciously cold, and the women soaked their dry bodies. Once they were done with their baths, they began to prepare the meal.

Lance's huge ham was brought up. Several of the older soldiers went in search of squaw cabbage while others found some wild plums. By the time the men had bathed, breakfast was ready and it was delicious.

The grass was long and lush on the side hills and the animals were picketed after they were watered. The men fell into their beds and were instantly asleep while the women went back down to the water to wash their clothes. They knew they would sleep better if they were fresh and clean.

Nearly everyone slept well into the day.

However, Sammy, who had dozed most of the night either on Badger's mule or in the wagon, was ready to go in just a few hours.

"Come on, Grandpappy!" he begged. "Let's go fishin'."

Badger opened one eye and grinned at the earnest little face. He slowly sat up, and they planned their strategy. As they went down toward the creek, Badger cut off branches and showed Sammy how to make a fishing pole.

"Ya have ta pick one with some give in 'er, Sammy. If'n ya was ta catch a bigun', yer pole has ta bend an' not bust." They walked up the creek from where everyone had bathed, sat down on the bank and threw in their lines.

Sammy was enthusiastic but not very coordinated. Finally, after Badger fished him out of the creek twice, Sammy caught a fish. It was only about eight inches long but Sammy was delighted.

Badger studied the fish, "Now that thur is a fine lookin' fish, Sammy. Why, I tell ya what. You'ins an' me 'ill jist cook that thar monster fer dinner."

Badger showed a fascinated Sammy how to clean the fish. He intended to bake it in the coals and that turned out to be a good plan. It was hard enough to gut a fish so small, let alone try to skin it.

As the smell of baked fish sifted through the camp, some of the men awakened to see who was cooking. They came up to the fire just as Badger was pulling the tiny fish out of the coals. Sammy was excited.

"Ya wanna try my fish? Me an' Grandpappy catched this monster in the creek an' we's gonna eat it now!"

Each soldier pretended to take a bite and smacked his lips as Sammy beamed.

The fish *was* delicious and it wasn't long before most of the soldiers were headed to the creek with handmade poles.

Sergeant O'Malley and Lance hiked up to Horse Thief Cave. It was so rough that the wagons couldn't be pulled that far. However, the cave was huge and would be a great place to spend the night. As soon as they returned to camp, O'Malley gave the order to break camp.

"Pack 'er up, men. We are going to move camp up to the cave. Unload those wagons and pack only the supplies that we need on the mules. We'll leave the wagons here and one man will stay with them all the time. You never know who else will wander in here."

The troops would trade sentries every four hours.

Lance and Badger offered to take their turns as well but O'Malley shook his head.

"We have the manpower to handle that. If you would make sure that the women have everything they need, that will be good enough."

The soldiers had caught quite a mess of fish. Once they were cleaned, Sammy and Badger showed Mrs. O'Malley how to bake them. They had more squaw cabbage and Private Smith found wild turnips. They had a delicious evening meal at 1700.

After supper, O'Malley wanted to meet with everyone to discuss the rest of the trip.

"We are a little over halfway to Julesburg. We can stay one more day here and rest up if you want. However, that means pushing for twenty-five miles each day for the rest of the trip. Or, we can pull out in the morning and go eighteen to twenty miles per day."

A chorus of voices voted to stay. Arikaree Breaks was like a wonderful vacation and no one wanted to leave it yet.

The next morning after breakfast, the women started washing clothes and bedding. Soon, all of the rocks and bushes were covered with clothing and blankets. They even washed the soldiers' clothes. However, they didn't pay attention to how they were sorted and soon all of the clothes were mixed up. It took a little bit of shuffling and trading to get all the pieces of clothing back to the right man. High-water pants and tight shirts were traded for longer pants and larger shirts.

Lance was amazed at Arikaree Breaks. It rose high above the flat plains. The Breaks appeared to be two to three miles wide and over thirty miles long. They were nearly impassable with a wagon but the area around Horse Thief Cave was like an oasis on the plains.

Lance grinned at Molly. "Enjoying your vacation, Molly? Water, trees, nothing to do—you'd better rest up because I don't think we will see this again the rest of the trip!"

Molly looked up from the pan she was scraping, and her gaze took in the clothes hanging on all of the bushes.

As her blue eyes began to shoot fire, Lance took the pan from her hand and pulled her toward him.

"Take a walk with me, Molly. I'll help you clean up when we get back."

He led her up to the top of a bluff and they watched the sun go down. The colors changed quickly from oranges and golds to pinks and blues. Finally, only part of a yellow globe could be seen as the sun dropped out of site.

Lance pulled her closer to him.

"Don't be so busy that you forget to enjoy all the beauty the Good Lord shares with us, Molly," Lance whispered softly as he kissed the top of her head.

Molly could feel the tension flow out of her as she smiled up at this man who had become her everything.

The next day at Arikaree Break was refreshing and slow. Everyone rested up and feasted on fish which was a nice change of diet.

Supper that night was relaxed with lots of talking and laughing.

Sergeant O'Malley was all business though.

"We will plan to leave tomorrow at 0600. I expect the wagons to be loaded, mules hitched and everyone mounted by then."

The women groaned but the soldiers knew better than to complain even though it meant awaking before 0500 to pack the tents.

"You men get this site cleaned up, and have my wood ready or there won't be any breakfast before we leave. I will cook or I will clean but I won't do both. Breakfast will be ready by 0500," Mrs. O'Malley hollered over her shoulder as she stomped toward her tent.

Mrs. O'Malley could shout orders every bit as well as her son. Sometimes, she even forgot that her son was in charge and she gave orders to him.

The men complied quickly. Besides being an excellent cook, Mrs. O'Malley was a master at cooking over an open fire.

By 0500, nearly everyone was ready. Some of the women were slower to move until the tent started to come down on them. Then there was a scurry of activity inside with soldiers grinning on the outside.

Mrs. O'Malley cut up the rest Lance's ham. She had hidden some eggs in one of the wagons and added the ham to her scrambled eggs. The reaction from the men when they saw the meal made Molly laugh.

"You men are truly moved by your stomachs, aren't you?" Molly laughed as the men lined up for breakfast.

Of course, Lance was literally drooling. He just grinned at Molly and held out his plate when she made fun of him.

Mrs. O'Malley was a tough woman but she loved "her soldiers" and she beamed as they gobbled up her food.

"I have just a little left. Who wants to clean up this last dab of eggs?"

Eight men charged her pot and Mrs. O'Malley held up her spoon in front of her face as she glared fiercely at them. She gave the last of the eggs to Private Most and Private Smith.

"Because they are the youngest," she explained with a smile.

The caravan turned to the west to go around Arikaree Breaks. The breaks extended about three miles that way but stretched further east.

"We are now in Colorado Territory," O'Malley told Lance.

"Julesburg is due north."

CHAPTER (42)

FLASH FLOOD!

THE SUN CAME UP BRIGHT AND WARM. Soon the clouds appeared and everyone knew that the rains were coming. O'Malley was watching the sky. They had several rivers and creeks to cross and he wanted to get over them before the rains hit.

"I haven't had much experience with flash floods but this terrain does look like it is ripe for it," he told Lance and Badger as they moved out.

The caravan crossed the first creek with little problem. The same two horses didn't want to cross, but Lance was ready for them this time. Badger and Lance brought up the rear and when the horses saw the rope come out, they jumped into the water.

"Those two are going to be a problem if the next river is deeper than this," Lance growled. Badger bobbed his head in agreement.

They covered about ten more miles and then it started to rain. The mules were sinking in the soft ground and the pulling was much harder.

Finally, they saw a river up ahead. As the small party gathered at the edge of the bank, they could see that the water wasn't that deep but it was moving fast.

O'Malley conferred with Lance and Badger.

"We can hitch one of my mules to each side of the wagons to keep them from sliding sideways behind the team. We should probably take them across one at a time just to make sure we don't have any wrecks. Put your best teamsters on the wagons and the ambulance," Lance suggested.

The packs were quickly removed and stowed in a wagon; then the ropes were attached. Lance kept the tension tight on the left mule and Badger handled the right. The mules' small feet made them more sure-footed, and they were less likely to lose their balance than the horses.

Lance's method worked well and they moved the first wagon across quickly. Again, his mules were unhooked and the ropes reattached to the second wagon. The water was now higher and it was more of a struggle to get it across.

Lance yelled at the riders, "Get in that water now and get across!"

The two skittish horses jumped into the water when their riders jabbed them hard with their spurs. Babe didn't want anything to do with the fast moving water, and Lance couldn't help as he was attached to the wagon. They almost lost it once but the left mule dug in his feet and the wagon righted itself.

As they rushed to untie the ropes, Lance looked for Molly. Babe was till stomping at the water's edge. Lance raced his horse through the water and yelled for Molly to hang on. He slammed his rope down on Babe's rump. She sprang into the air and almost unseated Molly. Then she straightened out and finally crossed.

The water was even higher now and Lance knew they were going to have trouble with the light ambulance.

"Ladies, you can't ride the ambulance across this river!"

Lance shouted at the soldiers on the other bank, "Four of you men get over here and grab these women. We need to get them across now!"

Privates Smith and Most were the first in the water, followed by Sergeant O'Malley and a burly soldier riding a large army horse.

Private Most reached his hand down and Emma quickly slid across the saddle in front of him. Private Smith did the same with Marion and the two men quickly pushed their horses to the other side.

Private Andrew had been a soldier for nearly twenty years. He blushed as he grabbed Mary Lewis.

"I plumb apologize, Ma'am. I know you ain't used to ridin' this way." He charged into the water as Mary hung on for dear life.

Sergeant O'Malley grabbed his mother. She was quite a bit of woman, but her son was able to heave her up on his horse with one hand. His horse staggered once and hit the water before she was settled. No one seemed to notice that she was cussing him in Gaelic all the way across. The sergeant's red face was redder than normal as he deposited his mother on the ground on the other side.

Lance and Badger had their ropes attached to the ambulance. Lance was downstream and he knew that if the ambulance broke apart or if the mules went down, he would need to release his rope quickly or he would be pulled down as well.

The mules plunged into the water followed by Lance and Badger. The light ambulance kept bouncing up as it was pushed sideways downstream.

Sergeant O'Malley charged into the water. He lunged for the ambulance seat and grabbed the lines from the startled soldier. He stood up and roared as he whipped the mules. They lunged forward as the water rose quickly.

The soldiers on the bank began to yell and point. A wall of water was coming down the river, pushing rocks, brush and debris in front of it.

Lance let go of his line and plowed through the water toward the mules. He hit the slowest one with his rope, yelling at the top of his voice. The lagging mule lunged and the lead mules pulled it up on the bank just as the wall of water descended on them. Lance and Badger barely made it to the bank. They were soaked and Lance's mustang had a cut on its hind quarter.

Molly's heart was pounding. She saw how close the water had come to Lance, and she thought he was going to be swept away. It was Lance's mustang that saved him. The edge of the wall of water hit his horse's rump, knocking it off balance and sideways. Had his horse not been so sure-footed, it would have gone down and Lance would have been lost under the fast-moving wall of debris and water.

Lance's hands were shaking and he clenched his fists several times as he counted heads. Everyone had made it over safely.

O'Malley was yelling at the men to line the wagons up. His horse had climbed up on the bank before the ambulance and was trembling.

Lance grabbed the reins of the frightened horse and angled it to where O'Malley was shouting orders. Once everyone was settled and the mules were tied again behind the wagons, the soaking wet column began to move down the trail.

Everyone was looking for someplace to take shelter as it was still pouring rain.

CHAPTER 43

WACKY WEED HANGOVER

PRIVATE MOST WAS OUT IN FRONT WHEN HE SHOUTED, "A CAVE!" and pointed to the right.

They were on the far northwestern edge of the Arikaree Breaks. At the base of one of the cliffs, Private Most had spotted a cave.

Lance rode back to where the private had halted his horse. "Have you ever been in that cave, Billy?" he asked.

Billy shook his head, "No, but I have been in some of the other ones. They can be shallow or go back a long way. Would you like me to check it out?"

Sergeant O'Malley had just ridden up and both looked towards the sergeant.

He waved them on, and they rode toward the cave.

Through the opening, they could see that it was tall enough for horses and it looked to go back a ways.

"We'll need a torch of some kind to see back in there," Lance commented as he slid off of his mustang.

He dug through his saddle bags for a match while Private Most reported back to Sergeant O'Malley. Once Lance lit the match, he saw a packrat nest just inside the opening. He shoved it on a stick close to the nest and lit it. He followed the cave back about fifty yards and could see another fifty yards.

"We'll have to keep an eye on Sammy but otherwise, this should work pretty well."

Lance moved his torch from side to side and saw quite a few more packrat nests.

"We'll have plenty of fuel to start a fire," he commented to himself.

A large pile of buffalo chips and a small amount of wood was piled close to the opening of the cave. Lance looked closer.

"Those are the side planks off a wagon." He shook his head. *We surely were lucky today.* As he thought about the trip, he shook his head again. "Actually," he muttered, "We have been lucky all the way through." Seeing the wagon boards reminded him that not every traveler was so lucky.

The wet and bedraggled group slowly came up to the cave.

Sergeant O'Malley immediately removed the covers of the water barrels to let them top off with fresh water. The barrels were about three-quarters full, and he was not one to waste a chance to catch fresh water when it was offered.

The men unloaded the wagons and then unhitched the mules. They left the wagons by the opening of the cave. There was little grass to be had so the animals were brought into the cave. They were rubbed down, watered and given some oats. A buffalo chip fire was started.

Mrs. O'Malley had never cooked with buffalo chips before.

She cocked an eyebrow as she looked at the chips.

"I never thought I'd see the day when I'd be cookin' with cac," Mrs. O'Malley growled as she studied the chips.

Private Smith laughed. "Don't worry, Mrs. O'Malley. They really do work, and they won't throw sparks up like wood. You can even tell a little bit about the diet of the buffalo." He broke one open to show her but she wasn't nearly as interested as he was.

Marion stepped up, genuinely curious.

"You can tell their diet by the kinds of seeds and fiber in their dung. Buffalo are on the move all the time so their diet varies as the vegetation changes." Private Smith explained.

When he was done, Marion gave him a bright smile and just for a moment, Private Smith forgot he was not going to be taken in by her charms.

"I think we should call this cave 'Buffalo Chip Cave'," Marion giggled as she looked at her mother.

Molly was glad to be out of the rain. *I feel as cold as I did those last ten miles to Manhattan*, she thought.

"What is it about rain that makes it so warm when you are playing in it, and so cold when you are riding in it?" she asked Lance as he returned from making a bed for them at the back of the cave.

Lance looked hard at her and then felt her forehead. "You're chilled, Molly, and you might even have a fever. Do you want me to move the bed out by the fire? It will be noisier out there but it will be warmer."

Molly shook her head. Her face was pale and she couldn't stop shivering.

"No, I'm really tired. Let's just add an extra blanket." She gave Lance a weak smile as her teeth chattered.

Once Molly was settled in the blankets, Lance felt her head again and he scowled.

"Please don't get sick, Molly," Lance whispered as he pulled her closer. He put his hand on her stomach and the baby moved.

"You just hang in there a few more weeks, little fellow. You wait for us to get home before you make your appearance." The baby kicked his hand and slid away as Lance laughed softly.

The rock floor was cold and it took Lance some time to get comfortable. He slid another blanket under Molly's hips and finally dozed off.

Lance awakened when Molly bumped him.

She was shivering violently. Her face was hot—even her arms were burning up. She looked up at him. "I am sssso cccold," she stuttered as she continued to shiver.

Lance picked her up, blankets and all, and carried her to the front of the cave by the fire. He pushed the blankets as close as he could without catching them on fire.

He knelt down beside her and called her name. "Molly! Molly! Wake up. I need you to drink some water."

Molly opened her blue eyes but they wouldn't focus. He put his hand on her stomach and the baby didn't kick it away.

Panic was rising in Lance. He turned his head and hissed at Badger.

"Badger, Molly is running a fever. I don't know much about fevers but she feels really hot."

Badger knew more about natural medicines and healing than anyone Lance had ever known and he needed Badger's help now.

Badger felt Molly's forehead and then left without a word.

Sergeant O'Malley awoke when Lance hissed and he followed Badger to the fire.

The sergeant gave Lance a damp cloth to sponge her off.

"Loosen her clothes, Lance, and apply the cool cloth to her chest. You need to cool her body down."

As Lance began to loosen Molly's dress, she grabbed his hands and began to struggle. Her eyes flew open and the terror in them broke Lance's heart.

He held her hands and whispered, "Molly, you are running a fever. I have to cool you down."

Molly stopped struggling as she stared up at Lance. Her eyes were unfocused. Her eyes slid on and off his face as he unbuttoned her dress.

"Please drink some water, Molly. You need to drink something for your fever."

"I'm not thirsty." Her eyes focused for just a moment. "Lance!" She stared at him intently and whispered, "I love you, Lance. I even love you when you make me blush!" she giggled.

Sergeant O'Malley looked up with surprise and then looked away quickly as a smile spread over his face.

Lance held Molly's hands and kissed her face. He was watching the cave opening for Badger.

"Where did he go?" Lance whispered as he tried to keep Molly calm.

Molly was beginning to thrash around and wanted to get up.

"Badger, you had better get back here soon," Lance grated out as he looked at his watch. It was about 12:30 a.m.

Finally, Badger appeared. He had only been gone about twenty minutes but to Lance, it seemed he was gone an hour.

 Badger was carrying a collection of plants and roots. He began dumping them into a pot and added water. When the pot was boiling, he added a few more plants. Then he took a cup, filled it with his concoction, and handed it to Lance.

"Have 'er drink this."

Lance sat Molly up. He handed her the cup.

"Molly, you need to drink this. Badger fixed it for you and it will make you better."

Molly smelled it and turned up her nose.

At Lance's insistence, she finally took a drink. She tried to spit it out.

"That's awful! I don't want any more." She looked at Lance and tried to wink.

"You drink it!" she joked with a loose smile.

Lance looked at Badger who signaled to drink it all.

Lance gently insisted. "Come on, Molly, do it for your baby."

Molly looked at Lance and gave him a silly smile. She leaned forward and whispered loudly,

"I'm pretty sure he won't like it either!"

Sergeant O'Malley laughed out loud and walked back to his bed.

Lance scowled, and then growled his words at her.

"Molly, you need to drink this now. You have a high fever and it needs to come down so it doesn't hurt you or the baby."

She stared at him for a moment and then frowned. "I don't like you when you're grumpy," she pouted. Then she took the cup and drank it quickly. She gagged and looked accusingly at Lance.

"That wasn't a very nice thing for you to do, Lance." Her eyes were going glassy when for just a moment, they opened wide.

"You're not Lance! Lance isn't mean to me."

Molly lay back down on the blankets. She almost looked drunk. She smiled up at Lance and spoke in a slurred voice, "Hey cowboy, why don't you climb in here and keep me company. I think I'd like to cuddle with you."

Lance blushed a deep red and Badger laughed.

Badger patted Lance's back. "She'll be alright, an' then you'ins cin do all the cuddlin' ya want!" He whistled a jig as he walked toward his bed, and Molly was almost immediately asleep.

Lance looked back at Badger and called softly, "What is in that?"

Badger gave an evil laugh as he answered, "A little o' this an' a little o' that. Mebbie some loco weed, some o' the seeds from them thar buf'lo turds, an' a few roots from them thar hills. She be right as rain by mornin'."

As Badger rolled up in his blankets, Lance stared toward him suspiciously. *The thing is,* Lance thought, *I'm guessing that he really did put all of those things in that concoction.*

Lance smelled the concoction and gagged.

"Molly was right. It does smell terrible; and if it tastes as bad as it smells, it's rank."

Molly awoke about six hours later with a headache but no fever.

Badger was up and winked at Lance who had barely slept all night.

"Jist a wacky weed hango'er," Badger commented with his wicked laugh.

Molly smiled sleepily at Lance. "You look tired. Didn't you sleep well last night?" she asked.

Lance grabbed her hands and pulled her close. "You woke around midnight with a high fever. Badger made you a concoction to drink, and it knocked you out." He paused. "Is the baby moving? I don't see your dress moving."

Molly looked down and gasped as she pulled the sides of her dress together.

Lance's neck turned red.

"I unbuttoned your dress and put wet clothes on you to try to cool you down. You had me pretty scared for a while there," Lance explained apologetically.

Molly stared at him and then shook her head. "I guess I don't remember anything," as she quickly buttoned her dress.

Lance laughed as he hugged her again.

"Be glad you don't. That concoction Badger made was rank but it worked. In fact, I think I will save the rest of it in case we need it again."

Mrs. O'Malley had just awakened and saw Lance digging in the wagon.

"Get out of my food stock, Lance Rankin!"

Lance gave her a sheepish look. "I was just looking for an empty jar, Mrs. O'Malley," he apologized.

Mrs. O'Malley continued to mutter until she found one for him. While she pulled supplies out of the wagon, Lance poured the rest of the concoction into the jar, sealed it down tight and stowed it carefully in the back of the ambulance.

He stood by the wagon and offered a silent prayer of thanksgiving, not only for Molly's recovery but for Badger's friendship as well. *That little man has tricks and talents like no one I know.*

As Lance turned to go back into the cave, he heard a lot of banging and yelling around the cook fire. He poked his head in and saw Mrs. O'Malley with her nose in her pot.

"Someone put a skunk in my pot!" she shouted. She raised her head up and she glared at the men. Her face was red and she was angry. "Who used my cooking pot?" she bellowed as she waved her spoon and looked around suspiciously.

Her eyes connected with Lance but he ducked back outside and disappeared.

Badger was laughing wickedly so she turned her wrath on him. Of course, that didn't bother Badger in the least.

CHAPTER (44)

HECK OF A SHOT

THE MORNING WAS BEAUTIFUL. The air was clean and everything seemed just a little greener.

Emma came to the opening of the cave. "Look! It's like the ground needed a drink of water."

Lance looked at her and smiled. "You are exactly right, Emma." The sun was rising and a blend of brilliant colors filtered across the sky.

Lance stepped out of the cave and whistled a happy tune as he went to check on the livestock.

Badger had moved the horses outside sometime in the early morning and had them hobbled on a small patch of grass. He had turned all of their mules loose to forage where they could.

Some of the soldiers were leading the army mules and horses to a little seep to drink.

Lance screwed the top back down on the water barrels. The sergeant's technique had worked. All of the water barrels were nearly level full.

The sergeant didn't seem to be in a hurry to leave.

"We will wait a day for the water to go down. We have a few more rivers to cross. Besides, the ground is too spongy to make any time today.

"Think you can shoot some meat?" he questioned. "We are running a little low."

Lance nodded in agreement. "I will head out now while it's still cool."

As he was saddling up his horse, Molly came to stand by him. Her stomach seemed larger and maybe a little lower. He didn't know that skin could stretch so far but he decided not to share that thought with her. When she found that he was going hunting, she immediately wanted to go.

Lance was tempted but he told her no.

"I don't know how far I will have to go. Besides, you ran a fever for a while last night. I think you need to take it easy today."

Molly frowned and then looked up with a puzzled look on her face. "You know, I remember not feeling well when I went to bed and being so cold but I don't remember anything after that."

Lance gave her a quick kiss and then cupped her face, "Molly, my love," he whispered. Then his eyes began to sparkle.

"Of course, at some point in time, you are going to have to pay up on all those promises you made me last night!" He laughed down at her and Molly blushed furiously.

Just as Lance loped away with one of his mules in tow, Private Smith strolled up. He turned to watch as Lance rode away.

"Where is Lance going, Molly?" he asked.

"He is going to try to shoot something," she answered.

Molly watched Private Smith hurry off. She turned to look after him and then she blushed a deep red as she thought of Lance's comment.

"Oh, I hope my promises had nothing to do with my dress being open!" she whispered to herself. Then she stomped her foot. "That man! He lives to embarrass me."

Private Smith rushed over to Sergeant O'Malley. He saluted sharply. "Permission to hunt with Mr. Rankin, sir!"

O'Malley growled a response and saluted him back.

Private Smith raced to his horse, saddled him and bounded into the saddle. The horse was almost at a full run before he had his seat.

Lance heard pounding feet. As he looked back, he saw Private Smith waving his hat with a big grin on his face.

"Sarge gave me permission to go hunting with you—what are we looking for?"

Lance liked young Private Smith. *He sounds so much like a kid this morning,* Lance thought.

"Well," Lance drawled, "I haven't decided. What sounds good to you?"

The private grinned at him. "Let's just ride and shoot what we see," he stated with enthusiasm.

Lance and Private Smith enjoyed riding, and it was a beautiful day. The ground around the narrow animal trail they rode was spongy from the rain, but the trail itself was firm. The elevation was increasing, and the hills were getting higher. It was still short-grass country but today it was green and lush after the rain. Both men rode listening to the sounds around them. It was a good morning for a quiet ride.

A mule deer walked slowly out of the rocks and crossed the trail. Lance and Private Smith were upwind of him as he tested the air, and he did not catch their scent. The large buck was followed by several does and three fawns.

Lance was debating if he had a clear shot when Private Smith whispered, "Let me take this one."

"Let's see what you can do," Lance whispered back with a grin.

It was a long shot at over four hundred yards but Private Smith's shot was true. The buck took a couple of leaps and dropped.

Lance took a long look at Private Smith and then at his rifle.

"That is not typical army fire power there."

Private Smith smiled and handed Lance the rifle. "I was a sharp shooter for the North."

As he took the gun back from Lance's admiring hands, he added quietly, "But I like to hunt for meat much better."

The men skinned and gutted the deer. He was huge and would provide a lot of meat. They wrapped the skin back round the carcass to keep it somewhat clean. Once the deer was tied to the mule, they headed back for camp.

Lance looked at Private Smith and his eyes twinkled as he drawled, "I think I just lost my job as the top hunter. That was a heck of a shot!"

Private Smith blushed. He knew he was an excellent marksman but Lance's compliment meant a lot to him.

CHAPTER (45)

Cold Water and Fresh Meat

SEVERAL OF THE SOLDIERS HAD EXPLORED DEEPER INTO THE CAVE and found a pool of fresh water. The animals refused to go back into the cave, so they were watered from the barrels. The barrels were then refilled from the pool.

Molly walked back to look at the pool with some of the soldiers, and Private Most handed her a cup of water.

"This water is delicious!" she exclaimed.

Private Most nodded. "There's probably an underground spring that feeds into it. That is what keeps it so cold and fresh-tasting." He took a drink himself and swirled the water. "Lots of rivers start in Colorado Territory," he added. "I think that some of the best water is mountain water."

More soldiers wandered back with Sergeant O'Malley behind them. They were eying the pool for a swim but the sergeant was adamant.

"No swimming. Caves can be tricky, and the pools in caves can be nearly bottomless. No point in taking a chance of someone drowning."

A voice shouted from the front of the cave, "We have meat for dinner!"

Molly hurried with the soldiers to the front of the cave. She saw the men standing around a large deer. Private Smith was blushing while Lance told an elaborate story about their great hunt.

"Why that deer was over four hundred yards away. Heck of a shot. Downhill and through brush. You don't want Private Smith to be hunting you, boys! "

Several of the men clapped the private on his back and nearly all of the soldiers began to pepper Private Smith with questions.

"Why don't you show us how to shoot like that sometime?" one of the privates asked.

Sergeant O'Malley walked up just as that question was asked.

"Why, didn't you know? Private Smith is going to be the Firearms Instructor when we get to Fort Sedgewick." He shook Private Smith's hand.

"Fine shot, Soldier."

There had been some downed trees in the little valley where Private Smith shot the deer and Sergeant O'Malley sent several troopers out to see what they could find. They came back with two mules loaded down with wood and Mrs. O'Malley was much happier to be cooking with wood again.

The venison was delicious. Lance and Badger cut into strips what wouldn't be eaten for supper and hung it up to dry. It wouldn't be ready by the time they left, but they could hang it on the side of the wagon. The air was dry so everything dried faster.

Supper was a little quieter as everyone was wondering what lay ahead.

Sergeant O'Malley barked, "Private Most, you're in charge of the water barrels. Make sure they are filled tonight and again after we water the animals in the morning."

Private Smith stepped forward, "I would be glad to help Private Most, sir," he offered.

Sergeant O'Malley nodded and the two friends began to haul water.

CHAPTER (46)

ROCKSLIDE!

THEY ROLLED OUT THE NEXT MORNING UNDER A SKY THAT WAS STILL GRAY. The sun was just coming up, and the air was cool and crisp. The mules stepped out easily, rested and ready to pull. Their ears were pricked forward as they picked their way over the narrow trail.

Sergeant O'Malley and Lance rode side-by-side and were discussing the rest of the route.

"We only made about six actual miles before we stopped at the cave last night since we had to detour around the Breaks," O'Malley stated. "We are over halfway and we've been lucky." He shook his big head, "Mighty Lucky."

Lance was thinking the same thing. He had traveled with Molly from Georgia to the Colorado Territory. She and her unborn baby were still healthy. Lance whispered a prayer of thanksgiving.

"I sure hope that little fellow stays put until we get Molly to the ranch," Lance commented. "If the baby comes early, that could add a whole new level of difficulty to this trip, especially for Molly and for him."

O'Malley frowned and then he shrugged. "Not much you can do either way. We'll just keep heading north." Then he grinned at Lance and added, "Of course, my responsibility ends at Julesburg—and yours will just be starting!"

Lance laughed as he agreed. He stared out over the prairie and then looked back to where Molly was riding. She gave him her bright smile and his stomach clutched. *I should have a backup plan but I don't. I'll just keep praying that she doesn't sick and that baby is not early.*

Emma stayed close to Molly, and the two of them talked often. Private Billy Most seemed to hang around Molly a lot when Emma was present. One time as the young soldier was being exceptionally helpful, Lance caught his eye and gave him a big grin. The private blushed a deep red but it didn't stop him from being "handy."

The trail they were taking cut below some rocky ledges. Lance looked up and his neck hairs stood on end. The rocks seemed to be tilted over the trail, ready to come down.

"Those rocks look a little unstable, Sergeant. Have you ever had any of them slide?"

Sergeant O'Malley looked up and nodded. "They do look like that, but I've been over this trail many times and so far, they've stayed put."

Mary Lewis was quite the picture in her sidesaddle. She had been in the ambulance the entire trip, and decided it was time to get some fresher air. Captain Lewis had sent her sidesaddle along, and her skirt was draped over the rump of her horse.

Lance studied her for a moment and then asked carefully, "Mrs. Lewis, are you sure you don't want to ride astride? It might be safer."

Mary Lewis stared at him and sniffed, "This saddle will do me just fine." Molly and Marion joined her and the three women rode together down the trail as they visited.

Mrs. O'Malley refused to ride a horse. When Lance suggested that she ride one of his mules for a change, she glared at him and folded her arms across her ample bosom.

"My God gave me two legs to walk upon. He did not give me four."

Emma had twisted her ankle the night before trying to climb to the top of the bluff. It was swollen and she couldn't get her shoe on so she was riding in the ambulance for the day with Mrs. O'Malley.

Private Most asked for permission to drive the ambulance, "to give Private Hedges a break," he quickly added with a smile as he attempted to appear nonchalant.

O'Malley wasn't blind, but he enjoyed young love and he agreed.

Private Billy Most jumped into the ambulance with the two women. He was quiet and shy, but Emma and he were having quite a conversation as he drove. She laughed often, and finally decided that it would be more fun to hang onto Private Most's arm than to try to grip the seat.

Billy looked surprised but he was pleased. He smiled and then patted her hand. "You hang on as tight as you want, Emma. You can hang onto my arm anytime," he whispered and they both blushed.

The women had asked that the canvas top be taken down and were enjoying the fresh air. Emma took off her bonnet and let the wind blow through her hair. Private Most smiled at her.

"You sure are pretty, Emma," he told her with a shy smile.

The trail widened out a bit as it went under a large overhang and Marion rode her horse up beside the ambulance to talk to her mother.

Badger moved up to ride beside the sergeant. Sammy was riding with him again, and had been talking non-stop as they left the cave area.

"Grandpappy, how much longer 'till we get to Wyomin'?"

As Badger started to answer, Sammy pointed up. "How do those birds stay up there in the sky? I jumped out o' the barn with a sheet but it didn't work," he told Badger with frustration. "Sissy told me it wouldn't but the birds can fly, so why cain't I?"

Badger's wise eyes twinkled over Sammy's head.

"Wal now, the Good Lord done made birds to fly an' you'ins ta walk on two feet. Now iffen you was a bird, you'd be a eatin' bugs an' worms. That's why they's so light when ya hold 'im. They don't like those stinky bugs no mor'n you do, but they have ta eat 'em iffen theys a gonna fly."

Sammy was quiet for a moment as he thought.

"So iffen I was ta eat bugs, I'd be able ta fly?"

Badger laughed. "Wal' I spose we'd have ta figger a way fer ya ta grow some wings then," and he grinned down at Sammy.

As they rode under the overhanging rocks, Sammy pointed up again.

"Them birds is fightin' over who gits ta set on that big rock!" As Badger looked up, the rock moved and he wheeled around in the trail to warn the rest of the group.

"Move those mules! She's comin' down!" Badger hollered as he kicked Mule.

As people paused to look up, the rocks began to slide. The mounted soldiers along with Molly and Mary Lewis were not yet under the ledge.

Lance was behind the two wagons and was able to whip the mules into a run.

However, the ambulance was behind the wagons and couldn't get out of the way. The rock-slide hit the ambulance, and the tipping ambulance slammed into Marion's horse, knocking it off of the trail. The panicked animal tried to catch its feet but lost its balance, falling sideways and sliding down the side of the steep bank. Marion was flung off her horse as it fell. The force of the rocks pushed the ambulance and the mules down the rocky embankment onto the rocks below.

Marion's horse was dead. It was struggling to get up when the ambulance rolled over the top of it.

One of the mules was not moving and one was down and thrashing. The sound of its frantic braying as it struggled to get loose was heart-breaking, and Molly covered her mouth in horror at the scene below her. There was no sound from the wagon.

The stunned silence was brief and then the men rushed to push the ambulance aside.

Lance could barely breathe. He turned to make sure Molly was okay and then raced his horse down the hill to help. As he rode, he whispered, "Molly had just been riding in the same position as Marion, and then had moved back so Marion could tell her mother a story!" He cursed under his breath as he dropped from his horse and grabbed one side of the ambulance to help lift it up.

As the men flipped the ambulance over, all were quiet. Both Mrs. O'Malley and Emma had been crushed. Private Most had his arms still wrapped around Emma, and he was dead as well.

When Sergeant O'Malley rode down, he could see that the three people were dead. Tears welled up in the eyes of the tough sergeant as he wheeled his horse to find his sister. Just moments before, they had all been laughing. Now two women and a fine soldier were dead with a third woman injured.

Marion was lying further up the hill. Her horse had thrown her clear of the rolling ambulance, but she was not moving. The sergeant raced his horse up the hill.

"Don't move her or let her get up until we check 'er over!" he shouted.

Private Payne was somewhat of a medic and he rushed to help.

Badger handed Sammy to Molly and dropped to the ground beside Marion. Her eyes were open but she wouldn't respond to anyone.

As Private Smith dropped from his horse and rushed to lean over her, she smiled, "I'm not dead?" she asked. He took her hands with a relieved smile, "No, you're not dead."

Marion was trying to get up. Badger put his hand on her chest and pushed her back down.

"Not jist yet, little missy. Ya got ta answer some questions first."

She looked confused but agreed. "Can ya move yur fingers an' toes?" Marion's feet moved and everyone gave a sigh of relief.

"How 'bout yur fingers?' Badger asked. "I don't see them a movin'."

"That is because Private Smith is holding them," she answered as she looked up at him.

Private Smith released her hands as his neck turned red, and her fingers moved. Marion struggled again to sit up. Then she looked around.

"Mother! I was just talking to her. Where is she? Is everyone all right?" Marion's eyes were wide and she was still struggling to sit up.

Private Smith moved to place his body between Marion and the crushed ambulance down the hill. He didn't want her to see the men removing the bodies of her mother, Emma and Private Most.

He held both of Marion's hands firmly but gently as he softly spoke, "Marion, your mother is dead. When the rocks collapsed, they rolled the ambulance down the hill, and your mother as well as Billy and Emma were killed." His eyes were red as he added quietly, "You were very lucky that your horse threw you to the side."

Tears poured down Marion's cheeks as she looked up at him.

Private Smith held her hands a little tighter while she sobbed, "Oh, what will I do without my mother? She was always just there."

As Private Smith talked to her quietly, his heart broke for her. He could almost see into her soul as she cried.

Finally, Badger determined that nothing else was broken. "Go ahead an' hold 'er. We'uns need ta find somethin' ta set this here leg with but other'n that, she's a goin' ta be jist fine."

Private Smith pulled Marion against his chest and patted her back as she cried. Tears always had made him feel awkward and irritated but somehow, this was different. Slowly, Marion's sobs subsided and she grew quiet.

Marion looked up at Private Smith. "Thank you for letting me cry on you," she whispered as she sat up. Her bottom lip was still trembling and her hands were shaking.

Private Smith looked at her seriously and then he smiled.

"Marion, you can always cry on me if you need to cry," he told her softly as he squeezed her hands.

Private Payne and Badger returned with a sturdy sapling.

The private had set his share of broken legs and stated, "I will need some help setting this. We are going to have to stretch it out and then hold it in place."

He looked at Marion and Private Smith. "It is going to hurt but it will be important that you don't move. We want your leg to heal correctly so you don't have a limp later."

Marion's face was pale and her blue eyes opened wide but when she looked at Private Smith, he smiled.

As he laid her back down on the ground, one soldier gripped her leg and two more secured her shoulders. With a great pull, they were able to move the bone back into place.

Marion gasped and she gripped Private Smith's hands so tightly that she drew blood. He never moved.

Badger tied the sampling in place with the reins from the downed team. "I'm shore sorry for a hurtin' ya, little missy, but this here tree needs ta stay in place. You'ins ain't gonna be jumpin' in an' outa wagons fer awhile neither."

Badger and Private Smith helped Marion up. She lurched to the side from the pain in her leg and she leaned hard on Private Smith as she staggered. He helped her to one of the wagons and lifted her up to sit on the open end-gate with her leg extended. Her leg hurt and her eyes were large, but she had a small smile for Private Smith.

CHAPTER (47)

A New Family for Sammy

SERGEANT O'MALLEY'S EYES WERE FULL OF TEARS as they carried the bodies of the women and the soldier up the embankment.

They buried Mrs. O'Malley in a grave by the trail and they placed Private Most and Emma in a grave together, with the private's arms around her as they had been found. Sergeant O'Malley read from the Good Book and then Badger offered some words.

"These here folks was good people an' I shore hope the Good Lord sees 'em as they was. Mrs. O'Malley were a fine woman an' a good cooker, an' the Lord musta' needed another cooker up thar. Private Most loved little Emma an' I reckon the Good Lord done saw fit that they should go ta the next world side by side. An' we thank the Lord fer lettin' us keep Marion. Aaamen."

Lance paused by the graves for a moment and then walked to where Badger was standing by Sammy.

"Badger, that was a fine prayer. We have been blessed to have you with us on this trip." Lance squeezed Badger's shoulder as he stepped up to stand by Molly. Had he looked at Badger, he would have seen the old man rub his eyes.

Little Sammy looked up at Badger. "I ain't got no one now, Grandpappy. No momma, no Papa, no Sissy." His eyes were full of tears and they left wet streaks as they ran down his dirty little cheeks.

Molly turned toward Sammy. Her blue eyes were full of tears as she knelt down on the ground in front of the little boy. "Sammy, how would you like to be my little boy? Lance will be your Papa and Badger will always be your grandpappy."

Sammy's little face lit up. "I'd like that just fine!" he shouted and jumped into Molly's arms so hard that she almost fell backwards. Lance helped her up and put his arms around his little family.

"I'd like that just fine too, Sammy," he choked as he hugged them close.

Badger smiled and his ornery eyes glistened.

"Sammy, are ya ready to git on down the road with 'ol Badger?"

Sammy paused for a moment and then looked up at Lance. "Naa," he replied, "I think I'll ride with my new Papa today."

Marion watched the exchange between Sammy and the Rankins with a tight throat. *Shame on me for feeling so sorry for myself* she thought. *I had my mother my entire childhood and this sweet little boy just lost everyone.* "Lord," she whispered, "I want to thank you for giving me my mother for so many years. Thank you for giving her the skills to teach me all that she did and the patience to tolerate me when I was bad. And thank you for finding Sammy new parents."

She stifled a sob. "Goodbye, Mother. I love you." Marion dropped some of the wild flowers she was holding on her mother's grave and laid the rest on Private Most's and Emma's grave. "Goodbye, Emma and Billy. I know you'll be happy together." As she struggled with her crutch and a sob caught in her throat, she felt someone take her arm.

Private Smith smiled down at her as he squeezed her hand and tucked it under his arm. *Oh Mother*, Marion whispered silently, *You always scolded me for flirting so much. You said the Good Lord would send the right man, and I think He just might have.* Marion looked up at Private Smith and gave him a tremulous smile as he squeezed her hand a little tighter.

There was very little in the ambulance that wasn't destroyed. The injured mule had to be put down. Some of the soldiers had pulled the traces off of the dead mules and put them in the wagons. Mrs. O'Malley hadn't wanted "that terrible concoction" that Badger had created riding with her so she had placed it on one of the wagons.

The wagons were repacked and a spot was made for Marion to lie down. Private Smith took over driving that wagon and it wasn't too long before Marion was riding on the seat beside him with her leg stretched out in front of her. Private Smith helped her stabilize it. It still hurt but it was better than being in the back of the rough wagon.

They were a subdued group as they once again started down the trail. It widened out a little as they moved away from the rock ledges and through the rolling hills. Sergeant O'Malley pushed hard that day and they made thirty miles. His eyes were red and he rubbed them a lot, but none of the men seemed to notice.

Mary Lewis and Molly cooked the evening meal. Supper was quiet out of respect for the friends and family they had lost that day, and no one remained around the fire long after eating. Private Smith led the other soldiers in the clean up after supper.

As they prepared the wood for the next morning, Private Payne spoke up, "I'll cook breakfast tomorrow."

The rest of the men were quiet and then one suggested, "Let's take turns. Mrs. O'Malley liked it when we helped her. I'll do the next day." The other soldiers nodded in agreement. Mrs. O'Malley's death left a big hole in their little group.

The sergeant told everyone at breakfast that they had one more difficult river to cross. "It's usually not too high but who knows with the rains. We should cross it sometime today. We have come around one hundred sixty-two miles. If we can pull two more twenty-mile days, we should hit Julesburg in a couple of days. If not, well, we will just be a little later."

A flutter of excitement went through the camp. Everyone was ready to be out of the wagons. Molly looked at Lance with a bright smile on her face. "Oh, Lance! We are almost to Julesburg and then on to your ranch," she whispered as she wrapped her hands around his arms. Lance laced his arms around her. "Our ranch, Molly girl. Our ranch," he answered as he smiled down at her and kissed the top of her head.

QUICKSAND AND SINKHOLES

THE SKY WAS JUST BEGINNING TO LIGHT the next morning when they rolled out at 0500. This part of the route was rolling hills but not as many rocks as before. The mules were pulling easily. After about three hours, they arrived at their last large river. The river looked deceitfully calm and shallow, although it was flowing fairly quickly.

Sergeant O'Malley had a map in his hand.

"We have to follow the route across exactly as it says here," he told the group. "This river is a mess of quicksand and sink holes. There may be churning water under the surface although it does look calm today. This will be the last large river we have to cross before we get to the South Platte. Anything after this will be dry or shallow as long as we don't get another heavy rain. It will be important that you follow the animal in front of you exactly. One small misstep and we could lose a horse or even a person."

Molly's eyes were huge. She knew that Babe did not like to cross water if it was moving and this was definitely moving.

"We will take the horses across first. Once everyone is across, the wagons will follow. You two soldiers with the skittish horses will be last.

"You'll come with Badger and the other livestock.." The stern sergeant paused as he studied his little group.

"Don't start the second wagon until the first one is pulling up the bank. I don't want a wagon sitting in the water any longer than it has to."

Lance rode up beside Molly. He had Sammy in front of him. He smiled at her.

"Babe is a good horse. She'll be fine and I will be right in front of you." He kissed her cheek. "Ready?" he asked and their horses began to tentatively step toward the water. They had to cross the small island in the middle of the river. The sergeant was again hollering orders.

"Stay on the route!"

Molly studied the river, "The water looks pretty shallow. It is scary to think that it looks so easy to cross but could be so dangerous."

Lance looked back "Just follow my mustang. Keep Babe's nose on his tail and you'll be fine." He looked down at Sammy.

"Now, Sammy, I want you to hang onto the saddle horn with both hands and don't you let go!"

Sammy stared and then slowly nodded. His blue eyes were huge and for once, he was not talking.

Sergeant O'Malley led off. Mary Lewis and Marion were behind the sergeant on mules.

Lance had insisted that Mary Lewis straddle the mule she was riding. She was horrified but Lance explained, "If we have any problems, you will be able to balance easier." Mary relented as she understood the value of a just argument even though she was appalled.

Marion's left stirrup had been lengthened to accommodate her splinted leg. Her mule pawed the bank, ready to go into the water. Lance was next followed by Molly. Four mounted soldiers followed them. The horses that disliked water would be pushed in last. They would wait until the wagons crossed and then Badger would help the last two soldiers to get their mounts into the water. If they followed on their own, they would join the end of the column.

Babe fussed a bit and then stepped daintily into the water. A small fish slid across her front leg and Babe reared. As she spun in the water to bolt for shore, Molly lost her grip. Lance wheeled his mustang and caught Molly. His arm slid above her stomach and he pulled her across his saddle as Babe went over backwards. Sammy was pinned between the two of them, his small frame pressed against Lance as Molly's body was thrust sideways onto the saddle.

Babe was down and thrashing, barely keeping her head above the water. The horses in line behind her were twisting and trying to buck.

With one hand on the reins and the other arm around Molly, Lance shouted at the soldiers, "Turn around! Try to wheel your horses to keep on the route. Don't let them step out of line as they turn!"

Lance spun his mustang and followed Sergeant O'Malley to the far bank. He swung Molly down and dropped Sammy beside her. Molly was crying and Sammy was terrified. Lance and Sergeant O'Malley raced back into the water, following the route backwards toward Babe. O'Malley stayed on the sand bar in the middle giving directions.

Lance dallied his rope and caught Babe's front legs. Badger had come from the other side and dropped a loop over her back legs. The men flipped Babe over, dragging her feet onto the more solid base of the riverbed below the designated route. As they released their ropes, she shakily regained her footing and stood up.

Lance watched her carefully. The likelihood that she had broken a leg was high. He studied how she stood. Although Babe was shaking, she didn't seem to be favoring a leg. Lance grabbed her reins and once again started on the route. This time she followed meekly, keeping her nose almost on the mustang's tail. Badger had the other horses hold up until she was almost across, and then the small line of horses fell back in line.

The two wagons followed the horses into the water, spaced out as Sergeant O'Malley had ordered. The mules almost seemed to feel their way across the treacherous water. At last, all but Badger's string of mounts and the last two horses were in the water.

Badger smacked one of the problem horses and it jumped into the river while the other horse pawed the water and snorted. Badger decided to play it safe.

"Here, put yer outfit on this here mule. We ain't a takin' a chance with that there hoss, not when we'uns have good mules ta ride."

Once his outfit was switched to the mule, Badger handed the soldier the lead rope to the skittish horse. "If that thar horse sashays outside o' whar we are, drop the rope. Don't try ta hang onto 'im."

Badger brought up the end leading the last two horses. They were army horses so were used to following in a column. He had them tied to each other and was leading the first one. The problem horse stepped tentatively into the water. Then something set it off and it exploded. As it turned, it jerked the rope from the soldier's hands and bolted for the shore almost hitting Mule. Mule reached his head over and bit the horse hard on the flank. It jumped up into the air and landed about four feet from where it had started. Lunging and bucking, it finally made it back to the shore.

Sergeant O'Malley hollered at Badger, "Leave that bloody horse! If it can cross on its own, it will come. If not, we are still one horse ahead of what we started with."

As the last of the wagons pulled out of the water, the skittish horse was still on the far bank. It neighed and raced back and forth. Still it refused to get into the water.

Once everyone was across, Lance dropped off of his mustang and ran to Molly. She was crouched on the ground, holding Sammy with one arm while her other arm was around her unborn child.

Lance gently helped her to stand up.

274

Sammy wasn't hurt, but he was terrified. His blue eyes were huge and big tears were rolling down his face.

"I thought you was goin' to die, Momma!" Sammy cried.

Lance put his arms around both of them. He was shaking as he pulled his little family close to him. He raised his eyes to the Heavens and gave a silent prayer of thanksgiving for yet another miracle.

"Are you okay?" he asked as he looked intently at Molly.

Molly's face was drawn down as if she was in pain.

Lance looked at her stomach with fear in his eyes. "Did I hurt you when I grabbed you?"

Molly shook her head. "I'm fine. I am having some cramping is all."

Lance lifted her up and started for the wagon. "You are riding in the wagon the rest of the day." He spread some of the blankets out and lifted her in so she could lie down on them.

Molly lifted her arms. "Come and lay down by me, Sammy. Let me hug you for a little while." Sammy reached up his arms and Lance lifted him into the wagon by his new mother. Molly wrapped her arms around him and Lance laid another blanket beside her in case they needed it.

As they headed up the trail towards Julesburg, several soldiers turned to look back at the last horse. They hated to leave it, but there was nothing they could do.

Hopefully, Lance thought, *it will cross on its own.*

Mary Lewis looked back. "Do you think that horse will make it across?"

Lance studied the horse and slowly shook his head. "I doubt it. The river is dangerous and that horse is just too skittish."

Then he winked at her, "But maybe I will be wrong! Who knows?"

She laughed and Lance dropped back to ride by the wagon Molly and Sammy were in. Molly's eyes were closed and it looked like both of them were asleep. As the cavalcade dropped over the next hill, the horse was still running back and forth on the far bank, calling to its mates.

CHAPTER 49

BLUE FEATHER

EXCITEMENT WAS BUILDING IN THE SMALL GROUP. Julesburg was now thirty-five to forty miles away, and everyone could see the end of their journey.

Sergeant O'Malley noted, "The next two days should be fairly easy pulling. However, the farther north we go, the more we need to keep an eye out for Indians. For the most part, they have been quiet this spring, probably too quiet so we need to be on guard."

Badger was riding point. His eyes were like those of a hawk and he liked to see what was coming. Lance was either at the back or riding back and forth along the column.

Molly had only stayed in the wagon for three hours and she was back on Babe.

Lance tried to convince her to stay in the wagon, but she just smiled sweetly at him.

Lance scowled and tried again. "Molly, I really think you should take it easy. I thought you were going to deliver that little one right there by the river."

She turned in her saddle and glared at him. "Seriously, Lance, do you really think that rough wagon is any better than a smooth riding horse?"

Lance couldn't argue with that and the discussion was over.

Mary Lewis decided that horseback was more comfortable than the rough wagon as well. Now that the crisis was over she was once again riding sidesaddle. Although Lance had insisted that she ride one of the mules for safety when the going was treacherous, now she was riding one because she liked it.

"Isn't she the picture!" Lance commented as he pointed to Mary Lewis and Molly giggled.

Mary had her full skirt draped across the mule's hind quarters, and was sitting poised and erect in her sidesaddle.

Lance grinned again. "All she needs are some white gloves and a big hat."

Molly laughed with him and Lance's eyes swept over Molly. She was reaching down to rub Babe's neck and gave him her glorious smile before she faced forward again. Molly rode astride and was relaxed and easy in the saddle.

"You are quite the rider, Molly Rankin," Lance said softly, his voice betraying his admiration.

Molly smiled up at him. She was tired but she seemed to have come through the river crossing with no lasting problems.

Badger held up his hand for the group to stop. As he rode back to Sergeant O'Malley, Lance cantered up to meet with him as well.

The little man pointed. "There's somethin' a layin' up ahead. It's off the road but it looks like an Indian gurl. Now we cin either go on by an' do nothin' or we cin stop ta see if'n she needs help. I advise goin' on by."

Sergeant O'Malley frowned. It was against his nature to not help those in need. Still, if she was an Indian, their help could be perceived as a threat.

Little Sammy was riding with Badger and his eyes were huge. "It was a lady an' she was just alayin' in the grass!" he exclaimed, his eyes large with excitement.

The Indian woman lay off to the left side of the road, and the small caravan moved to the right to ride around her—all but Molly.

"How dare you ride by this woman just because she is an Indian! I will not be part of leaving any injured person with no help."

Molly jumped off of her horse and ran to the injured girl. The girl opened her eyes but was silent. Molly offered her a drink from her canteen as the soldiers watched. The girl drank slowly.

Lance rode back. "Molly," he began carefully, "helping her could put us in danger if her people are following and perceive us as the enemy."

Molly glared at him. "We can't just leave her here. She is injured!"

Lance could see there would be no arguing with her so he lifted the young woman up and placed her in the back wagon.

Badger circled back to the last wagon. He looked at the Indian girl and then at Lance with a cocked eyebrow.

Lance grunted at him. "We were overruled."

As the column again moved down the road, Molly climbed into the wagon and sat with the injured girl. The girl spoke broken English. Her people were Arapaho. She was taken from her village by raiding Pawnee and then sold to some trappers. She had escaped about two weeks ago and was trying to make her way back to her tribe in southern Wyoming. When Lance stopped back by the wagon later, Molly told him what she had found out.

Lance stared at her. He knew where this conversation was going. "No, Molly. We will not take her with us to Cheyenne."

Molly glared at him again and the fire began to flicker in her blue eyes. "And how do you expect her to get home? She is sick, her leg may be broken and she is running a fever."

Lance shook his head and rode back up to the front of the column, muttering under his breath.

"I have never met such a stubborn woman--*and* unreasonable."

Badger grinned at him. "Make ya a little crazy, does she? Yep, that's what they does!" He was laughing evilly as he turned his eyes ahead and Lance glared at him.

Sergeant O'Malley looked over his shoulder at the women and then back at Lance and Badger.

"I don't think we should have picked her up either. However, she is in our care now and we have to do what we can to help her to recover."

Mary Lewis dropped back to ride beside the wagon. She asked, "What's her name?"

The young Indian woman responded, "I Blue Feather." She stared at Mary. "Why you ride so strange? Your saddle is broken?"

Mary blushed and then laughed. "No, it is called a side saddle. This way, I can look elegant." She put her nose up in the air and pretended to fan herself.

Blue Feather stared and then laughed. "I call you Bird Lady!"

When they camped that evening, Badger and Private Payne looked the Indian woman over. She appeared to be young, nineteen to twenty years old. Her upper leg had a deep cut. The bone was broken and needed to be set. The skin around the cut in her thigh was infected and was causing her to run a fever.

Molly tried to explain to her that they would need to set her leg and sew it up. The young woman's eyes were terrified and she vehemently shook her head, "Hiiko! Hiiko!"

Lance pointed at her leg. "Beeniini. "It is pus-filled."

Still she shook her head no.

Lance looked at Badger. "I do have some of the potion that you gave to Molly. That put Molly to sleep and broke her fever. And as an added advantage, she remembers nothing after she went to sleep."

Molly glared at him and Lance laughed.

Badger scratched his head, "We cin try it, but you'ins is goin' ta have ta get 'er ta drink it."

Lance brought the jar in from the wagon. He shook it up and poured some into a tin cup, and indicated for the girl to drink it.

The Indian girl pushed the cup away and shook her head no, "Ciibeh-bene!"

Lance pushed it back to her. "You have to drink. This make you better."

Again Lance indicated that she should drink it. Molly took the cup and pretended to drink. She let a little touch her upper lip so the girl could see that it was in her mouth. Just the smell made Molly want to gag.

Finally, the Indian girl took the cup. She turned up her nose. She took a small drink and gagged. As she pushed the cup away, she shook her head again, "Woxcoo!"

Lance agreed, "Yes, it tastes bad but it will make your leg heal. Drink." Again, he pushed the cup toward her.

Hesitantly she took the cup. "Wohei" she exclaimed and drank it up. She lay back on the blanket Lance had set her on and stared at them. Within minutes, she was asleep.

Badger jumped into action. "Let's git this here dog an' pony show started. We only got 'bout twenty minutes 'fore she kin feel again!"

Quickly, the men stretched her leg out to reset it. Molly could see the break though the cut on her leg. "Pull harder. It's still crooked." The men pulled again and the girl moaned.

Molly moved aside so Private Payne could check it.

Private Payne felt her leg carefully. "I'm not sure we have that in place and if it's not set correctly, it may not heal or she could walk with a limp." He pushed his fingers closer to the wound and shook his head. "I'm not sure. I think it's in place but I'm no bone cracker."

Badger felt her leg and agreed, "It'll have ta do. It's better'n it was. Now stitch 'er up an' leave a place at the bottom fer it ta drain."

Private Payne was struggling with the needle and finally, Molly took it from him. She made quick even stitches and pulled the two sides together. The bottom she left open.

Badger had gone in search of some herbs that could be used for a compress. When he came back, he mashed them and wrapped them around her leg, tying them on with a rag.

Molly looked around at the group. "Her name is Blue Feather and I think she might be someone important in her tribe. I couldn't understand her but I think she may be the sister to a great warrior or chief."

Badger and Lance were quiet. "I just hope that they believe we were trying to help her if they come up on us," Lance muttered quietly.

Blue Feather only stirred once during the night and moaned a little. After Molly gave her a drink, she settled down and didn't move again until morning. When Molly awakened, Blue Feather was staring at her leg with a confused look on her face.

Molly broke a stick in half. "Broken. Your leg was broken. We set it and I sewed the wound together," she explained as she pushed the two parts of the stick together and pretended to sew.

Blue Feather's eyes became large and she tugged at the compress.

Molly unwrapped Blue Feather's leg so she could see the wound beneath the compress. The inflammation was down and the stitches were holding. A stick had been tied to her leg to hold the break in place.

Marion came in and swung her broken leg out in front of her as she pulled up her skirt. "See, we both have a broken leg."

Blue Feather smiled. She touched Marion's leg. "Hohou. Heetei'eininoo!"

Lance laughed. "She said thank you and that she will be strong."

Marion and Molly were both delighted.

The men left and the two women stayed to talk more with Blue Feather. They had offered her a bunk but she pointed at the ground. They had the men make a bed for her on the ground inside the tent. That night, the men heard a fourth woman's voice softly laughing and giving broken replies to questions.

Molly asked, "Are you married, Blue Feather?" Blue feather smiled as she shook her head.

"Blue Feather see Gray Wolf but he no see her." She shut her eyes and stuck her chin up in the air.

The women all laughed and Blue Feather giggled.

"Look at him and do this," Molly suggested as she twirled her braid and batted her eyes.

Blue Feather's eyes became large and she laughed out loud. She tried to mimic Molly and soon, all of the women were pretending to try to catch Gray Wolf's eye.

The men looked toward the women's tent several times but they were pretty sure they didn't want to be part of whatever that conversation was.

The discussion amongst the men that night was all about the next day. They had traveled another thirty miles in spite of high water and Blue Feather.

The little group should arrive in Julesburg the following day.

GOOD TRADE

THE NEXT MORNING WAS DAMP AND RAINY. The dawn was just breaking when Lance's horse snorted. He rolled out of his blankets and grabbed his guns. Molly had come out of the tent during the night and lay beside him. Sammy was still asleep inside the women's tent. Lance flipped Molly up under one arm with his hand over her mouth and disappeared in the brush.

Badger was nowhere to be seen. Within minutes, the camp was surrounded by twenty Indian braves in war paint. They sat silently on their horses with spears and bows ready, staring at the small group of men. A few of them had guns.

One brave stepped his horse forward and stared at the soldiers. He spoke in broken English. "We come for woman." The brave's face was dark as he glared around the camp. "She my sister. You pay for what you do."

The soldiers were still in their beds. They had been caught off guard. Their guns were stacked away from the fire and all had been caught asleep.

Sarge looked out toward where the sentry should be and growled under his breath.

Lance stepped from behind the tree, and Badger's buffalo gun appeared through the trees on the other side of the clearing. Lance held his rifle ready to fire but with the barrel tipped slightly down.

"No, we help your sister. She hurt. Bad men take her. She escape. We find her and help her." As he spoke, there was stirring and noise in the women's tent.

Blue Feather pulled herself to her feet and stepped outside the tent. She was using a crutch that Marion had given her. The warrior pulled himself erect and stared at Blue Feather. Blue Feather began to speak quickly.

Lance could only understand a few of the Arapahoe words. "Drink... help... woman...stitch."

The warrior looked at Lance. "Where woman that stitch my sister?" Lance wasn't about to bring Molly out when she stepped from behind him.

The warrior looked at her and then at Lance. "Your woman? Papoose come soon. You sell her to me."

Lance shook his head. "She is my woman, but I will not sell her. She is my wife." The gun barrel moved up slightly.

The warrior smiled. "I take hair," and he moved toward Molly with his knife, followed by Lance's and Badger's gun barrels.

Calmly, Molly reached up, and took the knife from his hand.

The warrior appeared to be surprised and amused.

Molly took a lock of her hair and cut it off with the knife. She handed the hair back to the warrior and kept his knife.

"Now you have my hair. I keep your knife."

The Indians all began to laugh and slowly, the warrior smiled.

He looked at Lance. "She warrior. Maybe some night, she cut your heart out."

One of the warriors led up a horse with a travois behind it. Blue Feather climbed awkwardly onto the travois and sat down. The Indians filed out of the soldier's camp, with no sound.

The large warrior looked back at Molly again. "Woman of Rising Sun! You will make many warriors. Maybe someday, I see you again." he declared, his dark eyes full of something that may have been humor.

The Indians had been in the camp less than five minutes and now they were gone.

Badger moved out of the trees and looked at Lance, his eyes dancing with humor. "Mebbie someday she cut yur heart out!" he repeated, laughing as he walked away.

Lance turned to Molly.

She was pale but her blue eyes were sparking. "How dare he want to take my hair. Hmmf. Well, I have a fine knife so it was a good trade. Lance, you need to make me a holder for this so that I can wear it." Molly tossed her head. "Hmmf!" she repeated as she moved to the fire to help with breakfast.

Lance stared at her and then he laughed. "Molly girl, I don't know about you. That was either a foolish thing to do or a very brave thing to do.

Molly whirled around. "Well, I certainly wasn't going to let him cut off my hair. Who knows how much he would have taken!" She looked at the soldiers staring at her with open mouths and gave them a pretty smile.

"Would one of you fellows fetch me some water, please?" she asked as she turned back toward the fire.

CHAPTER (51)

ONE MORE RIVER

THE MEN WERE A LITTLE QUIETER AS THEY BROKE CAMP. Sergeant O'Malley went to look for the sentry. He found the man staked to the ground, with his legs and arms extended. His mouth was tied with rawhide to prevent him from making noise. Sergeant O'Malley cut the ties and Private Payne sat up. His eyes were huge and he was sweating.

"I just knew that I was dead. They came out of nowhere. Sorry, Sarge. I just didn't see or hear them."

Sergeant O'Malley growled a response and started to walk away. He paused and looked back at the young soldier.

"Stay alert, soldier."

Private Payne saluted him. "Yes, Sir."

Sergeant O'Malley found Lance. "I sure appreciate you two fellows bein' ready this mornin'. It was my fault the troop wasn't prepared. I have been too relaxed."

Lance looked at Sergeant O'Malley. He liked this man and so did the troopers. "I think we were all surprised but it would be a good idea for the men to sleep with their weapons and not sleep so soundly." He grinned at the sergeant. "You'll have them ready next time."

Sergeant O'Malley agreed and then added, "Indians can be unpredictable but they do like a good joke and a brave woman. Thanks for acting so quickly."

Private Smith followed the sergeant back into the clearing. As the sergeant turned, he saluted him. "All horses and mules accounted for, sir."

Sergeant O'Malley saluted the young private and then shook his head again. "Mighty unpredictable."

As the group rolled out at 0600 for the final day of their journey to Julesburg, spirits were high. Everyone was excited to find a real bed and take a warm bath.

They had only been on the trail for about a half an hour when they heard a horse racing up behind them. The wagons were quickly pushed together and the women were placed behind them.

The men fanned out in front of the wagons and turned to face this new threat rushing down on them. A horse's head appeared above the hill and as the horse topped the hill, they could see it was the horse that had refused to cross the river. One side of his body was covered in mud and sand but he was running without a limp. He raced up to greet the other horses. It was obvious that he was glad to be back.

Lance caught his halter and grabbed the rope. Once he was tied securely to the wagon, the little group moved back into formation. The men studied him and everyone wondered how he had crossed the river. It was something to think about and they all did as they turned toward Julesburg one last time.

A few hours later as they topped the last rise, they could see Julesburg across the South Platte River below them.

Lance pointed at the town and told Molly, "Indians plundered the first site of this town in January of 1865, and then burned it to the ground in February of the same year. A second town was staked out in March of 1867 on the south side of the Platte River near its confluence with Lodgepole Creek over there. When the Union Pacific Railroad decided to follow the north bank of the river, the town's residents moved their city again. This time, they moved it two and one half miles north and across the Platte River. We are looking at Julesburg, in its third location, and it's known as 'The Wickedest City in the West.'"

Molly stared across the dirty water toward the town of Julesburg.

"Lance, as long as I have a clean bed, I just don't care how wild this town is. Maybe I will tomorrow but I just don't today."

The small group of riders and wagons paused on the hill, and then moved down the long slope to the muddy river below. The South Platte was about one half mile wide and was rarely over three to four feet deep. It was the deepest on the sides with the shallowest part in the middle. Wagons and horses of every size and makeup were crossing, mostly from the south side to the north. The river was literally teaming with activity.

The bottom of the river was a combination of quick sand and gravel.

Sergeant O'Malley began barking orders.

"I want a six team of mules or horses on each wagon. Those wagons need to keep moving. You don't stop for anything once we are in the water."

Two of Lance's mules were hooked to the first wagon and his third mule plus one of the extra horses was hooked to the second wagon. The horse was actually one taken from the outlaws. It wore an army brand and showed the trace marks of a wagon horse.

Marian chose to ride a horse while Mrs. Lewis wanted to ride in the wagon. Marion's leg was healing well and she refused to let it slow her down too much. Her eyes were sparkling with excitement as she rode beside Private Smith.

"One more river and we will be in Julesburg!" she exclaimed excitedly.

Private Smith reached over to take her hand as he smiled at her.

"You are the prettiest girl I know, Marion O'Malley."

Marion blushed with pleasure and she sure didn't try to take her hand back.

Sergeant O'Malley hollered, "Fill your canteens and then get those animals watered. We are dumping these barrels to lighten up the wagons."

The men sprang into action and soon, the barrels were emptied and recapped.

Sergeant O'Malley rode in front followed by the first wagon. Lance rode beside the first team and Badger rode beside the second one. The riders were positioned beside and behind each wagon while Molly rode beside Lance. Sammy rode on the first wagon with Mrs. Lewis.

The problem horse, or "Hurricane" as he was now called, pawed the water a bit and then dove in. Babe was hesitant, but she too did not want to be left behind and followed Lance's mustang into the river.

The bottom was soft from all of the traffic, but the sure-footed mules kept the wagons on track.

"Keep them moving," O'Malley ordered. "Don't let them slow down but don't push them either."

It took the group over two hours to cross the river due to all of the sand bars and little islands that they had to navigate through and around. The teams pulled strong and steady though, and they crossed with no problems. As the little party climbed out on the north side, they joined other travelers as they cheered.

CHAPTER (52)

JULESBURG!

T HE TRAIL-WEARY GROUP PULLED DOWN THE LONG MAIN STREET INTO JULESBURG. Everyone was tired but excited. Sergeant O'Malley had the soldiers unhitch Lance's mules and they left them tied in front of the livery.

As they rode their horses slowly up the street, Lance told Molly a little about Julesburg.

"J.P. Allen built the first hotel in Julesburg, and that is where we will be staying while we're here." He paused and then added, "Julesburg is known as a pretty wicked town so I don't want you to go out on the street without Badger or me."

Molly nodded without arguing and Lance looked closely at her.

Molly's pretty face was drawn and she was holding her stomach again.

"Are you okay? Are you cramping again?" Lance asked.

Molly nodded. "I think I am just really tired," she answered, as she gave Lance a weary smile.

Lance touched her arm as he smiled at her. "We did it, Molly. We made the hardest part of the trip."

Molly smiled. She didn't feel like talking. "I just want to lie down, Lance," Molly whispered as he helped her off of Babe.

As they signed in at the front desk, a tired receptionist agreed to have water brought to Molly's room. Lance carried their bags in and then gave his wife a quick kiss.

""I am going to put the horses up and then get a bath. I'll take Sammy with me. You rest up after your bath and we will have some dinner."

Molly lay down on the bed and when Lance touched her arm, she was already asleep.

Lance stopped at the desk and asked, "Could you take that hot water to my wife in about three hours? She is already asleep."

The clerk nodded. "Hard trip?" he asked.

Lance nodded as he agreed, "A long and hard trip but it gets easier from here. Thanks so much."

Lance led Sammy out of the crowded hotel. He lifted him up into the saddle and then mounted his mustang behind Sammy. With Babe's reins in his hand, they headed for the livery.

Julesburg was crowded and rough. Men and women of all walks of life filled the streets and women offered their wares from the balconies and windows.

Sammy had lots of questions. "Why do those mommies just have on their underwear?"

Lance looked around at the "fallen doves" waving at them from the balconies and blushed.

"I think maybe they just woke up and forgot that they were in town."

Sammy pointed to a drunk, throwing up in an alley. "Is that man sick?"

"He sure is," replied Lance as he urged the horses to a faster walk.

"I just saw two men shoot at each other! Can I go to pee in the street too? I really need to go pee!" exclaimed Sammy excitedly.

Lance's face was red. "No, you cannot pee in the street. You can pee when we get to the livery."

Lance took a deep breath. "This is downright close to running a gauntlet!" he muttered.

They finally arrived at the livery and Lance led his string of horses and mules into the barn's cool interior.

"Can you give those horses and mules an extra ration of oats," Lance asked the hostler, "and rub them all down—including the mules."

The hostler was muttering about "pampered mules" but Lance didn't care. He had acquired a new liking for mules this last month and a half.

The hostler growled, "All this is going to cost you an extra two bits." Lance grinned at the man and nodded. "Those animals just carried us all the way from Kansas City, and I want to make sure they are sound on into Cheyenne," he explained as he tossed the hostler another two bits.

Lance then headed down to take a bath. Sammy needed a bath too, and since he had never given a little boy a bath, Lance figured they could just have tubs side by side.

As they passed a clap board building with Dry Goods written on the side, Lance turned in. "Sammy, I think you need a hat like me." The building didn't look like much, but the store was well-stocked.

Lance was able to purchase Sammy some britches, a shirt, a pair of shoes, and a small hat similar to Lance's.

Sammy was delighted. "Can I put these on now, Papa?"

Lance shook his head. "We'll take a bath first so you're clean. You can wear your hat though."

As Sammy and Lance entered the bath area, Lance asked for two tubs, side by side. Sammy had never taken a bath in that much water before and it was awfully quiet in his tub.

Lance finally looked over the edge.

Sammy was trying to sit down but the water was too deep. Lance scooped water out until Sammy could sit.

Sammy was very interested in everything that Lance did, and he kept standing to look over the edge of the tub. He would then mimic Lance's actions as he washed. Sammy tried to use the brush on his back the way Lance did and he rubbed the soap under his arms. When he tried to put his foot up on the side to scrub it, his bottom slipped and he slid under the water.

At first it was quiet in his tub, but soon it became louder and louder as the little boy began to enjoy the water.

Lance had forgotten his razor. "I think maybe that is a good thing," he muttered as Sammy laughed down at him again before he splashed loudly in his own tub.

Finally, they were both scrubbed and clean. Lance dressed quickly and then helped Sammy out of the tub. Once Sammy was dressed, Lance rolled up the dirty clothes and off they went back up the street.

Lance was bombarded with more questions while Sammy tried to mimic the way Lance walked. Finally, Lance put the little boy up on his shoulders.

Badger stepped in beside Lance. "Have ya checked on tickets yet ta Cheyenne?" Badger asked innocently.

Lance looked at him. "Not yet. I was going to go there now. Why?"

"Well, I think we need ta get 'em bought. They kinda overfill them thar trains. In fact, ya might want ta special request a seat," Badger added with a grin.

As they headed for the train station, Lance asked, "You are going with us, aren't you?"

Badger replied, "I am if'n ya cin hold off a day. Martha comes in on the train in the mornin' an' I'd kinda' like ta get hitched 'fore we head fer Cheyenne."

Lance came to an abrupt halt and laughed out loud. "Well, you didn't waste any time!" he exclaimed as he shook Badger's hand.

Badger replied with a wink as his blue eyes twinkled, "At my age, they's not any time ta waste."

Sammy piped up, "Is that the lady who's gonna be my grandmammy? Oh, Boy! This is gonna be fun."

The men headed to the train station. The train arriving with Martha was to be in at 9:30 a.m. the next day. The next train out after that would be 10:00 a.m. the following day. As they bought their tickets, Lance told the agent that he had a pregnant wife.

"I want to make sure that she has a seat," Lance stated as he looked hard at the agent.

The ticket master shrugged his shoulders.

"That I can't guarantee. We don't have reserved seats. I suggest that you be on the train as soon as it pulls in which will be close to 9:30 a.m.." He warned, "If you don't get on early, you will be one of the passengers riding on top of the cars. We fill it up."

Lance bought three tickets and arranged for two livestock cars. They would put the four mules in one and the horses in the second one. Lance didn't want to take a chance on Babe irritating Mule.

"Also," Lance added quietly as he looked seriously at the agent, "I would like to make sure that there are signs on our livestock cars. If people try to ride with those animals, they will get kicked and in the case of one of the mules, possibly killed."

The ticket master laughed and then looked up. When he saw that Lance was deadly serious, his eyes widened.

"I will make sure a sign is posted," he promised as he scribbled down a note to himself.

As Badger stepped up to buy his tickets, he cautioned, "Jist put 'Killer Mule from Kansas' on that thar car."

The ticket master looked up slowly. "I've heard about that mule. How do you intend to load him because I won't be doing that."

Badger grinned his evil grin. "Oh, he be fine long as no stranger teches 'im. I'll load my own dad blame mule."

"I think the extra day will be good," Lance told Badger. "It will give Molly an extra day to rest. She was pretty worn out when I left her at the hotel."

Badger nodded. "It were a puty tough ol' trip, but I'm not shore yur little gal is a gonna make it ta Cheyenne afore she drops that wee baby."

Lance's eyes went wide, and then he frowned. "Let's hope you're wrong," he told his friend. *Badger is right about a lot of things but I sure hope he is wrong about this baby*, Lance thought.

Badger left to find a sky pilot to marry him, and Lance headed back to the hotel to check on Molly.

She had just bathed and was dressing as they came in. Her face was bright and her eyes were once again sparkling.

Lance looked at her and smiled, "Well, good morning, beautiful!"

Molly blushed and gave him a dazzling smile.

She pulled her eyes away from Lance and looked at Sammy's clean little face. "Did you have a bath, Sammy?" she asked as she smiled at him.

"Papa give me one," Sammy answered.

Molly looked at the little boy. "*Gave* me one, Sammy. *Gave* me one," she corrected.

Sammy looked confused. "Papa give you one too, Momma?" he asked with big eyes. Molly laughed and the three of them went downstairs to find something to eat.

CHAPTER 53

LOVE AND LAUNDRY

THE BENCHES IN THE DINING HALL WERE ROUGH AND THE TABLES WEREN'T THAT CLEAN. Lance was pleased that the food was good though, and there was plenty of it. Julesburg catered to working men, and it showed everywhere in the town.

Badger joined them shortly after they finished eating.

"The weddin' will be at 4:00 tomorry'," he announced, beaming.

Molly's mouth fell open while Sammy shouted excitedly, "I'm agettin' me a new grandmammy! Ain't that nice, Momma?"

"Martha is arriving today, Badger?" asked Molly.

"Naw, she's acomin' in tomorry' at 9:30. I figgered that'd give 'er time ta freshin' up a bit."

Molly laughed and hugged him. "Badger, I am so happy for you," she whispered, and she kissed him on the cheek.

Molly looked over at Sammy and Lance. She smiled and her face softened. Both of her fellows were beginning to droop. "Lance, why don't we all go back to the room and take a nap. Sammy needs one, and I believe you could use one too."

Lance nodded in agreement and the three of them headed back to the hotel. The street was even more crowded around lunch time, and Lance once again lifted Sammy up on his shoulders.

"Say," Sammy hollered, "I can see everythin' up here. Why is that lady wavin' at you, Momma? Do you know her? I didn't know that big people blowed kisses to other big people."

Molly looked sideways at Lance.

"Before you state the obvious, I agree," he replied quickly, "What do you want to do with him for a day and a half? You know the wedding is not until tomorrow."

Molly chided, "We just need to find some other kids or a place for him to play. These streets are not suitable for women let alone a small child."

Lance looked at Molly and laughed. "Maybe we had just better take him fishing," he drawled as they scanned the busy road. "I don't see another kid on this street or a place that would even be good for him to play, although those gals do look friendly!" he added with a ornery grin as he nodded his head at the women waving from the balconies.

Molly's face turned a deep red as she whirled to face him. "Lance Rankin—" she started to say and then saw the humor sparking in his eyes. She stared at him for a moment and then giggled in spite of herself.

"You are a scamp of a man!" she exclaimed as he winked at her and took her arm.

Lance fixed up a bed on the floor for Sammy, and the little boy was asleep in no time. Lance had intended to talk to Molly, but he was asleep almost as fast as he fell across the bed.

Molly studied the stack of dirty clothes. She had no way to wash them herself, so she would have to take them down to the laundry area by the bathes. She gathered up everything dirty she could find and put it in the bag that Mrs. Barr had given her. It was so heavy that she just decided to wait for Lance to carry it for her. She took off her clean dress and climbed into bed in her undergarments.

"Just a quick nap," she told herself. The room was dark with the curtains closed, and even though it was loud outside, for several hours there was no sound in that room except for the breathing of three sleeping people.

When Lance awoke, he saw Molly's dress draped carefully over the chair. He quickly peeked under the covers and grinned. "My wife is finally going to let me see her in her underwear," he laughed.

As he stood up and stretched, he saw the large bag of dirty clothes. He added the clothes he had on to the pile. He was whistling softly to himself as he shaved in his cut-off long handles.

Molly awoke drowsily. When she realized that Lance was already up, she blushed. "I only meant to rest a minute," she muttered to herself.

Lance looked around at her. His face was partly covered in shaving soap with razor trails running through it. "You're sure looking pretty after your nap, Mrs. Rankin," " he drawled, laughing with those ornery eyes. "I see you made yourself comfortable."

Molly pulled the covers up toward her chin and asked in a meek voice, "Could you hand me my dress, please?"

Lance turned completely around and looked at her grinning. "Now I like to be accommodating to a lady but that is a request I am not going to follow. Guess you will just have to get out of bed and get it yourself."

Molly blushed a deeper red. "Sammy—" she started to say.

"His grandpappy picked him up about an hour ago, and I am betting they are fishing about now." Lance's eyes were a deep blue as he laughed at her. "It is just you and me, pretty lady."

Lance was still standing with his back to the wash basin with shaving soap on his face. He was totally enjoying this.

Fire flashed in Molly's eyes. She threw back the covers and marched over to her clothes. Sweeping them up, she turned to him. "Well then, you just watch. And maybe you can help me fasten my dress. I can't reach the middle buttons anymore, but you might want to finish shaving."

Lance had never shaved so fast in his life or cut himself so many times. He was trying to watch Molly and look in the mirror too. Finally, he positioned the mirror so he could see her behind him. Lance started whistling again, wincing as he nicked his face but still trying to watch. When the job was done he moved up behind Molly to help her with her dress. He wrapped his arms around her and placed his hands on her firm stomach.

"You are truly a beautiful woman, Molly Rankin," he whispered huskily.

Molly went still and then turned around to face him. She wrapped her arms around his neck and leaned her body against his as she smiled up at him.

Lance's eyes opened wide in surprise and then he pulled her closer.

Molly heard the key turn in the door to lock it, and that was the last she thought of anyone except Lance for the next hour.

As she lay in Lance's arms, she studied his strong face. She couldn't believe how her life had changed in just a few short months.

Lance pushed some hair back from her face and kissed her tenderly.

"Molly, you have changed me," Lance murmured in a hoarse whisper. "You made me a husband and a father. I want to be the best I can be for you."

They talked for a while longer and then Molly exclaimed, "The laundry! We have to get it down to the wash area. I'm not sure when they quit for the day and nearly all of our clothes are dirty."

CHAPTER (54)

MAKE ROOM FOR ONE MORE

LANCE STEPPED OUT OF BED AND ADDED THE CUT-OFF LONG JOHNS TO THE PILE. Molly covered her face which was dark red and Lance began laughing that ornery laugh he had when he knew he had made her blush. He pulled on his britches and picked her undergarments up off the floor.

"I'll arrange another bath for you tonight so you'll sleep well." He drawled and then added, "This marriage business is way more fun than I ever thought it would be!"

He grinned at her and winked as he sauntered out of their room, whistling as he strolled down the hall.

Molly jumped out of bed and hurried to dress. She *was* going to need his help fastening her dress as it stretched tightly over her stomach and she couldn't reach the hooks.

Lance was back quickly. He had a bath arranged for her at 8:00 p.m. and it was 3:00 now.

"I need some help with these hooks," Molly requested tentatively. As she faced forward, Lance seemed to be all fingers and thumbs.

"Lance, you are not even close to the hooks!" she exclaimed as she looked over her shoulder and giggled.

Lance grinned back at her and drawled, "Well, you know, I'm going to need some practice with these hooks. I don't recall helping any women get dressed before although I'm liking it just fine," as he gave her a squeeze.

When Molly was ready, Lance took the large basket in one hand, and he offered Molly his other with a deep bow. She wrapped her arm through his, and they were both laughing as they walked out of the hotel and into the street.

Lance guided Molly quickly down the busy street to the laundry area.

A large, red-faced woman looked up as they walked toward her.

Molly smiled as she pointed at the bag. "We have quite a bit of laundry. Is someone available who could do it today or tomorrow?"

The woman wiped her hands on her apron front. "Do ya want it done fast or do ya want it done gentle like 'cause you ain't gonna' get both."

Molly paused a moment and then smiled again, "I will take the gentle wash, please."

The woman turned her head and yelled over her shoulder, "Sadie, get up here! Ya have some customers!"

A young lady of about nineteen came up from the back. Her rough clothes didn't hide the curves beneath the loose blouse and full skirt. Her arms were raw almost to the elbows, and her hands were cracked from the harsh soap.

Molly's heart broke for her. *What a terrible way for a young woman to have to make a living*, she thought. Then, as Molly remembered the street, she thought in horror, *why this is her only option if she doesn't want to join those women on the balconies!*

A smooth-faced man in fancy clothes came strolling in. His long hair was greased back and the large mustache curling down around his mouth was oiled as well. He ignored Molly and Lance as he looked the young lady up and down with bold, cruel eyes.

"So Sadie, when are you going to come to work for me and make some real money?" he sneered.

Sadie tried to ignore him, but he wouldn't leave. He tried to take her arm, and she jerked it away as she glared at him. The man continued to bother her, and Lance stepped a little closer.

Molly could feel the anger building in him.

The man pushed in front of Lance and Molly, and Lance stepped around him to stand beside the young woman.

The man paused a moment as he stared at Lance. Then he shrugged and turned his attention back to Sadie.

"You keep telling me that your brother is coming but he hasn't shown yet," the cold-eyed man smirked.

"Mrs. Murphy tells me that you aren't fast enough to wash the volume of clothes needed to pay your rent, and you'll be out of a job soon." He put his smooth face closer to hers and tried to take her arm again.

Once again, Sadie jerked her arm away, and with fury in her brown eyes she retorted, "Clyde Johns, I wouldn't work in your whore house if I was starving."

As the man started to respond, Lance stepped forward.

He ground out, "Well, just maybe her brother has arrived. Now you get out of here and leave my sister alone."

Sadie's eyes opened wide and Molly tried not to smile.

Clyde Johns was a large man. He believed himself to be handsome but his eyes were cruel. He brushed off Lance's comment, but something in Lance's voice made Clyde look at him again.

He stared at Lance and then gave an ugly laugh. "Sure, I'll leave but you won't be here tomorrow."

He leered at Sadie again. "You will work for me and I'm not waiting much longer."

As Clyde Johns walked out of the laundry area, Lance's eyes followed him. "I believe I will have a conversation with that fellow," he growled as his hard eyes dug into the man's back. Clyde looked back once and the look he saw in the tall cowboy's eyes almost scared him. Then he shrugged.

"Nothing to worry about. No one stays long in Julesburg," he muttered. His cruel face broke into an evil smile.

"Except Sadie," he sniggered with triumph.

Molly put out her hand to Sadie. "My name is Molly Rankin and your brother's name is Lance," she laughed.

Sadie took Molly's hand with a shy smile. "It is so nice to meet you, Molly. I am Sadie Hayes." She smiled at Molly again.

Sadie turned serious eyes toward Lance. "I want to thank you for stepping in just now. This won't end it though. Clyde will be back tomorrow after you are gone."

She dropped her head. A sob caught in her throat and she swallowed.

Looking up, she continued, "He was right. I am too slow to make money washing clothes. My father was part of the rail crew. He came down with cholera and both of my parents died. That was several months ago. I took a job here to survive until I can afford to leave this rough town and start over someplace else."

Sadie paused and blushed. "I'm sorry. I don't mean to bother you."

Molly touched her shoulder and Sadie looked at her with tears in her eyes.

"I am a seamstress. I wish I could make a living by sewing, but there are not enough women or families here to make it work yet."

She straightened her shoulders, "I will just have to get faster." She smiled again at Molly.

"I can have these ready for you tomorrow morning by 10:00 if that works for you."

"That will be fine," smiled Molly.

Molly paused and then looked up at Lance with a question in her eyes.

He grinned at her. *Here it comes,* he thought with a wry grin. *Make room for one more person in the parade I'm taking west!*

Molly beamed. "Sadie, how would you like to come with us? I am going to need some help at our ranch and we will help you to get a sewing business started in Cheyenne."

Sadie's brown eyes looked surprised and then became a little confused.

"Oh, I could never ask you to do that. I will be okay," she replied softly as she took their clothes.

"Now that would be just a fine way for me to treat my long-lost sister, wouldn't it? You know, my wife makes really good pies, and I want her to have time to bake. We have a three-year-old son and this one will be here soon," Lance stated as he patted Molly's stomach.

"How about you come with us? We are taking the train to Cheyenne the day after tomorrow. I can get you a ticket when we leave here if you want. The train is filling fast though, so you don't have much time to think about it," he added.

Emotions flitted through Sadie's eyes from hope to confusion to excitement. She looked from Molly to Lance and then smiled at both of them.

"Oh, thank you so much! I have a little money saved and I will pay you back for the ticket. Let me tell Mrs. Murphy that my last day of work will be tomorrow. That way, I will have a place to sleep tomorrow night."

With another quick smile over her shoulder, Sadie rushed off to work on their laundry.

As they left the laundry area, Molly smiled up at Lance.

"Thank you for letting Sadie come with us. I knew I wanted to help her as soon as I saw her raw arms and bleeding hands."

Lance put his arm around his wife. "Yes, I saw that coming. I just didn't know that I would become a brother again so quickly," he drawled as he smiled down at his wife.

Molly and Lance turned back toward their hotel, smiling as they walked down the main street of Julesburg.

The train station came into view and Lance suggested, "Let's go get that ticket right away. I hope I'm not riding on top of those cars!" His forehead creased as he thought a moment and he added, "And then, I'd better wire Old Man McNary and tell him to send the buckboard. A buggy is going to be too small for the crowd I'm hauling."

Lance paused and then growled, "And you do realize that the men will get *zero* work done as long as Sadie is around?"

He pretended to scowl at Molly and she elbowed him as they laughed again.

CHAPTER 55

BLOODHOUND ON A TRAIL

LANCE WAS LOOKING ACROSS THE STREET WITH A SMILE ON HIS FACE when he saw someone he recognized. He leaned forward.

"Slim? Slim Crandell, you old cayuse! What are you doing here?"

A tall, good-looking cowboy with blond curls and blue eyes turned around. His eyes lit up, and he crossed the street to greet Lance.

"Lance! I didn't know y'all would be here! The Old Man sent me down to finalize the delivery of some cattle for the railroad. Their crews like our steaks, an' we've been movin' a lot of beef."

Slim grinned and his eyes were full of laughter.

"Our foreman should'a done it but it looks like he's been plenty busy," Slim added slyly as his eyes flickered to Molly's stomach and then back to Lance.

Lance clapped him on the back and the two men talked cattle for just a little bit. Then Lance turned to Molly.

"Slim, I want you to meet my wife. This is Molly Rankin. Molly, Slim Crandell."

Molly gave Slim her nicest smile and just like that, he was putty in her hands. Lance rolled his eyes. *These women are going to be the ruination of my ranch*, he thought with a scowl.

Then Molly gave him her bright smile and he gave it up. *I'm smitten*, he thought. *I can't expect the rest of the men to be unaffected.* Lance took Molly's arm again, and Slim joined them as they walked toward the train station.

Lance bought one ticket. Slim looked confused. His bright eyes studied Molly and then moved back at Lance.

"I bought ours earlier. This one is for someone else," Lance explained offhandedly as his eyes twinkled.

Molly started to explain but Lance squeezed her hand.

"Someone else?" Slim asked. "Is someone else comin' to the ranch?"

Looking closely at Lance, Slim's blue eyes sparkled as he asked casually, "Are they female? Y'all know, we could sure use more women around there."

Lance snorted. "There hasn't been a female on that ranch in a long time. I feel sorry for Molly." Lance grinned at his wife and refused to give Slim any more information.

As Lance stepped away from the ticket booth, Slim nonchalantly mentioned, "I have somethin' I need to do. I'll meet ya at the food tent over there if ya want to eat supper together. The crowd picks up around 7:00 so let's eat at 5:30."

He paused and then almost blushed, "Unless you'd rather eat alone—"

Lance laughed and clapped him on the back.

"No, we would love to catch up. See you at 5:30."

As Slim headed down the street, Lance was grinning.

"Slim is like a bloodhound on a trail. By the time supper comes around, he will know every place we've been and I will lay you odds that he will have already met Sadie."

Molly looked at Lance in surprise.

"Why, how could he?" she questioned. "No one knows us here," she added with a puzzled look on her face.

Lance laughed.

"Well, let me tell you a little bit about my friend Slim. He will backtrack us and talk to everyone we saw today. He will know everything we did and every stop we made. He'll charm the information out of the ladies and 'visit' it out of the men."

Lance chuckled, "And I guarantee you, he will have met Sadie. Shoot, he'll probably already have a date with her!"

Molly studied Lance's profile as he talked about Slim.

She asked softly, "How long have you known Slim? I can tell you value him as a friend."

Lance nodded as he stared off across Julesburg.

"Slim was already working at the Rocking R when I arrived. He hasn't told me much about his childhood other than his parents died when he was really young. He was sent with his little sister to live with an aunt." Lance laughed. "In Slim's words, a 'stuffy' aunt. He ran away when he was twelve and worked his way up to be a top hand on every ranch he worked."

Lance was quiet for a moment and then added, "He probably would have been foreman for Old Man McNary but I came along."

As Molly waited for him to continue, Lance added softly, "Slim is the best friend I have ever had. He wasn't jealous when I was made foreman." he added quietly, "I am going to make him our foreman once we get back and officially take over the ranch."

Molly smiled up at him and Lance laughed. "Besides being a better rider than just about anyone I know, the one thing Slim can do better than any of us is woo the ladies. He knows how to lay on the charm, and he has a different girl just about every month or so. He is funny and gallant and oh, do the ladies love him. I don't think he intends to break hearts. He just likes women and they like him."

Molly laughed as she agreed, "I can see that. He is quite charming."

Lance stopped and pretended to be shocked.

"More charming than me?" he asked in feigned surprise.

Molly giggled as she looked up at him. "No, but he doesn't make me blush," she answered as her cheeks turned pink.

Lance squeezed her and pulled her close to his side.

"I sure am glad you made me marry you, Molly Rankin," he drawled as the ornery lights glinted in his eyes.

Molly rolled her eyes and they continued on down the street.

They stopped at the telegraph office so Lance could let Old Man McNary know when they would be arriving.

Send buckboard June 19. 9:00 a.m.. Bringing Guests. Lance

Slim was waiting for them at 5:30. His blue eyes were twinkling and full of orneriness.

Lance grinned. He knew that Slim had been on a mission.

Molly glanced at Slim's hands. "Slim! What happened to your hands? Did you get them smashed on something?" she asked with concern.

Slim looked down at his hands and then at Lance.

With a slow grin, he drawled, "Shore did smash them on somethin'. But that somethin' looks worse than my hands."

Then he innocently asked Lance, "Say, ya don't mind if yore sister joins us tonight, do ya? She is over there savin' us a spot."

The look Molly gave Slim was priceless and Lance laughed out loud. He looked at Molly. "I told you he would have it all figured out."

As Molly headed toward the table where Sadie was seated, Lance asked, "Clyde?"

Slim answered seriously as he eyes twinkled, "Yep only he ain't so purty anymore. I ree-moved a couple of his teeth. I jist won't tolerate a feller talkin' rudely to a lady."

The friends grinned at each other and both sauntered over to join Molly and Sadie.

A loud, high-pitched voice could be heard. "I sayed, excuse me! I'm a comin' through. An' no siree' this here top hat ain't fer sale!"

Badger appeared at their table with a big grin and Sammy in tow.

Sammy ran up to Lance. "Can I sit by you, Papa?"

Slim choked on his drink and everyone laughed.

Lance lifted the little boy up. "Did you catch any fish with Grandpappy?" he asked.

Sammy's eyes were big and he proceeded to tell them an animated story with lots of hand gestures and eye movement.

Badger's eyes were gleaming as he laughed and agreed whenever Sammy looked at him.

When Sammy was done, they finally figured out that Badger and he had caught three catfish. Badger had them in a spare horse tank behind the livery to flush them in fresh water. Then Sammy and Grandpappy were going to cook them and *everyone* was invited.

The little boy looked across the table and realized there were some new faces there.

He seriously put out his hand and addressed Slim, "My name is Sammy Rankin. And you are?" Sammy used some of the same mannerisms that Lance used, and Lance looked proud as he smiled down at Sammy.

Slim laughed. "Why my name's Slim. I work with yore pa. In fact, I think I work harder than yore pa," he answered with an ornery smile and twinkles in his blue eyes.

Molly watched him and rolled her eyes as she laughed.

Sammy looked at Sadie. "Is she your wife?"

Slim shook his head. "Not yet!" and winked at Sadie.

Sadie blushed and Molly was amazed. *He is just like Lance,* she thought. *He has barely met Sadie, and already he is doing his best to make her turn red!*

Sadie put out her hand. "Well, since Lance is my brother, I guess that makes me your auntie. My name is Sadie."

Sammy's blue eyes became huge.

"I have a Momma and a Papa, a Grandpappy, and now an auntie! And pretty soon, I will have a baby brother." He patted Molly's large stomach.

"He's in there somewhere but I don't know how he's goin' to get out."

Lance choked and everyone tried not to laugh as Sammy climbed up on the bench to sit by Lance.

"Slim, tell me about the Rocking R. I have been gone for so long, I almost feel lost. Catch me up on what all has taken place."

As the men began to visit, Molly and Sadie shared stories. Badger and Sammy listened to both conversations and missed nothing.

A high-pitched squeal followed by, "Molly!" turned everyone's head toward the outside of the tent.

CHAPTER 56

A Moment of Inner Thought and Refection

MARION AND PRIVATE SMITH, AS WELL AS CAPTAIN AND MARY LEWIS were looking into the eating tent and smiling. Lance, Slim and Badger stood up to give the women their seats. They worked their way through the crowded tent to talk to the men and Sammy followed them.

As Sammy walked by two nicely dressed people, the man leaned toward him and smiled.

"Hello, son. What is your name?"

Sammy looked at the man. "My name is Sammy." He was about to put out his hand when the woman pushed him back.

"Get away from me, you dirty little boy."

Sammy stared at her for a moment and then asked, "Are you a grandmammy?"

The woman looked indignant. "No, I am not a grandmother, and keep your grubby little hands off me. You will soil my dress!"

Sammy studied his hands and looked from them to the woman.

"They ain't really that dirty. See, we was fishin' an' they got lots a water on 'em to clean 'em off." Sammy wiped his hands on his britches to be sure and looked closely at the woman.

"You look like a grandmammy but you ain't nice like grandmammies are 'posed to be."

Lance could see the exchange from where he stood and he pushed back into the tent just in time to hear what Sammy told the angry woman.

The woman's face turned red and Lance grabbed Sammy. Fire was shooting from his eyes.

Slim had followed Lance in. He reached over and plucked Sammy out of Lance's arms.

Slim drawled, "Just in case yore gonna share a 'moment of inner thought an' reflection' with this woman, it might be a good idea fer me to take Sammy."

As they walked away Slim asked, "How would ya like to have a sarsaparilla, Sammy?"

Sammy's eyes became very large. "I don't know what a sapgorilla is but I'd sure like to try one."

Slim put Sammy on his shoulders and they pushed their way up to the serving station.

Lance turned to the older woman who was still sputtering. His face was tight and his blue eyes were smoldering. The gentleman beside her quickly leaned around her. He stretched out his hand with a smile on his face.

"My name is William." He smiled and asked, "Are you by any chance Lance Rankin?"

Lance was startled and moved his eyes from the woman to the man who had spoken. The gentleman smiled again and patted the bench beside him.

"Please?" he asked.

316

Lance slowly walked around the sputtering woman and draped a long leg over the bench to straddle it.

"Yes, I am Lance Rankin. What can I do for you?"

"I apologize for my wife. "Sometimes she can be overbearing but she does have a good heart." He paused and waited for an answer.

Lance didn't respond but he thought, *well, you picked her so I guess you do this often.*

Still, the man did seem sincere. Lance let out his breath and looked directly at the gentleman.

He answered coolly, "I don't think you asked me to sit down to apologize for your wife."

The man blushed slightly and put out his hand. "My name is William Mosier. I understand that you buried my brother, Samuel and his wife, Josephine."

Lance looked hard at the man and nodded his head slowly. "Yes, there were three of us. Private Most who died on the trip, Badger there, and myself, " as he pointed to where Badger was standing outside the tent.

"My wife and I are traveling to California," William explained. "A friend of ours is a United States Marshall and he was sent after some outlaws in the Colorado Territory. He tracked them to my brother's house. The O'Tooles were there working, and they gave him the entire story. Of course, he telegraphed me. We were in Omaha and hurried out."

Lance was confused. *What was he doing out here? They were buried—there was nothing else to do.*

William smiled. "You are probably wondering how I knew you."

He looked over at Sammy and murmured softly. "He looks exactly like Samuel did at that age. When he told me that his name was Sammy, I took a chance on you."

Lance slowly nodded. "What do you want from me, Mr. Mosier? Your brother was buried on his farm. We took the two children with us. You saw Sammy and Emma was—"

William's wife whipped her head around to Lance as she interrupted him.

"You are one of those who buried my brother-in-law? Did they have much land? What is the value of it? Is it now lying idle or is it planted? What would the value of the crops be?" Her eyes were bright and hard as she snapped the questions at him.

William seemed to shrink back just a bit as his wife snapped out the questions.

Lance was furious. *Why, the woman hadn't even asked about Emma.* Lance leaned toward Mrs. Mosier and hissed his answers to her.

"Their land is five or six hard days from here by horseback. They lived in a house just a little better than a shack. They had two children. Emma was captured by the outlaws who killed her parents. She hid her younger brother and he was hiding alone for one-and-one-half days before we were able to find him. Emma had no desire to return to the homestead so she signed it over to their neighbors, the O'Tooles. Emma died when the army ambulance she was riding in rolled over a cliff—the same accident that killed Private Most. I have no idea if crops are planted yet or not. Either way is none of your affair. Perhaps you could show just a little concern for those who died and the little boy who was left with no family!"

Lance's face was next to Mrs. Mosier's and as she pulled back, he leaned in closer. When he finished talking, he pulled back, his face white and taunt.

He looked at her with utter distain and spat the words, "You, Madam, are a despicable woman."

Lance nodded to William and stood up.

Badger appeared beside the table talking loudly and jumping around. Then with no warning, the butt of Ol' Betsy slammed down on Mrs. Mosier's foot.

She shrieked and Badger grabbed his leg.

"She kicked me! This crazy old woman kicked me!" he squawked as he hobbled off.

Mrs. Mosier continued to shriek and her husband tried to calm her. Lance was confused as to what had just happened between Badger and the woman. He stared from one to the other. Badger grabbed his leg—the *other* leg—and hobbled out of the food tent.

The women had been deep in conversation.

Molly looked up as the woman began shrieking and saw Lance's face. She didn't know what had happened but she guessed the "accident" had something to do with the look of fury on her husband's face.

Slowly, Lance let his hands unclench. When he saw Molly looking at him, he gave her a brief smile and walked out of the tent.

CHAPTER 57

SLIM'S GIRL

MOLLY HAD MISSED THE EXCHANGE BETWEEN LANCE AND THE ANGRY WOMAN because Marion was sharing her exciting news.

"We were married this morning, Molly! Captain Lewis and Mary stood up with us. Johnny asked me to be his wife as we were crossing the last river." She blushed softly.

"Johnny said, 'Marion, I would like to cross the rest of the rivers in my life with you by my side. Will you be my wife?' My Johnny is so romantic. Isn't that the most romantic thing you have ever heard, Molly?"

Molly hugged her friend as she agreed.

"Oh, Marion, I am so happy for you. You have a wonderful man. Your mother would be so pleased, and I'm sure your brother is as well."

Marion nodded happily. Private Smith, or Johnny as Marion called him, had six more months of military service.

"We are hoping to go to Denver after that to work with Billy's father in his dry goods store. Billy asked Johnny to look up his father if he wasn't able to."

Marion's face clouded for a moment and then she added, "Johnny wrote Billy's father and shared some of the experiences they'd had together as best friends. He also told Mr. Most that his son had died trying to protect the girl he loved." Marion's tender eyes filled with tears.

"We haven't heard back from Mr. Most yet but we hope to soon."

Molly patted Marion's hand and she smiled at her. She glanced up as the woman began screaming and for a moment, she caught Lance's eye. Then he nodded at her and left the tent so Molly turned back to Marion.

"That would be wonderful, Marion. I'm sure that Billy would be happy for you to help his father since he can't be there," she agreed as she hugged her friend.

Private Smith was standing off to the side watching the crowd. He saw how rude the woman was to Sammy, and anger had risen in him as well. Everyone in that caravan had loved little Sammy. He walked over to where Sammy was sitting. He was in deep conversation with a smiling cowboy so Private Smith stood back for a moment.

Sammy was talking as he drank his sarsaparilla, and he smacked his lips after every sip. He looked earnestly at Slim.

"Do ya have a wife, Slim?"

Slim grinned and shook his head no.

Sammy asked, "Do ya have a girl?"

Slim slowly answered, "No, I don't have a girl. I guess I haven't met one yet that I want to stick with. There are lots a girls out there, ya know," and he winked at Sammy.

"But don't ya want kids?" Sammy asked.

Slim's eyes began to twinkle. *Now just where is this conversation leading* he wondered as he tried to look serious.

"Wal', I would like to maybe have kids but ya have to have a wife first," Slim drawled. "An' before she's yore wife, she has to be yore gurl!"

Sammy leaned forward eagerly. "I know a nice lady who could be your girl! You want to know who?" Sammy asked with his eyes shining.

Slim raised an eyebrow. "Who do ya have in mind, Sammy?"

"I think ya should have Sadie as your girl. She's real nice an' she's my auntie. Would ya like to be my uncle, Slim? I don't have an uncle yet."

Slim looked at the earnest little face with so much love and trust expressed there. He leaned forward and chucked Sammy under the chin. "I'd shore like to be yore uncle, Sammy," Slim told him sincerely, "An' if I could have a little boy of my own jist like ya, why I'd for shore get married."

Sammy grinned and Slim laughed.

"Ya shore have things all figured out, Sammy!"

Private Smith stepped up with a big smile on his face. He put out his hand. "I'm Private John Smith. I came up from Monument with Sammy here." He tousled Sammy's hair and then dropped down on one knee by him.

"Say Sammy, I have some hard candy in one of my pockets but I can't remember which one," he stated with a serious face as his eyes twinkled.

Sammy looked at Private Smith with his eyes shining.

"Would ya like me to help you find it? I'm purty good at findin' candy!" he exclaimed with an excited smile.

Private Smith grinned at him. "I tell you what, Sammy. If you can find some candy, you can have it. Of course, you might need to share it with your new friend."

Sammy pointed at Slim. "His name is Slim an' he's my new uncle. Sadie is gonna be his gurl!"

Slim blushed a deep red and Private Smith laughed. "Well, that would probably be all right," he agreed.

Sammy jumped down from the bench and starting searching in Johnny's pockets.

He found candy in all of them. With each piece, he would stop and hold it up in the air. When he had gone through all of Private Smith's pockets, Sammy had a huge pile of candy and an even bigger smile.

"Thanks, Johnny!" he mumbled happily with his mouth full of candy. Then Private Smith sat down, and the three of them enjoyed Sammy's candy and more conversation.

Marion was watching Johnny talk to Sammy.

"He's wonderful, isn't he?" she whispered softly.

She turned to Molly. "I think Johnny is the most wonderful man in the whole world."

Molly and Mary Lewis laughed. Marion was right though. Johnny was wonderful.

Lance was leaning on the side of the dining hall when William Mosier approached him. Lance stared him coldly, but said nothing.

Again, William blushed slightly but this time, he didn't bother to apologize for his wife.

"I was wondering," he asked softly, "if I could meet Sammy? He is my last living relative. I think you know that we are not interested in taking him in. However, I would like to meet my brother's only son." William waited nervously and shifted his weight as he fidgeted.

Lance looked at him coolly.

"I will introduce you as a friend. I don't want Sammy to know any more than that."

William nodded and Lance led the way to where Slim, Johnny, and Sammy were eating candy and laughing.

Sammy glanced up as Lance approached the table.

"Papa, look at all this candy! I found it in Johnny's pockets. And you know what else? Sadie is going to be Slim's girl!"

Slim choked on his candy and Johnny laughed.

Lance grinned as he looked at his friend. Slim had always considered himself quite the ladies' man. Few women could resist those blue eyes. He knew how to make each girl think she was his one and only.

Sammy has one up on Slim there, Lance thought with another grin.

"So Slim, when are you going to share that information with Sadie? It might be good if she knew too."

Private Smith laughed out loud and Slim blushed again.

Sammy blurted out, "I'll tell 'er right now!" and before anyone could stop him, Sammy was off the bench and darting through the crowd. He grabbed Sadie's arm and whispered in her ear.

Sadie went completely still while Molly covered her mouth and began to laugh. Marion looked surprised and Mary Lewis looked over at Slim with a shocked face.

Slim turned a darker red. He muttered "Good night," and disappeared into the crowd.

Sadie didn't look around but Molly did and she was laughing.

As Sammy came rushing back to their table with a huge grin on his face, Lance squatted down beside him.

"Sammy, I want you to meet someone. He knew your first Mommy and Papa, and your Sissy as well."

Sammy's little face became sober as he looked at the man beside Lance.

"They all died. Now Lance and Molly are my momma and papa. Sadie is my auntie an' Slim is gonna be my uncle. I don't know where he went, but Sadie is gonna be his gurl."

William smiled and leaned down to look at Sammy. "You look like your father did when he was a child, Sammy."

Sammy looked surprised. "Say, that's just fine. Momma says my papa is a good lookin' man!"

William smiled again and shook Sammy's hand. As he walked quietly away, Lance was thankful the Mosiers' didn't want Sammy. He shuddered to think of Mrs. Mosier as a mother.

At last, it was their table's turn to join the food line. Poor Slim missed his supper, and Sadie appeared to be looking for someone all during the meal.

At 7:30, Lance tapped his pocket watch and pointed at Sammy.

The little guy had his head down on the table and he was almost asleep.

Molly hugged both of the women. They all promised to keep in touch and to try to visit. Molly had tears in her eyes as they walked away.

"I wonder if I will see either of them again," she asked Lance.

Lance was quiet. They had met a lot of people on this trip.

"We might not see them again, Molly, but that doesn't mean that you can't stay in touch. Besides, you never know where people might show up—look at Badger."

He scooped up Sammy and offered his other arm to Molly. They were all tired as they walked back to the hotel; it had been a very full day.

CHAPTER (58)

AN EXCITED GROOM

BOTH LANCE AND MOLLY WERE UP BY 7:30 THE FOLLOWING MORNING. Molly asked Lance to help her with her hooks on her dress. Lance's hands fumbled everywhere but they were not on the hooks. Molly was giggling and Lance was laughing. Finally, he turned her around and tried to hook them while he kissed her.

Sammy raised his head up and asked, "Papa, are you tickling Momma?"

Lance dropped down and began to tickle Sammy. "Yes, I am. Just like this!"

Sammy giggled and wiggled until Lance collapsed beside him. Then he looked up at Lance.

"I love you, Papa."

Lance's heart was full. He picked Sammy up and hugged him tight. "I love you too, Sammy," Lance answered, the emotion thick in his voice.

He carried Sammy over to Molly, and Lance put his arms around both of them. As he kissed the top of Molly's head, he thanked God again that he "had been chosen" as the preacher had stated on their wedding day.

On their walk to the dining tent, Molly worried, "I barely know Martha. We only talked a little at the box supper. She seemed so quiet but Badger acts smitten. I hope we get along well. It will be so nice to have another woman just a few miles away."

Lance nodded. "I wouldn't worry too much. She has to be pretty special to turn Badger's head, and have a good sense of humor as well. I'm sure we will all love her like we love Badger."

Badger was waiting at the dining tent when the Rankins arrived, but he was fidgeting too much to stay seated.

Molly looked at him and laughed, "Why Badger, I believe you are nervous."

Badger gave her his ornery grin.

"Why, shore I am. I'm a marryin' my Martha today an' I want it ta be special fer her."

Molly giggled. "Well, I am sure she won't be able to resist you—you look quite dashing!"

Badger did look dashing in his new suit and top hat. He was freshly shaven, and he had even scrubbed his fingernails. He didn't eat, and it was the first meal that Molly had ever seen him willingly miss.

Lance began to tease him about his future wife.

"I hope you have a room reserved for your wife, Badger. She can't sleep in the livery, you know." Badger swore under his breath and raced back to the hotel.

"My Martha needs a bigger room!" he exclaimed as he bounced up the steps.

When Badger asked about a second room, the disinterested hotel clerk answered, "I have the wedding suite. It's bigger. One bed. It is on the top floor and has windows on two sides."

"I'll take 'er jist fer ta' night," Badger told the man.

The clerk asked if Badger wanted his clothes moved from the small room right away.

"Naw," he answered. "The weddin' is at 4:00 an' my bride needs 'er space ta prepare. But youin's kin put 'em in there after 4:00 'cause that's whar I'll be tonight," Badger stated with a wink.

The hotel clerk was a young man. There were not many weddings in Julesburg, and never had he seen anyone as old as Badger marry. The clerk eyed the old man suspiciously. Badger had paid up front though, so the clerk would do his part.

Feeling just a little more relaxed, Badger hurried back to the dining tent. Molly and Lance had just finished, and Molly linked her arm through Badger's.

"You surely do look handsome today, Badger. We are all excited to get to know Martha."

Badger patted her hand. "I know you'll love my Martha. She's jist 'bout the sweetest little thing I ever did meet. Mule even approves."

Molly laughed. "You are right, Badger. If Martha already won over the most difficult member of your family, she surely is the woman for you!"

Badger smiled at Molly and winked. "Ya know, little missy, I shore am glad that slow cowboy you'ins married brung you out here." He pecked her cheek and Molly hugged him.

Sammy wanted to ride on Badger's shoulders to the train station but Lance grabbed him. He tossed Sammy into the air and then put him up on his shoulders.

The train usually arrived somewhat close to the scheduled time. It was 9:15 a.m., and people were beginning to gather in front of the train station. A small group of men and women were in a tight cluster off to one side of the crowd, and Badger stepped over to talk with them. Lance couldn't hear what he was saying, but with all of Badger's hand movements, he knew that Badger had something special planned for his Martha.

The train whistled as it pulled into the station, and Lance could only stare. There were men riding on top of the cars-- not just a few men but a *lot* of men! It looked like the inside of the cars were standing room only as well. Rail workers, bartenders, lumberjacks, cowboys and "Ladies of the Night"—this train carried them all.

Molly was staring in shock as Lance growled, "We for sure have to be here early tomorrow."

Molly's pretty face was worried. "I don't think I can climb up there, Lance."

Lance squeezed her hand as he laughed. "Don't worry. Even rough men can be gentlemen. I'm sure you will have a seat but I'm guessing I'll be on top!"

Badger darted up the steps and into the train. With a huge grin on his face, he stepped out and waved at the motley group of people he had spoken with just moments before.

They gathered in front of the train, took out a variety of instruments and began to play, "Oh When the Saints Go Marching In" just as Martha stepped into the doorway. Badger stopped her there for just a moment. The small band was more enthusiastic than talented but the bystanders loved it. Everyone clapped and cheered.

Martha was beaming and flushed. She proudly took Badger's arm as he carefully helped her down the steps. He looked so smug that everyone around them smiled.

As the music died out, instrument by instrument, Badger rushed back into the train to collect Martha's bags—and Martha had a lot of bags. He staggered down the steps of the train and onto the platform. Lance stepped up to help, and Badger gave most of the bags to Lance. After all, Badger needed to escort his future bride.

When the jaded hotel clerk heard the band start to play, even he went to the doorway to watch. As Badger presented his future wife with pride, the clerk smiled. He grabbed a vase of wild flowers off of the counter

330

that he had picked that morning, and put the unruly arrangement in the wedding suite. They were starting to droop as most wild flowers wilt quickly but they smelled wonderful. He smiled again as he shut the door and hurried back downstairs.

CHAPTER 59

SAMMY'S NEW GRANDMAMMY

MARTHA SHUMAKER WAS A WOMAN WHO WAS USED TO LITTLE LOVE and no attention. She was tall for a woman and carried herself proudly. Martha dressed conservatively, and did nothing to draw attention. She had been rail thin when she was young, but now she was rounded out and "nice and soft" as Badger would say. She had been married to her husband for over thirty years before he died, and during that time, he had kissed her only a few times. He believed in no show of affection and certainly not in public. No children had come from their platonic relationship.

Walden Shumaker had been a banker in St. Louis before moving to Manhattan, Kansas where they lived the last ten years of his life. After he was diagnosed with consumption, he knew that he needed a drier climate. Martha wanted to go even farther west as Manhattan was still rather humid, but money was Walden's everything, and he stopped where the money was.

Martha never complained even though she was just someone to cook and clean as well as for Walden to put his feet on at night. She knew she had a loveless marriage but life for Martha had always been hard.

Walden had married her at twenty-eight years old and she was certainly a spinster then by everyone's account. She had never intended to marry. However, her parents died together in a buggy accident and as a single woman, Martha was not allowed to run the small dry goods store alone after their passing.

Walden thought he needed a wife to boost his career, and he saw in Martha a woman who worked with no complaining, as well as a wife who would be willing to stay in the background and be silent.

The one thing that Martha had insisted on in their marriage was that both of their names be on every investment Walden made. Martha didn't balk at much, but when she crossed her arms and refused to cooperate until it happened, Walden agreed.

Walden knew that Manhattan was a growing town, and he invested in property there. It was paying off but Walden never lived to see the full benefit of it.

After he died, Martha considered moving on, but Walden's investments kept growing. She was an astute businesswoman herself, and Martha added more properties to Walden's portfolio.

Martha always liked to help those in need, and she had grubstaked various miners. Some of those grubstakes were paying off as well but Martha didn't grubstake them for her benefit. She did it because they needed help.

Walden had refused to share his money with anyone, but Martha loved children. Sometimes, she slipped cash into passing wagons or luggage if she saw young families who were struggling.

Martha was quiet, unassuming and cheerful. Her life was a placid line from one day to the next, and sometimes she wished she had more excitement around her. If you had asked her friends in the small community of Manhattan about Martha, they would have told you that she was a woman with few needs. She lived simply. None of her friends knew she was wealthy.

When Badger stepped on her feet in church, everything changed. And when he leaned over with those ornery eyes and offered to buy her box lunch "if'n she were a good cooker", Martha's heart skipped a beat.

Badger brought sparkle into her life if only for that one day. When he proposed after breakfast the next morning, she gave him a resounding yes.

Her friends were appalled. Why the man was shorter than she was and older than her fifty-eight years.

"Widow women don't marry after fifty," one neighbor scolded, "and besides, you know nothing about him."

The widowed neighbor, Mary Todd, added, "How will you survive? He may have no means to support you. And that terrible, stinky mule. Why, it almost glares at people!"

Martha merely smiled. Walden had been a small man as well, but Badger had an energy about him that just drew her in. Besides, she loved his mule. Mule always tried to rub against her, and he closed his eyes when she rubbed his head.

Her life might not be perfect with Badger but it certainly wouldn't be boring anymore. As far as money went, he didn't need to be rich because she was quite comfortable. And Martha Shumaker had no intentions of ever turning her financial future over to any man again.

Badger loved to tease but never before had a woman called him out. He liked Martha's spunk and he *loved* her cooking. When Mule let her pat him and rubbed his head against her, almost purring with contentment as Martha scratched his ears, Badger just knew he had found his one and only. He had never loved a woman and had never married. He certainly didn't think Martha would say yes when he proposed that morning after breakfast.

"Martha, what if'n we was ta git hitched an' move ta Wyoming?'" Martha turned a deep red as she nodded her head. "Yes!" she exclaimed as she beamed at this little man who had rattled her life. Badger did a happy jig across her floor and kissed her soundly.

"I'll make all the 'rangements," he promised as he darted toward the door with his lunch in his hand.

He turned around at the door and blew her a kiss. As he hurried down the sidewalk, he jumped up in the air and kicked his boots together. Mule brayed and Martha's placid life would never be the same.

Badger led the way up the street with a beaming Martha on his arm. He stopped and proudly introduced her to everyone he met.

When little Sammy wiggled lose from Molly and rushed over to grab Badger's leg, Martha smiled down at the little boy.

"Grandpappy, is this lady gonna' be my Grandmammy?"

Badger grinned but before he could answer, Martha reached down and lifted the little fellow up.

"Why yes I am," she beamed, as she kissed his ruddy cheek, "And just what is my grandson's name?"

Sammy seriously put out his little hand. "My name is Sammy Rankin. And you are?"

Martha's heart melted. "My name is Martha Shumaker but after I marry your grandpappy, it will be Martha McCune."

Then she whispered in his ear, "Do you like donuts? If you do, you take that blue bag that your father is carrying. I made those just for your grandpappy, but you may carry them and share them with everyone."

Sammy wiggled down as fast as he could and started tugging on the blue bag.

Lance had to put everything down to get it for him.

Everyone was laughing as Sammy opened the bag. He pulled out a large donut with delight in his blue eyes.

"Looky here, Momma! My cake has a hole in the middle!" he blurted out as he held it up to his eye. He quickly stuffed it in his mouth. He then went around to everyone in their group and offered to share.

Badger took one. He stopped walking after the first b ite a nd proclaimed to Martha, "'Sakes 'live, Martha! You'ins sure is the best

336

cooker I ever met." Looking up at her and winking, he pinched her cheek. Martha blushed contentedly as they continued toward the hotel.

Lance watched Badger and Martha. He had met Badger for the first time when he'd had left his horses with him in Kansas City. Now he considered Badger a valued friend. Even as he struggled to carry all Martha's bags, Lance smiled.

"You know, Badger, you and Martha have a relationship built on mules!"

Badger grinned and Lance laughed. He walked faster and Molly moved up to walk beside Martha. Soon the two women were visiting like old friends.

A ruckus could be heard in the livery and heads turned that way. Men were running in all directions as Mule came kicking out of the barn. He rushed up the street braying and bucking. He stopped in front of Martha and laid his head on her arm. She hugged him and rubbed his ears.

Badger winked and addressed everyone present, "And that thar' boys, is how I knew this here lady were the woman fer me. Ol' Mule is a good judger a character an' he already loves my Martha." Martha blushed again and the happy group continued to the hotel, followed by a meek Mule.

CHAPTER 60

WEDDING IN JULESBURG

SLIM HAD OFFERED TO PICK UP MOLLY'S LAUNDRY THAT MORNING, and she accepted his offer with gratitude. When he showed up at the wedding with the pretty Sadie on his arm, Molly understood his helpfulness and she laughed.

Sammy tried to wink at him and Slim winked back.

Sadie started giggling, and Slim grinned at her.

"Now Sadie, ya know I was jist bein' helpful, an' ya jist happened to be there, handy like." His eyes were twinkling and Sadie rolled her eyes as he pulled her arm a little closer to him.

As Lance watched Slim and Sadie, he questioned their relationship, "I am wondering about those two. I've seen Slim work his charm on women but this seems a little different."

Molly replied, "Oh I warned her that he would toy with her feelings. I just hope she isn't drawn in by his charm and gets her heart broken. I have already given her some advice as to how to handle a charming man."

Molly giggled as Lance pretended to glare at her. Then he smiled and pulled Molly a little closer.

"So how do you handle a charming man, Mrs. Rankin?" Lance drawled softly as his blue eyes bore into her.

Molly giggled again and replied, "Not very well because he always makes me blush."

The wedding was small. Badger wore his coat with tails and was on his best behavior.

Martha wore a blue dress that she'd had made for her big occasion. She asked that it have pockets so she could hide candy in case any little ones were there. She even wore a large hat with flowers. It was out of character for her, but she was marrying an adventuresome man so she decided to be a little daring. Someone had left flowers in their room, and she made them into a pretty bouquet.

Lance and Molly stood up with the happy couple. Badger asked Sammy to hold Martha's ring. Badger had held his fingers up to Martha's until he found one almost the same size as her middle finger, and that was the size he bought. It was a simple gold band, but he had it engraved, "For my Martha."

Mule wouldn't go back to the livery so he stood in the door of the little church.

Sammy stood as still as he could. After five minutes, he began fidgeting.

He whispered loudly to Badger, "Ain't that feller 'bout done talkin'? Are we goin' fishin' after this?"

Badger grinned and Martha smiled.

Molly looked up at Lance as Badger and Martha repeated their vows.

He squeezed her hand and was swallowed up again by her blue eyes.

When the pastor announced, "You may kiss the bride," Lance kissed Molly too.

Mule brayed loudly and Sammy snorted. "*Now* cin we all go fishin'?" he demanded.

The McCunes' wedding reception was a picnic behind the church. Badger had offered to make a sizeable donation to the church fund if the church ladies would fix them a meal after the wedding. As the ladies began to carry out platters of food, Badger smiled proudly at his new bride. The church only had five members so the ladies had been busy.

The church ladies beamed at Badger and congratulated Martha.

"We are so glad you chose to marry in Julesburg. Will you be settling here?" one of them asked hopefully.

"No, we will be leaving on the train for Cheyenne in the morning, but thank you for letting us use your church and for preparing the meal. Everything was wonderful," Martha replied sincerely.

She made a point to thank each of the five women for all of their hard work. When they gathered all of the dishes and began to clean up, they found $20 slipped under the tablecloth.

Badger saw Martha lift up the cloth, and he winked at her as she slid the money under it. Martha blushed and Badger squeezed her as he kissed her cheek.

By 6:00, everyone was tired and Sammy was falling asleep in his ice cream.

Badger stood and smiled at his friends.

"We'uns would like ta thank ya fer comin' taday. Sammy needs ta go ta bed an' I want ta take my bride fer a walk."

His ornery eyes were glistening as he looked at Lance and Molly.

"We'uns 'ill shore see ya in the mornin'."

Lance reached for Badger's hand and the little man wrapped him up in a hug. He grabbed Molly and swung her around as he kissed her cheek.

Martha smiled happily as she hugged each of them.

She whispered to Molly, "I am so excited to have you as a neighbor and a friend."

Molly's eyes filled with tears as she hugged Martha back.

"I am so glad Badger found you, Martha. I was hoping we would have some women neighbors in Cheyenne."

Lance picked up Sammy and offered Molly his arm. Slim and Sadie followed them back onto the street.

As they left, Slim heard Badger talking excitedly to Martha.

"Martha, all my bestest friends was here ta see us married off. Now lets us go have us a talk 'bout what we'uns is gonna do when we git to Cheyenne. I wanna tell ya 'bout our little ranch an' the names a all our mules."

He grabbed 'Ol' Betsy and off they went toward the river, arm in arm.

"So what would ya think 'bout raisen' mules? I'm a thinkin' that thar's a market fer 'em out here."

Martha agreed and then added, "I worked in a dry goods store when I was young. I think maybe I would like to open my own dry goods store in Cheyenne someday. I would need help though and I don't know anyone. I do think I would like to combine it with a women's clothing shop. I could hire a seamstress. What do you think?"

Badger's eyes gleamed. "I like that thar idear. An' if'n you'ins need any help with the money end, I have plenty."

Martha smiled. "I have plenty too."

They both laughed and continued on their walk.

Martha smiled at Badger. "Where were you forty years ago? We should have married as kids!"

She squeezed his arm and Badger grabbed her. He swung her around to music that only the two of them could hear.

CHAPTER 61

RIDING ON TOP

LANCE PUT SAMMY IN HIS BED ON THE FLOOR. The little boy had fallen asleep during the short walk back to the hotel and he didn't move at all as Lance laid him down. The water arrived for Molly's bath and Lance helped her out of her dress. As he turned her around to face him, she shook her finger at him and pointed at Sammy. Lance grinned and pinched her as she tried to slip by him.

"Molly girl," he said thickly as he caught her, "you are prettier than a new foal on a spring morning." Molly laughed softly and kissed him.

As he tried to pick her up, she backed away, pointing again at Sammy. "Don't you wake him!" she warned as she dropped her undergarments and slid into the tub.

Lance was so tired that he fell asleep before Molly stepped out of the tub or Sammy would have been awakened.

Train time was 10:00 a.m. and Lance had lots of travel details to finalize before then. He was up at 5:00 a.m., shaved and in the livery barn by 5:15.

When he led the livestock up the street a few minutes later, Julesburg was already awake and beginning to team with activity.

Lance tied one mule in front of the hotel to haul their bags. The rest were taken to the train station. The cars were open and names were on the designated cars. All of the mules would ride together.

Badger and Martha were at the station by 7:30 with Mule. Martha was beaming and Badger looked ornery and contented.

"I believe marriage agrees with you, Badger!" Lance laughed as he studied the two of them.

Badger loaded Mule and then followed Lance back to the hotel to get their bags. Molly had everything packed and stacked by the door. She led an excited Sammy into the street.

Badger and Lance packed the mule as high as they could with bags for both families and both men still had their arms full as well. Lance didn't know what all Martha had brought but she certainly wasn't traveling light.

"I think she has even more things than last night," Lance muttered to Molly as he worked up a sweat with the large load.

Molly laughed and offered to help but Lance shook his head.

He grinned down at her. "Naw, you better save your energy in case we decide to get frisky tonight."

Molly blushed and sputtered. "Lance Rankin!" she hissed and Lance laughed.

He had received the reaction he wanted, and somehow the load didn't seem as heavy.

Slim arrived with a glowing Sadie. Lance looked at him curiously. Sadie was laughing and looking up as Slim talked to her. He was flirting outrageously, but he listened closely as she answered, and the ornery cowboy was very possessive as he moved her through the crowd.

As Lance watched them more closely, he commented, "Molly, I think Slim has fallen for Sadie!"

He turned around to see her response, but she was talking to Badger and Martha. Lance didn't have time to think more about it though as they were caught up in the hustle of the crowd.

The bags and packages were unloaded from the mule and stacked on the ground. Lance loaded the last mule on the train, and the group moved to the dining tent for a quick breakfast before their long train ride.

The train arrived with men riding on top and standing room only in the cars. Lance shook his head. "This is going to be a long twelve hours," he muttered nervously as he looked at Molly.

Molly's face showed some tiredness, and Lance patted her arm. *It has been a hard trip for everyone*, Lance thought as he looked around at his friends, *but even more so for Molly.*

"Feeling okay this morning, Molly?"

"I'm just tired and my stomach is cramping some. I feel fine though," she answered as she smiled up at him. She paused and then gave Lance a concerned look.

"I'm really worried that I will have to ride on top!" she whispered.

Lance squeezed her. "I know you won't have to ride on top. I am afraid that it will be really crowded though."

When the train stopped, people rushed to unload as more pushed to get on. When they finally pushed through the crowd, Lance saw that there were no open seats. As the seated men inside saw the women, several stood and offered their seats.

An older gentleman was the first to rise. He took Molly's hand and pointed at his seat. "Please take my seat," he invited. His seat was against the side so she would be able to rest a little easier. He gave her his blanket as well. As she smiled in appreciation and murmured a thank you, he nodded at Lance and climbed on top of the cars.

All of the young men in the car were smiling at Sadie and she had many offers of seats. When the man next to Molly offered his, she accepted it with a smile and squeezed Sammy in between the two of them.

Finally, all of the women were seated. Sadie was beside Molly while Martha was across the aisle.

Martha held out a bag of donuts to the man next to her. "Sir, would you be willing to trade your seat for some donuts?" she asked. The man looked confused so Martha opened the package.

His eyes opened wide and he exclaimed, "Bear sign! I'd sure trade this seat for a bag of bear sign!" He tipped his hat and took the bag as Badger slid into the open spot.

Other men began to offer to trade their seats as well and Martha beamed.

Slim scowled as he watched all the men try to talk to Sadie. Lance laughed and Slim glared at him. The whistle blew and the two men quickly climbed on top of the cars to find a place to ride.

The train stopped at every town. Lance watched the train work crews and their wagons as they hauled supplies from stop to stop. The rails were moving quickly west.

Slim sat relaxed with his hat tipped over his face. Lance growled, "This train makes enough stops that we will surely be able to find a seat sometime during this trip."

Slim looked up and replied, "Or y'all could jist shut up an' go to sleep."

Lance chuckled but it was good advice.

The sun was hot on top of the train but with the wind, Lance decided that it wasn't too bad. He checked on Molly at each stop. Martha, Molly and Sadie seemed to be getting along well and Lance was thankful.

After about three hours, Badger climbed up and traded with Lance; around 3:00 p.m., Lance traded with Slim. It was 6:00 p.m. before enough seats opened inside the car to seat all of the men.

Bathroom stops were hard and even more so for the women. Lance had helped Molly on several stops to find a little privacy. They had to take turns though as the empty seats needed to be watched at all times.

As Lance was bringing Molly back in around 8:00 p.m., he could see Slim facing a dark haired man with a long mustache and tied down guns. The man wanted to sit next to Sadie and Slim was not in agreement.

Lance quietly helped Molly to her seat before he asked, "Problem here?" The man turned at the sound of Lance's voice. His eyes narrowed and he shook his head.

"Next time," he threatened Slim.

"Anytime," Slim answered his face hard and tense.

The man tried to stare down Slim but when it didn't work, he walked away. He climbed out of the car and found a spot on top.

"Did you know that man?" Lance asked Slim.

"Yeah, Clay Allison. He's from my part a Texas. He always was a troublemaker. Thinks he's fast with a gun now but he knows I cin beat 'im. He's a little crazy so I'm glad he's on top."

"Looks like little Sadie has herself a big, handsome protector," Lance drawled as he grinned at Slim.

Red crept up Slim's neck and Lance laughed. He slapped his friend on his back.

"Well, she is a pretty sweet girl and easy to look at too."

Slim's face was serious, but his eyes sparkled as he agreed, "Why shore now, I'm jist bein' the gentleman I always am."

The two men leaned back in their seats, glad to be riding inside.

CHAPTER 62

SLIM AND SADIE

SADIE WAS VERY INTERESTED IN SLIM. He had wandered into the laundry area the day she met him with a dirty shirt that was missing a button.

"Cin ya wash this here shirt an' sew a button back on fer me?" he asked with a charming smile.

"When would you like to pick it up?" Sadie asked.

Slim's blue eyes glinted with humor as he answered nonchalantly, "Oh, I'm not a hurryin' feller. I'll jist wait."

Sadie agreed but as she began to pluck the old thread out, she could see it had been cut off.

She tried to hide the mirth in her eyes as she asked casually, "How did your button come off?"

Slim saw that she was onto him.

He grinned and replied, "Wal, I couldn't think of a better way to get a date with the purtiest gurl in Julesburg than to have 'er sew my button fer me whilst I talked to 'er!"

Sadie had laughed out loud and the button sewing took way too long.

Slim told her that he worked with Lance and when he invited her to go to the wedding with him, she agreed.

Now here she was on a train headed to Cheyenne, and she would be living on the ranch where he worked.

Curly blond hair, blue eyes that are full of mischief, tall, muscular. Sadie caught herself and shook her head slightly.

Molly had told her that Slim had lots of girls. Molly had advised, "The best thing is for you is to play a little hard to get."

As Sadie peeked at Slim from under her lashes, she thought, *I don't want to be hard to get. This man makes me want to be "got."*

Sadie was a beautiful woman and men noticed her. Even as a washerwoman, she received multiple proposals each day. Sadie had never been interested in any man until Slim had come along.

She looked across the aisle at him. He was asleep with his hat over his face so he couldn't see her. She hated games; they were so exhausting, but she couldn't just throw herself at him either.

She sighed and turned to look out the window.

Slim wasn't asleep. He was watching Sadie from under his hat. He wished there was an open seat beside her.

He muttered to himself, "If any of those folks leave, I'm goin' to acquire a new seat."

Slim remembered his pa telling his ma that she was built like a brick outhouse. Slim had been six at the time and he thought that sounded terrible.

His Pa had laughed. "But a brick outhouse would be fine, solid and easy to look at. That is how I see your mother," his pa answered softly as he put his arm around Slim's shoulders.

Slim had never forgotten that conversation and as he studied Sadie he thought, *she's like a brick outhouse too—fine, solid and easy to look at.*

Slim knew that Sadie had probably been told that he moved through women like water through a glass. He frowned. *Yeah, but that was only* 'cause I ain't met one yet who was interestin' enough to hold my 'tention, Slim thought to himself. *Now I meet the best lookin' gal I've ever seen an' she's the whole package. An' that means ever' guy in Cheyenne an' fer sure the rest of the Rockin' R cowhands are goin' to be after 'er too.* Slim groaned internally. *How'm I gonna beat off all those fellers if I don't have a head start*, he moaned to himself.

Sadie turned her head to look at Slim.

Big brown eyes like pools of dark chocolate, he thought.

Just then, Molly stood up. They were coming to a stop. Slim put his hat on his seat but instead of getting off the train, he slid into the seat next to Sadie. She looked up and smiled at him.

"Wal, I waited 'most the whole durn trip to sit by ya," Slim drawled as he grinned at her.

She could see the humor in his blue eyes and she laughed. "I have been here the entire time," she replied softly as she smiled.

"Now, Sadie, ya know all those durn cowboys are gonna be after ya when we get to the ranch. I'm just tryin' ta figure out how to make ya notice me so's I don't jist blend in."

Sadie laughed out loud. "Slim, I don't even know your last name but I am pretty sure you have never blended into a crowd a day in your life!"

Slim grinned. He took off his hat, stood up and bowed.

"Slim Crandall at yore service, Miss Sadie, an' I reckon I'm a gonna enjoy this ride."

Soon they were talking like old friends and they never did run out of things to talk about. Both thought the last two hours of the train ride were the best.

CHAPTER (63)

MAGIC CITY OF THE PLAINS

WHEN THE TRAIN FINALLY PULLED INTO THE CHEYENNE STATION a little before 10:00 p.m., everyone was exhausted. Cheyenne originally was called *The City of Tents* because it sprang up so quickly. However, because it continued to grow rapidly as a result of the railroad workers and the troops stationed at Camp Carlin, it earned the name, *Magic City of the Plains*.

Molly stepped off of the train and looked across the new city of Cheyenne and then stepped back, surprised. Actually, she was appalled.

Lance was exhausted but excited to be so close to home.

As he looked at Molly's expression, he patted her arm. "Don't worry. We'll get a room in the Rollins House. Stay here with Badger while Slim and I run up the street to beat the crowd."

Lance and Slim raced up the street and into the Rollins house. They were able to get two small rooms, one for the men, and one for the women. As they walked back to the train, they grinned at all of the people climbing off the train and wondering where they were going to stay.

The men unloaded the livestock and this time, they packed two mules with all the bags. Once they were unloaded, Slim offered to take care for the livestock so Lance and Badger could get the women settled. Slim was a little nervous around Mule so Badger and Mule had a discussion. Slim watched Badger hold Mule's head and then talk to him as one would talk to a child.

Slim muttered to Lance "The funny thing is that durn mule seems to understand!"

Lance laughed.

"When you get to know Mule better, you will see he understands a lot of things," Lance agreed as he headed toward the hotel.

Mule snorted as Badger moved away. Slim gingerly took the lead rope and Mule walked along meekly.

The livery was not as full as Slim was afraid it would be. He was able to put the two mules in one stall and the horses in another. Mule he turned loose in a smaller stall by himself. After giving the hostler instructions on how Badger and Lance wanted their animals cared for, he started to walk out. He paused and then turned around.

"Shore now, I wouldn't go into the stall with that there single mule. He's on the cantankerous side, and he ain't so nice all the time."

The hostler's eyes opened wide. He was only helping out for the weekend and wasn't familiar with mules. He moved slowly up to Mule's stall to study him closer. The mule was standing quietly.

"He doesn't look so bad," the hostler commented, reaching to adjust the lead rope hanging over the stall door. Mule charged the door and the hostler barely pulled his hand back in time. The man hollered and rushed back to the front of the barn while Mule returned to his meek position. If it were possible for a mule to pattern the characteristics of its owner, one could almost say that Mule was laughing wickedly.

Lance gave Molly a little of the history of Cheyenne as the two couples walked toward the hotel.

"In 1867, the first lots in Cheyenne sold for $125 -$150 each. A month later, lots were selling for $1000 and the price continued to go up. By January 1 of this year, three hundred businesses opened and are operating. Cheyenne's population now is over four thousand and many of the original tents have now been replaced with wooden buildings," he told her proudly.

They look more like shacks, thought Molly, although even she could feel the vibrancy of the growing city.

One of their reserved rooms in the Rollins House had two beds and that room was given to the women. The men dumped all of the bags and parcels inside the door.

Lance took Sammy by the hand and led him down the hall to the second room. He made beds on the floor for both of them. By the time Slim arrived, everyone was snoring. Slim collapsed on the bed by Badger and none of them moved until morning.

The Rollins House prided itself in comfort and the women were grateful to Lance and Slim for arranging the room. Talking didn't last long and all was soon quiet in the women's room as well.

6:30 came early, and all of the men were up.

Even Badger shaved that morning. He just grinned at Lance as he took out his razor.

"Didn't knowd I owned one, did ya?" he asked with a grin.

Lance laughed and soon Slim and Badger were headed to the livery.

Lance, with Sammy in tow, knocked on the women's door. A sleepy Molly answered and opened the door with a smile. She hugged Sammy and kissed Lance. Lance couldn't help but stare at his wife. Her hair was down and fell well below her shoulders. Her firm stomach was large but beautiful. Lance leaned over and kissed her round stomach and the baby inside moved quickly away. Molly looked startled and then smiled.

"We are headed to the Ford House for breakfast. I can take Sammy with me now if you want. You can join us there as soon as you are ready. We have a long ride out to the ranch."

Molly quickly grabbed a clean shirt for Sammy and washed his face. Lance pulled out his comb and Sammy was headed down the hall with his father.

The Ford Restaurant was run by Barney Ford, an ex-slave from South Carolina. It was known for its good food and was the most popular eatery in Cheyenne. Barney knew his customers not only by name, but where they liked to sit and what they usually ate. The Rocking R ate there often, and Barney gave Lance and Slim their usual table. The men ordered coffee for themselves and milk for Sammy. Then, they settled in to wait for the women.

Badger was all smiles and Lance couldn't help but grin along with him.

"So you're liking married life so far, huh Badger?" Lance asked innocently.

Badger tried to look nonchalant but then he grinned. "My Martha is the warmest li'l thing I've ever cuddled with. Why I just didn't get cold a'tall ta'other night."

Lance laughed and neither he nor Slim followed up on that comment.

The women caused quite a stir as they walked in. Molly's beautiful hair was once again wound around her head and even pregnant, she drew the eyes of all the men in the room. Martha was beaming and smiled at everyone. Sadie was shyly following and had three marriage offers before she even arrived at their table.

Lance was watching Molly but something in Slim's expression caused him to move his focus to his friend.

Slim was watching Sadie with an almost jealous look on his face and Lance ducked his head to grin. *The tables sure have turned on Slim*, Lance thought as he laughed to himself.

Horses could be heard racing down the street and then a barrage of men's voices laughing. The Rocking R ranch hands had arrived.

When Lance sent the wire to clean up the buckboard, they were all suspicious of who he was bringing home. Old Man McNary left a couple of the older riders at home and gave the rest of the crew the day off. The buckboard, driven by the Old Man himself, was coming but moving slower.

Sixteen riders pushed through the doorway looking for their foreman. When they spotted Lance, they headed for him in a rush. As they saw the three women with him, they stopped and became quiet. Every hat came off, and the loud riders looked as meek as mice.

Lance introduced the women first and then Badger. Sammy kept pulling on his leg and asking to be held. Finally, he lifted Sammy up and put his arm around Molly.

He added with a proud smile, "And this is our son."

The men stared and then moved to congratulate Lance. Barney moved some tables so the men could all be seated. Eating was a serious event and the tables where the riders ate were quieter until they were finished.

The men kept looking at Molly and then grinning at Lance.

"Boss didn't waste no time once he decided to settle down, did he?" grinned one as he nudged another.

The second cowboy was so taken by Sadie that he didn't answer until his partner elbowed him for the third time.

Lance grinned. *The ride back ought to be interesting,* he thought.

Once the meal was over and they all moved outside, the riders crowded around Lance. It was obvious to Molly that the men liked and respected Lance. Lance for his part was delighted to be home.

CHAPTER 64

MY SON IS HOME

THE MEN WHOOPED AND POINTED AS A BUCKBOARD CLATTERED UP THE ROUGH STREET.

Old Man McNary was dressed in his Sunday best. He had a feeling that Lance was bringing home more than just *guests,* and he wanted to put forth his best foot.

Lance walked to the buckboard and the two men shook hands. To everyone's surprise, Old Man McNary gave Lance a bear hug. "Welcome home, Lance." *My son is home* he thought as he stood with his hands on Lance's shoulders.

"Boss, I want you to meet my family. This is my wife, Molly, and our son, Sammy." Lance's smile almost spit his face.

The Old Man looked the three of them over. "Well," he beamed at them, "Lance was never one to waste time gettin' a job done. Welcome to the Rocking R, Mrs. Rankin."

Badger had stepped up beside Lance and Old Man McNary grabbed his hand. "Badger, you old shyster! Welcome to Wyoming! How long are ya stayin'?"

Badger's sharp eyes twinkled. "Why we's a movin' here! I bought out yur neighbor ta the south, an' Martha an' me are a gonna raise mules."

Badger pulled the beaming Martha up beside him. "This is my Martha."

Old Man McNary was speechless for one of the few times in his life. Then, he threw back his head and laughed.

"Mary Gooden never did want to live out here, but John didn't tell me who he sold to when they left. He said, 'I had a fair offer and I'm headed east to keep Mary happy.' Welcome to Wyoming, Mrs. McCune!" Old Man McNary exclaimed as he shook Martha's hand.

Sammy tugged on Old Man McNary's britches. "Are you a gonna be my grandpappy too? Badger promised that I would have two grandpap-pies when we got to W yomin'."

The Old Man looked down at Sammy and then he picked him up. "I would love to be your Grandpappy, Sammy. I would like that just fine." The Rocking R riders had never seen the Old Man tear up for anything but there was definitely a tear in his eye that day.

The men had all the bags loaded and the women were helped into the buckboard. Molly was on the front seat while Martha and Sadie were on the back seat. The riders were all arguing about who would drive them but the Old Man just climbed in and took the reins. The arguing then changed to who would get to ride the closest to Sadie.

Lance shook his head. *Yep. They are all stirred up and we won't get any work out of them for weeks*, he thought with a grin.

It was a twenty-mile ride back to the Rocking R and none of the hands opted to stay in town on their day off. The Old Man showed no expression but his eyes were twinkling.

Molly was entertaining to talk to and after ten miles of conversation; Old Man McNary understood exactly why Lance was so smitten. *Molly is intelligent and loving with a great sense of humor. And beautiful to boot,* the old man thought.

He rubbed his chin. "You know, Molly, I asked the Good Lord to help Lance find a wife so he wouldn't be an old dried out bachelor like me. I shore am glad he found you."

Molly blushed and kissed his cheek. "And I am glad our children will have another grandfather, and one so close!" she replied softly as she held onto his arm to steady herself.

CHAPTER 65

BROKEN KNIFE'S WELCOME

SIX BRAVES IN WAR PAINT APPEARED IN FRONT OF THE **RIDERS.** Their horses filled the road, and the Old Man cursed quietly as he reached for his rifle.

"Broken Knife!" he growled. "He's the worst of the worse."

The cowboys closed in around the buckboard and conversation ceased. Molly looked closer and then stood up.

"Blue Feather!" she cried as she climbed out of the buckboard.

An Arapaho woman dropped to the ground.

"What are you doing here? How is your leg?" questioned Molly.

Blue Feather flexed her leg. "Leg healed. Stitches good," she answered with a smile. She smiled bigger and blushed.

"Blue Feather has husband," she whispered as she pointed at the brave she had been riding with.

Molly's eyes opened wide, "Is that…?"

Blue Feather laughed and nodded. "Gray Wolf," she whispered as she batted her eyelashes at Molly.

Molly laughed out loud. She looked up.

"Hello, Gray Wolf. It is nice to meet Blue Feather's husband."

Gray Wolf showed no expression but his eyes glittered with pride.

Broken Knife pushed his horse closer to Molly. He held up a strand of red gold hair in a small braid.

"Still have hair from Woman of the Rising Son."

Molly pulled his knife from inside of her pocket. "And I still have your knife."

Broken Knife handed her a piece of deerskin beaded with a large sun. The sun was yellow and the crooked rays that encircled it were red. "This for you. You hang on barn if you need Broken Knife. Our peoples are friends." Broken Knife swept his hand in a circle around the group of riders and braves. His eyes focused on Molly and then on the group of riders.

Molly paused and then she turned to Martha.

"Martha, do you have any donuts left?"

Martha pulled out a large package from the bag she was holding.

Much to the riders' dismay, Molly presented the entire package to Broken Knife.

"Bear sign."

Lance showed Broken Knife in sign language what she had given to him.

Broken Knife grinned. He turned to Lance, "I see she no cut your heart out yet."

With a fierce glare at the cowboys, Broken Knife swung his horse around.

Blue Feather's husband grabbed her arm, swung her in back of him and the braves swept away.

The riders were all looking at Molly in disbelief.

Lance laughed. "They met before and Broken Knife wanted her hair. Molly took the knife out of his hand, cut off a piece of her hair, gave it to him and kept the knife." His grin became bigger as the hands stared at Molly with gaping mouths.

"Guess they are friends now," he explained proudly as he smiled at his pretty wife.

One of the hands commented dryly, "Your wife is either brave or crazy, Lance."

When Molly glared at him, the rider shrank back in his saddle with a sheepish look on his face.

Lance laughed. "Nah, she was just mad. Let that be a warning, boys. Don't make her mad!"

Lance chuckled as he looked down at Molly. Her blue eyes had fire in them but she laughed as well.

Old Man McNary rubbed his back. "I think I need to get out of this darn buckboard."

He looked around at the riders as his hard eyes twinkled.

"Slim! Let me have your horse and you drive this thing awhile."

Lance was helping Molly up and she suggested with an extra sweet smile, "Sadie, why don't you ride up front. I would like to talk to Martha for a bit if you don't mind."

Sadie blushed but moved forward quickly.

Slim was off of his horse and in the wagon so fast that all the riders started laughing. They knew they had lost round one, but they wouldn't give up that easily.

Slim, for his part, knew he had better make the rest of the ride count because the competition was going to be tough.

The buckboard moved slower those last ten miles as Slim used all of the charm he could put forth to win Sadie over. By the time they turned down the road that went by the ranch house, Sadie had her arm looped through Slim's lean arm, and was giving him dazzling smiles.

Molly and Martha were pretty sure he had hit every rock he could to keep Sadie bumping into him.

Lance was grinning. *Slim is working to win her over, but he's the one who has already falle*n, Lance thought as his grin became bigger.

It was midafternoon when the group arrived at the ranch headquarters. The Old Man had built a cabin off a distance from the house and moved his things out there. The ranch house was clean and ready for Molly and Lance to take over.

Sadie would take the extra bedroom with Sammy. Her pretty eyes were sparkling and every rider was already in love with her.

After they unloaded the bags that stayed, Badger took over the reins to the buckboard. His ranch was five miles farther south, and he was excited to show it to his Martha.

As they drove away, Martha called back, "Come over next week, and I will make more bear sign."

The men stared and then one of the riders stated, "I think I'm goin' to like havin' women 'round here."

CHAPTER (66)

NOMI

MOLLY HAD HER HAND ON HER STOMACH as she sat down at the rough kitchen table.

Lance squatted beside her. "Everything good?" he asked.

Molly nodded. Her face was a little pale but her eyes were sparkling.

"Oh, Lance, I am so glad to be home. Your ranch is beautiful," she whispered.

Lance kissed her hands. "Our ranch, Molly girl. This is your home too."

He paused as he proudly smiled at her, "And our baby will be the first little one to be born here!"

Molly smiled. She took his face in her hands and kissed him.

"I'm so glad you rescued me, Lance. I can't imagine my life without you," she whispered tenderly.

Lance's heart thudded in his chest as he hugged his wife.

Molly's smile froze and he felt her body tense. She breathed deeply several times and then relaxed.

"Would you mind taking care of Sammy? I would like to take a quick nap."

Molly's face was tired and Lance was reminded again of the hard trip his wife had just completed.

Lance helped her up and guided her into their bedroom. As he helped her into the bed, she looked around. The room had been freshly painted. Molly smiled up at Lance.

"Your men love you, Lance, and so does Old Man McNary."

Lance's neck showed color as he answered huskily, "Well, we are all pretty close here. Now, you get some sleep and I will check on you in a few hours."

Molly lay back on the bed. Her stomach had been cramping for the last hour and her back was aching. She rolled onto her side and closed her eyes.

By evening, Molly was in full blown labor. Her face was sweating and she was struggling with each contraction.

"Molly, shouldn't this be moving faster?" questioned Lance with concern.

Molly frowned at him. "This is my first too, Lance, so I don't know how it is supposed to go," she grunted as another contraction hit her.

Lance sat down by the bed and kissed her head.

"I've sent for Badger. He should be here soon. In fact, Tiny just rode in—Badger might be with him."

Lance walked out into the yard. He looked at Tiny in surprise.

"I thought you went after Badger. Where is he?"

"Badger warn't home. The buckboard was gone an' there warn't nobody 'round. I rode 'round an' hollered but I couldn't raise nobody. I even took the long way 'round to come back but I couldn't find 'em."

Lance was trying to remain calm but he had counted on Badger's help.

He turned to the small man next to him.

"Take the fastest horse we have and ride into Cheyenne. Don't come back without that doctor. If something is wrong, we need to have him here."

The rider, Frank Jones or Jonesy, as the guys called him, raced out of the yard. He was back in three hours with an orderly who knew just a little about birthing babies.

"Doc is out of town and won't be back until next week," the orderly explained as Lance looked at him in question.

The orderly checked Molly's stomach and looked carefully at Lance. "Let's go outside and talk."

Lance stared at the man and then slowly followed him out of the house.

As they stepped outside, the orderly turned to Lance with worry in his eyes.

"I think the baby's backwards. It's head should be coming first but it's bottom is trying to come first instead. That is called a breach birth."

As Lance stared hard at him, the orderly cleared his throat and continued, "Some women can deliver that way and others can't. Your wife is pretty small and sometimes, that makes it harder. A doctor might be able to help you but I can't," the trembling man stated quietly.

Lance's eyes opened wide. As fear rose from his stomach to his heart, his face went white.

"What can I do? Is there something we can do to make it turn?"

The orderly shook his head. "A doctor might try it but I don't know how. I am not even sure what to look for. I am only guessing that the baby might be backwards. I read about breach births in one of Doc's books."

The orderly patted Lance's shoulder and walked back into the house.

Lance was frantic. There was no one who could help. As he realized that he could lose this woman in childbirth, his heart clenched. He looked up towards the Heavens.

"Lord, please help us," he begged. "Molly needs to have this baby, and I don't know how to help her." Lance's voice caught in his throat.

Molly was calling for him and he went to her side. Her eyes were full of pain but she took his hands and kissed them.

"Lance, don't forget about Sammy. He is going to need you," she pleaded as her eyes filled with tears.

Lance grabbed her hands.

"Molly, no! Don't talk like you won't be here."

Molly began to cry softly.

"Oh Lance, I so want to spend my tomorrows with you, but if I can't, don't become bitter. Keep your joy for life and pass it on to Sammy. Please. Do it for me."

Lance held his wife as she sobbed. Tears formed in the corners of his eyes, and he blinked hard to hold them back.

Then they offered a prayer together. They asked God to save both Molly and their baby. They also asked for strength.

It was now almost dawn and Lance went to check on Sammy.

Sammy was not in his bed and Lance rushed outside. Sammy was on top of the barn. He was working to spread out the deerskin that Broken Knife had given to Molly. Grandpappy Badger had shown him where they should put it if they needed help. Sammy was slipping and sliding around on the roof as he pulled and tugged the hide.

Lance rushed to the roof. He grabbed Sammy and carried him down.

"Sammy! You can't climb that high by yourself. You could fall." Lance's voice shook as he hauled Sammy back to safety.

Lance was so exhausted that at first, he didn't see the tears running down Sammy's face.

"Momma needs help," Sammy sobbed, "and Broken Knife told us to put out the cloth if we needed him."

Tears were trickling down Sammy's face and his blue eyes were red as he looked up at his father.

Lance's eyes took in the deerskin. It was bright and beautiful on the top of the roof.

Lance hugged his little boy. His voice was husky as he responded, "Thank you, Sammy. That was a wonderful thing for you to think of. We will tell Momma, and she will be so proud of you."

Slim quietly came forward and lifted Sammy out of Lance's arms.

"How 'bout we go find Badger today, Sammy? Would ya like that?"

As Sammy nodded his head, Slim squeezed Lance's arm hard and walked away. Lance's men feared the worst.

Lance slowly walked back to the house. He could hear Sadie talking softly to Molly. Molly was calling his name with panic in her voice. Lance paused and looked toward the Heavens before he hurried to his wife's side.

"Sadie, let's get some water heating. Slim will find Badger, and Badger will know what to do."

As he sat down by Molly's side, she stared up at him.

Lance pulled her close, and huge sobs silently shook his body.

Molly smiled weakly at him. Love pushed aside the fear she was feeling as she looked at this man who was her everything.

"Don't be sad, Lance. You have given me so much," Molly murmured.

Just then, one of the riders shouted, "Indian's comin'!"

Lance released Molly and stepped to the kitchen door.

Broken Knife pulled his horse to a stop. He reached behind him and dropped an old Indian woman to the ground.

"Broken Knife think Little Warrior come. He bring Nomi. She help."

Nomi looked at Lance and grinned. She was missing quite a few of her teeth. As she shuffled toward the house, Nomi pointed to Lance and then nodded for him to come.

Molly was still sweating, but she was moving less now. Her huge blue eyes searched Lance's face for some hope. Nomi pushed the orderly aside and shooed both him and Sadie from the room.

The orderly began to protest and Lance shoved him out the door.

As Lance started to close the door, the orderly exclaimed, "You can't let an Injun help. Why who knows what shenanigans she might pull."

Lance yanked the door open. All of his frustration and fear went into the punch that connected with the man's chin. The orderly dropped without another sound and Lance slammed the door shut.

Nomi's grin was even bigger as she signed for Lance to cover the windows. She set a bag on the floor and began pulling plants from it. She mashed some herbs and signed for hot water.

Sadie already had water heating and by the time Lance returned with the water, Nomi was burning some kind of herbal mixture. The scent was unusual but pleasant. She took some of the mashed herbs and mixed them in a cup of hot water.

Nomi pushed the cup to Molly's lips, but Molly refused to drink it.

Lance knelt down by Molly.

"Molly, we asked the Lord for help, and He sent Nomi. Now you have to drink this," Lance stated firmly as he blew on the mixture.

Molly's eyes moved from Lance to Nomi for a moment and then she drank the sweet-smelling liquid.

Lance could almost see her body relax.

Nomi then mixed more herbs and began to rub Molly's stomach gently as she sang a song in Arapaho. She felt all over Molly's stomach. Her hands paused close to the bottom swell. Nomi gently pushed down with her hands and gave a twist.

Molly cried out but Lance saw the baby move.

Nomi continued to rub Molly's stomach and sing. Molly's stomach was cramping harder now. Nomi took Lance's hand and signed for him to make Molly stand up.

Lance looked at her incredulously. Nomi signed again.

Lance took Molly's arm. "Stand up, Molly. Nomi wants you to stand."

Molly tried and finally was able to move out of the bed.

Nomi had Molly squat on the floor, and she signed for Lance to hold his hands under his wife.

As Lance squatted beside her, Molly pushed hard and the baby's head came out followed by the shoulders and the chest. When Molly pushed again, the baby dropped into Lance's hands.

Lance stared in amazement at this little person he was holding.

Nomi immediately lifted the baby up to Molly and helped her to stand. Molly was trembling and shaking as Lance helped her to sit down on the side of the bed. She stared at the beautiful little boy she held in her arms. She looked up at Lance with pure love and joy in her eyes.

"Paul," she whispered softly. "Let's call him Paul."

Nomi waited until the cord quit throbbing before she bit it in two. She handed the baby to Lance, and the little boy began to squall in a loud voice. Nomi again rubbed Molly's stomach with her mixture and had Molly squat a second time.

As Molly delivered the afterbirth, Lance looked on in awe. He had never been part of anything so amazing.

Nomi took a cloth from beside the bed and wiped off the baby. She wrapped the healthy little boy in a beautiful, soft deerskin. She grinned at Lance and pushed him toward the door.

As he looked at her in confusion, she gave him another push and a big grin as she pointed outside.

CHAPTER 67

A FINE WARRIOR ON THE ROCKING R

LANCE STEPPED OUT TO SEE SIXTEEN RIDERS GATH-ERED IN FRONT OF THE HOUSE. Old Man McNary was there along with Broken Knife and three braves.

A buckboard was racing into the yard with Badger and Martha while Slim and Sammy were riding beside it on horseback. Badger hauled back on the reins and dropped out of the wagon while it was still moving. He literally lifted Martha down as he ran. The look of panic on his face slowly changed to joy when he realized that everything was okay.

He moved up to look at the baby. "Well, would ya looky there. Ain't he a handsome fellar. Kinda looks like his grandpappy, an' I ain't a talkin' 'bout Old Man McNary neither," he stated as he grinned at Lance.

Old Man McNary eased out of the crowd and peered at the baby Lance was holding. Paul opened his eyes and stared intently. The Old Man talked softly to Paul and the baby clenched his finger.

He looked at Lance with pride. "He's a fine boy, Lance. A man should always take pride in his children."

As both of them stared at Baby Paul, something passed between the three of them. Lance knew that this man who had helped him realize his dreams in so many ways would always be the father he missed.

Old Man McNary squeezed Lance's shoulder and stepped back quietly.

Lance held up the little boy to his friends. "Meet Paul Rankin! Paul *Broken Knife* Rankin," he announced as he looked directly at Broken Knife.

Broken Knife stalked up and stared at the baby. "Fine Warrior. Your woman makes fine warrior."

Everyone cheered and Lance offered a prayer of thanksgiving to the Maker who had heard his plea this day. He looked at Broken Knife and held out his hand. "Brother."

Broken knife took Lance's hand. "Brother," he replied.

As they pressed their hands together, Lance knew that he truly did have another brother.

Nomi came out of the house and signed to Lance that the baby needed to eat. Her signing was so unmistakable that everyone understood what she was telling Lance. Some of the men laughed and others were almost embarrassed.

Paul was mouthing Lance's shirt and beginning to cry loudly. Lance turned toward the house. As he reached the door, he turned around and looked at everyone again.

"Thank you, all of you," he called as his voice cracked.

Nomi was grinning at him and he gave her a one-armed bear hug. He kissed her cheek. "Hohhou."

She grinned again. Broken Knife pulled her up on his horse, and they were gone.

Molly touched Paul's soft cheek as he nursed. She smiled up at Lance and he caught his breath.

"I have never seen anything so beautiful," Lance whispered to her as he watched. "And I think we'll make sure Nomi is here for every birth," he commented softly as he smiled at his wife and son.

The devils began to dance in Lance's eyes and he looked slyly at his wife.

"The only question is, when do we start working on the next one?" he asked with an ornery grin. His blue eyes were soft as he stared at Molly.

Molly blushed a dark red and tried to glare at him, but her laughter spilled out. She rolled her eyes.

"You really are a scalawag, Lance Rankin."

Lance pulled up a chair by his wife and watched with amazement.

"You grew this baby inside of you, birthed it on the floor and now you're feeding it milk you produced with your body." He shook his head—he was truly in awe.

Molly smiled up at him as he kissed her forehead.

"Sammy!" Lance called. As the little boy came running into the bedroom, Lance grabbed him and placed him on his knee. "This is your little brother, Sammy. What do you think of him?"

"Well, I like 'im just fine. An' I think you're right, Papa. You should get started on another one. I like babies," Sammy declared as he leaned forward on the bed and rubbed the baby's head with his dirty little hand. Lance laughed again and Molly smiled contentedly as she patted Sammy's hand.

Lance could hear Martha in the kitchen bustling around as she prepared a meal for the large crowd and Sadie's soft laughter as she helped. The men's voices ebbed and flowed outside as they talked, argued, and laughed.

Slim stuck his head in the door. He grinned at the happy parents and sauntered into the room when Lance waved at him.

Molly had the baby over her shoulder and was patting his back to burp him.

Slim stared at the baby's back for a moment and smiled at Molly. He squeezed Lance's shoulder. Ornery lights began to flicker in his eyes as he grinned at Sammy.

"Sammy, jist so ya know, Sadie is my gurl. We talked about it last night, an' she agreed." He winked at Sammy and Sammy bounced off Lance's lap.

Slim strolled out of the room, looking quite pleased with himself, and Sammy raced after him.

"Oh, boy! I knew it! I just knew it! I'm a gonna tell my Grandpappies!" he shouted as he raced out the door.

Lance stretched out his long legs and leaned back in his chair.

"I think I will just take a little nap. This birthing babies is exhausting business!" he drawled as he pulled his hat over one eye and grinned at Molly, looking at her from the other.

The blue eyes that pulled Lance in the first day he'd met Molly swallowed him up again. His family was safe and Lance Rankin was a contented man.

CPSIA information can be obtained
at www.ICGtesting.com
Printed in the USA
JSHW040904161122
33215JS00003B/13

9 781643 180049